CONQUEST

ANNA MARKLAND

CONTENTS

Conquest 1

More Anna Markland 5
1. A New Year 9
2. A Cursed Year 15
3. Homecoming 19
4. A Wrong Righted 31
5. Our Seigneur Is Dead 35
6. Who Will Weep? 41
7. Treasured Possession 47
8. A Betrothal 51
9. Exploring Montbryce 55
10. First Meeting 61
11. The Right Decision? 73
12. Ruffled Feathers 81
13. He Does Not Want Me 85
14. Regrets 89
15. Discreet Meddling 93
16. She Knows Her Worth 99
17. Duke William's Visit 109
18. Building The Fleet 117
19. Stamford Bridge 121
20. The Invasion Begins 125
21. The Patriot 135
22. Preparing For Battle 139
23. Carnage 147
24. Aftermath 155
25. The Healer 163
26. Farewell 167
27. Blindsided 171

28. Confrontation 177
29. Ascha 183
30. Dire Tidings 197
31. Alensonne 201
32. A Wedding 207
33. Allegiance 213
34. Wedding Night 219
35. A New Dynasty 231
36. Flight 243
37. Ellesmere Takes Shape 251
38. Rebellion 257
39. Morwenna 261
40. Sons 265
41. Accident 275
42. Recovery 283
43. Conspirators 287
44. Poison 291
45. In Need Of Protection 301
46. Normandie 307
47. Plans Laid 315
48. Abduction 321
49. Cadair Berwyn 331
50. Ransom 339
51. The Dream 347
52. A Perfect Match 351
53. Amber 353
54. No Future 361
55. Yuletide 369
56. Birth 371
57. Death 375
58. Negotiations 379
59. Don't Go 387
60. The Bridge 393
61. For Wales 403
62. A Fortunate Fool 409
63. Sequel 413

64. Postscriptum 419
65. Defiance ~ Book Ii 421
66. Anna's Story 427

CONQUEST

THE MONTBRYCE LEGACY

ANNIVERSARY EDITION
BOOK ONE

By
ANNA MARKLAND

The ruling passion conquers reason still
~Alexander Pope

For Don, my Conqueror.

Conquest by Anna Markland

Book One, The Montbryce Legacy, Anniversary Edition

(Parts of this story were originally published under the titles Conquering Passion and Defiant Passion)

www.annamarkland.com

Cover by Dar Albert

MORE ANNA MARKLAND

The Montbryce Legacy~Anniversary Edition (2018)

I Conquest—Ram and Mabelle, Rhodri and Rhonwen

II Defiance—Hugh and Devona, Antoine and Sybilla

III Redemption—Caedmon and Agneta

The Montbryce Legacy~First Edition (2011-2014)

Conquering Passion—Ram and Mabelle, Rhodri and Rhonwen (audiobook available)

If Love Dares Enough—Hugh and Devona, Antoine and Sybilla

Defiant Passion-Rhodri and Rhonwen

A Man of Value—Caedmon and Agneta

Dark Irish Knight—Ronan and Rhoni

Haunted Knights—Adam and Rosamunda, Denis and Paulina

Passion in the Blood—Robert and Dorianne, Baudoin and Carys

Dark and Bright—Rhys and Annalise

The Winds of the Heavens—Rhun and Glain, Rhydderch and Isolda

Dance of Love—Izzy and Farah

Carried Away—Blythe and Dieter

Sweet Taste of Love—Aidan and Nolana

Wild Viking Princess—Ragna and Reider

Hearts and Crowns—Gallien and Peridotte

Fatal Truths—Alex and Elayne

Sinful Passions—Bronson and Grace; Rodrick and Swan

Series featuring the stories of the Viking ancestors of my Norman families

The Rover Bold—Bryk and Cathryn

The Rover Defiant—Torstein and Sonja

The Rover Betrayed—Magnus and Judith

Caledonia Chronicles (Scotland)

Book I Pride of the Clan—Rheade and Margaret

Book II Highland Tides—Braden and Charlotte

Book 2.5 Highland Dawn—Keith and Aurora (a Kindle Worlds book)

Book III Roses Among the Heather—Blair &Susanna, Craig & Timothea

The Von Wolfenberg Dynasty (medieval Europe)

Book 1 Loyal Heart—Sophia and Brandt

Book 2 Courageous Hearts—Luther and Francesca

Book 3 Faithful Heart—Kon and Zara

MYTH AND MYSTERY

The Taking of Ireland—Sibràn and Aislinn

17TH CENTURY

Highland Betrayal—Morgan and Hannah (audiobook available)

CLASH OF THE TARTANS

Kilty Secrets—Ewan and Shona

Kilted at the Altar—Darroch and Isabel

Kilty Pleasures—Coming soon

Novellas

Maknab's Revenge—Ingram and Ruby

Passion's Fire—Matthew and Brigandine

Banished—Sigmar and Audra

Hungry Like De Wolfe—Blaise and Anne—Kindle Worlds

Unkissable Knight—Dervenn and Victorine

A NEW YEAR

ARQUES, NORMANDIE, NEW YEAR'S DAY 1066 A.D.

Lady Mabelle de Valtesse removed her grease-spattered apron with a weary sigh, rolled it up, and gathered a meagre blanket around her shoulders. Exhausted, she sank onto the stale rushes strewn on the hard stone floor, tucking the apron under her drooping head. Her snoring father, the exiled *Seigneur* of Alensonne, lay sprawled across the space allotted to them both in the Great Hall.

She had been careful not to step on the slumbering forms—human and animal—in the communal sleeping area of the castle at Arques, a task rendered more difficult by the half-light of the early morning hour. A pall of blue smoke from the long dead fire in the hearth hung in the air, irritating her tired eyes. She startled when her unpredictable father asked loudly, "Why are you so late to bed?"

Mabelle gritted her teeth and stiffened her shoulders. Waking him was the last thing she wanted. "I was not allowed to leave the kitchens until everything had been tidied. The banquet for the New Year was larger than usual. I'm tired to the bone."

"It's intolerable," he replied, making no effort to keep his voice down. "The only daughter of Guillaume de Valtesse working like a peasant in the kitchens."

"Papa, please, not now," she whispered. "The castle steward made it plain we must contribute if we want to avail ourselves of their hospitality."

Her irritating father considered it beneath him to contribute anything.

"Hospitality," he sneered. "Where is the chamber I should have, as befits my rank?"

"Hush there," someone called. "It's the middle of the night."

Valtesse bristled and shouted back, "Don't tell me to hush. I am Guillaume de Valtesse, the *Seigneur* d'Alensonne."

The retort came quickly. "We don't care if you're the King of the English."

This sentiment was quickly supported by the complaints of others awakened after a day spent toiling for their master. Dogs yapped. Startled cats scurried away, screeching displeasure at having their nightly foraging disturbed.

Mabelle well knew the potential for the argument to escalate. In their wanderings, she had seen her father thrown out of many a hall because of his inability to control his tongue and his temper. She squinted at him. "This is why we are exiled. If you hadn't lashed out and blinded the *Seigneur* de Giroux during the argument six years ago, we wouldn't be in this predicament."

Her father spat into the rushes. "If your bastard half-brother had not aided the Giroux family in their quest for revenge, they would never have captured Alensonne and cast us out."

Mabelle rubbed her weary eyes. "Well, Arnulf rules there now, while we—"

"I will not sleep with ignorant serfs," her father began, fumbling to retrieve his sword.

A dull ache began in her temples. "Papa, hush, please. I must sleep. You never cease complaining."

He sat up. "You are too impertinent, daughter. Young noblewomen don't speak to their fathers so rudely."

Mabelle rolled her eyes, itching to point out that her impertinence and resourcefulness had saved his miserable skin many times. She had told him often enough she believed the only person with the power to end their exile was their overlord, the *Comte* de Montbryce.

Muttering, Guillaume gathered his blanket over him, turned onto his side and seemed about to fall back to sleep, but suddenly rasped, "Be ready at first light. We leave for Montbryce."

"*Oui*, Papa," she murmured, trying not to sound surprised. It would be a mistake to get her hopes up. In the beginning, when she was three and ten, she had followed her father without question, learning quickly which servants to befriend. If she couldn't coax leftover food from a kitchen wench when a lord's hospitality was meagre, she filched it. She shared food with hungry stable boys and was rewarded with oats for their horses. Aiding laundresses in their tasks provided her with clean clothing. She listened to gossip, and used what she learned to her advantage.

Living by her wits had been easier when she was a

young girl. There was always something to trade. Six years later, it was more difficult. The drab peasant garb she wore concealed the body of a woman, despite her efforts to hide it. Men now wanted something in return that she had no intention of trading. In a constant game of cat and mouse, Mabelle rarely felt like the cat any more.

For all his faults, her father had shown he was aware of the growing dangers and was quick to protect her, but his volatile temper often led to confrontations and a curtailing of some of her freedom. She appreciated his protection, but was afraid of his inability to control his temper. For the past year he'd repeatedly ignored her attempts to set him on the path to his liege lord. She sometimes fretted he was happier in his misery.

Now he had agreed to go. What had made him change his mind? Perhaps the rumors concerning the recent death of Edward, King of the English, had prompted him to take note of the winds of change blowing in Normandie. Every Norman knew their Duke William had been promised the Confessor's throne usurped by Harold Godwinson. The *Comte* de Montbryce might be willing to be the instrument to help regain her dowry, lands lost to Arnulf, and now of strategic importance to the duke.

Her father's loud snores indicated he was not lying awake worrying. She wrinkled her nose, pressing a finger and thumb over her nostrils, shutting out the unpleasant odors emanating from the rushes. Tucking her knees to her belly, she hoped sleep would come quickly and that on this night she would be too tired to dream of fine clothes, rich food and the comfortable bedchamber that had been hers at Alensonne—before Arnulf had usurped the castle.

Despite her exhaustion, sleep proved elusive as her

restless mind thought of the journey to Montbryce. Would this be the means to at last regain the life of respected nobility to which she had been born? She pushed away the insistent notion that if her dowry couldn't be won back, then marriage to a nobleman would be the only solution. How to accomplish such a thing? Did she truly want to exchange one overbearing noble for another? She could only pray the Year of Our Lord One Thousand and Sixty-Six would bring a change of fortune for her as well as their duke.

She curled into a tighter ball and covered her ears against the grunts of a peasant who had taken advantage of his unexpected awakening to rut with his bedmate.

A CURSED YEAR

ALENSONNE, NORMANDIE 1066 AD

A thin sun heralded the first day of the year, its rays barely penetrating the hovel wherein Simon Hugo sat, staring at his daughter's body. If he needed further confirmation that this would be a year cursed by God, he had only to shift his reluctant gaze to the tiny bundle lying atop his daughter's lifeless frame.

"At least his soul is preserved," the village midwife had muttered before wrapping the stillborn child in an old rag. "Such are the wages of sin."

Then she'd left him alone with his grief and anger.

Estelle was the one precious thing he had, a living reminder of his wife, dead in childbirth fifteen years before. His daily life was a hard grind, ploughing a few acres with his ox, planting and reaping. His sole pleasure at the end of a grueling day, the only thing that sustained him, was the sight of his daughter's angelic face.

Then his *Seigneur*, the greedy Arnulf de Valtesse, Lord of Alensonne, had filled her with a bastard.

He'd failed as a father. Why had he not paid heed to the whispers among his fellow peasants? Arnulf was known to prey on young maidens, yet Simon sent his daughter to the castle to deliver turnips, grown on the meagre plot of land he tenanted. Arnulf was debauched and decadent, though not cursed with the fiery temper of the father he had ousted from the castle. At least with Guillaume de Valtesse peasants had been able to prosper if they avoided angering him.

Simon's gut twisted when he remembered the night his daughter returned to their hut, disheveled and sobbing. He had known the awful truth before she told him and had relived that night over and over, the words haunting him. Eventually he found his voice, averting his eyes from her dirty, tear-streaked face. "We'll tell no one," he muttered.

For a long while the only sound was Estelle's sobbing. Simon clenched and unclenched his fists, his heart broken. "You'll never have to go to the castle again. Arnulf is a pig."

What words could he have uttered? How could he have comforted her? "It's not your fault, daughter. I've failed to protect you."

Her silence worried him more than her wrenching sobs. He wanted to rush to the castle and kill Arnulf, but could only pound the crude table with his fists, knowing such vengeance would result in his being hanged and Estelle left alone. He was a powerless cottar, a peasant. His lord owned the ox and plough. He could do nothing.

Eventually, it became evident she had conceived. Village gossips heaped censure on her, intensifying his anger.

Now she was dead. Coward that he was, he'd crouched

outside the hut, pressing his cloak to his ears, unable to shut out her screams while the sour-faced midwife kept up a steady commentary of dire predictions.

He resolved now to make a promise of his own. Someday Arnulf would pay for his crime.

HOMECOMING

ST. GERMAIN DE MONTBRYCE, NORMANDIE, APRIL 1066

Rambaud de Montbryce stood in the stirrups and rubbed his hard saddle muscles. "After the years I've spent on horseback, my backside shouldn't ache as it does," he complained to his brothers.

Antoine and Hugh chuckled their agreement. They had ridden out from their father's castle to welcome him home as he approached with a large contingent of Montbryce men-at-arms.

Ram smiled, always happy to see his siblings. "When did you arrive with your brigades? You must have been more anxious to get home than I."

"Yesterday," Antoine replied. "But we didn't have as far to come. We were in Caen."

Ram wiped the dust from his lips with the back of his hand. "I hope you have a tall tankard of ale ready. It's been a long ride from Rouen."

Hugh smiled. "Father has it in hand."

Ram's heart lifted as the welcoming walls of the family castle at Saint Germain de Montbryce came into view.

Surrounded by fertile meadows that stretched as far as the eye could see, the imposing edifice sat atop a strategically important promontory at the junction of two river valleys. It watched over the *demesne* that included extensive apple orchards. The serfs brewed a fine apple brandy for their lord, which was famous throughout the Calvados region, as was the golden honey and *fromage cremeux* they produced.

In the bailey, Ram dismissed his men. At his signal, an excited crowd surged forward to welcome the knights as they dismounted, kissing wives and hoisting children onto their shoulders. It was a happy scene, yet as Ram eased his weary six foot frame from the saddle, he quickly shoved aside the pang of regret that the only person who came out to greet him and his brothers was their father.

"Good to see you, my boy," *Comte* Bernard declared. "It's been too long. You look fit. Campaigning has toughened you up."

He punched his son in the shoulder, and Ram feigned injury. They clasped arms and embraced, his father pounding him on the back. "Your hair is too long. Don't you shave it for military duty?"

Ram laughed, stretching as he combed his fingers through his hair. "Vaillon shaves it for me when necessary. I encourage my men to do the same, though they don't need me to tell them it's more comfortable under a helmet. But my hair grows quickly."

"I wish I could say the same for myself," his father lamented, running his hand over the few remaining grey wisps. He laughed and tousled Ram's hair. "No wonder they call you *Rambaud le Noir*." He pointed to the threatening skies. "Let's go inside."

Ram winced, throwing irritated glances at his grinning brothers, who had no doubt taken great pleasure at his father's teasing. "I believe the nickname *Rambaud the Black* has more to do with the discipline I expect of my men," he retorted.

His father seemed to sense his discomfort. "It's good to have the three of you home together. I'm proud of you all. You're carrying on the noble military tradition of this family, in the service of Normandie. That you've stayed alive in these dangerous times is proof of your prowess. Many noble families haven't been as fortunate."

Sixteen when he first fought at his father's side, Ram remembered fondly the pride in his sire's eyes as they faced the Angevins together. "We learned from you, Papa. You are a great warrior."

Antoine and Hugh voiced their agreement.

The *Comte* slapped Ram on the back. "If only I could still join you boys. With the dire news from England, I sense you will be going to war again."

Ram concurred. "Duke William is incensed Harold Godwinson has claimed the Confessor's throne. You're right. It will mean war."

"Then your many abilities will be even more important to the duke."

When they reached the solar, Ram dropped into a chair and used his feet to drag over a footstool. "William is now our undisputed ruler. During my last visit to the ducal court, every major family had sent a representative. However, military prowess won't be enough. If he becomes King of the English, he will need capable administrators and I want him to see me as more than a warrior."

Two maidservants entered and served tankards of ale.

Their father waited until the women left. “As my heir, whatever effort you put into the efficient running of our estates will benefit you. You’ll continue our proud heritage as descendants of the original North Men.”

Ram offered a toast. “To the honor of the Montbryce family.”

“Montbryce…*Fide et Virtute*,” the others echoed.

The four sat for a while, drinking contentedly.

Ram licked his lips and belched, thumping his chest. “Good ale. Just what I needed after the long journey.” He turned to his father. “I’ve asked the duke if I can spend time assisting you with the administration of our estates. Before we go to war, I’ll make sure all is in order.”

Comte Bernard looked indignant. “You think I’m getting too old for the job, eh?”

Ram exchanged a glance with his brothers, shook his head and smiled. “It will be good to leave the military life for a while, and the duke recognizes you’re an able tutor. He knows we’ve already learned much from you.”

Relaxing in the comfort of the castle where he had grown up, Ram had to admit his father had aged quickly after the death of their mother, a loving woman who always deferred to her husband. He hoped for such a wife, if ever he decided to marry.

His father had carried on talking while he had been lost in thought. “Well, there is a matter in which I must involve you.”

Ram waited, curious to know what could be so important it had to be discussed now.

His father walked over to the window, took another draught of his ale, then fidgeted with the lace on the cuffs of his tunic. Finally, he cleared his throat and began. “The exiled *Seigneur* of Alensonne, Guillaume de Valtesse, has appealed to us with complaints his bastard son, Arnulf, has usurped his lands. Valtesse and his daughter, Mabelle, were forced to flee. At first, it seemed a minor problem. You boys may not recall the uproar. Guillaume de Valtesse was a competent lord, but unpredictable. Now those lands have become strategically more important, and Arnulf is forming alliances with our enemies, his Angevin neighbors."

Antoine leaned forward. "I believe I've heard something of them in my travels. A *jongleur* in Caen performs a *ballade* that tells the tale of Valtesse blinding another nobleman. That can't be true."

Their father corrected him. "Nigh on six years ago, there was an acrimonious dispute over land. Valtesse is an irascible fellow. He lost his temper and lashed out. As well as blinding Charles de Giroux, he cut off the unfortunate devil's ears. It drove Giroux to madness."

Hugh held out his empty tankard. "I've never heard this tale. What about Arnulf?"

Their father refilled their tankards. "If only it were a tale. Seeing an opportunity to advance his own wealth, Arnulf sided with the Giroux family. They challenged Valtesse to come out and fight, but without the support of his own son, his courage failed him. He surrendered and was exiled, taking his daughter with him, at Arnulf's insistence."

"He and the girl have wandered ever since?" Hugh asked.

"*Oui*, the only life his daughter has known is that of an outcast, regarded with scorn, and probably mistrust, as the landless daughter of a vicious murderer and mutilator."

"Murderer?"

"There are suspicions Guillaume de Valtesse killed his wife. She was strangled."

Ram scratched his head. Why had his father turned the conversation to the girl? "This woman—what's her name, Mabelle?—is either as evil as her father, or she has intelligence and has learned how to survive, despite his madness."

His father seemed intent on continuing the story. "There's no doubt she's lived a hard life. I believe coin has been a problem, and they've been forced to depend on the code of hospitality. Imagine a young woman, born into nobility but unable to take her rightful place. She's never had the opportunity to be who she was born to be. The only way to regain her position would be—marriage."

Ram didn't like the speculative look in his father's eyes. "Who would marry a landless refugee with no dowry, and what does this have to do with us?" he asked cautiously, putting down his tankard.

His father shrugged, winking at Ram. "I may not like the horrid man, but he is my vassal and the rightful lord of the lands in question. We can't have impertinent sons usurping their fathers' estates, can we?"

"*Non*, I suppose we can't," Ram said with a chuckle. Like him, his father was probably offering up a silent prayer of thanks for the unspoken bond of trust that would ensure nothing of the sort ever happened to the Montbryces. In such uncertain times, family treachery could put everything at risk.

His father's voice broke into his musing. "Besides, it's time for you to take a wife."

Ram bristled. The ale suddenly had a bitter aftertaste.

He stood, stiffened his shoulders and faced his father squarely, folding his arms. His brothers shifted nervously in their seats. This was not the first time their father had insinuated he should be considering marriage, but he had never done it so blatantly.

Ram resolved to stay calm. "First of all, I have plenty of time for such matters." He acknowledged inwardly that he was past the age when most young men took a bride, but he soldiered on. "In any case, William will try to oust Harold and there will be war. This is not the right time to be marrying. And what does this have to do with the Valtesse problem?"

His father took up an equally challenging stance. "You are five and twenty—past time to be married. You should be siring children while you're in your best years. Besides, I'm getting old and would like to see my grandchildren. Mabelle de Valtesse has grown to womanhood."

Ram's hackles rose but he preferred not to lose his temper. He had managed thus far to deflect his father's attempts to get him to marry. He liked the freedom of his bachelor life. "Why would I want to wed an urchin who has spent her life wandering, and who has no inheritance, titles or dowry? She wouldn't make a suitable *comtesse.*"

"One day she may have those things. Come, Valtesse expects us in his chamber."

"He's here? Now? But—"

"*Oui*, now."

Ram itched to object. He'd just arrived home, but once his father made up his mind, it was useless to argue. Though he had no desire to meet this dubious nobleman, he wouldn't disobey.

"Let's get it over with then," he grumbled, glaring at the grinning Antoine.

"I won't attend, if that's acceptable?" Hugh offered. "I haven't finished my ale."

"Fine. No need for you to be there, but Antoine, you should come."

Antoine's grin disappeared as they followed their father to the chamber allotted to Valtesse. Introductions were made. Valtesse's arrogant posture and scowling face added mistrust to Ram's annoyance. And where was his daughter?

Bernard de Montbryce explained that his sons would undertake to travel to Alensonne to negotiate with Arnulf. Ram arched his brows and looked at Antoine, who seemed equally perplexed and confused. Wary of what he had learned about the wandering nobleman, he approached the matter carefully. "Tell me, *milord*, your son—"

Guillaume glared at him. "Arnulf is a fat, lazy bastard. He stole my lands from me, and from Mabelle, my rightful heir. He took the part of the Giroux family to further his own ends and must be ousted. He has no right to the estates he occupies."

"Is Alensonne fortified?" Antoine asked.

Guillaume's eyes bulged as he paced. "All my castles are fortified. Arnulf forced us to flee south to nearby Anjou. We had to leave there because of Angevin animosity towards Normans."

"But—"

"Because of Arnulf and the *Seigneur* de Giroux, we've been denied our rightful position and have wandered from Caen to Fécamp, from Arques to Avranches. What kind of life is that for my daughter? At times, she's had to assist the cooks in the kitchens. My only daughter, a servant. It's intolerable."

"My father has suggested—"

Valtesse made no effort to listen and carried on, his mouth now twisted into an ugly sneer. "My daughter and I have been forced to sleep on pallets in musty, unused chambers, if we were lucky enough to find such."

He stretched out his arms and threw his hands in the air to gaze at the beams as if to seek vindication from whatever spirit lurked there.

Ram opened his mouth to speak again, but Valtesse resumed his pacing and his rant. "Other times the stale rushes on dirt floors have been our resting place. The *Seigneur* of Alensonne, Belisle and Domfort, sleeping with servants and serfs. God has abandoned us."

It was as well the bishop was not present to hear this heretical tirade about God's mistreatment. Ram glanced at his father, who merely shrugged. Antoine was biting his fist, apparently finding the situation amusing. Ram felt sorry for the people of Alensonne if this raging fanatic did regain his lands. He experienced a momentary pang of pity for the young girl who had been forced to traipse around Normandie with her irascible parent. She was probably as angry and twisted as he.

As they left the contentious meeting, Antoine and their father started towards the Great Hall, but Ram turned in a different direction.

"Aren't you supping in the hall?" their father asked.

"*Non*, I have an appointment elsewhere."

His father shook his head and walked away.

Antoine wagged a finger at his brother. "Ah, the provocative Joleyne," he teased.

Ram tapped a forefinger to his lips. "Lower your voice."

Antoine snorted. "You think Papa doesn't know? Besides, Mabelle de Valtesse will likely be in the hall. Don't you want to meet her?"

"Nothing will come of the idea of my marrying her. She's not suitable. Why should I forego a long-awaited tryst to spend an hour making conversation with an uneducated urchin?"

Antoine frowned. "Joleyne isn't *suitable* either. She's a peasant, a woman to bear bastards, not heirs."

Ram's jaw clenched. "I'm aware of that, and I've no intention of fathering bastards with my mistress. I love you, brother, but I don't meddle in your *many* liaisons. I'll be dining privately with Joleyne. By the morrow, Father will have forgotten about Guillaume de Valtesse. I bid you goodnight."

~

Ram was proven wrong the next day when his father remained insistent. He and Antoine had no choice but to set out for Alensonne to force a solution to the problem of the contested lands.

The weather had deteriorated considerably. The brigade of Montbryce knights made slow progress along the road, harnesses jangling. Though he rode proudly at the head of the well-armed column, Ram peered through the rain with a sour gaze at the muddy track.

Why is Papa adamant about this matter?

"I'll be relieved when we reach Alensonne," Antoine

complained. “Curse these April rains—they turn the earth to muck.”

Fortis snorted, seemingly in agreement as he pulled his great hooves free with each step. Ram could see no good reason why he should deal with this trivial mission. He had been home only a day. At least he’d had the chance to enjoy Joleyne’s talents. The memory of their tryst soothed his discontent.

A WRONG RIGHTED

A cloaked figure squeezed through the tiny postern gate of Alensonne, and paused to listen, his eyes darting from one darkened corner to another. The moonless night suited Simon's plans. Heavy clouds threatened more rain, but the deluge had stopped for the moment.

He had learned from recent gossip in the bailey that Rambaud de Montbryce, son of his overlord, was due to arrive on the morrow. The guards would be more alert, and Montbryce would bring his own men. Now was the time to avenge his daughter's death. It had been long enough.

Creeping through the darkened bailey, he was glad he had waited and taken time to plan. It was close to midnight. Guards would still be on the turrets. He clenched the calloused fists with which he intended to restrain his victim. There was nothing more to lose. If he was hanged for the murder he was about to commit, so be it. This lord had no honor, no morals.

It's a cruel man who wrests from young maidens the only thing of value they have.

Two sentries paused as their paths crossed on the battlements above. "*Mon vieux,* how are you this dark night?"

"I wish I was tucked up in a warm bed with my wife, *old friend.*"

"I wish I was tucked up in a warm bed with your wife too."

Simon smirked and leaned his head back against the wall. His hood protected him from the rough stone. He suspected the two men had exchanged this same jovial greeting many times over the years. Both snorted their laughter as they parted to continue their vigil. He was relieved their attention was on their jest and not their duty.

Moving stealthily through the darkened bailey, he hugged the high stone walls, breathing more easily when there was no guard at the heavy door to the keep. Things were as lax as always. The hinges of the oaken door creaked as he inched it open and paused, waiting, alert, his thick fingers gripping the time-worn wood.

No-one challenged him. His aged boots made no sound on the steps as he climbed to the chamber where all knew the master slept. He paused again to steady his breathing as his fingers touched the vial concealed in his cloak. Reassured, he smiled grimly and edged the door open.

Loud snoring assailed his ears as he entered the chamber, and his disgust intensified. "*Cochon,*" he murmured.

The *pig* was a man of thirty years, whereas Simon had weathered two score and ten. However, the dissolute nobleman would be no match for strength bred from years of toiling in the fields for this cruel wretch and his father before him.

An echo of his daughter's last desperate wail of agony in the throes of death pressed in on his memory as he waited for his eyes to become accustomed to the darkness. He had been helpless then, but he wasn't helpless now. Rage coursed through him as he tore open the drapery of the enormous bed and grunted, "*Cochon!*"

Arnulf startled and struggled to sit up, confusion apparent in his half-open eyes. Anger threatened to choke Simon. He seized his prey and dragged him to the head of the bed, pressing his knee into his victim's chest. Forcing Arnulf's head against the backboard, he used his big hands to pry open the ugly mouth, silencing the scream that threatened to escape. Reaching into his cloak with one hand, his fingers closed on the vial. Deafened by his own heartbeat, he eased off the stopper with his thumb and slowly and deliberately poured the wolfsbane between Arnulf's protesting lips.

The wretch tried to move his head, his fat legs kicking frantically, but Simon increased his grip and brought his whole weight to bear on his lord's chest. A foul odor filled the air and he took grim satisfaction in knowing his victim's bowels had failed him.

It took but a few minutes for the struggling to cease. Arnulf's eyes were wide with the knowledge he would soon be a dead man, and his paralyzed body could do nothing. Simon looked into the dying gaze and smiled grimly.

I have righted the wrong, Estelle. Vengeance is yours.

Then it was over.

Simon stepped back and lowered the lolling head to the pillow. He wiped the dead man's sweat from his hands on the linens as he heaped them over the body. He forced himself to wait until his breathing steadied, confident it would be hours before anyone became alarmed.

“Sleep well, pig,” he rasped, his heart finally at peace. “It was your destiny to die this night. It’s too late to help my Estelle, but I pray other souls will benefit from your death.”

OUR SEIGNEUR IS DEAD

"I'm getting curious about this Mabelle," Ram admitted to Antoine as Alensonne came into view. The prospect of a possible marriage to an unknown refugee filled him with misgivings. War was imminent. It was not a good time to marry. "How can a girl who has spent her youth wandering from place to place with a man like Guillaume de Valtesse make a suitable *comtesse*?"

"If you'd supped in the Great Hall, you'd have seen her," Antoine replied with a grin. "Perhaps there'll be no treaty with Arnulf, and Mabelle will never inherit any part of her father's lands. You'll be free to marry someone more to your liking, someone more *suitable*, who'll bring you a rich dowry. Perhaps then I'll pursue Mabelle."

Ram cast a puzzled glance at his brother. "You already have too many women in your thrall. How do you keep track?"

Antoine chuckled. "What can I say? I like women, and they like me. What's wrong with that?"

"Nothing, I suppose."

How alike he, Antoine and Hugh were in many ways. Yet Antoine had attractive females at his beck and call, whereas Ram doubted if the shy and gentle, happy-go-lucky Hugh had ever bedded a woman.

He shook his head, sending water droplets flying. "It's ironic I'm given the task of playing the diplomat on a mission I'd prefer not succeed. I'm sure there are prospective brides who have a more suitable background than this Mabelle."

Wiping the rain from his face, he thought again of Joleyne. She brought him relief from his physical needs, but it wasn't a satisfying relationship on any other level. He meant nothing to her beyond providing a means to fulfill her considerable passion. He paid her well for her discretion. Whenever he summoned her, she came to a secluded chamber he kept for such trysts, not wishing to soil his own nest.

He smiled at the thought of his solar, furnished with military souvenirs and trophies. He loved to run his hands over the prized swords and shields mounted on the walls. It was his refuge. He was sure his father was aware of his mistress, but it was a liaison he didn't flaunt. Few in the castle knew of it. Compared to Antoine he was a monk.

An errant thought suddenly occurred. He turned to his brother. "Imagine being a married man with a beautiful wife who is yours alone. A woman who returns the love you feel for her."

"Enough," Antoine replied good-naturedly. "What are you thinking? Has the mud clouded your brain? You're the eldest son of the *Comte* de Montbryce. You'll have no say. None of our comrades in arranged marriages are in love with their wives. It's a foolish notion to expect that from a marriage. We all know it. Though I'm the middle son, my bride will be chosen for me. That's one reason I'm enjoying myself now."

"You're right. Look at our friend, Pierre de Fleury."

"Exactly."

A cold shudder shook Ram as the possibility of a similar fate loomed. "Poor Pierre. How does he bear it? How can he lie with his shrew of a wife?"

He frowned, trying to recall what his father had said about Mabelle. He hadn't paid attention—perhaps he should have. It was his responsibility to secure the succession of his family. He had to trust his father to ensure that the woman who became his bride would bring them increased wealth and influence. Happiness was not an issue. Neither was passion. That could be found with the likes of the tantalizing Joleyne.

They rode at last into the Alensonne bailey, but no one came to tend their tired mounts. Blathering women ran hither and thither. Men shouted, with no apparent purpose. Indignant hens dodged the stampede. Dogs barked. The torrential rain added to the wretchedness.

What was the commotion about? Ram's body tensed as he gritted his teeth. He had pushed men and horses through the deluge to get to shelter, yet they were being ignored.

"This Arnulf doesn't have his servants trained in the code of hospitality," he grumbled as the damp seeped into his bones.

Antoine nodded his agreement, shrugging his shoulders.

"You there," Ram shouted to a lad scurrying by.

The boy stopped but kept his gaze fixed on the muddy ground.

"What's going on here? Is there no one to tend to our mounts?" he asked angrily, rainwater dripping from his helmet and chain mail.

"*Mi—milord*," the ragged urchin stammered, taking the reins, fear oozing out of him. "Our *seigneur* is dead. He's dead. No one knows what to do."

"Dead? Arnulf de Valtesse?"

"Oui, milord."

Ram and Antoine exchanged glances. "How did he die?"

The lad glanced around furtively, as if looking for a means of escape. "No one knows, *milord*. His valet found his body in bed."

"He died in his bed?"

The urchin seemed confused by the question. "Our lord often slept late, but his servant became alarmed when the hour for the noon meal approached, and he hadn't risen."

The boy, his hair plastered to his head, was almost hysterical, apparently overwhelmed by the presence of two scowling knights accompanied by a brigade of men, and the hubbub around him.

"A lord who sleeps till noon," Ram remarked to his brother as he dismounted, knowing from experience the successful running of a castle required a leader who rose with the sun. Servants and serfs learned discipline from their masters.

Grooms finally emerged to take the reins of their mounts.

"Make sure the horses are dried thoroughly," Antoine ordered.

"I am *Vicomte* Rambaud de Montbryce. Who's in charge here?" Ram asked the boy, who pointed timidly to a short, bearded man, standing with a group in the bailey, about twenty feet away. He was scratching his head, shoulders hunched, trying to coax shelter from a small overhang by the door. As the brothers sloshed angrily through the puddles, he raised his head and immediately hurried towards them, his consternation evident.

Antoine smirked. “He’s realized who we are, and that he’s failed to provide an appropriate welcome.”

The man bowed. “*Mes seigneurs*, forgive me. I’m Michel Cormant, steward of Alensonne. As you see, we’re in confusion here. Our master is dead, the body recently discovered. We have therefore failed to give you the proper welcome, and we beg forgiveness.”

“I am Rambaud de Montbryce. This is my brother, Lord Antoine. Your master was told of our visit. Have preparations been made for my men?”

“My son, Paul, will show them to their quarters, and I myself will take you to your chamber.”

WHO WILL WEEP?

The Montbryce brothers followed the steward into the keep. They ascended winding stone steps to the second floor of one of three towers. They were shown into a well-appointed, circular room with two large beds, heavy draperies and exquisite tapestries. Ram nodded his approval to Cormant, then, confident no servants were about, asked, "How did your master die?"

"We're not sure," the steward replied, shrugging rounded shoulders and shaking his head. "Perhaps some kind of fit."

"We'll need to see the body."

Cormant hesitated a moment, then replied, "Of course, *milord*. It's still in his bed. Follow me, please."

Ram was reluctant to perform the gruesome duty in wet clothing. He gave permission for two servants to enter, carrying their trunks. "Leave us now, Cormant. We'll send our chain mail, swords and gambesons with these servants to be dried. Return within the hour, and we'll go together."

He didn't want to hand over his sword. He felt naked

without his *arme blanche*, a gift from his father, but it would rust if not taken care of. He had dubbed it *Honneur* and pledged it to the honorable service of his duke.

Cormant bowed and left.

"He hesitated when you asked to see the body," Antoine remarked, bouncing on the edge of the mattress.

"*Oui*, but he quickly dismissed his misgivings. He's no doubt relieved someone from the family of his liege lord has arrived at this time of crisis."

They stripped off their wet armor and clothing with the help of the servants, who hurried away with it. Ram found two drying cloths draped over a chair and tossed one to Antoine, who tucked the long cloth around his waist and rubbed his legs. Espying a bone comb on a table by the bed, Ram tugged it through his wet hair, and then handed it to his brother.

"*Dieu!* I grow to look more like you every day," Antoine lamented.

"What's wrong with that?" Ram retorted good-naturedly. "There's less than two years between us, and we both look like our father. Good thing your eyes are green."

Antoine shrugged. "Perhaps next time I shave my head, I'll keep it that way, so people don't keep mistaking me for you."

Ram smiled. "Strange, I've never been mistaken for you."

The friction of the cloth warmed him. He spent long hours in the training yards to keep fit, battle-ready. His body was all muscle, yet lean. He rubbed dry the smattering of curly hair on his chest and worked his way down the faint line, to the thick nest of curls at his groin.

"I'm soaked through," he said with a shiver. As he

rubbed, Joleyne's erotic comments came to his memory. "You're so big, *milord*," she would croon. "I never saw such a weapon."

He was jerked from his self-absorbed reverie by the flick of a damp drying cloth against his buttocks, administered by his grinning brother. "Admiring yourself, Ram?"

He retaliated and they spent a few minutes indulging in their playful antics, gleefully chasing each other around the chamber, as they had when they were boys. Then they sobered as they remembered the unpleasant task they were to perform. "Better get on with it," Ram muttered.

"You're right."

They took fresh hose, linen shirts and woolen doublets from the iron trunks and dressed quickly, each assisting the other since they hadn't brought a valet. They had no choice but to lace on wet boots.

A polite rap at the heavy door heralded Cormant's return, and they followed the steward down the steps and across the hall to another tower, where they again mounted to the second floor. Cormant opened the door of this chamber after tapping.

"Why would he knock?" Antoine whispered.

"Habits of a lifetime," Ram murmured.

The steward bowed. "After you, *mes seigneurs.*"

Their chamber was finely furnished, but the one they strode into now was opulent. An enormous, heavily-curtained bed sat on a raised platform, dominating the room. The drapery was open, a shape visible. The bedspread had been thrown back. The pungent odor of human excrement cut the air like a sharp knife.

Ram approached the body resolutely, aware of Cormant still at the door. "No overabundance of mourning family members," he whispered sarcastically to Antoine, who stood at the other side of the bed, a hand covering his nose and mouth.

He clasped his hands behind his back and looked at Arnulf's ugly body, reluctant to touch it. "He looks surprised. Death came unexpectedly. But was it by natural causes, or foul play?"

Antoine kept his voice low. "No blood. No weapon in evidence."

When a lord died suddenly and mysteriously, all were suspect. Ram was thankful they had arrived after this death and sympathised with Cormant's obvious nervousness. "Has a physician been summoned?"

"*Oui, milord.* He came shortly after the alarm was raised and isn't sure what happened. An attack, he thinks. An apoplexy. The lord had enjoyed a rather heavy meal last evening."

Looking at the fat jowls and bloated belly, Ram could believe this pig of a man might have died from his excesses. It confirmed his low opinion of the whole Valtesse family. "It's evident no one will miss such a poor specimen of humanity," he whispered to his brother, who had moved to stand beside him as they conferred. "Or be sorry he's dead."

"His unexpected death might solve problems for the house of Montbryce."

"But what if someone murdered the wretch? In his own bed. Should an enquiry not be held?"

Antoine gestured to the body. "You know as well as I the likelihood of finding the true killer, if one exists. It's far more probable some innocent scapegoat would be punished instead."

Ram turned to the steward, trying not to wrinkle his nose. “We must arrive at a decision as to our course of action and get this corpse cleaned up and buried.”

“*Oui, milord.* However, I don’t have the authority. You’re the highest ranking noble.”

“I don’t want to waste time conducting an enquiry into this death,” Ram confided to Antoine. “I’ve more important things to do for father, and for Normandie.” He made a decision. “I declare his death to be of natural causes, in concurrence with what the physician has observed. We’ll bury him on the morrow. Cormant, you’ll see to the arrangements.”

He glanced over to Antoine, who nodded his agreement.

“*Oui, milord,*” Cormant replied, relief evident in his voice.

Ram regretted what had to be said next. “Brother, we’ve just arrived, and it’s a long journey, but I suggest you leave on the morrow to take the news to Montbryce. I’ll stay to assist Cormant for a few days.”

Antoine gritted his teeth. “I’ll leave after the interment.”

~

At the funeral the next day, Ram wondered how a man from a noble family could come to such a pass—most of the people in attendance were the knights of a baron’s sons who hadn’t come on a social call.

People from the castle attended—Cormant, his wife and three sons, the cook, the chatelaine, the stable boys, servants, and village folk. All looked on with disinterest, though one ragged peasant made no effort to hide his smirk. Arnulf was interred with seemingly endless solemnity by the Bishop of Alensonne. It took eight burly men-at-arms to lift the enormous lead coffin.

Antoine whispered to his brother, "I wonder where they managed to find that monstrosity?"

Ram shook his head. "I hope there are more to mourn my passing when the time comes, and that they care about my death." His father was aging and it wasn't likely Ram would die first, unless he fell in battle.

Who will weep for me?

He resolved to leave this castle as soon as possible. Shifting his weight, he looked up at the sky. "Praise be to the saints the rain held off. It's good to be dry for a while. A few days here will ensure the steward has everything in place for the successful management of the castle until Guillaume de Valtesse can return."

"Cormant seems a good man," Antoine agreed. "Even with Arnulf as his master, the steward appears to have kept things running reasonably well. But it's hard to tell whether he and the rest of the servants and serfs are looking forward to the return of their rightful lord or not."

TREASURED POSSESSION

Mabelle had never seen her red-faced father so excited, or for that matter, so happy. Antoine had brought the news of Arnulf's death a few hours ago and her sire had ranted gleefully ever since. Despite her relief, this was not a suitable way to react publicly to news one's son had died. She determined to behave with more dignity than her father. She barely remembered Arnulf and was not saddened by his death, since it was he who had cast her out. His convenient demise meant her dowry would be regained.

Her father calmed down sufficiently to have a conversation. "Didn't I tell you, daughter, your accursed brother would get his comeuppance? Didn't I tell you we would return to Alensonne in triumph and regain possession of our rightful lands? I can't wait to discover what that miserable miscreant has been squandering my money on."

"Is it safe to go back? Is the castle ours again?" she asked, noticing he gave her no credit for pushing him to seek support from Montbryce. Would she always be a cipher as far as her father was concerned?

"Of course it's ours," her father roared. "The *Comte* de Montbryce has guaranteed it in writing. His sons signed the documents, confirming Arnulf's death was from natural causes. I am the *Seigneur* d'Alensonne, without question—and of Belisle and Domfort."

As if the mention of his name conjured him, the *comte* appeared, and Guillaume bowed low. Mabelle curtsied, sinking to her knees.

Comte Bernard proffered his hand. "Rise, dear child."

Guillaume rushed to his side. "*Milord Comte.* I can't tell you how grateful I am for your succor and support over this difficult time, and now you've guaranteed the return of my lands."

"I've done nothing on your behalf, Valtesse. It's a coincidence your son died as my sons were embarking on their attempts to arrive at a diplomatic solution."

"But, *Milord Comte*, honor dictates I thank you for your help," Guillaume replied.

Mabelle was certain he was deliberately not listening, as usual.

"I wish to repay you, by giving you my most treasured possession."

Comte Bernard's eyes widened. "And what might that be?"

Mabelle held her breath. With her dowry regained, she could pick and choose her suitors. Perhaps she could find someone to love and honor her?

Her father avoided her gaze. "Now that my beautiful daughter is heiress to my lands and titles, she'll be a much sought after bride. But I offer her to you, in betrothal to your son, Rambaud."

Should she laugh or cry? He had never told her she was beautiful, and now he was anxious to be rid of her.

"Papa—"

"*Silence*, child. I know what's best for you," he hissed. "So, *Milord Comte*, do you agree to my proposal that we join forces? Mabelle will bring to the marriage a formidable amount of land, power and influence in Normandie and Le Maine."

Comte Bernard hesitated only a few moments before walking over to Mabelle. Placing his fingers under her chin, he tilted her face to his view. "You're a beautiful woman, and you'll make an exceptional wife for my son. You have strength, pride, intelligence, and perseverance. The future *Comte* de Montbryce will need such a woman at his side in the turbulent times I foresee for Normandie. There's no doubt His Grace too will be pleased at the strategic lands that will come under our control. We must get some new gowns made for you."

Mabelle had never heard such words of praise from her own father. She wanted to throw her arms around the *Comte* and kiss him. He had seen qualities that her sire had never considered. Perhaps strengths she hadn't seen in herself? She looked at her father and was suddenly afraid he might start strutting around the room crowing like a cock. He had heard nothing of what *Comte* Bernard had said.

She should have been happy but had a sinking feeling she had quickly lost the long-desired control over her own life. Had she indeed exchanged one authoritarian for another?

A BETROTHAL

Mabelle was thankful the next day for her mother's insistence she be taught to read. She could also sign her name, but was determined not to let anyone see her trepidation when the documents for the marriage contract were brought into the Chart Room by the scrivener. Wearing a new linen chemise and dark green surcoat, tailored hastily by a castle seamstresses, she signed her name with care. To *Mabelle de Valtesse*, her father insisted the monk add *and of Alensonne, Belisle and Domfort*. The intended groom had not yet returned from Alensonne, and his father signed in his stead.

She had lain awake, worrying she knew nothing of this man to whom she had been given. Consequently, she had arrived late for the ceremony, much to her father's chagrin. No one had asked her opinion. Life with her father was hard, but few paid her much attention most of the time. She was a person of no consequence. There had been a chance, with her birthright regained, that she could return to her beloved Alensonne. Now another man, a stranger, would control her life. His brothers had been warm and welcoming, but what was Rambaud like? She and her dead half-brother were very different.

At the celebratory banquet, she teased her father. "Now, Papa, the *jongleurs* will sing a new *ballade* about the Valtesse family."

He actually smiled, a rare event, and tweaked his mustache. "And now, daughter, we're seated *above* the salt."

The dark red wine and ale were plentiful, the courses many. They dined on roasted pheasant flavored with tarragon from the herb gardens, pigeons sprigged with rosemary, and suckling pigs. The woman who reigned supreme in the kitchens, known simply by the name of her calling, *La Cuisinière*, had roasted piglets on spits. Mabelle, used to wandering in and out of kitchens, had watched her brandish a large wooden spoon at anyone who tried to steal the crisp crackling of the succulent meat. *La Cuisinière* used a secret recipe to produce a memorable dish with trout caught by the steward's men. There was yellow cheese in wedges, the famous *fromage cremeux* de Montbryce, and coarse black bread.

Her father's voice dominated, and Mabelle was content he was happy, enjoying the honor he felt was his due. But she worried about her betrothed. Why had he failed to appear in the Great Hall the night he had been home? *Comte* Bernard had apologized for his son's absence, obviously embarrassed by it. Antoine had muttered some excuse about an appointment. She had an idea of what that meant. There was a more important female in his life.

She should be relieved her father had given her to a wealthy family. She would become the wife of a liege lord when her future husband inherited the title of *Comte*. Wasn't it everything she had wanted for a long time?

~

"A messenger has arrived from Montbryce, *milord.*" Cormant handed the missive to Ram and turned to leave.

Ram clenched his jaw, hoping the letter didn't contain what he suspected. "A moment. I may need to send a reply." He unfurled the letter, scanned it, and swore.

"I trust it's not bad news from home, *milord*?"

Ram scratched his head. "I'm betrothed. To a girl I've never met. I'd hoped it would come to naught, but my father has signed the betrothal documents."

Cormant seemed ill at ease with this moment of familiarity. "It's often the way, *milord,* for the sons of great families."

Ram shrugged. "I wish I'd at least met her. You know her perhaps? The daughter of your lord."

Cormant looked at him with surprise. "Mabelle de Valtesse? I remember her as a child, before her father's ouster brought us Arnulf."

"So, you have no knowledge of her upbringing, her education? I'm not sure about her—suitability."

He felt uneasy. Perhaps he'd already said too much to this servant. He made an effort to explain. "I've met your lord—my future father-by-marriage, it seems."

Cormant remained silent. Ram looked him in the eye. "I don't envy you the task of dealing with Valtesse when he returns."

Cormant's face gave away nothing.

Ram read the missive again and rolled it up. Holding it

in one hand, he tapped it absent-mindedly against his thigh. "Send the scrivener to me. I'll dictate a reply. I might remind my father this is not the time to be marrying."

"Is there ever a right time to marry, *milord*?"

Ram smiled. The man had mistaken his meaning. "I'll be off to war."

Cormant looked impressed. "You'll be accompanying His Grace in his quest for the English throne?"

Ram squared his shoulders, proud he could slap the steward on the back and declare, "*Oui*, of that I'm sure." Then his thoughts went back to the news of his betrothal. "We must redouble our efforts to secure Alensonne now it's part of my betrothed's dowry. Seems I have no choice. My inevitable wedding is in a sennight."

EXPLORING MONTBRYCE

Mabelle wanted to explore the castle where she would live and rule as the future *comtesse* when she and Rambaud married. "Perhaps if I can find my way around, it won't seem so overwhelming," she suggested to *Comte* Bernard.

He instructed the steward to conduct a tour. Mabelle was grateful for a knowledgeable guide such as Fernand Bonhomme. They viewed halls, galleries and chambers. Mabelle had spent the last six years in one castle or another, but she had not seen such beauty, nor felt such comfort and warmth, since her childhood in Alensonne.

"It's beautiful," she kept saying to Bonhomme. "Very impressive." It was hard to believe it would soon be her home.

They arrived at a stout oaken door. "And this, *milady*, is the chamber of your betrothed."

Mabelle hesitated before stepping over the threshold. It was a man's room, without a doubt. Red predominated in the hangings and furnishings. Weapons and shields adorned the walls, wolf skin rugs warmed the floor. A woven Flemish tapestry depicting a battle covered one wall. She ran her hand over the rich brocade of the bed coverings, snatching it away when she became aware of the tall steward's eyes on her.

The thought of sharing this bed with a man she had never met was overwhelming, and her belly turned over. She had little knowledge of men, despite the harsh life she had lived. Her father was a difficult man, but he had protected her. Would Ram be patient? Would he treat her well? The room seemed very masculine, with no place for a woman. Would he expect her to sleep elsewhere?

"Shall we continue, *milady*?"

They toured the kitchens, the smithy, the chapel, the brandy distillery, the bee hives, the stores, the larder, the smokehouse, the herb garden, and even the chicken coop, though Bonhomme carefully avoided the manure pile. In the stables she found her mare.

"Sibell will love her own clean stall," she confided to the steward, who was also stroking the horse. "I used to bring her morsels from the tables. She'll be better taken care of here."

"*Oui, milady*. The Montbryces pamper their horses."

He assisted her to ascend the stone steps to the ramparts, from where they looked down on the vast stretches of land surrounding the castle. "This is the Montbryce *demesne*," he declared, spreading out both his arms expansively. "As far as the eye can see."

Mabelle smiled. "You're proud of it."

"*Milady*, I've been the trusted steward of the Montbryce estate for many years, taking over from my father before me. One of my sons will succeed me when the time comes."

"Oh, look," she exclaimed, pointing out to the west. "Over there—a patch of bluebells, at the edge of the forest."

She closed her eyes, remembering the warm springs and summers of Alensonne, tucked away in the south west corner of Normandie on the river Sarthe. She heard again her mother's tinkling laughter as they gathered armfuls of bluebells in the open fields surrounding the castle. Now the wildflowers were a dim and distant memory, like her mother. "Is it safe to go there?"

"*Oui, milady*. Provided you don't go too far into the forest."

"I'll be careful. Has there been any word from my betrothed?"

Bonhomme shook his head. "Not that I know of, *milady*. But don't worry, he's very punctual."

Punctual? I suppose that's a good thing. Unless he expects it of me.

He took her hand and helped her descend the steps.

"*Merci,* Fernand. I appreciate your taking the time to show me everything. It's a big castle, and you run it well."

His face reddened. "*Merci, milady*. My pleasure," he gushed as his wife joined them.

She bowed to Mabelle, a sign of respect she would have to get used to. "*Milady*, the seamstresses await you in your chamber."

Madame Bonhomme accompanied her to the fitting. The servant seemed friendly as she chattered on. "The dressmakers have never worked so hard. They've been plying their needles from morning till night, preparing shifts, nightgowns, wimples, hose, chemises and dresses for you. The *pièce de resistance* will be the gown for the ceremony itself."

The woman was seemingly unable to take small strides, and Mabelle had to run to keep up with her.

"I've never worn anything as fine. There have been so many fittings, pinnings, twirlings, and adjustments, I'm beginning to feel like a pincushion. Is there word from my betrothed?"

It bothered her she seemed driven to ask about him.

"Not that I'm aware, but *milord* Rambaud is always—"

"I know—punctual. But what is he like?"

"Oh, he's a handsome devil. A decorated warrior, counsellor to Duke William, despite his youth."

Was he kind, thoughtful, or a tyrant? She couldn't voice these questions aloud to this loyal Montbryce servant.

When they reached the chamber, Mabelle submitted once more to the ministrations of the dressmakers, and the steward's wife took her leave. Mabelle looked down at the peasant woman adjusting her gown. Again, curiosity got the better of her. "Tell me, Bette, what is my betrothed like?"

The girl blushed and giggled. "Oh, *milady*, forgive me for saying, but *milord* Rambaud has eyes that can make women do foolish things."

"Ouch!"

"Sorry, *milady*, just a pin."

The pit in Mabelle's belly widened further. She had

been chewing her nails—a new habit. She hastily curled her fingertips into her palms. Doing foolish things with a man was something beyond her comprehension. It was likely he would want to dominate her. Would she grow to love him? She had to meet him first.

FIRST MEETING

The evening before the wedding, a message from Rambaud arrived with assurances to his father he was on his way home, and would arrive in time for the ceremony.

"He expresses frustration at being delayed in Alensonne. He wanted to ensure all was as it should be since those lands and titles will be part of your dowry, Mabelle," *Comte* Bernard told her as they dined with Antoine and Hugh in the Great Hall. "He received the message of the betrothal two days after we signed the document. He needed to investigate any lingering threat from the Giroux family but has heard no rumors of this. He sends you greetings."

"Greetings," she mumbled, struggling to control her disappointment that she would not meet him until their wedding.

Doubts nagged as the interminable night dragged on. She woke from a fitful sleep before dawn on her wedding day, feeling tired and irritable, bemoaning the state of her fingernails.

She needed fresh air. Suddenly, she remembered the field of bluebells espied from the battlements. Bonhomme had assured her it was safe. Perhaps that was what she needed—an hour alone to recall happier days.

She leapt to her feet and dressed quickly, as she'd done for years, in a homespun chemise and sage green surcoat with ample skirts down to her feet. She tied the braided woolen belt at her waist, pinned up her hair, and stole out of the bailey, carrying a basket from the kitchens. Peasant garb had proven over time to be the surest way to pass unnoticed among servants already up and busy. People would be looking for her soon enough to prepare for the ceremony.

Once outside the walls, she followed the path across the meadow. The fragrance of the apple blossom from the nearby orchard filled the air. Tension melted from her body as her bare feet touched the dew-laden grass. Turning to face the rising sun, she shielded her eyes, catching a glimpse of a lark high in the sky, filling the air with its tribute to the dawn. Then, in a whirl of feathers, the bird was snatched from the air by a swooping hawk. A chill swept over her. She stiffened her shoulders, blinked away tears and hurried on.

She reached the carpet of blue and stooped to pluck the squeaky, hollow stems of the wildflowers, humming as the bunch grew in her basket. She tried in vain to think of something other than her impending marriage. Wandering in penury, she had longed to be free to make her own decisions. Now that seemed unlikely, but at least she would no longer be sleeping on stone floors or working in kitchens.

Bees buzzed busily among the bluebells. She became flushed as the unseasonably warm April sun rose higher, and obliged her to seek the shade of the white-barked birch trees at the edge of the forest, lured by the cooling sound of the warm gentle breeze rustling the leaves.

The basket became unwieldy. She set it down and bent to resume her gathering. She had strayed far into the forest and was on the point of turning back when a glint of sunlight caught her eye. Venturing a few steps further, she smiled at the sight of a shimmering lake.

It was private and inviting, surrounded on three sides by sheer, moss-covered rocks. The clear water didn't appear to be deep. She was hot. Out of sight of the castle, she felt secure no one could see her. It would not be the first time she had bathed in a lake or stream.

Glancing around nervously, she removed the belt and dress, setting them down on a rock. The distant chirping and warbling of birds, newly hatched hungry nestlings, brought a smile to her face. She could hear no other sounds. The air was still. The chemise quickly followed the dress, and she waded gingerly into the refreshing water, gasping as the chill assailed her body.

Not a strong swimmer, she waded, moving her arms to and fro, her breasts bobbing on the surface, nipples hardening from the initial shock of the cold water. A tingle snaked through her as she modestly cupped her breasts.

Before this day is out, I'll be married. Rambaud will expect his rights as a husband. Will he be gentle? Will he want me to call him Ram? Will he like me? Everyone says he looks like his handsome brother, Antoine, who has been kind to me since I came here.

She yawned, the long night and early rising catching up with her.

I must make my way back. It will take a while for the sun to dry my skin.

She strode out of the water, spread the surcoat on the grass and lay down, unpinning her hair to let it flow over her shoulders, easing her feeling of exposure. She spread the chemise over her body and gathered up a bunch of bluebells to clutch at her breast. The water had calmed her. With a smile on her face, she drifted off, dreaming of what it might be like to be kissed.

~

After riding at a steady pace for several hours, Ram was confident he would arrive home in plenty of time for the wedding, punctuality being one of the things he prided himself on. His muscles ached. He had been riding with his body tense, preoccupied with the frustration of this unwanted marriage. The duty chafed. He had his future planned, and this would interfere. He decided to take time to stop at his favorite lake to swim, not wanting his betrothed's first impression of him to be the unpleasant odor of horse after a two-day ride.

As the castle came in sight, he signaled his men to go ahead and veered off to take the familiar path into the forest, slowing his horse, then stopping and dismounting a short distance from the lake. He tied his stallion to a nearby birch tree and propped his helmet on the pommel of the saddle. "Fortis, old friend, you'll soon be back in your own stall, where you can have a rub down, some delicious hay and a well-deserved rest."

He walked briskly towards the inviting water, unsheathing his sword, eagerly stripping off his boots, padded chausses, surcoat, hose, undershirt and braies. He tossed them into a pile, placed his sword carefully on top, then slipped soundlessly into the water. It was bracing, but felt good against his skin. He swam lazily for several minutes, then floated on his back looking up at the clear blue sky, listening to the sounds of chirping birds, inhaling the fragrant apple blossom.

I love this place. Maman used to bring us here when we were boys.

The mysteries and frustrations of Alensonne melted away, and he began to look forward to his marriage. He had never bedded a virgin. Considering the life she had led, was Mabelle untouched?

Reluctantly deciding he should make his way home, he strode from the water and perched on a flat rock, rubbing his hands through his hair, waiting for his body to dry. After a few minutes, he wandered over to his clothing and pulled on his linen braies. Catching sight of a mound of blue in the grass nearby, he wondered idly what it might be. He sauntered over, fiddling with the ties of his braies. He discovered a basket of freshly picked bluebells.

He smiled and crouched down to touch them, but then his brow creased as his warrior instinct warned of a possible threat; he had let his guard down.

Merde! My sword is with my clothing.

He stood, listening, but then the smile returned as the notion struck him only girls picked flowers. His spine tingled at the recollection of floating on his back, naked. Had a woman watched him?

Surely I would have sensed?

He crept forward and his mouth fell open when he caught sight of a scantily clad maiden, half-hidden by the long grass. She had covered her body with a chemise, and appeared to be sleeping, but her arms and legs had escaped the garment's folds. He licked his lips at the sight of her glorious golden hair and white shoulders. One long arm lay outstretched at her side. The other was bent, hand tucked into the side of her face. The steady rise and fall of the wildflowers covering her chest drew his eye. Her bare feet were slender. He could see only part of her thigh, but her legs were long. They had fallen open, the chemise bunched between them. Were the curls of the triangle at the top the same golden color as her tresses? Rosy cheeks and open lips, curved into a trace of a smile, gave her the face of an angel at rest. He inhaled sharply as his body responded fiercely.

Was she a vision? He squeezed his eyes shut, then looked again, taking in another ragged breath. Long eyelashes fluttered at the slight sound. She rubbed her nose and stretched, arching her back and bending her knees. The chemise came tantalizingly close to slipping off her breasts.

Icy heat rushed through Ram's body. The fearless *Rambaud le Noir* felt something tighten in his chest. He had never seen a more desirable woman. Crouched like a cat, he had an urge to spring up and pounce on her. Swallowing hard, he clenched his fists, struggling for the cool control that had made him a decorated cavalry commander. In the blink of an eye, a maelstrom of thoughts flew through his head.

He was to be married this afternoon. The clothing he now caught sight of indicated the woman was a servant.

Having his way with her before going to the altar to meet his betrothed would not be suitable behavior for a Montbryce. He intended to be faithful to his new wife, and though his lust for the vision argued fidelity could come after the vows were spoken, he knew he would not take advantage of this woman.

He wasn't married yet, didn't want to marry. This was not the right time to be marrying. However, he was not a ravisher of women. This stunning wench had aroused him, but he didn't intend to take her against her will. His legs were starting to cramp. He should move away before she—

Her eyelashes fluttered again. At first she didn't see him. Then she sat up, clutched the chemise to her body and exclaimed with a gasp, "Antoine! What are you doing here?"

The fruity huskiness of her voice startled him, and the taste and aroma of apple brandy suddenly filled his senses. He stood quickly, gooseflesh marching up and down his spine, his mind whirling. She stared at him, eyes wide, mouth agape, obviously nervous, but not afraid.

She struggled to her feet, clasping her arms over her breasts, and glanced down, then back at him. He groaned inwardly when the long golden tresses fell forward across her shivering shoulders. Embarrassment turned her body pink. He imagined her nipples hardening beneath the chemise she clutched. His already rigid arousal throbbed.

Striving to cover herself without revealing any more of her body, she looked vulnerable, in need of a champion. He wanted to be that man. No wonder his philandering brother was bedding this delectable woman—the devil. Thank goodness he had donned his braies, but they were not adequate to conceal his arousal, and the wench's gaze seemed fixated on his groin. His clothes were with his sword. He resisted the urge to move his hands to cover his erection and looking down would make matters worse.

He put his hand on his chest and shook his head. "I'm not Antoine. You're waiting for my brother?" he rasped.

"Your brother? You're—"

"I'm Rambaud de Montbryce. Who are you? I thought I knew all the servants. You must be new?"

"Ram?" she gasped.

He was on the point of remonstrating with a servant for using his given name, and the familiar form at that, but then she stammered, "I'm Mabelle."

A cold chill swept over him. He was speechless for a moment then exclaimed, "Mabelle de Valtesse? My betrothed? What in the name of all that's holy are you doing here, lying naked in the woods? Are you waiting for Antoine?"

Would my brother betray me thus?

The anger blazed in her eyes. "How dare you accuse me of such a thing? I wasn't naked. I came to pick flowers. I bathed," she cried. "I fell asleep, dreaming."

"Dreaming of Antoine, no doubt," he spat, not sure why anger had taken hold of him and why he wanted to hold on to such a preposterous idea.

"I dreamt of—"

"Clothe yourself, woman!" He turned his back to her. "You're supposed to be a future *comtesse*. I've said repeatedly your behavior would be suspect."

She struggled breathlessly to hide her nudity, then her voice broke into his confused thoughts. "And what, pray, are you doing here, almost naked, watching a girl you don't know? On your way to wed me, you intended to bed a whore."

He wanted to turn back to her, to explain how her beauty had bewitched him, but his anger and confusion held him in its thrall. His state of undress and obvious arousal left him feeling vulnerable. It was not a feeling *Rambaud le Noir* was used to. He was offended she thought so little of his honor. The word *whore* on her lovely lips sounded like an obscenity. It was a word a *comtesse* would never utter. What's more, it was unacceptable for a woman to argue with him. "You must learn to be more obedient, and not answer me back," he spluttered, crouching in an effort to conceal his arousal.

"Obedient?"

She pushed him then with all her might. Her strength took him off guard. He lost his balance, staggering into the water, falling full length with a great splash, cursing as he resurfaced.

Grabbing the rest of her clothes, she ran, but stumbled over his sword. Her belongings fell to the ground as she picked up the long, heavy weapon with both hands, straining to hold it out in front of her. He stopped a few yards away and raised his hand to calm her, unsure as to what she might have in mind for his beloved sword. His heart raced at the incredible sight of this desirable woman, the thin chemise clinging to the curves of her body, bluebells tangled in her hair.

He had to admire the way her heaving breasts thrust forward as she braced her feet, turned, and tightened her buttocks, gathering strength to heave the weapon. Through the thin fabric, he saw the outline of her bottom.

"*Non! Arrête!*" he yelled as she hurled the blade into

the water.

She retrieved her clothing and fled. He watched her disappear into the forest, blonde hair flowing like a cloak behind her, wanting to pursue her but knowing he could not leave *Honneur* where she lay.

"She's stronger than she looks," he said to the trees.

Swearing a silent curse, he waded into the water and began searching the muddy bottom for his weapon, shaking his head.

This is not how I envisioned our first meeting.

~

Frantic, angry and breathless, Mabelle paused, listening. How far had she run in her panic? There were no sounds of pursuit. She gasped when she looked down at her soiled chemise. She shrugged on the dress, hands fumbling with her belt, fervent prayers falling from her lips, mind racing. She wound the wimple round her head and tossed the ends over her shoulders.

She had known as soon as Antoine's name was out of her mouth that she was mistaken. The strapping athlete before her was older and taller than Antoine. Antoine's eyes were green, not ice blue like the ones burning into her.

Dread and heated embarrassment crept up her spine. She groaned, remembering how she had stared open-mouthed at the broad-shouldered, black-haired giant who had leapt to his feet to stand before her, like a purebred stallion. He wasn't naked, but he might as well have been.

This was Ram. This ruggedly handsome knight was her future husband. The reality seemed to hold far more promise than she could have hoped for. She had done nothing wrong. She could have explained, but he hadn't given her a chance.

His angry voice had rumbled over her like thunder, raising the hair on her nape. She had never felt the least *frisson* when approached by men before, yet had quivered like a wanton in his presence. The storm of desire had swept over her, and for the first time in her life, she knew what it was to want a man. But then lightning had struck, and she had known in a blinding moment of clarity that this proud, arrogant male she had angered and embarrassed was her betrothed. She wanted to weep when she thought how furious he would be about his sword.

What an astounding sight he was, water dripping from his hair, running in rivulets down his broad chest, wet braies moulded to his very male body, his eyes burning with disbelief as she threw the weapon.

No wonder they call him Rambaud le Noir. But he thought I had a tryst with Antoine.

She cursed aloud and made the Sign of the Cross. "It's a spell I've brought on by picking the Fairies' Thimbles. The lark was an omen. God save me."

She made for the wall, half running, half walking, chewing her nails. As she stumbled into the bailey she almost collided with Madame Bonhomme.

The woman eyed the peasant garb. "*Milady*, we've been looking everywhere for you. Are you ill?"

"*Non,*" she gasped. "I'm well. All is well. I fell asleep in the meadow, and now I'm late. I'll go to dress—for the ceremony."

She felt the eyes of the steward's wife on her back as she walked away on unsteady legs.

THE RIGHT DECISION?

Mabelle's head was full of thoughts of Ram when she came at last to her chamber. She'd hoped to find a moment of quiet sanctuary, but an excited voice startled her.

"*Enfin*," cried her maid. "Finally, you're here, *milady*."

"It's not to be," she sighed, gulping air.

Giselle eyed the peasant garb then immediately got busy undressing Mabelle

"I'm proud to have been chosen as your personal maid. I'm a widow, *milady*. My husband died many years ago in a skirmish, fighting for the duke."

Mabelle nodded, only half listening, grateful the maid had said nothing about her attire. Once undressed, she stepped into the wooden tub that stood ready.

Giselle dipped her fingers in the hot water. "I was worried your bath water would be too cold."

This diminutive woman, her red hair flecked with grey, was respected by the whole household. It would be wise not to alarm her.

"I've two grown sons, *milady*. People say I talk about them too much, but they are soldiers in the duke's service, and I rarely see them. Let me help you. You've got weeds in your hair."

Soon the scented water and Giselle's soft chattering about her sons and their exploits calmed Mabelle and one certainty emerged from her jumbled thoughts. No one must ever find out what had happened by the lake. She would keep the truth hidden and was confident Ram would too. Yet, her agitated heart was in turmoil. They might never have trust, or friendship, between them. Anger, something she had lived with for too long, was not a good beginning. Ram wanted obedience. She craved love and acceptance.

Giselle helped her from the tub, grasped the drying cloth with tiny hands, and dried her new mistress briskly and efficiently. The little maid was spry, despite a thickening waistline.

The seamstress arrived to help Mabelle into the wedding gown. The sleeves of the fitted white undertunic were made too long, so they could be pushed up, to give a wrinkled effect, which was prettily revealed by the shorter sleeves of the dress itself. The hem, sleeves and neckline were embroidered with ornamental bands of blue flowers. She traced fingertips over the embroidered silk girdle that hugged her hips before falling in a V to her mons.

"The satin emphasizes your curves, *milady*," the seamstress observed proudly.

"*Milord* Rambaud is a lucky man," Giselle whispered with a smile.

Giselle combed the tangles from Mabelle's long hair, and Bette pinned the finely wrought opaque veil on her mistress's head, drawing it over her face. The veil cascaded to the floor. Satin slippers were placed upon her slender feet. She felt beautiful and giddy.

"What's *milord* Rambaud like?" she asked Giselle nervously, aware the woman had watched Ram grow up in the castle. She had been a loyal servant to the Montbryce family for many years, having served Ram's mother until her death.

"Ah, *milady*, those blue eyes." Then she giggled. "Just like my own boys."

Mabelle took another big gulp from the goblet of dark red wine Giselle had brought to steady her nerves. She remembered the anger in those blue eyes.

~

It had taken Ram several frustrating minutes of diving to find his treasured sword. Its weight and the distance his betrothed had managed to throw it had embedded it into the muddy bottom of the lake. He was anxious not to step on the sharp blade. Cursing, he carried it to shore and dressed hurriedly, his hands fumbling with the points as he tried to reattach his hose to his wet braies. Running to his horse, he shoved his helmet back on his wet hair, mounted and rode at a gallop to the castle, his mind preoccupied with the vision of the angry beauty throwing the sword.

"*Milord*," shouted the groom, when he careened into the bailey. The boy reached for the reins, grabbing the sword as Ram thrust the hilt at him.

"Dry my sword at once. I don't want it to rust. Then lay on the oiled leather—not too much."

"*Oui, milord*," the lad replied. His frown betrayed his

curiosity as to how the magnificent sword had become wet and muddied.

Ram took the steps to his chamber two at a time. Mabelle was not what he expected. The vision he had stumbled upon filled his head. He had lost his temper, angered by her mention of Antoine's name and his own embarrassment. He'd envisioned a waif, a stray. His future wife was a woman of incredible beauty and perhaps deep passion. He had indeed been bewitched, more or less accusing her of being a whore. No wonder she'd been angry.

But she would have to learn obedience. That was just the way of it. He didn't want a wife who would stare back at him defiantly, did he? A woman who was brave enough to shove him into the water? The whole thing was a big mistake.

Vaillon had laid out his wedding finery. The valet arched his brows when Ram stripped off his wet braies and jumped into the bath he'd prepared.

He scrubbed his body quickly, then vaulted out and dried himself vigorously. He hoped the rubbing would help dry his hair. When he was ready to be dressed, Vaillon picked up the wet braies and looked at him curiously.

"Milord?"

"I went for a swim," he mumbled.

Soon, clad in pale hose with a long black doublet edged with gold worn over his cream linen shirt, he thought he looked presentable. Vaillon laced up his best black leather boots.

"Hmm," Ram mused, running his hand over the crest embroidered on the doublet. His finger traced the Latin motto. "*Fide et Virtute*. It's a good motto. *Fidelity and Valor.* I hope I'll do nothing to dishonor it today."

Vaillon adjusted a short black cloak around Ram's shoulders, fastened it at his neck, and drew a wooden comb through his hair. He brushed off his master's doublet and then stepped back. After a thorough inspection, he announced his satisfaction with his lord's appearance.

But Ram had reached a decision. There were too many things bothering him about this arrangement. He needed to speak to his father.

The breathless stable boy came with his refurbished sword. Ram had just sheathed the weapon when a soft tap at the door heralded Hugh and his father.

"All is in readiness, my son. You should be at the door of the chapel before your betrothed arrives. I haven't had a chance to speak to you until now. I hope you'll be as happy as your mother and I were together. Mabelle has had a difficult life but I'm confident you can erase the memory of those years for her. Come."

They embraced. Ram marveled his father would share anything intimate concerning his relationship with his dead mother, saddened by the knowledge of how much his father missed her. He had never heard such words from his sire, and wondered how Mabelle had managed to reach his father's heart.

Hugh clasped his hand and smiled as he gave him a brief embrace. "This is it, brother. No turning back now."

"About that, *mon père*—a word please. Hugh, find Antoine."

"But he's waiting for you at the door of the chapel."

"Find Antoine and bring him here."

~

Mabelle's heartbeat echoed in her ears. Her face felt flushed. She was confident she looked lovely in her wedding finery and hoped it would impress her betrothed and make up for the incident at the lake.

"Stop biting your nails." Her father's gruff, impatient voice echoed off the stone walls as he hurried his daughter to the chapel door.

There was no turning back now, though she'd been tempted to call the whole thing off, convinced discord was not a good beginning. She was to be married to an arrogant man she'd angered, a man who had aroused feelings in her she had never known before, a beautiful man.

Her breath caught in her dry throat as she rounded the corner. Her eyes fell on the unexpected sight of the *Comte* de Montbryce standing stony-faced, his hand on the hilt of his sword, his three sons behind him.

Perhaps they're upset because I'm tardy?

Antoine chewed his bottom lip, his face contorted in anger.

Hugh scratched his head, his attention on his feet.

Ram looked stunning in a black doublet and cape, but his expression was unreadable. His legs were braced, shoulders squared, ready for action, eyes fixed on Guillaume de Valtesse. She heard her father swear loudly as he reached for his sword.

She didn't hear exactly what *Comte* Bernard said, didn't need to. The only sounds that came to her ears were the thin metallic wail of swords drawn from scabbards, and her own anguished cry, "*Non*, Papa. Don't kill him, please don't kill him."

Then she fainted.

~

When Mabelle came into view outside the chapel, Ram wanted to take back everything he had told his father concerning the necessity of a postponement. He wasn't sure in his own mind why he'd asked for such a thing. The expression of nervous anticipation on her beautiful face turned to one of utter dismay. His gut clenched. He tore his gaze away to concentrate on her volatile father.

When Guillaume drew his sword, Ram's brothers responded, freeing him to rush forward to catch Mabelle as she fainted. He gathered her up into his arms, filled with an urge to beg her forgiveness.

Glaring at him as if he had two heads, Giselle picked up the trailing veil and unfastened it from Mabelle's hair. Her tresses fell free, prompting a desire to run his hands through the golden curls. His betrothed felt light in his arms, her head nestled against his chest, yet his heart was heavy. What he had done would turn her against him. He wanted her with an intensity that shook him, but he pushed the ache aside. Glory and wealth beckoned.

RUFFLED FEATHERS

Ram reluctantly left Mabelle in Giselle's care. He had to explain, though what he'd say…

On his way back to the chapel he encountered his father and a very angry Guillaume de Valtesse. Ram regretted disappointing his father, but the other man's fury raised his hackles.

"You've shamed my daughter, Rambaud de Montbryce," Valtesse screamed, spraying spittle across Ram's face. "I've killed men for less. Jilted at the chapel door. I'll have to send her to a nunnery."

Ram wiped his face, trying to keep his anger in check. "I haven't jilted her. I'm requesting a postponement, a time for us to prepare for this momentous step. I'll soon be going off to war and it isn't fair—"

Guillaume threw his hands in the air. "Rubbish! Many women will be sending their men off to fight."

Ram ran his fingers through his hair, the other still on the hilt of his sword. "But, Mabelle and I only met today."

Guillaume snorted derisively. "Many noblemen meet their wives for the first time at the chapel door."

Ram took his hand off his sword and opened his arms in a gesture of conciliation. "I need more time. Will you not grant that?"

Guillaume strode off towards the door. "*Non*, the betrothal will be cancelled and she must go to a nunnery."

The threat rendered Ram speechless. His feisty betrothed would wither and die in a convent.

His father intervened. He looked at his heir as he spoke. "My dear Valtesse, we all, including my son, are aware this marriage will benefit the Montbryces, your family and Normandie. Does it matter if it takes place now or in the future, as long as it takes place? We're on the brink of war. Ram is one of the duke's closest counsellors. He's perhaps right that he should not be distracted at this juncture by a new bride. It would not be fair to Mabelle, or to our duke. And if you send her to a nunnery, the Church will inherit your lands."

This last ploy seemed to resonate with Valtesse. After pacing for several minutes, he agreed to a postponement. "I'll take Mabelle with me to Alensonne."

Ram couldn't let her go. "*Non*, she'll stay here."

His vehement refusal clearly took his father by surprise, and he was afraid Valtesse would lose his temper again, but his failure to continue the argument was proof the *Seigneur* no longer wanted to be burdened with his daughter.

Ram sensed the nobleman was close to capitulating. "We can't come to know each other if she's in Alensonne. She'll be chaperoned here and won't be shamed. I'll oversee what she does and whom she sees."

Before Valtesse could object, Ram turned and strode out of the chamber.

HE DOES NOT WANT ME

Mabelle preferred to remain in a stupor. Then there were no tears. When she was awake, they came unbidden and she couldn't cease sobbing, despite Giselle's best efforts to console her. For two days she couldn't speak of her humiliation. Then she could only stammer, "He…he…does…doesn't want me."

Giselle sat on the edge of the bed and stroked her mistress's hair. "He's conflicted, *milady*. Young men don't like to rush into marriage."

Mabelle shook her head. "He…he doesn't…want me."

Giselle sighed. "*Milord* Rambaud isn't a cruel man. It's a postponement."

Mabelle blew her nose. "He…does…not…want…me, any more than my father did."

"Soon there'll be war with Harold of England. *Milord* Rambaud must concentrate on his duty to Normandie."

"But he doesn't like me."

A fit of hiccups followed this outburst.

Giselle continued to stroke her lady's hair. "*Non*, that's

not true, *milady*. He's come several times a day to ask about you. He carried you here when you fainted. I've known *milord* since he was a boy. He cares for you."

Mabelle lay back against the bolster. "He abandoned me at the chapel door. I wish my father had killed him."

"Hush, *milady*. You know that's not true. You must eat something. That will improve your spirits."

Mabelle shook her head. "I can't eat. I'll be sick."

Giselle rose and went to fetch a goblet. "Drink then, a sip of ale."

After another day, Mabelle grudgingly accepted broth, but refused to leave her bed. In the years she'd wandered with her father she had never known such humiliation. She had allowed herself to hope, to have feelings, and Ram de Montbryce had ground her into the dirt. She disgusted him. He would never feel anything for her, and yet she still desired him, couldn't get the picture of him at the lake out of her head.

Eventually, Giselle coaxed her into a soothing bath. She felt better with her hair washed, but when the maid searched through her garments for a suitable dress, she espied the wedding gown and declared loudly, "Get rid of it. I never want to see it again."

~

Ram bumped into Giselle as she came out of the chamber clutching Mabelle's wedding gown. He folded his arms and frowned. She bundled the dress more tightly to her body and turned away.

He fingered the material. "Don't worry, Giselle. I understand her hatred of the gown."

"You heard, *milord*?"

"*Oui.*" He ran his hands through his hair. "I didn't think she'd be this upset."

Giselle snorted. "She's a woman, *milord*, a woman you rejected at the chapel door. How do you imagine she feels?"

Ram bristled. "She'll just have to get used to me. She's wilful."

Giselle snorted. "How do you know that? You only spent two minutes with her, and she was in a swoon for most of that time."

He looked away, realizing his mistake. "I mean, from what I understand…from what Antoine has told me."

She frowned. "Antoine? He barely knows her either."

Ram hoped that was true. He'd been reluctant to broach the topic with his brother and didn't like that this mistrust stood between them. Had she been waiting for Antoine in the meadow? He and his brother had always had a close bond, sharing everything. But he didn't want to share Mabelle.

Why does she rouse such strong feelings in me?

He had reacted badly at the lake, but her beauty and state of undress had taken him unawares. Now he stammered on, driven by a need to justify his actions to this little maid who knew him well, and who cared for him. "I'm told she rides her mare all over the estate, mounted astride. This isn't the behavior of a future *comtesse*. She must comport herself in a suitable manner, something she evidently hasn't been taught. She must learn to be a Montbryce."

"But her mare is one of her few pleasures, *milord*."

He soldiered on. "Nevertheless, when she recovers, I'll

speak with her. We'll come to an understanding of whose wishes and desires rule in a marriage. I must have obedience."

Giselle stared at him, open-mouthed.

"What? What's wrong?" he shouted to her back as she stomped off.

REGRETS

A sennight passed before Mabelle would agree to eat in the Great Hall with everyone else. Ram cringed when he saw her unhappy face. The spark had left her eyes, and she chewed her bottom lip nervously. She looked tired and ill-at-ease, but his manhood hardened at the sight of her.

This woman never fails to rouse me.

He took her hand and indicated the seat next to him. "Sit here by me."

She didn't withdraw, but her fingers were stiff. "That's not my place, *milord*," she replied coldly. "I'm not your wife. I have no right to sit at the head table."

He tightened his hold, drawing her to the seat. "You're still my betrothed. Please obey me and sit here."

She raised her chin and looked him in the eye. A flash changed the warm brown, rich as the earth of his homeland, to an angry blaze, and he remembered her reaction at the lake to the mention of obedience.

Good, the fire is back in her eyes.

She took her hand from his, sat demurely, back rigid, hands folded in her lap. He suddenly missed the warmth of her skin, but resisted the urge to grab both her hands, press them to his face and kiss the palms.

She glanced over at Hugh and Antoine, seated further along the table, and smiled. Both returned the smile, but Antoine winked, sending pangs of jealousy searing through Ram. He wanted to leap up and pound his brother into the ground. Trying to control his temper, he turned to speak to Mabelle, ignoring Hugh's barely concealed snorts of laughter. "I'm glad to see you've recovered."

She shrugged her shoulders lightly and shook her head. "I'll never recover."

There was no anger in her voice, only resignation, and he regretted being the cause. Putting his hands squarely on his knees, he leaned towards her slightly and offered, "Let me explain my actions. Perhaps then you'll not think so ill of me."

She looked up into the rafters. "I'm all ears, *milord*."

Ram fought the urge to tell her she should not treat him with such sarcasm. "I requested a postponement. We will marry when I feel the time is right."

"And when might that be, *milord*?"

She's a feisty filly.

The notion brought new blood rushing to his manhood. He cleared his throat. "I'll be off to fight in England. The duke relies on me. Until then, you and I can come to know each other, perhaps repair some of the mistrusts, reach an understanding."

She turned to look at him. "An understanding of what?"

She looks me right in the eye when she baits me.

He coughed again, rubbing his forefinger briefly over his top lip. “Well, of certain standards, codes of behavior for a future *comtesse*.”

She looked away. Even to his ears, his words sounded inane, but he couldn’t seem to stop. He waited, *hoping* she would turn those disturbing eyes on him again. When she looked back at him, he held her gaze, wanting to make sure she knew he was determined. Their eyes locked. Could she tell a wave of heat had rolled over him? He might drown in those brown eyes. “We must talk about your mare.”

She lowered her long lashes and looked away and he felt her tense beside him. Still he pressed on. “I can’t allow you to go riding alone all over the *demesne*.”

She looked back at him, her eyes boring into his. “Why not?”

Again she questions me. Keep calm.

He took a deep breath. “You ride astride. It’s not seemly. And it’s not safe.”

She stood. “Excuse me, *milord*. As you’ve said, I’m not a *seemly* woman. You wish to deprive me of my only pleasure. I can no longer sit here.”

He got to his feet, shoving his chair back so abruptly it toppled, crashing to the floor. “Mabelle…”

But she flounced off, head high, back rigid, and he didn’t intend to embarrass himself further in front of his grinning brothers.

Her only pleasure.

The challenge in those blazing eyes held the promise of passion, and he wanted desperately to be the one to introduce her to many other pleasures.

DISCREET MEDDLING

"Milady, you seem upset," Giselle observed a sennight later when Mabelle stormed into her chamber yet again, slamming the door with both hands.

Mabelle whirled around, shoulders heaving. "You love my betrothed like a son, but he's the most infuriating…"

"He's a man, *milady*."

Mabelle walked towards her bed, fingertips pressed to her forehead. "But he wants to control everything I do. First he forbids me, *forbids* me to ride my mare. That's not considered *comtesse*-like behavior.

"Then it was how I dress. Next he forbade me to express my opinion of the conflict with Anjou. He scolded when I told him what I overheard people saying about the duke in the castle at Arques."

She sat on the edge of the bed. Giselle sat down beside her, put an arm around her lady's shoulders and took hold of her hand. "Rambaud wants to live up to what he sees as his father's expectations. He believes his parents' marriage was dominated by his father, and to the outside world it was. But I can tell you differently. The *comte* respected his wife and never made a major decision without seeking her opinion. Rambaud's view is women are for, well, obedience. And bedding—and the begetting of heirs, but he'll change, as did his father."

Mabelle leaned her head on Giselle's shoulder and blushed. "I don't think the bedding will be a problem. I have to admit we seem drawn to each other that way. When he looks at me with those startling blue eyes, I want to surrender, to be obedient, to agree with everything he says. And he knows the power of those eyes to make a woman do foolish things. His voice is like the beat of a tabor drum rolling through me."

She blushed and paused, fiddling with the sleeve of her gown, afraid she'd betrayed too much of her intense feelings. She rose from the bed to sit in a chair. "I long to bear a child I can love. But what Ram wants is dominance."

Giselle massaged her lady's shoulders. "He's a soldier, *milady*. Above all else he's a warrior. But he's ambitious and such men believe they have to control everyone. His life has revolved around discipline."

Mabelle leaned her head on her hand. "But I can't sit all day doing nothing. If I'm to be a *comtesse,* I need to learn things about the castle, the estates, the world. Ram will let me do none of that."

Giselle knelt in front of her mistress. "Rambaud is a good man, *milady*. Sometimes, men rebel when they think they've been forced into a marriage, though their hearts tell them it's what they want. They feel they have to assert their authority. Rambaud has never been cruel, or unreasonable. He'll come to see you're not a threat, but you must make him see you can help him achieve his ambitions."

Mabelle moved her head from side to side as Giselle stood again and kneaded her tense neck muscles. "How did things get so complicated? I want a husband who can love me for myself, let me be myself."

"Don't give up hope, *milady*. Someday Rambaud de Montbryce will be that man. Help him grow."

Mabelle placed her hand atop the maid's. "Thank goodness I have you. I would feel alone here without your guidance."

"You seem upset, *mon fils*—again," *Comte* Bernard remarked to Ram when he stormed into the solar, slamming the door. "That's the second loud bang to echo through the castle this evening."

Ram whirled around. "This woman you want me to marry is insufferable. She's wilful."

His father smiled. "*I* want you to marry? Sit down. What has she done now?"

Ram sat, but on the edge of the seat. "You think highly of her, *mon père*, but she must learn to be more obedient."

To his annoyance, his father rolled his eyes.

"Don't you find her pleasing?"

She pleases me so much I can't control my arousal whenever I'm near her.

He stood again and paced. "*Oui*—er—she's pleasing—I agree—but—"

His papa stretched out his legs and crossed his feet at the ankles. "Don't you think she's intelligent?"

"*Oui*—very—but—"

"Would you prefer an empty-headed wife?"

"Well—*non*—"

"Is she not beautiful?"

Ram sank back down into the chair. "She's breathtakingly beautiful, but, for example, it's my right to decide what should be done with Alensonne when her father dies, isn't it?"

His father stood, walked to the hearth and stared into the flames. "Alensonne is her birthright, Ram. True, it's part of her dowry, but she grew up there. She lost that childhood home when she was a girl." He turned to face his son. "Why do you want to deprive her of a say in what happens to it?"

Ram had no answer. He got to his feet again, and resumed his pacing, his arms folded across his chest. "I didn't think of it that way."

A reassuring hand landed on his shoulder. "Mabelle isn't a threat to you, unless you turn her into one. She has survived worse tyrants than you, and is wily. If you want her on your side, you'll need to be more subtle, more appreciative of her talents and opinions. If you're not, she'll find a way to achieve what she wants, despite you.

"She'll make a much better ally than enemy. She has listened to gossip in castles the length and breadth of Normandie and may have a better idea of people's sentiments than even our duke. Mabelle is an exquisite rose and roses have thorns, but we tolerate the slight pain they may cause so their intoxicating beauty can enrich our lives."

He considered the wisdom of his father's words, but change never came easy. "I suppose I could indulge her a little more."

Waiting in the gallery, *Comte* Bernard greeted Mabelle's maid when she arrived punctually for their appointment. The woman had worked for his family for most of her life and he trusted her implicitly. He shook his head when she curtseyed. "Please be seated, Giselle. How fares your lady?"

She made herself comfortable in the upholstered chair, feet swinging free of the floor. "Just as she has for the last fortnight. She's frustrated with *milord* Rambaud's insistence on obedience."

He shook his head. "And my son is still complaining about her wilfulness."

"*Milady* has agreed to be less confrontational, to try to get him to understand she can be a support to him and not a threat."

Bernard chuckled. "And Ram has agreed to be more *indulgent*. He said nothing about his former mistress, of course, but I've heard she has another *patron*."

Giselle wrinkled her nose. "Ah, *oui*. I don't think he ever had feelings for Joleyne."

"Nor she for him."

There was a silence between them, and *Comte* Bernard sensed her hesitation, but he knew this diminutive woman well. Sooner or later she would say what had to be said.

"I hope my advice to her is correct. I'm only a maidservant but I love *milord* Rambaud like my own sons and don't want to see him destroy his prospects of marriage to this intelligent young woman."

Bernard nodded. "I'm glad she has you as a confidante.

My dear wife relied on your good sense, as do I. You're much more than a maidservant."

Giselle inclined her head. "*Merci, milord.*"

Satisfied to hear of some progress, he stood and offered his hand to help her out of the chair. "I hope my son will soon understand that love and respect will bind Mabelle to him, not *indulgence*. She's the kind of woman whose support Ram will need in the turbulent times ahead. You and I won't always be here to guide them."

Giselle indicated her agreement. "Perhaps they'll one day see how fortunate they are to have each other."

He chuckled. "We can but hope, and perhaps continue our discreet meddling?"

The maidservant was about to take her leave, but turned back to face him. "Do you ever get a sense there's something else between them?"

He frowned. "Such as?"

"I'm not sure. I have the feeling something happened on the morning they were to wed. Perhaps I'm imagining it."

SHE KNOWS HER WORTH

On the morrow, as golden streaks of dawn lit the sky, Mabelle stole down to the stables, saddled her mare quickly, a skill born of necessity and learned early in life, and rode out into the fields.

"Sibell," she exclaimed gleefully as the mare tossed her head. Urging the horse to a canter across the meadow, she headed for the apple orchards. The wind caught her hair and ballooned in her cloak. Exhilarated, she tossed her head and laughed with joy. "I've missed you, little horse. Let's gallop until we get to the trees. We can't allow an overbearing nobleman to come between us and our fun, no matter how preoccupied we are with him."

Once in the orchards, she dismounted and led the horse by the reins, inhaling the scents of late spring, remembering ruefully the last time she had been in the woods beyond the orchards. "I'm confused, Sibell. I can't get my thoughts off Ram de Montbryce but I'm afraid to trust him with my feelings. I'm nervous whenever I'm with him, I can't think properly."

Sibell whinnied and pricked up her ears. Mabelle looked around nervously. Had the horse sensed someone? Seeing no-one, she calmed. "It's good to be out of the castle for a while. I feel Ram's presence everywhere there. He's a complicated man. Will I ever understand him? Will he ever understand me?"

~

Ram had spent most of the night tossing and turning, the restful sleep he usually enjoyed in his own chamber eluding him yet again. Thoughts of Mabelle's generous breasts and beautiful hair kept intruding on his thoughts. If he had gone ahead with the marriage, he would now be suckling her nipples, wrapping golden tresses around his body, held tight in the grip of those impossibly long legs, as he plunged deep—

Abandoning any hope of sleep, he rose in the predawn darkness, donned a linen shirt, tied his hair back with a leather thong, and pulled on breeches and boots. He climbed to the battlements as the sun rose, hoping the fresh air would clear his head. Looking out over his family's *demesne* gave him a sense of peace. But he tensed as an unknown rider trotted out of the bailey, waving to the guard.

It can't be!

He watched in disbelief as the mare cantered and then broke into a full gallop, heading for the orchards. Mabelle's cloak ballooned behind her and the wind whipped her wheaten hair like a blazing banner, liberating her long legs from her skirts. He remembered the last time he had seen her hair streaming behind her, down to her *derrière* as she fled him at the lake. She looked back over her shoulder for a moment, revealing the naughty grin on her sunlit face. Then she turned back and bent low, one with the horse.

She looks magnificent.

In less than five minutes he was mounted bareback on Fortis, pursuing her. Once in the orchards, he proceeded more slowly, following her trail. It led him into the woods and he suspected she had gone to the lake. He dismounted and edged forward stealthily, confident the horse would remain where he was.

She was perched on an outcropping, close to where he had first found her, feeding something to the horse, crooning soft words.

He froze.

She looked peaceful and happy, her tangled tresses covering her cloaked shoulders.

He longed to bury his face in her hair, inhale the intoxicating scent that was peculiarly Mabelle.

She tucked a stray lock behind her ear and he imagined running his fingertips along the edge of that dainty ear, taking her head in his hands and drawing her lips to his. He stilled, afraid her horse would sense him. She pulled the cloak tighter around her shoulders and glanced around, peering into the trees. Had she felt his presence? Did she know his scent as he knew hers?

Is she plotting how to be free of me?

Why was he intent on denying her this simple pleasure? Why did he feel such need for control?

She sat for a good while, laughing as the horse nudged her, begging another morsel. Ram wished he could make her laugh. He became rapt in his gazing and when she stood abruptly, it took him off guard. She saw him. He hated the flicker of fear that flashed across her face as she stopped, looking for an avenue of escape.

"Don't be afraid, Mabelle," he said softly as he stood, holding out his hands to her. "I'll never hurt you."

"*Milord.*" She bowed her head briefly and then looked directly at him. "You have a habit of watching me in the woods." Her eyes raked over his linen shirt and tight breeches and her mouth fell open. He was being devoured and it excited him. Slowly, he rolled the loose sleeves of his shirt to his elbows, braced his legs, pulled the thong from his hair, and put his hands on his hips.

"I asked you not to ride, Mabelle."

She looked at the ground. "You did."

"Yet here you are, wilfully disobeying me."

She shrugged then looked right at him. "I *am* wilful, as you've often said. I'm not suited to be a *comtesse*. You should free me from our betrothal so I can seek another husband who will think my dowry *is* suitable."

My father was right. She's wily and knows her worth.

He strode toward her. The proud jut of her chin indicated a determination not to show nervousness. She tucked the errant strand behind her ear, never averting her eyes from his. Her courage excited him. He wanted to touch her, to gather her up in his arms, but she shuddered when he put his hands on her shoulders. Her lashes fluttered and she closed her eyes but didn't pull away as he had feared.

"Mabelle, you infuriate me, yet I find myself longing for your company, for the touch of your hand in mine. I want to know how your lips will feel as they open to me."

Her face reddened and the heat rolled through his body. He felt her trembling.

"Please don't make fun of me, *milord*."

"My name is Ram," he breathed, pulling her body to his. Her spine went rigid. Her sensuous mouth enticed him. Would her lips be warm or cold? How would she taste?

"You rouse me, Mabelle. You are my betrothed, yet we've never kissed."

He brushed his lips over hers. Their moist warmth made his skin tingle. She moved her mouth away from his lips, but he held her against him, his arms now around her shoulders.

"Please don't tease me—Ram."

She seemed more afraid now than when she thought he was angry. He held her away from his body and rasped, "Are you wishing it was Antoine and not me kissing you?"

"*Non*," she murmured, shaking her head, tears welling. "Why do you torment me with this?"

He kissed her again, more deeply, his tongue coaxing her to open to him. He sucked her lower lip, bit it gently, then darted his tongue once more over her lips, whispering, "Open your sweet mouth for me."

The fight seemed to go out of her. She opened her mouth and twirled her tongue around his. Her deep groan reverberated through his body. His hand went to the back of her head and he raked his fingers along her scalp. She groaned again and then sucked his tongue into her mouth.

"Mabelle," he rasped when he could breathe again, "You certainly know how to kiss a man."

He immediately regretted the words.

She stiffened. "Of course I do. Have you forgotten? I'm a whore."

His grip on her shoulders tightened. "Don't utter that

word. You're not a whore. I didn't mean—aagh—by the saints, Mabelle, why is it that when I'm with you—?"

He shook his head, and moved away. He paced, running a hand through his hair, unsuccessfully willing his arousal to abate. "I'm a decorated cavalry commander, a counselor to the duke. One day I'll be the *Comte* de Montbryce. I've faced many dangers, and yet I can't say or do the right thing when I'm with you."

She swayed and leaned against Sibell, her eyes closed. "It's the same for me. I've survived all manner of trials and tribulations but you—make me—quiver. I've—never—I've never kissed a man before."

His mind struggled to reconcile the idea he was the first to kiss her with what he suspected to be true—that she was no longer a maid. But the taste of her had excited him. She looked vulnerable, leaning dejectedly against her horse. What had happened to the spirited woman he had seen ride out from the castle? He preferred the idea of the feisty Mabelle. He wanted to reignite that flame.

He strode towards her, captured her mouth again and kissed her deeply, his hand at her throat, his thumb caressing her neck. He swirled his tongue around the inside of her mouth, feeling the warmth, the textures. She drew his tongue into her body, welcoming him. Her chest rose and fell as her breathing became more rapid. His hand moved down slowly until he cupped her breast, lifting it, feeling the weight of it.

"I've wanted to hold your lovely breasts from the moment I first saw you," he whispered. "You fill my hand."

"Ram—" she breathed, as his thumb and forefinger fondled her nipple through the fabric and he felt it harden.

Were her nipples pale or dark, their haloes large or small? He shook his head and gently pushed her body away, afraid he would soon lose control of his arousal.

"I want to possess you, but not here, not like this. I'm an honorable man. When our bodies join, it will be in our marriage bed. The wait will be purgatory, but it'll be worth it."

It's a purgatory I've brought on myself. We could have been married by now.

"If Harold hadn't stolen the English throne, things would have been much simpler. Duke William will be here within a sennight to discuss the coming invasion of England. I must stop touching you, or my proud words will be for nothing, and I'll take you right here. I'm close to the point of no return. You inflame me."

She gasped and swayed slightly, her mouth, swollen with his kisses, still open. She looked dazed.

Sibell ambled over and nudged Ram.

"She likes you," Mabelle whispered.

"I like her too," he said with a smile, "and I know you love her."

It would be a simple thing to grant her this happiness.

"I'll *allow* you to ride her, provided you never ride alone."

At first she seemed upset, but then murmured, "Astride?"

He hesitated. "If you wish."

She kissed his palm, held it to her face. "*Merci*, Ram. That means so much to me."

Waves of heat radiated up and down his spine. "Perhaps sometimes you and I can ride together."

Have I ever ridden with a woman?

"I would enjoy that, Ram. Sibell will love it. She likes Fortis."

For the first time since their meeting, Mabelle's face blossomed into a smile. She was stunningly beautiful. He wanted that smile bestowed on him every day of his life. Something tightened in his chest and he coughed to conceal the tumult that had coursed from his heart, down through his belly and into his groin. "This talk of riding is —stimulating, Mabelle. We should go back."

They rode in silence as far as the meadow, where Ram reined in his horse. "I lost my temper concerning Alensonne. I wasn't thinking about how important it is to you, to your childhood. This castle, my home, means everything to me. I should have understood."

"*Merci*, Ram. I'm sometimes impatient. I didn't mean to question your decisions."

"I want us to be friends." He reached over and tucked the curl, his finger lightly touching the edge of her ear. It sent another jolt of desire through him.

"We can be friends—if there's trust," she replied, then urged Sibell to a gallop.

He sat atop Fortis, watching her disappear into the bailey, shaking his head, wishing it was him she rode.

Mabelle trembled from head to foot when she arrived in the bailey. She could barely dismount and had to lean her head against Sibell while she regained her equilibrium. The feelings Ram's touch had aroused in her were so intense she was afraid she might swoon.

If he had not been honorable, if he had wanted to take

her in the woods, would she have surrendered herself? She was inexplicably drawn to him, but what made her giddy was the notion he wanted her.

As she'd grown to womanhood, she had seen men lust for her. She knew the signals and had learned to be wary of them. Ram's every gesture had spoken of desire and when his thick, glossy hair sprang free from the thong and fell to his shoulders, she was lost.

The heat of his hands on her had travelled down to her toes. She had never been kissed, and the intimacy of Ram's tongue shocked her. But she had suddenly understood what kissing was all about as the ache grew between her thighs, and her own tongue became a thing beyond control. She wanted to suck him right into her mouth, to join their bodies in some way. He tasted of apple brandy, the unique scent of his maleness on the stubble of his morning beard, excitingly rough against her face.

What came over me?

When he withdrew and forced her body away from his, she felt bereft, cold. It wasn't lost on her that this proud man had been willing to concede to her wishes concerning her horse and her childhood home. But William was to arrive soon, and above all, Ram was a warrior, sworn to his duke.

She looked up and watched him ride in. Sweat beaded her upper lip and she breathed heavily as chills chased down her spine. He had looked at her as if he wanted to eat her. The touch of his hand cupping her breast, the playful squeeze of her nipple—*when our bodies join*—dizziness overwhelmed her again at the persistent memory, still tugging deep in her belly.

He desires me. Me, the unsuitable Comtesse.

DUKE WILLIAM'S VISIT

"Everyone in this castle is in a state of nervous apprehension," Ram exclaimed to his brothers with exasperation, watching the flurry of activity in the Great Hall. "Just because Duke William is coming. He's been here before."

"But never on an official visit and never at such a turbulent time in Normandie's history," Hugh retorted.

Antoine put a hand on his brother's shoulder. "Worry not, Ram. *La Cuisinière* is in full command, bellowing orders to the scullery maids and serving wenches, making sure everything is in preparation for the finest meals ever concocted in her kitchen.

"Madame Bonhomme has an army of maids and houseboys cleaning every last nook and cranny. Chambers are being swept, rugs and tapestries beaten, draperies and bedding aired, cobblestones scoured.

"Fernand is making sure the stables are spotless, the horses immaculately groomed, the men-at-arms properly uniformed and equipped, new *enseignes* run up the flagpoles and overseeing everything else about the preparations. He even has boys up in the oak beams of this hall, sweeping out the cobwebs."

He took a deep breath, pointing to the urchins perched precariously above them.

Antoine was right and Ram was pleasantly surprised to see Mabelle assisting in any way she could. She seemed to enjoy the work and was friendly to everyone, unlike when he spoke to him.

He dragged his thoughts back to the business at hand. "William is coming to speak to us specifically about the future. He'll no doubt be commanding us to accompany him to England for the invasion to oust Harold. Father has pledged all of us to his service."

"I'm sure you're right," Hugh replied, helping himself to a tankard of ale from the servery. "But I expect it's you he wants as his right hand man during the invasion. Your rewards could be rich."

"Whatever honor and rewards we earn are for the advancement and glory of the Montbryce name," Ram replied, aware Hugh's observations were probably correct.

I must get Mabelle off my mind and concentrate on what's important.

~

The sun was high in the sky when William, proud descendant of the Viking Rollo, first ruler of the Normans, rode to within sight of Montbryce Castle at the head of an impressive force of one thousand well-armed men. Sixth Duke of the Normans, he had held that title since the age of seven. Green and gold *gonfanons* emblazoned with the

Papal cross snapped in the steady breeze, creating music to his ears. He furrowed his brow and squared his jaw as befitted a man on a mission.

The steeds of the mounted knights behind him snorted and pranced. The spears and shields of the infantry clattered. The archers moved as one, longbows over their shoulders, newly fletched arrows rattling in their quivers. He knew it was an awesome sight and that his leonine features only added to the fear and respect his army inspired.

He left the bulk of his troops to pitch camp in the freshly scythed meadows, knights under canvas, men-at-arms out in the open. In the bailey he and a small retinue were greeted by all the men of the Montbryce family down on one knee, and the women of the castle in deep curtseys, their wimpled heads bowed.

"Not bad for the bastard son of a duke and a tanner's daughter," he chuckled as he dismounted. "And Ram's betrothed. What a beauty! Why hasn't he married her yet?"

He'd been gladdened by the news of their betrothal. It would bring a great deal of strategic land in both Normandie and Le Maine under Montbryce control.

"*Non*, rise, *Comte* Bernard de Montbryce. Your family has served me, and Normandie, well. You need not bend the knee to me. Let's enter and enjoy your hospitality and discuss how we'll teach Harold a lesson he won't soon forget."

"Welcome, Your Grace," *Comte* Bernard replied, rising stiffly with the help of his youngest son. "You do us great honor. Ram will show you to the chambers we've prepared for you. I trust they'll meet with your approval."

Later, when his trunks had been taken to his chambers

and his servants had bathed and dressed him, William descended the stone steps in the company of his senior knights to the Great Hall. A feast was served that he suspected was more sumptuous than any other meal eaten there before.

The immaculately groomed servers were resplendent in their green tabards with the Montbryce crest. The mutton meatballs were excellent and the roast chicken glazed with eggs delectable. So many multicolored boars' heads made an appearance, the iron pans in which they reposed held aloft by brawny lads, William wondered if there could be any boar left in the Montbryce forests. *La Cuisinière's* signature dish of rainbow trout was the *pièce de resistance,* and everyone sighed as the succulent juices of the golden baked apple flesh of the *pommes d'orées* dripped from their mouths.

The renowned Montbryce apple brandy was a favorite of William's and he savored it as he watched Ram and Mabelle. Leaning over to his trusted commander, he jested, "Ram, *mon ami*, I'm heartily pleased for you that your upcoming nuptials have been welcomed, a far cry from the torment my own marriage to my tiny wife Matilda caused."

"*Merci*, Your Grace," Ram responded, though not with the enthusiasm William had expected. He wondered if there was a problem he wasn't aware of, but the urge to repeat the tale of his own marriage carried more weight.

He had regaled Ram many times with the story but appreciated his friend would humor him as he retold it. "With a princess of Flandres as my wife, I would have the Flemish as my allies. She at first refused me, saying she would rather become a nun than marry a bastard. Hah!"

He took a sip of apple brandy before continuing. "However, once I went swiftly to her side, I rapidly convinced her to change her mind." He winked knowingly. "Pope Leo was enraged by the marriage and excommunicated us both, as well as the whole of Normandie, when I refused to annul it."

Ram smiled. "I recall it took the persuasive powers of our staunch friend and ally, Lanfranc, to convince a new Pope that returning Matilda to her father would be seen as a gross insult, and Nicolas relented."

William chuckled. "*Oui*, but it cost me a pretty penny because the Pope insisted I build a monastery and a nunnery as my penance, which I built in Caen, not to mention the hospitals I had to construct. That reminds me, I'll have to repay Lanfranc in some way once I get rid of the scheming Harold in England. Perhaps Archbishop of Canterbury might suit our friend?"

William enjoyed the feasting and suspected he would eat no such fare in England. He so relished the food, he sent his compliments to the kitchen, particularly regarding the trout dish.

Watching Ram and Mabelle, he saw the fire in their eyes when they looked at each other. Did they recognize the alchemy between them? He regretted the coming war would mean separation for them but was gladdened his friend Ram had found his perfect mate, even if he didn't know it yet. He leaned over to ask the question that had bothered him all evening. "Why haven't you married her, Ram? I thought the nuptials were—"

His question was interrupted by the voice of *Comte* Bernard. "Your Grace, on behalf of our family, my eldest son will propose the toast."

Ram stood, goblet in hand. "Your Grace," he began, "you have done us a great honor by visiting our humble castle. You are the pride of Normandie and we salute you. We wish God's blessings on your voyage to fight the Saxons in England, where you will take your rightful place as the king. Every Montbryce knight will do what he can to further your cause."

He turned to the assembly and raised his goblet. "Fellow knights of Montbryce, rise and join me in a toast to our beloved *Duc de Normandie*, soon to be William the Conqueror."

"Duke William the Conqueror." The toast echoed around the cavernous room, followed by a resounding cheer and loud banging of tankards and goblets on tables.

He stood to reply. "Thank you, Ram. It's only because of families such as yours that Normandie is a great power. With your family's help we drove out Henry, King of France when he dared to invade our borders."

With a wave of his hand, William indicated *Comte* Bernard. "Your father distinguished himself at the great victory which decimated our enemies at Mortemer, and though you were a mere lad at the battle of Varaville, you helped us soundly defeat the Angevin dogs. We will similarly punish these puny sons of Danes, who have usurped the throne promised to me by my cousin. Our legacy wherever we conquer will last forever. You have pledged many knights and your brothers to our campaign and they will cover themselves with honor and glory."

Applause and cheering broke out.

"However—" William raised his hand, and the cheering stopped, as he'd known it would. He paused to make sure his words had the desired effect. "However, there is one Montbryce for whom I have a special honor and responsibility."

A hush fell over the large hall. William loved theatrics and knew how desperately Ram wanted to accompany him on his campaign. He was aware of the pride his courageous and capable friend took in being his counsellor.

"It will take many months to build our fleet to invade England. I've left Normandie ungoverned while overseeing the preparations. Too many have taken advantage. I can't be worried about trouble at home while I'm preparing to fight the accursed Harold the Oath-Breaker."

A hint of murmured agreement stole round the room.

"I must have a capable commander in charge of finishing my fleet, someone I can trust implicitly."

He turned to Ram, seated beside him. "Rambaud de Montbryce, you are that man. You'll oversee the completion of our great fleet and the gathering of men, weapons, horses and provisions. Your decisions will be my decisions. You and your family have never failed me. You've supported me against the rebellious barons who would take Normandie for themselves, including my own uncles.

"You served brilliantly in our successful campaign to extend our influence into Le Maine, a few short years ago. Your skills as a negotiator helped bring Harold Godwinson into our grasp when he was shipwrecked on the lands of Guy of Ponthieu—*without* our paying a ransom for him."

He slapped Ram on the back and the laughter and cheering echoed in the room. "Too bad we let him go then —we would not be in this predicament now."

More cheers, laughter and agreement.

Ram rose and bowed deeply, his hand over his heart. He cleared his throat. "Your Grace, I will build a fleet of ships so mighty and gather an army so great, it will strike terror into the hearts of the English. The honor you do me, my betrothed and my family is humbly accepted." He turned to Mabelle and held out his hand. She rose and bowed.

"You're fortunate, Rambaud de Montbryce, to have such a beautiful and capable woman to support you in your formidable task. *Mes seigneurs et mesdames*, a toast to Mabelle de Valtesse."

The toast echoed around the room. "Mabelle de Valtesse."

Custom dictated she reply. "*Majesté*," she began, swallowing hard.

William was pleased and flattered by the exalted name she used to address him.

"Your Majesty, I thank you from the bottom of my heart for the honor you have bestowed on my betrothed. I know he will serve you, our beloved Duchess Matilda, and Normandie well."

She raised her goblet, took a sip, licked her lips and looked into his eyes, and then, nervously, at Ram.

The Duke of the Normans inclined his head in acknowledgement, relieved his ducal robe concealed his arousal.

BUILDING THE FLEET

For most of the next four months, Ram was away, supervising the building of the ships. He rode home whenever he could and kept his family apprised of his progress, challenges and frustrations. The surprising realization gradually dawned on him that it was a desire to see Mabelle and share these matters with her that drew him home. She was often present when the Montbryce men discussed the preparations, and he came to see, as his father had indicated, that she was intelligent and pragmatic. Her insights were often impossible to ignore.

"We're felling the trees from the forests around the coastal town of Dives-sur-Mer. Shipwrights shape the wood into vessels, armor and weapons. The building will be more or less completed at the mouth of the Dives and then the fleet will move to Saint-Valery-sur-Somme."

"I suppose that will make for a shorter crossing," Mabelle remarked.

When the move to Saint-Valery was undertaken, it was hampered by foul weather and several men drowned. Ram was angry and upset, worried the same might happen when the day came for the invasion. It was Mabelle who reassured him. "You won't be forced to launch the invasion during bad weather," she soothed.

During one of his visits, they were discussing the comet which appeared and remained visible for fifteen days. "William has taken it as a good omen. His astrologers declared this portends the transfer of a kingdom. I'm to start gathering horses."

"You're taking horses?" she asked with surprise.

"*Oui.* William and I have discussed it with the commanders and we believe it's essential we take them."

"You're right. How can you win without your horses? Normandie's strength is in her elite mounted troops."

Ram's heart swelled with pride that she recognised the importance of his life's calling.

On another occasion, the men were seated around the table in the Map Room, discussing the landing in England. "We're concerned about our arrival on the coast," Ram explained. "We'll need a fortification of some sort, but that will mean time lost gathering materials, building and the like."

They pondered the problem for a while. Mabelle sat off to one side, saying nothing until she suddenly suggested, "Why not build a fortification here in Normandie and take it with you in pieces?"

Ram scratched his chin. It was brilliant.

"What an intriguing idea," Hugh exclaimed with a smile.

By early September, Ram was close to the breaking point. He paced back and forth in the Map Room. "I have seven thousand men and six hundred and ninety-six ships ready to move, yet we've had to sit and wait for an interminable five and thirty days for the wind to shift from north to south, to fill our square sails. The wait is driving me out of my wits."

He strode over to Mabelle's chair and went down on one knee before her, taking her hands in his. "Thanks be to the saints I have you to listen to my interminable ramblings. William is becoming maniacal about his *crusade* and maintaining morale is difficult."

Mabelle stroked his hair. He wanted to rest his head in her lap. He felt better sharing his frustrations with her. It was an odd feeling. He had never confided in a woman before. "Horses and men have to be fed, and I've forbidden pillaging. William doesn't want the ordinary people of Normandie trembling at the sight of his soldiers. It might have been easier if they were all Normans."

She stopped stroking his hair, and he instantly missed the soothing gesture. "You have men who aren't Normans?"

He took her hand, kissed her fingertips and put it to his forehead. "My head aches."

She massaged his temples with her fingertips. He let out a sigh and slumped to sit at her feet. "That feels good. *Oui*. Many of them are mercenaries, allies and volunteers from Bretagne and Flandres. A few have come from other parts of France and some from as far away as the Norman colonies in Italy. I've maintained strict discipline but it's not an easy task when old hatreds and feuds reassert their ugly heads."

I could sit here all day, letting her massage my head.

Mabelle's next words brought him back to reality. "Does King Harold know you're coming?"

He didn't want to tell her spies had informed them Harold had assembled a large force on the south coast of England to repel any attack.

Despite a conviction it was foolish to trust Ram, Mabelle looked forward to his visits and to discussing preparations for the invasion with him. She suspected he too was surprised at the way they fell into an easy give-and-take of ideas. She'd never had such a relationship with a man and didn't know what to make of her growing need to bask in the glow of his approval.

Ram was confident in his decisions, a leader of men, and yet he seemed to increasingly value and even seek her opinions.

While she shared his fervor for the invasion of England, she began to dread the day it would come to pass. Then he'd be gone and life wouldn't be the same without him. In the event of a successful campaign, it was unlikely he would return for many a year, if he survived.

If he fell in battle…

She didn't know whether to be relieved or bereft that nothing would ever come of their betrothal.

STAMFORD BRIDGE

Harold Godwinson, King of the English, sat in stunned disbelief in his headquarters on the south coast of England, where he had gathered his forces to await William's arrival. He swallowed hard, handing the message that had sent chills down his spine to his frowning brother. "King Harald Hardråda has landed unexpectedly on the north east coast near York with a force of more than fifteen thousand men. He's come for the throne."

Gyrth scanned the parchment. "What's worse, if this is true, our wretched half-brother has apparently joined with Hardråda."

"Tostig is evidently incensed I drove him out of his earldom of Northumbria after he rebelled against me," Harold replied, taking back the parchment. "What did he expect?" He crushed the missive in his fist, aware the trap carefully laid for William was now in serious jeopardy. "What's your advice? Do we stay here and wait for the Norman, or make haste to York?"

"We must oppose your Norwegian rival," his brother

replied without hesitation. "The threat from him is real. William is still waiting in Normandie for the wind to change."

Harold had been of the same mind. "You're right. We have no choice."

The forced march north was grueling. The strategic northern town of York had surrendered to Hardråda on the twenty-fourth day of September. In an effort to avoid battle, Harold arranged a meeting with Tostig, but no agreement was reached and the battle was joined the next day at dawn at Stamford Bridge. The opposing forces fought hard until noonday. The Norwegians were forced to retreat under the weight of superior English numbers. They were driven across the Ouse, where they made a fresh stand. A lone Norwegian giant took up a post on the bridge over the river and hewed down more than two score Saxons with a battle-axe. This stayed the advance of the English army for many hours.

Watching the massacre from his command post, Harold asked his commanders with exasperation, "Who is that formidable warrior?"

"No one knows, Sire," replied one of them, with equal irritation. "But we cannot advance with him there. I have a plan to send a boat beneath the bridge, and skewer him with a spear from below."

Harold looked at him sceptically, then shrugged, "Sometimes the simple plan is the best."

To the king's surprise, this ploy was successful, and the Norwegians were overrun. Harald Hardråda was killed by an arrow through the throat.

Gyrth gloated. "We've thrashed the Norwegians. Of their three hundred ships, only four and twenty are returning with their wounded, and Tostig, the traitor, is dead."

Harold scratched his head and adjusted his gold coronet. "We've defeated one rival, but now we're hundreds of miles from the south coast where William might arrive any time. Our army is tired, bloodied and aching to return home."

THE INVASION BEGINS

As she watched the elderly *comte* bid *adieu* to his three sons, Mabelle's heart bled for the man whose faith in her had changed everything. He seemed to have aged considerably in the few months since their first meeting.

She was aware he had spoken to each of them individually in his solar the previous evening, but now the moment of final farewell had come. The winds had finally changed.

Every servant braved the chill of the bailey to bid their *seigneurs* farewell. Giselle was crying and she wasn't the only one. Fernand Bonhomme stood rigid, his mouth a tight line. The distraught wives and children of knights stood shoulder to shoulder with the families of common soldiers, all united by pride and dread.

His face pinched and pale, Bernard de Montbryce shook the hand of his youngest son. "Go with God, Hugh. I pray you'll soon return safe and sound after a glorious victory."

Hugh embraced his father. “We are prepared. You’ve taught us well. We’ll celebrate together.” He turned to Mabelle, brushing a kiss on her knuckles. “*Au revoir, ma soeur*. We’ll bring him home in one piece.”

She could only nod in reply, afraid she too might dissolve into tears if she tried to form words from her dry throat. That the gentle Hugh already considered her a *sister* was humbling.

The *comte* poked his second son’s chest. “Watch out for those Saxon women,” he teased.

Antoine embraced his father but seemed unable to reply. He turned to Mabelle, bending close to her ear. “I don’t understand why my brother hasn’t yet married you. He’s a fool. Be patient.”

She swayed, afraid her knees might buckle at any moment as he pecked a kiss on each cheek.

Ram embraced his father. “I pledge to you that those who don’t yet know the name Montbryce will be aware of it once this righteous campaign is done and victory is ours. The Saxons will quake whenever they hear it.”

The old man stiffened his spine and nodded.

Ram took Mabelle’s hand, glaring at Antoine. “Papa needs you. I know you’ll take care of him,” he whispered. “You’re a good woman. I’m sorry—”

She shook her head, fighting the tears that threatened to spill. “Don’t leave with words of regret on your lips, Ram. I understand.”

Their gazes locked, the determination in his blue eyes piercing her to the heart. She prayed the lead ball lodged in the pit of her belly wouldn’t come up her throat. Were these the last moments they’d spend together? This wasn’t the time for recriminations. The Montbryces were off on a quest for glory. But she would miss him—keenly. Despite his arrogance, she was drawn to him. He had awakened feelings she'd never known.

He took her by surprise when he pressed his mouth firmly on hers, his big hands on her shoulders. She opened without thinking and leaned against him as their tongues mated. She didn't know what to do with her hands, afraid to touch him.

"I will carry the taste of you with me," he said when they broke apart, "until I return."

The *comte* linked his arm in hers and leaned on her heavily as they watched the three warriors mount their steeds and lead the Montbryce knights out of the bailey.

"Come back to me," her heart whispered. "Come back to me."

Ram rode proudly at the head of the Montbryce host as they made their way to where the fleet lay ready to sail. He was fulfilling his destiny to serve his duke in the fight for the English crown, to cover himself with glory. A grateful William would reward him well with lands and titles in the vanquished country. He and his brothers would return home as heroes. This was no time to look back.

Yet, an urge to turn Fortis around and gallop home to the castle consumed him. A dreadful premonition that he would never see his father again lay like a lead weight in his gut.

And what of Mabelle? He burned for her. Could he expect her to wait? She would likely never forgive him for his disregard, and pining for her would distract him from his mission. If it was God's will, they would be together.

None of these thoughts helped ease the discomfort of the hard arousal that had sprung to life when he'd kissed her.

The prospect of the short ride to St. Valery loomed like a trek to Constantinople.

~

As the winds of change blew across the Narrow Sea between Normandie and England, William and his army of seven thousand, the Montbryce brothers among them, boarded their longboats, after loading the horses, armor, weapons, provisions and wine.

"An army can't be victorious if it runs out of food," Ram had told Mabelle, "and we'll be a long way from the fertile fields of Normandie."

The deafening sounds of drums, trumpets and pipes filled the air as they set sail.

"If Harold is waiting on the coast, he'll surely know we're coming now," Ram jested.

William smiled. "According to reports delivered to me yesterday, he's moved his forces to the north to repel an unexpected attack by Hardråda. You and I will sail through the night aboard the *Mora*, and land on the morrow, as day breaks. Is the muster roll complete? Do you have it?"

"*Oui*, Your Grace, it's complete and in the good hands of the clerks who assisted me to compile it. Every man fighting for you is listed."

When all was in readiness, William ordered the signal to be given by use of a lantern on the mast. "Matilda gave me this ship, Ram. See the figurehead? It's a young boy with a bow and arrow pointing towards England."

Watching the setting sun, Ram held his breath, his heart beating erratically as the hundreds of ships he had helped build set sail on this momentous undertaking. All seemed to be going well, but, as darkness fell, the smaller flagship got too far ahead of the main fleet. Ram sensed his friend didn't want to appear perturbed as he calmly issued commands. "Cast out the anchor. We'll break our fast while we wait for them to catch up. Bring some spiced wine also."

Servants scurried to do his bidding, and soon Ram and his duke were savoring the wine. "You know, old friend, when I visited Edward in England all those years ago, he promised me the throne as a lawful gift. I sometimes wonder why he sent Harold to us as an ambassador. Did the wily old Confessor think it humorous to have two rivals size each other up?"

He cupped his goblet in both hands and inhaled the aroma. "I regret I'll have to kill Harold. I like the fellow. He's tall and handsome, has remarkable physical strength, courage and eloquence. He's known for his ready jests and acts of valor. But what's the use of those gifts without honor? It infuriates me he swore an oath of loyalty to me two years ago, over the relic of a saint's bones. He claims he was not aware of the bones, and in any case had crossed his fingers when he took the oath. You were there, *mon ami.*"

The wine was beginning to ward off the chill of the sea air creeping into Ram's blood. "I was indeed, Your Grace." He knew what came next.

"When he came to Normandie, I greeted him with

splendid hospitality after his difficult journey. He was shipwrecked, as you know, and we rescued him from Guy de Ponthieu. He assisted us with our campaign against the Bretons, saving two of our commanders who had fallen into quicksand. I knighted him for that."

William took a long draught of the wine and bit into a pastry. "He swore an oath, of his own free will, that he would represent me at Edward's court and do everything in his power to ensure the throne came to me, after the Confessor's death. He promised to garrison my troops in the castle at Dover, and anywhere else I might choose—at his expense, I might add."

"I can testify to that, as a truthful and honorable man who was present." Ram had heard the story many, many times over the course of the past six sennights, and his attention was more on the play of the moonlight on the rippling water. Did Mabelle watch the same moon?

William suddenly threw his empty goblet down angrily, and it rolled back and forth with the swell. "Then comes the unwelcome report that this insensate Englishman has not waited for public choice, has broken his oath, and has seized the throne of the best of kings on the very day of his funeral. But, unfortunately for Harold," William laughed, "the Pope doesn't approve of oath-breakers and has given my crusade his blessing."

Watching the rolling goblet made Ram's stomach clench and he felt the bile of *mal de mer* rise in his throat. He wondered if William would be as free and easy with his confidences and friendship if he did become king. Only six years separated them in age but William had ruled Normandie since he was a boy.

"I'm not naive, Ram. I recognize the real reason most

of the Norman nobility has supported my *crusade*—the promise of titles and lands in England, for anyone who would help me regain my throne."

He jumped to his feet and braced his legs against the movement of the ship. "I'm offering them the investment opportunity of a lifetime. If we can take England away from Harold, we'll divide up the kingdom. The Pope has legitimized our violence as necessary, in a just cause, to depose an oath-breaking upstart."

He raised his hand and pointed. "He's even given me this fine consecrated Papal banner."

Both men became lost in their thoughts as the longboat bobbed in the waves. Ram was not a good sailor and, if he had to be in a boat, would prefer it wasn't anchored. He didn't wish to retch in front of William. The duke was probably envisaging thrones and crowns and coronations. Ram thought of Mabelle, and his father's magnificent castle, his home. He wondered if and when he would ever see them again.

As dawn broke, they heard the cry from the prow, "We've sighted the fleet."

"Signal to regroup, and continue on to the coast." William sat, legs wide, hands on his knees, his back rigid, as the longship resumed its journey.

At Pevensey they heaved the longboats up on the shore, but when William stepped ashore, he slipped and fell into the mud. Trying to avoid the accident being perceived as a bad omen, Ram quipped, "His Grace already has the earth of England in his hands."

William smiled his thanks and raised his fist full of the muck. Everyone cheered, obviously relieved the awkward moment had passed.

"This is a good omen, Ram. We've had a safe crossing, and Harold has no one here to oppose us. Our spies were correct. He didn't expect us to come so late in the year."

Knights and nervous horses poured out of the boats.

"They are relieved to be back on dry land," William commented.

"As am I," Ram agreed.

When all were ashore, William summoned his commanders to his tent. He pointed to his half brother. "Eude will send out men immediately to raid the surrounding countryside for supplies. We'll move a few miles inland to the east, to Hastings, and erect the temporary wooden stockade we brought with us in pieces. An excellent idea of yours, Montbryce."

Ram squared his shoulders and jutted out his chin as he inclined his head in acknowledgement.

Merci, Mabelle.

William paced as he went over his plans for what Ram felt must have been the hundredth time. "Then we await Harold's inevitable arrival. We could advance on London, but it would be better to lure Harold to the coast. We have a sheltered harbor here. It's a good defensive position, and Sussex is Harold's territory. He'll ride to defend his people from our harassment. We must attack property in the vicinity, incensing Harold and drawing him here quickly.

"Once we have the south in our grasp, we'll turn our attention to bringing the rest of the country under our dominion. I've heard the Saxons have never managed to quell the rebellious Celts who live in the mountains of Wales. That might be a job for you, Rambaud de Montbryce."

Ram inclined his head, elated the duke considered him worthy of such a task.

"This castle feels empty without my boys," *Comte* Bernard said sadly, as he and Mabelle supped. "They've gone off to fight before. I should be used to this by now."

She understood his concern. His life revolved around his sons. They were the hope of his family's future. He seemed to have aged further in the few days since the departure of the fleet.

"We'll pray daily for their safe return, *milord*." She kept her voice calm, but her heart thudded in her ears, her head ached and she was filled with a sense of dread.

Pray God he returns to me.

But her heart knew it was a hopeless prayer. If he survived and prospered in England, it was unlikely he'd return for her.

They had received no word of the crossing. Had the ships arrived? How had Ram weathered the sea journey? Was he safe? She couldn't get him out of her head, couldn't forget the taste of his lips, the feel of his hands. It had been challenging and stimulating to sit discussing the preparations for the invasion, but now it was a reality and the potential loss to the Montbryce family, and to herself, overwhelmed her. An atmosphere of nervous expectancy, tinged with fear, pervaded the castle.

THE PATRIOT

DEEP IN THE MOUNTAINS OF WALES, AUTUMN 1066

Prince Rhodri ap Owain had received messages two days before with news that the newly crowned king of the English Saxons was on his way back to the south with his army. They had won a hard-fought battle in the north of England, defeating the Norwegians. Now Harold Godwinson journeyed to face another threat on the south coast.

William of Normandie waited with a fleet to invade England, intent on seizing the throne which he claimed Edward the Confessor had promised to him. The wind had only to change.

The ominous tidings spawned the usual nightmares, the keening laments of the dispossessed, gaunt faces of hunger and desperation.

Rhodri sat up abruptly, drenched in sweat, filled with foreboding that the nightmare would soon be reality. He shivered, combing his fingers through matted hair. Had he cried out? A deer hide separated his niche in the hall of the mountain fortress from the communal sleeping area of his men, but sounds travelled. He was their leader now after his father's untimely death. They looked to him, despite his youth. He must never show weakness.

He stretched his arms around his bent legs, and pressed his forehead to his knees, willing his body to cool and his heart to slow. Hasten the day the fortress would be completed, then he would have his own chamber, as he did in his small but comfortable castle in Powwydd.

He held his breath and listened. The wind moaned through the timbers in its relentless descent from the surrounding crags. The sounds of men deep in slumber filled the air. They slept the sleep of the dead after long back-breaking hours spent erecting this impregnable fortification in the mountains of Wales. It had been no easy task, but they needed a secure, hidden base for their attacks on the arrogant Ango-Saxons. Cadair Berwyn was the perfect location, tucked away where no one could find it.

Here they could speak their native *Cymraeg* without caring that the hated Angles called it *Walhaz*. It might be foreign to them, but to Rhodri's people it was part of the identity they had fought to protect for hundreds of years. Here they could be the children of *Cymru*.

Rhodri lay down on his side and pulled the *brychan* over him, the October air chilly on his naked skin. The amber beads around his neck shifted. He fingered his mother's gift lovingly. "A memory of me," she had whispered. "After I'm gone."

Now his whole family was indeed gone, swept away by a pestilence that had scythed through the hills and valleys. Had Rhodri not been at Cadair Berwyn, he too might have succumbed to its merciless march through the villages of Powwydd.

The aroma of frying food wafted into his nostrils, though the stone kitchens were some distance away from the wooden fortress. The cooks must be up and about. Dawn would break soon, bringing another day of challenges as the champion of an oppressed people.

Rhodri did not lack for courage but felt keenly the solitary nature of his position as Prince of Powwydd. It was a lonely life. No woman wanted to live with a rebel chieftain, hidden away for months in the mountains after raiding forays into lands they had once called their own.

At the funeral for his family, his father's ally, Morgan ap Talfryn, had raised the possibility of a betrothal with his daughter. Morwenna had been present at the rites in Powwydd. She was a girl of eleven, eight years his junior, but he had been reluctantly drawn to her promising breasts and long blonde hair. Her smile had been—alluring.

Restless, he pulled the *brychan* off his arms and settled it round his waist. The wool irritated the knotted designs newly etched into his biceps—symbol of his chieftaincy. He turned onto his back and stretched, cursing that his thoughts of generous breasts had aroused him. He cupped his *ceilliau* and shifted his weight to relieve the ache. Perhaps he should take Morgan up on the offer—but there was something about Morwenna made him hesitate.

He could not put off rising much longer. He must not be the last abed. He was reluctant to rise this day, a foreboding hanging over him they would receive bad tidings. His premonitions were not often wrong.

He scratched the stubble of his morning beard. The consequences for his people of either enemy being victorious weighed heavily on his mind. Harold's army would be tired after the battle and the long trek back to the south.

But the Saxons were a formidable fighting force, their shield wall impregnable, battle axes lethal.

From what Rhodri knew of William, Duke of the Normans, his strength lay in his mounted knights. He had a reputation as a brutal man who brooked no opposition. Heaven help *Cymru* if the Normans triumphed. But how could they get their horses across the Narrow Sea? In any case, a horse was no match for an axe.

Better the enemy you know.

Rhodri clenched his jaw. So many greedy men. Would his people ever be left in peace to live their lives in their own country, or would they be driven further into the wild mountains?

He thrust the *brychan* to the floor, pulled on his tunic, leggings and boots and strode off to break his fast with whatever it was that smelled so good.

PREPARING FOR BATTLE

Bands of Harold's forces began arriving back on the south coast throughout the day on the thirteenth of October. The king, his younger brother and several other knights met in his tent to plan strategy. "These men won a hard-fought battle a mere eighteen days ago two hundred and sixty miles to the north," Harold declared. "And now we expect them to meet a different enemy."

"Despite the hardship, morale is high," Leofric assured him. "Soundly defeating Hardråda has boosted confidence."

Harold tapped his chin. "But our numbers might not be sufficient despite recruiting many to our cause on the trip south, and collecting fresh troops in London. I assume a battle is inevitable since no form of parley has been offered. I've made the decision to challenge William before he can consolidate any further."

Leofric put his hand on his brother's shoulder. "You're the king the people of England want. They didn't want

Hardråda, and they certainly don't want William. Edgar the Aetheling is much too young. You're the dead Confessor's brother-by-marriage. He intended you to sit on the throne."

"I believe you are right," Harold replied. "The decision of the Witan to support me instead of Edgar has nothing to do with the Aetheling's age. The Archbishops of Canterbury and York and the other powerful members of the Witan recognize I am the more capable monarch."

Leofric nodded his agreement. "Now you need to clear your head after the long ride from the north and concentrate on the coming conflict."

Harold clenched his jaw. "Even my mother has advised we wait before joining William in battle, but I am adamant."

He hoped the confidence in his voice would resonate with his commanders as he faced them squarely, one hand on the hilt of his sword, his back rigid, his crowned head held high. "We can't afford to give William time to form alliances in England with Normans who've dwelt here for years. My decision to surprise the Norwegians is what brought about their defeat."

One knight raised his hand, as if to speak, but Harold's glare silenced him.

"We will fight William *now*. We need to choose the location of the battle with care."

He looked around for any further signs of opposition but saw none. "I've opted for Caldbec Hill for a number of reasons. It gives a natural advantage because of its all round visibility. It's protected on each flank by marshy ground, and there's a forest behind it. It's easy to reach from London and is close to William's position."

Many voiced their understanding and agreement.

"The Old Hoare Apple Tree is a well known landmark and will make an excellent rallying point. By nightfall, I estimate at least seventy-five hundred of our men should have arrived. Preparations must be laid to challenge William as soon as possible. He's in Hastings. Tomorrow is Saturday. I was born on a Saturday, and my mother has always said it's my lucky day."

After a sleepless night, he watched his army set off at first light. The common soldiers wore conical leather helmets, the wealthier helmets of iron and as much clothing as possible under their hauberks, to serve as padding. The rich knights had hauberks with hoods worn under the helmets. All were on foot, well-armed with battle-axes, swords, shields and spears. The impressive sight bolstered his confidence in the successful outcome of the battle.

Gyrth approached and went down on one knee. "Harold, there will be great danger in the coming battle. Let me take your place to lead the army against the Normans. You're too important to expose yourself, especially tired as you are after Stamford Bridge. England can't risk losing her king."

Harold took Gyrth's hand and pulled him to his feet. "I thank you for your love and concern, brother. William is deliberately victimizing my people in Sussex. It's personal now. I will lead our victory against him."

~

Prayers were offered in the Norman camp throughout the night prior to the impending confrontation, and men confessed their sins. Ram sought out his brothers and they received the Sacrament of Penance together. He wanted to clear the air, once and for all, between Antoine and himself. He had never truly believed his brother had dallied with his future wife, but the unfounded jealousy was there, in the back of his thoughts. Mabelle had uttered Antoine's name at the lake. He and his brother could both die during the coming battle. Antoine had sensed his coolness, he was sure. The crackling campfire held their gazes.

"Brother, there's no easy way to ask you this, but I must."

"I know something's on your mind, Ram. It has bothered you for months."

"It's Mabelle."

Antoine shook his head. "I've never understood why you didn't marry her that day. I was ashamed, I have to admit. You're lucky she still speaks to you."

Ram hesitated. "You're part of the reason I didn't."

Antoine looked startled. "Me?"

Here was the point of no return. "I chanced upon Mabelle in the woods, on my way home that day. She seemed to be waiting for someone."

Hugh and Antoine looked up suddenly. "And you thought it was me? Why?"

"She spoke your name."

"My name? What do you mean?"

"When she first saw me, she thought I was you."

Antoine straightened his back. He stared intently at Ram. "I'm confused. You saw her in the woods, and she thought you were me?"

Ram shifted uncomfortably on his camp stool. Now he would have to tell the whole story. "She was sleeping."

"In the woods?"

"She'd been bathing…at the lake…and fallen asleep."

Antoine exchanged a glance with Hugh and both men burst out laughing, drawing the curious stares of other knights nearby. Hugh almost fell off his stool.

When Antoine could speak again, he stammered, "What you're trying to tell us, older brother, is that you stumbled across Mabelle lying naked in the woods and—but, wait a moment—did you know who she was?"

"*Non*. And she wasn't naked. Not quite, anyway."

"So, let me see if I have this right." Antoine held up his thumb. "One, on the way to your wedding, you stopped to watch an unknown, *almost naked* maiden?"

He held up his forefinger. "Two, you became angry with me?"

His middle finger popped up. "Three, you were so furious with her, because she thought you were me, that you called off the wedding."

Another fit of laughter from Hugh caused Antoine to pause.

"I *knew* something had happened that day. I could tell there was tension between you," his younger brother said.

"Four," Antoine continued, "you're an idiot, and five, you should fall to your knees and ask the woman's forgiveness." He thrust his five outstretched digits in front of Ram's nose.

His brothers continued to mock him, and soon he was laughing and shaking his head at his own folly. He stood and dragged Antoine off his stool and into his embrace, choking back tears. "I'm sorry. Forgive me. When I'm near Mabelle, I lose my senses."

"That's called love," his brother replied.

Ram's spine stiffened. "I have no time for love."

"You're a fool if you drive her away," Hugh said gently.

They talked for another hour about their father, their beloved castle and its orchards. Each swore to bring honor to the Montbryce name. Despite their earlier laughter, Hugh's wide eyes, tense lips and crossed arms told Ram his brother was terrified.

"Hugh, there's no shame in feeling fear. I'm afraid, as is Antoine. My gut is in knots. Any man who tells you he's not afraid this night is a liar. The important thing is not to let the fear control you. Bravery is born of fear. Engrave our family motto on your heart, as it is on your shield, *Fidelity and Valor*."

Hugh nodded. "I know. I can't stop shaking but I'm not a coward."

~

William ordered a pre-dawn Mass to be said, during which he placed around his neck the relics on which Harold had sworn his oath. He assembled his army, and informed them what was expected. Astride his destrier, he proclaimed, "It's all or nothing. There's no going back without a victory. We will win because we are the righteous side."

He intoned a *laisse* of the Song of Roland to inspire his soldiers with that warlike example.

His castles all in ruin have you hurled,
With catapults his ramparts have you burst,

Vanquished his men, and all his cities burned.

Apprised by scouts of the Saxon position, the Normans set off from the coast in a long column, because of the forested terrain, their wagons loaded with sharpened weapons, armor and provisions. Startled birds took flight as the horde marched through the trees. No words were exchanged.

Did each man ponder his future, or his past, as Ram did, hypnotized by the muffled sounds of horses' hooves and leather booted feet, as they made their way to the inevitable horror ahead? Did every rider focus on the swaying tail of the horse ahead, sphincter muscles clenched?

They followed the Papal banner for nine miles then William selected a location for his command post behind the cavalry. Ram joined him astride Fortis.

"It's as well the situation is coming to a conclusion. Morale is beginning to wane amongst the foot soldiers," William confided. "They're more concerned with staying alive than with moral crusades and promises of wealth to the nobility."

Ram carefully checked his equipment, the hooded hauberk and iron helmet, spear, shield and trusty sword in its scabbard. He smiled at a brief memory of Mabelle heaving *Honneur* into the lake, but quickly banished the thought. He couldn't afford to be distracted from the dire business at hand. His hauberk, with three layers of metal circles, looped and soldered together, would give him good protection, especially with the extra rectangular breastplate of chain mail secured to protect his chest. The bottom of his hauberk tunic, split at front and back, covered his thighs like a skirt, and made riding more comfortable. He wished it covered the lower part of his long legs but would have to make sure the pointed end of his tapering wooden shield did that. He was proud of his leather covered shield, one of the few with a coat of arms. *Fide et Virtute*.

Vaillon had shaved the back of his head. He would be sweating a lot this day, and couldn't afford to have his vision obscured. The nosepiece of his helmet, protecting his nose and eyes, was enough of a distraction.

William positioned his army looking towards the steep hill Harold had chosen. Ram's gaze ranged slowly over the front ranks of archers, then to the six rows of infantry behind them, and then to the cavalry, the fearsome Bretons on the left, the Flemish contingent on the right, the Normans in the center. As he surveyed the daunting sight, Rambaud de Montbryce knew with dire certainty this would be a different fight from any he had been in before. It would be a mighty battle to the death that would change the course of history. His own, his country's and his duke's.

Immense pride and sheer terror coursed through his veins.

CARNAGE

"We will meet his challenge," Harold shouted decisively when he saw the Normans take up their position. "Move the men down from Caldbec Hill to within five hundred yards of the enemy. The Normans won't deploy a shield wall."

He scanned his army. The *housecarls* in the front rank were responsible for forming the shield wall, developed by Alfred the Great and used ever since. This tactic was particularly effective against the initial onslaught in any battle. Behind the *housecarls* were the *fyrd,* or militia, ten deep, led by the thanes who carried swords and javelins. Many of the peasants they'd recruited were armed with iron-studded clubs, slings, reaping hooks, scythes and haying forks.

He set up his command post behind them, centrally positioned to provide an elevated view of proceedings. Confidence coursed through him, heating his warrior blood. He ordered the signal to be given. His standard bearer raised the Wessex Wyvern dragon and waved it proudly. Suddenly on the air came the Saxon battle cries, "*Godemite*", "*Oli Crosse*".

The Normans responded with a plea for God's help, "*Que Dieu nous aide*."

Trumpets sounded. The pivotal battle began.

~

"What's that fool doing?" screamed William, as one of his men broke ranks to rush forward *alone*, juggling swords, to attack the Saxons. He was quickly cut down, after managing to slay a standard bearer at the front of the astonished enemy soldiers.

"Loose the arrows," he commanded.

The Norman archers let fly their arrows in a concentrated barrage. This had limited success against the shield wall.

A serious problem soon became apparent to Ram. "Your Grace," he shouted breathlessly, when he arrived back at the command post. "I'm not sure why, but the English are not using archers, and we require an exchange of arrows to keep the ammunition levels up. We'll soon run out."

William cursed. "If that happens, our archers are not trained for hand to hand fighting. Bring forward the crossbows."

Ram shook his head. "But, Your Grace, the Pope has forbidden the use of crossbows. We're fighting Christians."

William clenched his fist. "We must defeat Harold. That's our only concern, and crossbow bolts are more effective against shields."

Ram had no alternative but to obey.

With prearranged hand signals, William ordered his foot soldiers forward. The English did the same. The quiet of the countryside soon filled with the clang of swords, the sickening thud of clubs on helmets and bone, the battle cries of the living, and the groans of the dying. Iron helmets and weapons clashed.

The English on the high ground had the advantage. The Saxon line remained virtually untouched, the arrows having done little damage to the impenetrable armored monster that was the shield wall. The barrage of traditional weapons as well as rocks from slings, caused serious problems to William's men.

"We'll need the cavalry earlier than I would have wished," William shouted. "Too many heavy casualties." He turned as Ram galloped into view. "Montbryce," he yelled, "order the cavalry to charge on the shield wall, before it advances much further."

Heart pounding, Ram rode at full speed into the bloody mayhem to deliver the order to the cavalry. Both his brothers were among the mounted Norman ranks. He encouraged his horse, knowing the weight, speed and impact of Fortis might prove to be his best weapon against the unmounted Saxons. Secure in the large saddle, raised front and back to give him a solid seat, he used his spurs sparingly on the beloved horse. "I'm thankful it's you beneath me, Fortis. Many questioned the wisdom and necessity of bringing horses on the ships, but I would wager they see the right of it now. You could be the difference between victory and defeat."

It was puzzling that the English army had no cavalry. Perhaps neither the horses nor the men were trained to fight as one. As a youth he had learned to fight from horseback as a noble pursuit. The idea of a mounted elite was a heroic notion in Normandie and Bretagne, as Mabelle had rightly observed.

But now, hard as the Normans tried, they could not break the shield wall. The Saxons brought down riders and horses with a single blow of their lethal Danish battle axes. The slope quickly became a muddy slide, making the ascent difficult for the horses. Fortis struggled as Ram swung and hacked with his sword, severing limbs and heads.

The much feared Bretons, on the left, were having a particularly difficult time. They retreated back down the hill, and Ram watched in horror, left with no alternative but to go back to the command post. The muscles of his sword arm were on fire, his face spattered with blood and muck. His heart raced. He turned back to look at the scene of chaotic terror and caught sight of another Montbryce shield, the knight carrying it still mounted. Was it Hugh or Antoine?

"The retreat of the Bretons leaves us vulnerable to a pincer attack," William bellowed when Ram returned to his side. "Our men are panicking." He cursed and Ram sensed he could see his dreams of taking the English throne in serious jeopardy.

Ram feared he might never see Mabelle again.

Why do my thoughts go to her?

Panic was widespread amongst the Normans. The Bretons were in full retreat back down the hill but were slowed down on the lower slopes by the stream and marshy ground below, giving the Saxons more opportunity to inflict casualties.

"Your Grace," Ram panted, swallowing hard, pointing to the cavalry. "Eude is rallying his men."

Two of William's commanders, one his half brother, the other Eustace of Boulogne, had indeed seen the action on the left flank, and were rallying their confused cavalry. They galloped towards the Saxon infantry who turned tail, broke off battle and tried to return to their lines. The uphill trek proved to be too far, and they were cut down by the Norman cavalry. Ram suddenly caught a glimpse of his gentle brother Hugh hacking down an enemy soldier, but then lost sight of him.

Ram sensed William was at his lowest ebb, trying to plan a new tactic to break down the Saxon defenses. "The cursed Saxons will win if they hang on until dark. We can't stay here all night. We would have to retreat, and retreat means defeat. The terrain makes it difficult," he shared with his commanders gathered around him. "We can't attempt a flanking movement, because of the trees and marshes on either side. Harold chose this place well. We can't break the shield wall. Perhaps we can feign a retreat and draw the Saxons forward?"

Most of his commanders were doubtful it would work. Ram wiped the bloody muck off his face and urged, "It's our only chance. We need to lure the Saxons forward by giving the impression it's a genuine retreat, and not a tactic. Normans have used it successfully before."

William thought for a while, shifting impatiently in his saddle. "We'll resume the battle. Montbryce, order the infantry to advance, and then lead the cavalry, at speed, up the hill behind the infantry. Engage the Saxons, and then turn around and make it appear we're running. You'll have to choose the moment carefully, so as not to arouse their suspicion it's a trick."

Ram rode back into hell, his blood pumping so fast his heartbeat echoed in his ears, in time with his steed's hoof beats. The sound had an oddly comforting cadence to it, "Ma-Belle, Ma-Belle, Ma-Belle."

The duke had already lost three horses in the melee. Ram thanked God Fortis still lived. He clutched the leather straps of his shield tightly, couched his spear like a lance, and leaned into his horse.

The infantry advanced with limited success. Ram regretted he could not inform them of William's plan. Most would be killed, sacrificed for the greater good. Yelling the battle cry *Fide et Virtute* at the top of his lungs, he led the cavalry at a gallop up the hill and engaged the Saxons, narrowly avoiding being decapitated by a gigantic Saxon wielding a battle axe. He felt the cold draft of the huge weapon as it swung close to his ear, heard the *whoosh*. For a moment, he couldn't understand why he wasn't looking at his own bloodied head on the ground instead of into the startled, disembodied gaze of the Flemish knight who had ridden at his side. He thrust his spear into the Saxon's throat, then pulled hard to retrieve it. A quick glance over his shoulder showed the moment was at hand. Shifting his shield to cover his back, he bellowed the order to turn, hoping to give the impression they were retreating.

To his immense relief the Saxons broke ranks and followed. He quickly turned his men and attacked. The enemy had no footing on the slippery slope and were easily cut down.

Ram became vaguely aware of arrows flying overhead.

He surmised William must have sent his archers forward to retrieve the arrows loosed earlier. Wheeling round, he saw King Harold raise his hands to clutch an arrow that had struck him in the face. The monarch fell to the ground.

"Your Grace, Harold has fallen! He has fallen!" Ram's throat was so dry he hoped his strangled cry had reached the duke's ears.

Reining in his horse and swiveling in the saddle to look at where Ram pointed, William yelled, "This news will cause widespread confusion. We must launch a full frontal attack now."

News of Harold's demise spread like wildfire through the Saxon ranks. They fled up the hill into the forest on the other side. Exhausted and wounded English warriors were pursued relentlessly and cut down in the woods or trampled beneath thundering hooves.

AFTERMATH

After the battle, the dead and injured of both sides and the carcasses of Norman horses littered the battlefield. Severed body parts lay everywhere on the bloodied earth, now churned to mud. The Saxon line had broken. The mangled bodies that had been the flower of English nobility covered the ground as far as the eye could see. Only the King's *housecarls* were prepared to continue the fight. They surrounded their dead king, armed with battle-axes and swords, and fought valiantly to the last man.

The Normans at last broke through to where King Harold had fallen. They had won against the odds, but, as darkness fell, William uttered his dismay at the sight of so many promising young men, both English and Norman, lying dead or maimed on the field of battle. Only the cawing of scavenging crows intruded on the eerie silence.

As they picked their way through the carnage, William confided to Ram, "If Harold had waited only one more day for his full force to arrive, the outcome of this battle may have been very different. If he'd been patient, it would have been more difficult for us to maintain our position here, far from home."

He gazed distractedly at the Wessex Wyvern dragon banner, still fluttering limply in the breeze, and Harold's personal standard of the Fighting Man, captured near his body. It was sumptuously embroidered with gold and precious stones. William pointed to it. "I want that standard borne to the Pope."

Ram saw the exhaustion etched into his friend's face and suspected he looked equally haggard.

"By the way," William said, "speaking of impetuous, who was the fool that charged the Saxons alone, at the outset of the battle?"

"According to rumor, a *jongleur* named Taillefer," Ram replied.

"Hmm. The man must have had a death wish. I suppose *troubadours* will be singing about him soon. He'll be more famous than I."

Ram de Montbryce and his future king looked at each other and laughed.

~

As soon as William gave leave, Ram searched frantically for his brothers. To his great relief, they had both survived the slaughter. The three stood together for long silent minutes, arms around each other's shoulders, except that Hugh's left arm hung at his side. He had suffered a sword slash to his bicep, which had been tended by one of the camp physicians.

They spent time calming and reassuring their horses,

knowing the important role the steeds had played in keeping them alive. It was significant the three Montbryce horses—his own Fortis, Hugh's Velox, and Antoine's Regis—had survived. Few Normans could claim that, and it was a testament to the care with which they were chosen, and the attention lavished on them.

"My body stinks," Antoine lamented. "It disgusts me. I'm for the river."

They stripped off their armor with the help of their squires and joined many others who were trying to wash away the stench of blood, sweat and their own waste. They enjoyed a moment of wry humor at the sight of Hugh trying to keep his wounded arm dry.

"I'll never be clean again," Ram complained as they dried off.

He got no sleep that night, and as dawn broke the following morning joined the other survivors summoned for the solemn reading of the muster roll. Ram was saddened to discover his handsome friend, Pierre de Fleury, had lost his life.

"He'll no longer have to lie with his ugly wife," he said bitterly to Antoine. "Perhaps he'd rather be alive and lying with her, than stone cold dead on this bloody field."

The Montbryce brothers left the marshaling area after the ceremony and huddled under the canvas hastily erected by their squires. They looked out over the distant battlefield, sickened by the scavengers still combing over what remained of the bodies. "We should be grateful our rank saved us from the duty of searching for spoils," Hugh murmured.

"My squire has scrubbed my armor with vinegar and

sand, but I can still smell the stench of blood. It clings as do fleas to a dog," Antoine scowled.

"It's the piteous moans of the wounded I find the hardest," Hugh murmured. "We were lucky to escape as we did."

His brothers grunted their agreement. They sat in strained silence. Eventually Hugh spoke, his voice full of anger. "The duke has arranged for the proper burial of the Normans who fell and Bishop Eude is to say a Mass. A few Saxons took their dead away, but most of the English corpses are being buried in a mass grave."

Antoine looked hard at Ram. "There are rumors His Grace wanted to verify the identity of the body they thought was Harold's. It was so mutilated his face couldn't be recognized. William ordered Harold's mistress, Edith Swanneck, to attend and verify identifying marks which only an intimate would know."

"That's true. I can vouch for it. The body was a gruesome sight," Ram admitted, shaking his head. "The woman was distraught."

"What about the other rumor, that Harold's mother sent messages offering the weight of her son's body in gold, if she could be allowed to bury him, but William perversely refused?" Hugh asked.

"That's also true, I regret to say. He ordered Harold be buried in an unmarked grave, near the sea shore he'd fought so hard to protect. Even I don't know the location."

The three were silent for a long while, holding their hands to the warmth of the campfire. Ram spoke first. "I'd hoped to return home to Normandie," he told them, "but William is sending me to Ellesmere, in the west where there has been trouble for many years between the Welsh and the English. News has arrived from Normans who settled in the area years ago that there have been more recent raids on the Welsh borders. A rebel by the name of Rhodri ap Owain has been attacking the towns and villages near Ellesmere. William has promised me an earldom there."

Antoine and Hugh were delighted for their brother and shook his hand. Ram accepted their congratulations, knowing they were genuine, then continued, "William wants us to assert our authority now over the rebels. I'm to reconnoitre the area and inspect my castle at Ellesmere at the same time. I'll request you be assigned to accompany me. Your wound shouldn't prevent you from traveling, Hugh?"

His brother's hand still trembled.

"*Non, mon frère*. I'll be fit to travel. Thank you for your words of courage before the battle."

Ram nodded. "Hastings has taken a heavy toll. We will never forget this battle as long as we live. I wouldn't admit this to anyone else, but you're my brothers. I miss Mabelle. I want to share the victory with her—perhaps confide something of the terror and disgust I felt, and tell her the news of the promised earldom. I want to lie with her, bury my head in her breasts, fill her with my seed and feel whole again. You're right, Antoine. I was a fool many times over not to marry her."

His words seem to resonate with Hugh. "Why is it the thing a man feels compelled to do after courting death is lie with a woman? Most of the survivors in my brigade are hobbling round trying to hide tree trunks at their groins. Look at me." His trembling hand went to his bulging manhood. "I can't help myself."

Antoine shifted uncomfortably. They believed Hugh had never lain with a woman. Ram thought his young brother might be close to his breaking point. "Much as I would like to hasten home to wed Mabelle, I'll have to do the duke's bidding, if I want to keep the title he's promised. At least we'll have each other's company as we travel to Ellesmere, and I'll know you're safe. I'll dispatch a messenger to Montbryce."

~

William was incensed. "Since Hastings I've waited a sennight for the Witan to formally surrender the English throne to me, and now we have news they've proclaimed Edgar the Aetheling king. They have the gall to support the Confessor's grand-nephew. I give my oath, Ram, he'll never be crowned, as long as I draw breath. We'll evidently have to take London by force."

Ram's heart fell. This would mean another delay before he could return to Normandie. He struggled not to let his agitation show. William was upset enough. "It seems ironic Stigand and the others now want to support Edgar, when they were previously willing to favor Harold as king over him."

"You're right. It makes one question their resolve. First we march to Dover. It's strategically important and we must secure it."

In Dover an epidemic of the flux broke out among the troops after they ate tainted meat and drank the water. Many died, and still more had to be left behind in Dover to recover as the invading force advanced to the religious center of England.

After taking Canterbury, they marched on London, where the core of resistance was centered on Edgar. Meeting fierce opposition at London Bridge they circled to the west of the city, setting fires and leaving a trail of devastation.

"We'll cross the Thames at Wallingford," William ordered. "Wigod, the Lord of Wallingford, is a Norman sympathizer."

At Wallingford, Stigand abandoned Edgar. The Aetheling's forces were dwindling rapidly. He met William at Berkhamsted, with a group of English nobles, and offered him their fealty, bringing to an end the Anglo-Saxon kingdom that had lasted for hundreds of years.

THE HEALER

HAMLET OF ELLESMERE, BORDER MARCHES.

Rhonwen Dda had never met her father. Everyone in the Welsh village where she was born was aware she was the natural child of a Saxon lord and the local healer. The shame had driven Myfanwy to take her skills as a healer and her babe to the hamlet of Ellesmere, in the border Marches, where they weren't known.

Rhonwen had no memory of Wales.

Over time, Myfanwy's reputation spread, and she was sought after for her knowledge. People spoke in hushed tones of her mystical healing powers. As Rhonwen grew, she often assisted her mother with the preparation of herbs and salves. She longed to master the secrets of healing and observed her mother closely.

Myfanwy was a patient teacher who delighted in her daughter's wish to follow in her footsteps. "It's glad I am you'll be a healer, Rhonwen. I'm getting old, and the day will come when you'll need to take care of yourself."

The meagre brazier flickering in the centre of the hut had melted the November frost, but their breath still hung in the air as they prepared cures. Rhonwen's shoulders stiffened as she shivered. She slid her hands from the warmth of her sleeves and touched her mother's arm, stilling the grinding of dried herbs. "You're not old, mammie."

But her mother had not been a young woman when she had conceived. The arm Rhonwen held was thin and boney. She shivered again. Her mother was her protector, her teacher. How could a girl of ten fend for herself?

Myfanwy's face was grim. "There is danger everywhere in these uncertain times, daughter, and healing skills are what will protect you, give you standing. We must hope these victorious Normans will appreciate our talents when they come to the Marches."

Her mother resumed her task. Rhonwen's heart fluttered again. She took a deep breath. "How do you know they'll come?"

Myfanwy put aside her mortar and pestle and took Rhonwen's hands. "They will come. This William of Normandie will be as greedy as the Saxons. Now he has slain King Harold, he will want to control everything and everyone in his path. I pity the Welsh who have struggled so valiantly against the English Saxons. I fear life under the Normans will be much worse."

Rhonwen threw herself into her mother's arms. "Can we not flee? Where can we go to be safe?"

Myfanwy hugged her tightly and whispered, "Nowhere will be safe. We must make sure we are needed. Good healers are highly prized by warriors."

Rhonwen inhaled her mother's scent. It was the comforting aroma of healing herbs and potions, the smell of hope and freedom from pain. She nestled her head into her mother's breast and Myfanwy rocked her, crooning a soothing Welsh lullaby.

FAREWELL

Mabelle was distraught. News of the costly victory at Hastings had reached Montbryce, but no word of her betrothed and his brothers. Rumor was rife that hundreds of Norman knights had lost their lives; the remainder had been stricken by the flux and the campaign was not going well in other parts of England.

Comte Bernard paced the hallways on the rare occasions he wasn't closeted in his solar, brooding. The one man who'd been her champion was lost in his own anguish. Sometimes he seemed not to know who she was.

Giselle talked about nothing but her sons and fretted for news of them.

It was Mabelle's darkest hour. Was Ram alive or dead? Why did she ache for a man she should loathe?

There was no happiness for her at Montbryce. Ram would never love her. She'd longed for years to return to Alensonne, and not a sennight went by without a missive from her father urging her to come home. Now was the time.

However unlikely it might be that a letter would reach Ram in England, she couldn't simply leave without explanation.

She summoned a scrivener. After several attempts to express her feelings to the impatient monk, she approved the final version.

To Vicomte Rambaud de Montbryce

In the great hope that you and your brothers yet live, I send you this missive.

Montbryce is a place I have known only humiliation and unhappiness. Will any of you ever return?

I must turn my attention to my beloved Alensonne, where by all accounts my father is making life difficult.

You must marry a bride more suited to you. I release you from your obligation. You will not now receive Alensonne, Belisle and Domfort in dower, and I don't yet know how to resolve that problem, as I'm sure they are lands you covet.

Perhaps my diplomatic father will have a solution.

Mabelle de Valtesse (and d'Alensonne)

Having set her seal, she dismissed the supercilious cleric and set off in search of the *comte*, not looking forward to telling him of her decision. She found him sitting before the hearth in his solar, staring into the flames, and stammered out her intention to leave. He eventually dragged his gaze away from the fire, looked at her as though bewildered, patted her hand and told her she must do what she thought was best. She left unsure if he'd understood her words or not.

She then sought out the steward and gave him the letter. "For my betrothed," she explained. "You'll know the best way to make sure he receives it."

"*Oui, milady,*" he replied, taking the letter with uncharacteristic brusqueness.

"Is something wrong, Fernand?" she asked, worried he might have guessed the contents.

He tucked the parchment into his tunic. "Forgive me, *milady*. Vangeline and I are trying to do too much. Many of the servants have fallen pray to the pestilence spreading through the village."

Giselle had told her of the illness afflicting some of the neighboring villages. Perhaps it was her duty to stay. She was probably needed at Alensonne, though her father had mentioned nothing. Not that he would care if servants fell ill. "You'll make sure my letter is sent," she reminded Fernand as he bowed and hurried away.

BLINDSIDED

Ram and his brothers left the main army after the historic surrender. The three Montbryce men had escaped the ravages of the flux but were sickened again by the excessive brutality of the victory at Wallingford. Guided by Normans who'd settled in England years before, they set out with two hundred of the best surviving knights and men-at-arms from Montbryce, to make the journey from the River Thames to the Welsh border region. Ram deemed the force a sufficient number to deter any attack from disgruntled locals. It was unlikely there'd be any threat from armed militias, most of whom had joined Harold's army and perished at Hastings.

Ram told Hugh, "We should cover the seven score miles to Ellesmere in four days, if we're lucky and the December conditions don't make the track difficult. Pray for cloudless skies."

Their route took them through the fortified burgh of Oxford. The inhabitants fled upon catching sight of their small army.

"News of our victory has traveled fast," Ram observed. "William has spoken often of this place, founded two centuries ago by Alfred the Great. He's considered building a castle here and I'll report it's a good idea, given the location."

"I'm impressed with the way the streets are laid out in an orderly pattern," Antoine added. "I'd guess there are about a thousand houses, which probably means there are close to five thousand inhabitants."

Hugh agreed. "The Danes burned the town fifty years ago, so I suppose much of what we see has been built since then. The town seems prosperous."

They left Oxford in good spirits and followed the Cherwell River, bound for Warwick, another walled town William had his eye on for a castle. The three agreed a piece of land on a sandstone bluff overlooking the River Avon would be an ideal location for such a project.

Ram began to feel more optimistic. "Such important pieces of information might turn this inconvenient journey to my advantage, and augment my importance in William's eyes."

He was glad of the company of his brothers. He could keep an eye on Antoine and Hugh, and the presence of family bolstered his hopes. They had proven themselves as warriors in the hell of Hastings, but Hugh had withdrawn into uncharacteristic moodiness. The seemingly uncontrollable tremor in his younger brother's hand was worrisome.

Passing through Bridgnorth on the River Severn, Ram resolved to ask William for this town as part of his holdings. Though somewhat far removed from Ellesmere, it was a good location, and William hadn't mentioned it for a royal castle.

They decided to stop at Shrewsbury to ascertain the latest news of Welsh incursions, learning from Norman sympathizers that Rhodri ap Owain had been creating havoc around the town of Oswestry.

"This is surprising," Ram remarked to his brothers as they left the meeting. "I understood winter normally keeps the Welsh in their mountain hideaways. Perhaps they're changing their strategy? We'll investigate once we've inspected Ellesmere."

~

A day later, Ram surveyed the crumbling Anglo-Saxon timber fortification that was Ellesmere Castle. It guarded the only dry approach to the town, which seemed to exist in a sea of mud.

He and his brothers were frozen to the bone, thanks to the incessant bitter wind sweeping down from the snow-capped peaks to the west.

"They say Welsh rebels survive all winter long in those bleak mountains," Antoine observed, "but that can't be true."

"Must be hardy men," Hugh added.

Drowning in disappointment, Ram looked at his shivering brothers, their noses as red as winter beetroots, aware they were avoiding voicing what had to be said. "Go ahead and say it. So much for my earldom. The place is a *fyking* disaster."

"It'll need work," Antoine agreed.

"Work," Ram exclaimed. "More like a miracle."

"You simply have to accept it will take a few years to

build another Montbryce here," Hugh retorted. "But you have the ambition and the intelligence to do it."

"And you'll have Mabelle," Antoine reminded him. "She's survived hardship before."

Ram looked to the mist-shrouded mountains. "This is a good location for forays into Wales. I suppose I have to be patient and face the reality it will be a long while before this place is habitable. I certainly can't bring a wife here the way it is now."

"You intend to marry Mabelle then?" Hugh asked.

"As soon as William gives me leave to return to Normandie," Ram replied, swearing a silent oath to build a magnificent castle for Mabelle at Ellesmere that would be warm and welcoming, instead of this abomination, and to return to her side as soon as he could. What more did he want in a wife? The prospect renewed his hopes for the future. "Let's get the men out of the wind and see what's inside this so-called castle."

~

They spent two days deciding what to burn or demolish. Hugh mastered a few words of the native tongue and assured Ram there were many peasants who'd come looking for work. It seemed the majority were glad to hear of the demise of the Danish king. It was a good omen. Normans had much to offer, especially in terms of government, commerce and architecture, and Ram began to envisage Ellesmere as a prosperous market town.

But he was impatient to reconnoiter the surrounding area. There'd been more reports of raids by Welsh rebels and he wanted to let local folk know he and his army were in the vicinity to stay and intended to put a stop to the raids. They were far from London and William had placed a great responsibility on his shoulders.

He was about to ride out with Gervais and his brigade when his lieutenant noticed a small group of riders approaching.

Antoine had come to see him off and was the first to recognise among them the messenger they'd sent to Montbryce after Hastings.

Ram hadn't really expected a reply. "You delivered our missive?" he asked. "Our father knows we are safe?"

"*Oui, milord*, although he was too ill to dictate a response."

Ram's heart lurched. "Too ill?"

"A pestilence, *milord*. Many in the Calvados are suffering."

"But he will recover?" Antoine asked.

The messenger took a parchment from a satchel slung across his body. "I'm sure of it, *milord*, but he said you would understand once you read this missive from *Milady* Mabelle."

Ram took the letter, but hesitated.

"Open it," Antoine urged.

"Mabelle wouldn't have written unless it was bad news," he replied, slipping off the ribbon.

He unfolded the parchment, scanned the contents and immediately understood his father's distress. His sire had been correct. Mabelle recognized her own worth, something he had failed to see. He wanted to tell her about Hastings, about his promised earldom, but that wouldn't come to pass now.

He didn't blame her, but the loss cut deep. However, he

couldn't give vent to his anguish with his men looking on. He refolded the letter. "She's left me," he said to Antoine.

His brother grabbed the parchment. "What?"

Perhaps if his trembling legs functioned and he managed to mount Fortis and ride away on his mission, some of the pain might dissipate. "Remain here. I'll be back in a few hours."

Antoine followed him. "You can't accept this. She'll come round. Ask for permission to return home. Father is ill. The duke will grant leave."

Ram swung himself into the saddle, anxious to be anywhere but in the windswept courtyard. "She's made her decision. I have to learn to live with it."

He signaled Gervais and rode out towards the distant mountains.

CONFRONTATION

Rhodri had forewarned his men their latest foray into the Marches would be dangerous, but they needed the grain. The farms near Ruyton were the likeliest place to find it. They did not expect to encounter Saxons. According to rumor, most of the English nobility had been massacred by William of Normandie at Hastings, the rest at Dover, Canterbury and Wallingford.

The Normans would come, but it was not likely they had reached the Marches yet. From all reports, William seemed to be concentrating his merciless campaign in the south, and Rhodri had led several raids without encountering any opposition. He hoped Ruyton, the furthest point they had travelled from their hideaway, would be the same.

Taking the grain went without a hitch. The terrified farmers offered no resistance. Rhodri was careful to leave them sufficient for their own families and they were grateful. They had no overlord to satisfy now. He hoped the Woolgar brute who governed nearby Shelfhoc Hall was one who had perished at Hastings. It was probable, since the man had been a *huscarl* of King Harold. It was said they had fought to the death rather than surrender to the Normans.

They loaded the surefooted ponies that would carry the grain safely back to Wales. This raid would be the last for a long while. Rhodri tarried with a handful of his men, sharing ale with the farmers, trying to coax what news they might have about the Norman invaders. They confirmed Caedmon Woolgar's death at Hastings.

"I pity the Mistress of Shelfhoc," one of the farmers said. "Lady Ascha is better off without her brutish husband, but 'tis no time for a woman left alone, especially with them Welsh—"

He stole a glance at Rhodri who snickered and slapped the man on the back. "I don't attack defenseless women. Besides, Shelfhoc is a difficult place to assault with its ditch and rampart. Much better to prey on farmers."

They smirked, then looked at him strangely. Rhodri thought he'd best leave. "I thank you for your hospitality, and your grain. Were we treated like men, we could farm our own land, but as it is—anyway, fewer will starve now."

He mounted his pony and led his band at a gallop westward across the plain.

~

Ram relished the cold wind on his face and ignored the numbness of fingers frozen inside leather gauntlets. He wasn't even sure how far they had ridden when they caught sight of a distant group of riders galloping west.

"*Milord*," Gervais shouted excitedly, "I would wager those are Welsh rebels fleeing Ruyton."

Ram had no notion where Ruyton was, but here was an opportunity to rid himself of the fog in his brain. "*Oui*, you're probably right. We'll give chase. If they are headed for those hills yonder, they have some way to go and won't be expecting pursuit. Give the command to pursue."

The veteran Norman soldiers eagerly spurred their horses and had closed the gap on the Welsh band significantly when the lead rider, a mountain of a man, turned and saw them. He alerted the others, and they increased their speed. The moorland terrain was rugged. One false move could result in a horse's hoof plunging into a pothole in the rolling landscape.

Suddenly, the leader's horse lost its footing, and animal and rider went down. With incredible agility, as if it were an everyday occurrence, the huge warrior quickly found his feet and had his dagger out. One Norman soldier fell from his horse with a bone-chilling scream as the barbarian slashed the dagger across his belly, almost severing the lad in two with the power of his thrust.

Ram's warrior blood rushed to his head. "Gervais, continue the pursuit. I'll deal with this ruffian," he yelled, reining in his snorting horse, dropping from the saddle and unsheathing his sword in one fluid movement. The men continued on after the fleeing rebels.

Ram yanked off his helmet, threw it to the ground, and faced the barbarian, noting with surprise his opponent didn't show signs of fear. Ram had the advantage. His enemy had no sword, but he'd seen what the man had done with his dagger and would have to be wary. He pulled off his gauntlets and blew on his cold fingers.

Perhaps facing him alone wasn't a good idea.

The two warriors squared off—Ram trying to make the thrust with his sword that would disarm the rebel, the powerful Welsh barbarian attempting to plunge his dagger into a momentarily unguarded part of his body. It occurred to him he rarely came face to face with an enemy who matched him in height.

"I am Rambaud de Montbryce, Earl of Ellesmere. On the authority of King William, I command your surrender," Ram declared with calm assurance in Norman French.

The barbarian grinned, and to Ram's surprise responded in the same language. "I am Rhodri ap Owain, Prince of Powwydd. Ellesmere has an earl, you say? The Norman bastard isn't my king, not anyone's king yet, therefore I cannot and will not surrender to you."

Ram became more determined now he knew his opponent's identity. Without their fabled leader, the Welsh would falter. He thrust again and Rhodri deflected the blow. Sword and dagger became braced together as the two men struggled, their intense gazes locked on each other. He decided to use a well practiced maneuver and pulled away from the deadlock, taking Rhodri unawares. His sword flicked the dagger out of the Welshman's hand. He advanced on the unarmed man, again offering him the chance to surrender.

"You don't understand, Norman invader. Welshmen don't surrender," Rhodri sneered. Suddenly he lunged at Ram, knocking the wind out of him and *Honneur* out of his hand. He fell backwards onto a rocky outcropping. Pain lanced into his skull.

I survived Hastings to fall here?

His knees buckled and he reeled into oblivion.

Rubbing his bruised shoulder and gasping for breath, Rhodri retrieved his dagger and whistled for Ariel. It wasn't the first time he'd fallen from a speeding horse and he'd learned to keep his body loose and roll. He thanked his ancestors for the intelligence of the loyal pony that had known enough to stay close. He remounted with difficulty, sickened by the ghastly memory of almost severing the Norman lad in two with his dagger. Fodder for more nightmares.

He galloped west, filled with a dread he had not seen the last of the arrogant Rambaud de Montbryce. Earl of Ellesmere, indeed!

ASCHA

Ram didn't recognize the unsmiling face of the woman bending over him, but her eyes showed concern. Weren't angels supposed to be smiling when he reached paradise? He sank back into the murky haze.

"If I'm in heaven, why does my head feel like it's broken?" he murmured groggily when he awoke some time later.

"That's because you're not dead, *milord*."

"Gervais?" he muttered, half opening one eye.

His lieutenant stood at the foot of the bed on which he lay.

He lifted the linens to discover he was shrouded in a nightshirt several sizes too big.

"*Oui, milord*. I'm relieved you're awake. *Non*, don't try to get up. *Milady* says you must rest. You suffered a severe blow to the head."

"*Milady*? Who is *milady*? I trust it was not she who removed my clothing?"

Gervais scowled as if the notion of him allowing such

a thing was preposterous. "Her manservant assisted me to get you into bed. Lady Ascha Woolgar is mistress of this manor, *milord*. We brought you here because it was close and we were afraid you wouldn't make it to Ellesmere. This is Shelfhoc Manor, near Ruyton. I have sent word to your brothers."

"I don't understand what happened," Ram said with great exasperation.

"*Milord*, it's not good to get agitated. When the barbarian lunged and knocked you off balance, you hit your head on a sharp rock. You have a large gash on the back of your head. The wound bled a great deal. We were on the way back and I saw what happened, but couldn't get there in time to aid you. The rebel's horse wasn't hurt, and he remounted and fled. I had to decide whether to follow them, or help you. We had killed two of their men, but three of ours had fallen. I didn't think it wise to pursue them into Wales."

Ram felt like an incompetent fool. So much for the prowess of the great warrior *Rambaud le Noir*. The scourge of the border, the threat to peace had been at his mercy. He wondered why the Prince of Powwydd hadn't simply finished him off. "You did the right thing, Gervais. He must have laughed his way back to Wales. Who is this Woolgar woman?" he demanded, his head throbbing. He remembered Mabelle's soothing touch on his aching temples.

"She's a Saxon noblewoman, *milord*."

He was in the house of an enemy, but too tired to protest. He dozed off again and awoke later, sensing a presence. He didn't know how much time had passed.

"Gervais?"

"I'm Lady Ascha Woolgar. This is my home," a soft voice replied.

Ram opened bleary eyes and saw the woman he had previously thought was a vision. She looked to be about the same age as he. What he could see of her hair peeking out of the edges of the wimple was brown and curly. She was slender and her long thin fingers held a bowl and spoon. She bore a look of resigned defeat.

"I've brought you a nourishing vegetable broth," she said without emotion. "You should eat only broth for a few days, until you feel more recovered."

She was polite but didn't smile, doubtless resentful of his intrusion into her life.

"You speak my language," he replied.

She shrugged. "Many Saxons of the nobility speak Norman French. The Confessor encouraged it."

"Lady Woolgar, I thank you for allowing my men to bring me here," he said coldly.

"They didn't give me much choice, my Lord Montbryce."

"I regret—"

She raised her hand. "Don't worry. It's a reality I must accept. I'm a Saxon, a widow. You're a Norman. You're the conqueror, I'm the conquered."

Normally an articulate man, he struggled to marshal a reply. He tried to sit up but dizziness overwhelmed him and his stomach roiled. He closed his eyes and waited until the fog cleared. "Dear lady, we're Normans, not savages like the murderous Danes. Our king, your king, wishes peace and prosperity for his people, Saxon and Norman."

He mouthed the words but knew in his heart that William's plans for the total subjugation of these lands would result in great bloodshed. He wondered why he was bothering to justify his duke's actions to a woman, especially a Saxon.

She bowed her head slightly. "I'll let you finish your broth yourself. A manservant will see to your needs."

An elderly man entered a few minutes later, assisted Ram to stand so he could relieve himself, and then removed the chamber pot. He too was polite but the undercurrent of Saxon resentment was palpable. The dizzying effort exhausted Ram and he slept again, relieved he had managed not to retch.

A warm hand on his forehead woke him. It felt good.

"Mabelle," he croaked, still half asleep. He raised his hand and lay it atop the one on his forehead.

"It's Lady Ascha."

Ram's eyes shot open, sending pain arrowing through his head. He quickly removed his hand.

The lady seemed to pay no attention to the abrupt movement. "There is no fever. You're fortunate, Lord Montbryce."

Ram's head throbbed, his throat was dry. "Please, Lady Ascha, my name is Rambaud," he said wearily.

"As you wish, Lord Rambaud. Who is Mabelle?"

"She's my betrothed." No that wasn't right. "She was my betrothed—in Normandie. When I felt your touch, I was half asleep and I thought it was she."

Surely I'm not blushing?

"Were you dreaming of her?"

"Perhaps I was," he admitted, thinking it a strange question.

"But you're no longer betrothed?"

"*Non*," he said, swallowing the lump in his throat, unwilling to share his torment with this foreigner.

For a few minutes she gazed down at him, not with animosity but with a strange sort of interest. He felt uncomfortable, and wished he wasn't lying in a bed.

"I don't dream of my husband," she whispered, and her eyes glazed with unhappiness.

"You told me you're a widow."

"Yes. My husband was a warrior, a thane of the king. He's dead."

A feeling of dread crept into Ram's gut. Many Saxon nobles had died on the field at Hastings that terrible day.

"You don't want to ask me, so I'll tell you, since there's no shame in it. My husband, Sir Caedmon Woolgar, was a *huscarl* to King Harold. He died at Hastings. At least, we assume he did, since he hasn't returned home."

Ram thought of the mass grave where Harold's *huscarls* lay buried. They had been determined to fight to the last man. Could the Saxon giant who had come close to removing his head have been Sir Caedmon Woolgar? He saw no point in avoiding the truth.

"I fought at Hastings," he said forthrightly.

"Yes," she replied quietly, smiling an enigmatic smile.

Convinced though he was of the righteousness of William's conquest, this woman's plight brought home to him the often terrible consequences of war for those left behind. Men fought for glory and honor, and often to protect what was theirs, but there was no doubt women were often left to bear the burden of sorrow, and the weight of castles and manors with no man to defend them or provide.

None of this would have happened if Harold hadn't broken his oath.

By the next day, the dizziness had abated, and he left his bed. The manservant assisted him to dress. "Lady Woolgar will receive you in her solar, if you'll follow me."

Ascha was seated on a wooden bench by the window, the oiled covering drawn back, despite the chilly air. The embroidery on her lap lay untouched as she gazed out at the surrounding lands. A maidservant sat by her side, sewing.

"Leave us, Enid," she said softly when she saw Ram enter.

"Lady Ascha, I trust you're well today?" he ventured.

She didn't look up at him. "As well as can be expected."

"I would offer my condolences, but we both know it would sound hollow. I was your husband's enemy. I strove to kill him and his comrades. I don't regret it. I may have been the one to deal his death blow."

Had her expression softened slightly?

She looked him in the eye. "I don't lay blame at your door. My husband was a fierce warrior. He gloried in war. He died doing what he was born for. In a conflict there must be winners and losers. Sir Caedmon wasn't on the winning side this time."

Sad grey eyes distracted him momentarily, then he recalled his concerns. "What of your manor, Lady Ascha? I don't wish to add to your burdens, but it's our king's wish that we strengthen this border region against the

Welsh. You're not in a position of strength here, through no fault of your own. Many would covet such a manor. Rhodri ap Owain was close by, as you know. Gervais tells me you hold more than five hides of land, and that there's a church, a kitchen and a fortress gate. While you do have a rampart and ditch, he doesn't believe you could hold off a large attack."

She fidgeted nervously. "I don't know what will happen, Lord Rambaud, the grief and uncertainty is too new. I'm a woman alone."

Her grief touched a nerve. He too was alone, abandoned by the one woman he wanted. Perhaps…

She sobbed, so quietly he wasn't immediately aware she was crying. The embroidery fell to the floor. He strode across to sit by her side, hesitant to take her hand, not knowing how to bring comfort.

He retrieved the embroidery, but as he returned it to her lap, their fingers touched. She seized his hand and gripped it with both hers. Trembling, she leaned into him and he nervously put his arm around her shoulders, trying to bring comfort.

As the sobs wracked her slender body, the wimple slipped from her hair, and brown curls tumbled to her hips.

She's younger than I thought. And beautiful.

His body responded. He ran his fingers through her silky hair.

She appeared embarrassed by the crack that had appeared in her armor, but he continued to murmur soothing words and soon her weeping subsided. She blushed when she glimpsed the bulge in his leggings.

He cleared his throat, extricated his hand, withdrew his arm, and came to his feet. "Lady Ascha, I'll place you and your manor under my protection. I don't intend to take this place for myself, but others will no doubt try. I'll station a contingent of my men-at-arms here, and provide a steward to help you manage your estate."

He suspected fellow Normans might be more of a threat than the Welsh, but said nothing of this.

She stared at him, open mouthed. "I thank you for your unexpected compassion but I can't accept. I've nothing to give you in return, Lord Montbryce."

"I want nothing in return, Lady Ascha. If my future wife was in a similar position, I'd like to think some champion would protect her."

"Your future wife?" she murmured.

He clenched his jaw. "I misspoke. Our separation is recent. It will take some time to get used to."

Antoine had insisted he pursue Mabelle, but if she cared about him she would have stayed, wouldn't she? An alliance with a Saxon widow might prove beneficial. Ascha Woolgar was beautiful and in desperate straits. He doubted she would reject the notion of marriage to a Norman earl. Why then did the prospect not sit well with him?

His mind in turmoil, he took his leave and returned to his chamber, hoping things would seem clearer on the morrow.

~

Ascha liked the sound of the word *champion* but not Rambaud's slip of the tongue regarding his future wife. Perhaps he had loved the woman, though few noblemen of her acquaintance cared a whit about their wives, and certainly she and Caedmon Woolgar hadn't married for love.

She was drawn to this Norman warrior deposited into her care in a way she'd never been attracted to a man before. He had a sensitivity her brutish husband lacked. She'd held on to his hands like a rock in her sea of fear and uncertainty, and the unexpected intimacy of his arm around her shoulder had sent a warm shiver through her body.

And he's not married.

~

Still dressed in nightgown and bedrobe, Ascha wasn't cool and detached the next morning. "I wish you weren't leaving. Head wounds can be dangerous and the effects often linger. You should rest here longer, Lord Rambaud," she cajoled when he told her of his decision to leave forthwith. Her hand lay on his arm as she spoke, and she looked directly into his eyes.

Ram met her gaze, surprised at the intimacy of the gesture, and the use of his given name, not to mention her attire. Desire flickered in the grey depths.

She's lonely. She desires me.

The thought aroused and dismayed him. She was an attractive woman who had been without a man for a considerable time.

What harm could a kiss do?

He had been celibate for months. After meeting Mabelle, he'd lost interest in Joleyne—but his lovely refugee had left him. Perhaps he and Ascha were destined to meet. William had talked often of the importance of marriages binding Saxon and Norman. In these dangerous new lands he could be killed before he made it home to Normandie. Hugh was right about war rousing a man's libido. Since Hastings he seemed to be constantly hard, constantly needy.

"Lady Ascha," he murmured as he bent his head to kiss her.

His lips brushed hers as she breathed, "Lord Rambaud."

They kissed. Her soft warmth sent blood rushing to his groin. His tongue coaxed her lips and she allowed him entry. The kiss was sweet and gentle, and she clung to him as he pressed his arousal to her body. "I didn't love my husband," she whispered. "War was his life. He didn't understand the needs of a woman."

Intense emotions, pent up since Hastings, swept over him—the terror of the battle, the horror and stench of the bloodshed and broken bodies, the sickening brutality, the constant homesickness, the exhaustion of travel, the heavy responsibilities put upon him by his duke, the unbearable aching for his infuriating Mabelle, the frustration of Rhodri's escape, the concern for Hugh—all conspired to render him senseless, his only instinct a need to possess and be possessed. He held a woman in his arms who had admitted never knowing the pleasures of passion. It was more than he could resist. He wanted to tear the clothes from her body and take her on the floor, to liberate her from the sexual frustration she had endured.

He ran his hands over her body, along the swell of her breast, the curve of her hip, the flesh of her thigh. He gathered her up, intending to carry her to the chamber where she had tended him. He felt a momentary dizziness as he rose, but braced his legs and steadied himself. She curled her arms around his neck and rested her head against his chest.

Once in the chamber, she disrobed quickly, then inflamed him further by helping him remove his clothing. She gasped and licked her lips when she saw his rigid manhood and her eyes burned with wanting.

He didn't have to spend long preparing her. As a spasm of release tore through her body, he raised himself above her, positioned his shaft at her opening, and groaned as he slid inside. They quickly found each other's rhythm and she smiled, her hands reaching up to his chest, thumbs brushing his male nipples. In a moment of clarity, he rasped, "Have no fear, I'll spill myself outside your body."

She dug her nails into his shoulders. "No, Rambaud."

"But—"

She gripped his hips fiercely, pulling his body to hers. "No! Fill me! I can't keep you. I want every bit of you. These moments are all I have."

The intensity of her words inflamed him. He shuddered and bellowed his euphoria as his seed pulsed into her body.

Later, as his wits slowly returned, a vivid image of Mabelle lying by the lake, barely covered by her chemise, rose up in his mind. He abruptly turned away from Ascha. "This was wrong," he said hoarsely. "You're a widow. It was dishonorable to take advantage of you."

But his greatest regret had little to do with taking advantage. How could he have sacrificed what he wanted to give to Mabelle by bedding another woman, no matter how great her need, or his? Mabelle was his destiny, brought to him through some miracle he didn't understand, which he had tried to deny. Though she had broken the betrothal, he felt guilty for betraying her with this woman. What he had experienced with Ascha was simply physical release. Antoine was right. If he wanted Mabelle, he'd have to fight for her.

"You didn't take advantage of me," Ascha whispered languidly. "I took advantage of you. I sense you're a man in love. My husband didn't love me, didn't understand the importance of touch for a woman. I thank you for the gift you've given me today. The memory of it will help see me through many difficult days. I don't regret what we've shared. I don't expect you to love me."

Confusion whirled in Ram's head. "I must leave now. I'll be your champion but I can't be your lover."

She grew agitated as he dressed, and came to her knees on the bed, wrapping the linens around her body. "Rambaud," she stammered, "I lied. I need you—please. Stay a few days."

He shook his head, desperate to be gone from this manor. "I cannot."

He strode out of the chamber. She would be safe under his protection, but he prayed she would find a good husband some day. She was a woman with a deeply hidden passion Woolgar had been unable to ignite, and he silently thanked God for Mabelle and the erotic joys her touch and her kisses promised. A chill went up his spine when he thought of telling Mabelle about his liaison. Honor demanded it. Had she been faithful to him? He wanted to believe she was still a virgin but, given the life she had led, the odds were…

His fury grew at the idea of Mabelle sharing another man's bed, and he was dismayed he had bedded this woman and was now hurrying away. This was not behavior worthy of a Montbryce. His heart was in knots. Had the brutality of war destroyed his honor?

A vague dread he might have impregnated Ascha wriggled like a worm in his belly, but he reasoned that was unlikely after only one coupling. She had no children. It was possible she was barren anyway.

He left soldiers to guard Shelfhoc but the contingent that rode away with him was still a force to be regarded with respect. As he made for Ellesmere, he deliberately pushed away the tantalizing vision insinuating itself into his head of a maiden with golden hair, lying on a grassy bank. He had tried to deny his passion for Mabelle, but Ascha's words echoed over and over—*I sense you are a man in love.*

~

Through the window, Lady Ascha Woolgar watched until the Normans were completely out of sight, her fingers absently rubbing the oiled window covering. From the moment she had set eyes on the magnificent Norman, feelings had stirred within her she had never known with her husband. She had tried unsuccessfully to deny them.

She sank to her knees sobbing, swathed in bed linens, feeling more fulfilled, yet more bereft than she had ever felt. It was unlikely she would ever see Rambaud de Montbryce again, but she would remember the feel of his touch, the fulfillment of his manhood inside her, forever.

DIRE TIDINGS

His brothers were solicitous upon his return to Ellesmere, but a preoccupation with their father's illness overrode their curiosity and they seemed satisfied with a cursory explanation. They agreed to ride to Westminster, where they received permission to return home. William was distraught at the news the *comte* was ill; Ram deemed it wiser not to tell him about Mabelle.

They rode to the south coast where they took ship for Normandie. A sennight after receiving Mabelle's missive, the Montbryce brothers were galloping into the bailey of the castle, long after sunset.

Fernand Bonhomme appeared and grooms came to take their mounts.

"Fernand," Ram embraced his trusted steward, "you look haggard."

To his consternation, the man began to sob. "*Milord.* Forgive me. We are desolate. Your father…my wife…"

It took a moment for the terrible truth to dawn. His gut roiled as a chill raced up his spine. The walls seemed to be closing in. He couldn't speak. His beloved father couldn't be…

"Our father is dead?" Hugh rasped.

Fernand nodded. "Two days ago. The same day as Vangeline. A pestilence. Many have died all across the Calvados. Thank God you have come, but we've already laid him to rest in the crypt. I thought…"

They stood in stunned silence for several minutes. It had never occurred to Ram that his father might die. Did Mabelle know?

Antoine put a hand on Fernand's shoulder. "You did the right thing, as always. We are distraught at the news of your wife's death."

"*Merci, milord.* Vangeline was a good wife and help-mate. We'll miss her sorely. And your father—it was a desperate time, but he succumbed quickly and didn't suffer. Now you're the *comte, milord* Rambaud."

Ram tried to marshal his scattered thoughts. He wanted desperately to cry out his anguish in Mabelle's arms. "*Oui*, Fernand, but I would prefer our dear father was still with us. The hour is late. I suppose my betrothed has retired to her chamber?"

"*Non, milord*. She's gone."

He felt like a fool. How could he have forgotten? He swayed, fearing he might retch. Antoine linked arms with him. "Walk with me, brother."

They came to the Great Hall, a place of many happy memories, now dark and empty. Giselle appeared, her face grim. She tearfully embraced them each in turn. Ram understood the grief that choked off her words.

"*Milord* Ram," she finally cried after blowing her nose, "I tried to persuade your lady to stay, but she wouldn't listen. She was unhappy here and believed her place was at Alensonne."

"I suppose that's where she's gone?"

"Oui, milord."

Ram hadn't really believed she had left him until this moment. Filled with an urge to vent his rage, he leaned his forehead against the wall and pounded the cold stone with his fists.

"Be calm," Antoine shouted. "You can go after her, convince her to return."

"There won't be time. I must return to England for the coronation. She's left me, and no wonder. But I'm not a man to go crawling on my hands and knees."

Hugh put his trembling hand on Ram's shoulder. "Let's go down to the crypt. I want to pray by father's tomb."

A few minutes later, Ram stood in the cold, candlelit crypt, flanked by his grieving brothers, his arm around Hugh's shaking shoulders. They felt their loss keenly, but his heart ached too for Mabelle, the beautiful refugee he had done his utmost to alienate.

The three returned to the hall, where they reminisced together until after midnight, then Ram decided to clear his head out on the battlements before retiring. If he slept at all, it would be from sheer exhaustion.

He came at last to his chamber and took out the crumpled parchment he'd carried since the day he'd received it at Ellesmere.

He read it again, then pounded the bolster over and over in frustration, until he collapsed onto it. "I don't want to be released, Mabelle. I don't covet your lands, I covet you. I want you as my wife, the mother of my children."

Antoine and Hugh greeted him the next day when he arrived in the Great Hall to break his fast, still tired after a sleepless night.

They couldn't hide their excitement.

"What scheme have you two plotted now?" he asked wearily.

Antoine grinned. "If you leave immediately and ride at a gallop, you can reach Alensonne in a days. One day to get there, one day to persuade Mabelle to return with you, one day back, a day to wed her and bed her, two days to get to Westminster. *Voilà,* you'll arrive a day before the coronation on Christmas Day."

Ram shook his head. "Antoine, if I'm not at William's coronation, I can bid *adieu* to my earldom. We could miss the tide, encounter the wrong winds."

"The choice is yours. The earldom or Mabelle de Valtesse. Hugh and I are willing to ride with you. You may need some protection from her father. Or perhaps from Mabelle."

Ram hesitated. What if he went to Alensonne and she rejected him? But he had to try. If he didn't go now, he could be mired in England, possibly for years. "Tell Bonhomme to get provisions ready for the journey. I'll get the horses saddled and the men-at-arms organized."

ALENSONNE

"Normandie is abuzz with the news of the upcoming coronation of our duke as the King of the English," Guillaume de Valtesse announced to his daughter as they broke their fast. "It's to take place on Christmas Day. His victory over the Saxons has earned him the name of *Conqueror*."

His words sent Mabelle's mind reeling back to the banquet at Montbryce, when she had returned the duke's toast. "Ram foretold he would be known as the Conqueror," she whispered.

"I'll never understand why you broke the betrothal. You're obviously smitten with the man, and we'll be in great difficulty here if he comes to claim his dower rights," he mumbled as he shuffled out of the hall.

She would never understand him. It was he who had urged her to come home, yet they had argued long and hard after her arrival. Hoping to find peace here, all she could think of was Ram de Montbryce—the feel of his lips on hers, his strong arms around her, his hands fondling her hair, her breast—she couldn't erase the memory of him at the lake, standing almost naked, his arousal obvious.

She longed to run her hands over his thighs, his chest, his shoulders. She ached in places she had never ached before. Her body tingled when she thought of him, and she longed to see him *sans* braies.

However, she had made her decision. There was no going back. He would not want her, never had wanted her. How angry he must have been when he read her letter—if he received it.

The sound of raised voices disturbed her reverie. Her breathless father reappeared, Steward Cormant with him. "I told you he would come for his due. Your former betrothed is at the gates with his brothers, demanding entry."

He's alive?

Her heart lurched when her father began issuing orders for the men-at-arms to ride out against the visitors.

"*Non,* Papa, I don't want to see blood spilled. We'll allow him entry, and perhaps negotiate some settlement for the lands. Leave this to me. You're too apt to lose your temper. Cormant, pass the word the *Vicomte* de Montbryce is to be allowed entry. Show him to the Great Hall."

She hurried there and climbed up on the dais, hoping she looked like the *Milady* of the castle, in control. She wiped her sweaty palms on her dress.

Don't bite your nails.

"He's bigger even than I remember," she murmured when Ram, Antoine and Hugh entered the Great Hall five minutes later, looking like they had ridden hard and fast.

What has he done to his hair?

She balled her fists, trying to still the wild beating of her heart. The sound filled her ears, and she was sure everyone else could hear it. She held out her arms to the three men. "*Mon seigneur*, *Vicomte* de Montbryce, my Lords Antoine and Hugh, welcome to my home. Welcome to Alensonne."

Ram's stare was unnerving, but Antoine's hoarse words shocked her to the core. "Ram is *comte* now, Mabelle. Our father died."

Ram's grief was etched on his face. She longed to embrace him, to hold him while he grieved. "I am devastated by the news," she said. "I loved—" The words stuck in her throat when Ram clenched his jaw.

Antoine and Hugh moved quickly to her side and embraced her. "Mabelle," Antoine whispered close to her ear, "be patient with him."

She smiled. "He looks like his blood is boiling because we're whispering."

Hugh laughed out loud.

Ram stiffened his shoulders. "Mabelle, I've come about our betrothal."

"You wish to discuss the dowry?"

"*Non,*" he exclaimed. "I haven't come to discuss the dowry."

"What he means is he's here to beg you to come back," Antoine began.

"I haven't come to beg," Ram interrupted.

"He has come to *ask* you to return to Montbryce."

"I'm capable of speaking for myself. Why not go tend to our horses, dear brothers?"

"I'm sure the steward—"

"Go! Leave us."

Antoine and Hugh shrugged their shoulders and left, scarcely able to contain their mirth.

Mabelle took a deep breath. “You seem comfortable giving orders here, but Alensonne is not yours yet.”

She fought to control the excitement flooding through her as Ram quickly crossed the space between them. Would he touch her? Take her in his arms? Cradle her to his chest?

He took her hands. “I don’t care about Alensonne. I want you to return to Montbryce with me so we can be married.”

She swayed as she struggled to control her voice and the threatening tears.

“*You’ve* decided this is the right time?”

“My father pledged me to you. It would dishonor his memory if I reneged.”

Her heart sank. She pulled her hands away from his grasp. “I told you, I’ve released you from that pledge. I have no desire to dishonor your father. I loved him. But I don’t want to be wed to a man who is marrying me for the sake of duty.”

She sensed his agitation at her words. He paced nervously for several minutes, running his hand over his short hair. She had to resist the impulse to rush over and tell him of her relief he was alive, that she would be his wife under any circumstances, that she couldn’t bear the thought of losing him.

He turned to face her. “Mabelle, you’re the woman I want, the woman I need. I am sure of it now, after Hastings. You were my talisman. After the battle, I burned to join my body to yours, to lose myself in you. I can be overbearing but I’ll try to—why are you crying?”

He brushed a tear from her cheek with his thumb.

"Ram," she whispered.

He kissed her fiercely, making her body cry out for him. He put his hands on her waist and pulled her to him. She felt his hard male length against her belly, and the pent up longing burst over her.

"Ram," she whispered again, her breath catching in her throat as she reached up nervously to run her fingers lightly over his shaven head. "You're alive—but what have you done to your beautiful hair?"

He laughed and put his arms on her shoulders. "Vaillon shaved it for battle. It will grow back, but it feels strange."

She leaned on him, her arms around his waist. They clung together for long minutes. She could hear his breathing, feel the beating of his heart. She had never felt so safe.

"Return to Montbryce with me, Mabelle. Come be my wife, my *comtesse*."

She swallowed hard. She had run away, denied her attraction to this man, but he was her destiny. "I'll return with you. I invite you to rest here a few days. You've had a long journey and the grief of your father's death. Enjoy Yuletide at Alensonne with me for a while."

He kissed her knuckles. "It would give me great pleasure to get to know your childhood home for a while longer, but I've been summoned to the duke's coronation in Westminster on Christmas Day. I want to take you there as my bride."

"But that's only a few days away."

"William has promised me an earldom in England, but if I'm not at the ceremony—"

"You risked it to come here—to get me?"

"You're the woman I want to marry."

He had spoken no words of love but he wanted her enough to risk what was important to him—lands and titles. He would make sure she was safe. Alchemy drew them to each other. They would at least have passion.

"Then we must summon Cormant to prepare for our departure on the morrow. I'm used to traveling fast and light."

A WEDDING

Hugh and Ram walked together to the door of the chapel of Montbryce Castle where Ram took his place with the bishop and Antoine. The two brothers clasped forearms in a familiar gesture. Antoine slapped him on the back and smiled. Ram kissed the bishop's ring as he bowed to the cleric.

He wished with all his heart his father still lived and regretted deeply he had deprived him of the satisfaction of seeing him wed. The trio waited a few minutes in nervous silence, then heard a rustling of gowns along with female whispers.

Ram's breath caught in his dry throat when Mabelle came into view on the arm of her father, who had insisted on riding to Montbryce with them. She seemed to be carefully studying the elaborately tiled floor. He licked his lips.

Valtesse, smiling for once, passed her warm hand into his and Mabelle stole a glance at him when a jolt passed between them. He would happily drown in those brown eyes.

As the long ceremony progressed, Ram became aware that the tall woman holding his hand tightly with her long slim fingers, was swaying. Was she going to faint? His head filled with images of running his hands over her full breasts and shapely hips that promised fertility and many healthy children.

"Do you, Rambaud de Montbryce, wish to take this woman, Mabelle de Valtesse, de Belisle, d'Alensonne and de Domfort, to be your wedded wife?"

The bishop's voice brought Ram back to reality. Immersed in his daydream, he had lost track of where they were in the ceremony.

"I do so wish."

Mabelle let out a long breath.

She thought I might betray her again.

"Do you, Mabelle de Valtesse, de Belisle, d'Alensonne and de Domfort, wish to take this man, Rambaud de Montbryce, to be your wedded husband?"

This may be the moment she's chosen for her revenge.

"I do so wish," she whispered, her head bowed.

He slowly exhaled the breath he hadn't realized he'd been holding.

"I now declare, to all present, they are husband and wife. *Comte* Rambaud de Montbryce, you may kiss your bride."

They both stood perfectly still for a moment before turning to face each other. His heart racing, he lifted the veil and smiled, scarcely able to believe the erotic passion she provoked in him. Then the unhappy thought came again that he had come cross his bride lying barely clothed in a meadow. *Had* she been expecting someone? It wasn't Antoine, but perhaps another man? But then he had something to confess as well. His smile turned to a frown. Why was she so cool? He bent his head to kiss her. At first she didn't respond, but as he darted his tongue into her mouth, she opened to him.

Ah oui. She definitely feels the passion.

"Mabelle," he whispered, "you're beautiful."

"*Milord* Ram," she faltered. "*Milord*, you are—what an impressive weapon," she giggled, pointing to the sword she'd hefted into the lake, a naughty grin on her face. "Is it a family heirloom?"

The bishop eyed her curiously. Ram suppressed a chuckle at the confused perplexity on the cleric's face. *L'évêque* was not a man who showed any emotion. Ram doubted he'd ever known a new bride openly admire her husband's weapon.

He bent to whisper in her ear. "*Oui*, Mabelle, my weapon is a family treasure," he replied with a smile. "It's always ready to be of service."

She reddened and averted her eyes, though none of the guests had heard the exchange.

They signed the book of records and led the procession out of the chapel to the Great Hall. Ram gripped her hand, momentarily nervous she might loudly denounce him. Or perhaps he should accuse her, cast her off? But that would mean never experiencing the fulfillment of the needs she aroused in him. No, the die was cast. He dismissed his worries as the confused ravings of a newly married man, and there would be time enough to confess his dalliance with Ascha Woolgar.

Mabelle risked a glance at Ram when a spark passed between them and her throat went dry. During the long nuptial ritual she lapsed into a daydream. A tall, dark, naked man rose in a glittering spray of water from the depths of a pool, his manhood erect—

"*Arrête,*" she chided inwardly, opening her eyes, trying to get back a sense of what was next in the sacred ceremony, not sure of how long she had been distracted.

She felt his hand twitch and close tightly around hers when she spoke her vows and breathed a sigh of relief when Ram gave his promises. She would not need the dagger concealed in the sleeve of her gown, ready to thrust into him if he betrayed her again.

By the time the rest of the ceremony was over, the vows completed and the ring blessed and placed by Ram's large, firm hand on her trembling finger, she was worried that when he lifted her veil, she would be withered by his look of mistrust.

Was that what she saw as his smile turned to a frown? When he kissed her, she tried not to respond, but the wanton, aching feelings returned. She couldn't help herself when he darted his tongue into her mouth. Then the courage which had helped her survive for many years came to her rescue, bolstered by the wine drunk rather rapidly a short time before, and she made a remark about his weapon, clearly shocking the bishop.

Relieved no one else had heard the exchange, she was glad to see Hugh hurrying to embrace Ram. He took her hand in his, bowing slightly as he bestowed a kiss upon it. "Welcome to our family, Mabelle. I'm confident you'll make your husband very happy."

"Patience, dear sister. You will need lots of patience," Antoine teased.

Their remarks warmed Mabelle's heart. She'd never had a brother who cared.

Her father shook Ram's hand vigorously, and then gave his daughter a perfunctory kiss on the cheek. "I depart for Alensonne on the morrow," he informed her.

Soon invited guests were pressing around, congratulating the newlyweds. They became separated.

She lost track of her husband, until she saw him a while later, beckoning to her from the dais, a hint of uncertainty in his blue eyes. She had to admit grudgingly she was happy to find him again, having felt strangely bereft without him at her side.

He deemed her behavior inappropriate, yet, on his way to his own wedding, he had hidden in the woods, watching a scantily clad maiden. It was immaterial that she found him attractive. It was a betrayal. Then he had abandoned her at the chapel door. He claimed she was his *talisman*—but could he be trusted? Did he have some ulterior motive for marrying her? She steeled her emotions as he approached.

"The servants are ready to serve the feast, *milady*. Please come and take your place by my side." She allowed him to lead her to the head table, saying nothing. The touch of his hand made her incapable of speech. This would never do. She would need to be wary.

ALLEGIANCE

The festivities began. The servants brought out large platters laden with food from the kitchens. Two liveried serving lads appeared, carrying on their shoulders a large iron pan with the traditional boar's head. There was crusty fresh bread. *La Cuisinière* had spared no effort to provide a sumptuous spread for the wedding of their *comte*.

A serving dish of roasted chicken was placed on the head table between the newlyweds, a symbolic shared first meal. Ram tore off a wing and offered it to Mabelle. She accepted with a nod, eyelashes fluttering, and bit into it, the succulent juices dripping on to her trencher. She licked her lips and fingers, savoring it.

"I've eaten nothing all day," she whispered.

Ram's manhood—hard since their kiss—pulsed. He pressed his thigh against hers, wishing it was his fingers she licked. She seemed to sense his arousal as she stole a blushing glance at the tight bulge in his hose. He wondered how he would get through the next few hours of food, wine, ale, ribaldry, *jongleurs,* toasts and speeches without ripping the clothes from her body and making love to her on the tables.

It was a heady thought that he had married a passionate woman. He could stir her with his kisses, his touches. But she harbored resentments, and it sobered him. He had some groveling to do, but she too had things to explain.

There was a sudden flurry of activity. Antoine and Hugh were up on their feet, indicating to the diners in the hall something was about to happen. People were being ushered into lines.

"What is it, Ram?" Mabelle asked nervously.

"We're going to have a ceremony," he replied, rising from his seat.

She frowned. "Ceremony? We just—"

"Allegiance. Everyone will swear their allegiance to me, as their new *comte*. And to you."

"To me?"

Ram turned to her. "Mabelle, you're now the *Comtesse* de Montbryce. I would expect my people to honor and respect and serve you. They're your people now."

Mabelle quickly wiped greasy hands and lips with a napkin, her heart racing. It was the first time he had acknowledged she could be a good *comtesse*. Vaillon came forward to refasten the short cloak Ram had shed during the meal. Her husband took her hand and led her to stand at the front of the dais. He drew his sword, braced his legs, pushed the cloak further back on his shoulders and took up a stance with his sword pointing down, his left hand on the hilt.

He looked at his wife. "Place your right hand on top of mine."

She obeyed, her knees turning to water. He put his right hand on top of hers. His hands were warm, and soon those hands—

Ram gestured to Antoine. "Begin."

Antoine came first, followed by Hugh. Each brother bent the knee, placed his hand atop Ram's, and pledged, "In the name of our Lord, and in the presence of all gathered here, I acknowledge that you, Rambaud de Montbryce, are my *comte*, and my liege lord, and I am your loyal man, and I acknowledge that you, Mabelle de Montbryce, are my *comtesse*, and I am your loyal man."

The knights and men-at-arms followed suit. When all had pledged themselves, Ram turned to Mabelle and declared in a loud, authoritative voice, "I'll accept your pledge now, *comtesse*."

Her instinct was to refuse. Ram wanted to use the occasion to demonstrate his dominance. But what choice did she have? In a deep curtsey before him, she placed both hands on his, looked into his eyes, and made her pledge, hoping her voice didn't betray her nervousness. "In the name of the Lord, and in the presence of all here gathered, I acknowledge that you, Rambaud de Montbryce, are my *comte* and my liege lord, and I am your loyal woman."

I am your woman.

The words echoed in her head, and her mouth went dry. She was this man's woman. A baron she barely knew was her future, her forever. Ram bowed slightly, a smile tugging at the corners of his mouth. He took her hand and helped her rise, and she silently thanked God for the strength she felt in his grip. She assumed he would lead her back to her place, having established his superior position.

Instead, he handed her the sword, placed her hands on the hilt, covered them with his own, and knelt on one knee before her. Staring at her intently, he gave his oath. “I, *Comte* Rambaud de Montbryce, in the name of the Lord, and in the presence of all here gathered, acknowledge that you, Mabelle de Montbryce, and de Valtesse, and d’Alensonne, and de Domfort and de Belisle, are my *comtesse*, and I am your loyal man.”

The room filled with loud cheering as everyone resumed their places, and the feasting recommenced. Ram rose, took Mabelle’s hand and led her back, never taking his eyes from hers.

Her tears had started as soon as he knelt before her. She recognized what the gesture cost him. Perhaps there was more to this man than she thought. He reached over as he took his own seat and, with a smile, wiped away her tears with his thumbs.

Hours later, taking her hand, he whispered, “It will soon be time for the bedding ceremony, Mabelle. I’ve tried throughout this interminable evening not to recall the vision of you lying in the grass, your legs half open—inviting.” He pressed his thigh against hers again. Her nipples tingled and warmth flooded a very private place. Feverish heat washed over her.

I must be ailing for something.

They listened to the toasts given by Antoine, then by her father, who, to her embarrassment, rambled on about traitors and rights and redemption. Then Ram raised his goblet and toasted his bride. "I drink to the health of my beautiful wife, Mabelle de Montbryce. I'm confident she'll be a good and willing wife."

He winked at her, and she thought he had probably drunk too much wine.

Such arrogance. Good and willing? We're back to that.

She rose to her feet to return the toast, hoping her trembling legs would sustain her. She too had imbibed more of the excellent wine, not to mention a sip of the fine apple brandy brought from the cellars. She felt somewhat unsteady. She was also nervous about the journey they would undertake on the morrow to England, having never sailed before.

"I thank you, *mon seigneur*, and I drink to your health also." She sat down but not until she had winked at him, or at least tried to. Winking didn't seem to be a skill she possessed at that moment.

He looks disappointed. Good.

She had heard gossip in many castles about bedding ceremonies, but had never attended one, being an unmarried woman. They could apparently be affairs bordering on mass hysteria, where the bride and groom were both stripped naked and forced to copulate in front of the whole assembly. Bloodied sheets were then hoisted up the flagpole.

Or, they might be polite and discreet occasions. The bride's maids dressed her in her nightgown, the groom's men undressed him, and then the bishop blessed the marriage bed, the gathering tucked the happy couple up in bed, and left. She fervently hoped something along the lines of the latter would be the case now.

Ram reassured her, “Don’t worry, Mabelle, there’ll be no running sheets up flagpoles in this castle.”

He had understood her concern, and tried to make her feel better. Or was it that he had made sure there would be no public display, because he suspected she was no longer a virgin and there would be no bloodied linens?

He still thinks me unchaste.

WEDDING NIGHT

The assembled gathering was merry but not bawdy as they lifted a broadly grinning Ram and a blushing Mabelle, and carried them to the bridal bedchamber. A carved wooden screen had been placed at one end, and she and Giselle stepped behind it so the maidservant could help remove her gown, chemise, shoes and hose. The veil had long since fallen away.

She gasped at the flimsy nightgown that a gleeful Giselle carefully pulled over her head. Ram, and everyone else in the chamber, would see through it. But Giselle wrapped a warm bed gown around her, and pulled the belt tight.

"Only for *milord's* eyes, in my opinion. Not those who want to ogle," whispered the feisty maid.

Thank God for the loyalty and common sense of this serving woman.

Giselle combed out her hair, then tucked her into bed and propped a pillow behind her.

Ram's friends and brothers were divesting him of his

clothing, tossing it here and there; despite her determination not to peek, she caught a glimpse of a bare hip as he eased into a black silk bed robe held out by Vaillon. He cinched it lightly around his waist. Smiling and waving to the cheering crowd, he strode proudly across the room and joined his nervous new wife. The robe barely came to his knees, and she couldn't help but be aware of his muscled thighs as he walked. She averted her eyes quickly, hoping he hadn't noticed her interest.

The bishop intoned a brief prayer of blessing, and sprinkled the bed with holy water.

Despite ribald urgings from the guests to *"Get on with it"*, Ram ushered them out with an imperious wave of the hand, and gradually they left.

"*Allez, tous!*" he commanded with mock seriousness. "Be gone, all of you."

Their eventual leaving, urged out by Vaillon and Giselle, created an overwhelming silence in the big chamber. Ram slipped off his bed robe. Mabelle averted her eyes as he raised his hips to free the silk from under his body. He threw it nonchalantly to the floor. Turning onto his back, he stretched out an arm to the table for one of the two goblets of mead. She stole a glance at his well-muscled chest and the trail of black hair leading down to his navel and—he turned back to her and offered the goblet.

"Something sweet for my bride?"

She shook her head, her face on fire.

"Too nervous?" he asked.

"*Oui,*" she whispered, scarcely able to speak, her insides churning. She was aware of the long relationship he'd had with his mistress, though there was talk Joleyne had left St. Germain. Mabelle had never for one moment assumed Ram would come virgin to their bed, whereas she had no experience of men. Would she satisfy his male needs?

Propped on one elbow, he took a sip of the honeyed wine and licked his lips. "You should try some. It's bad luck not to."

He raised the goblet to her lips. His eyes seemed to darken as he watched her sip the mead, and he frowned slightly. "More?"

"*Non, merci,*" she murmured as the lukewarm mead trickled down her throat.

He smiled, took another sip, then replaced the goblet on the table, licking the stickiness off his fingers. A peculiar urge to taste his skin seized her.

Turning once again on his side, his head propped on his arm, he said seductively, "Well, *ma belle,* will you let me see that irresistible body without my begging?"

"You weren't going to beg at the lake." As soon as she uttered the words, she regretted them.

He bristled. "*Non*, you're right. Would I have had to beg? I got the feeling you were ready to give yourself up without much protest."

But my dream was of you—of your kiss.

His words cut into her heart, but his next question raised her hackles.

"What trick do you have in mind to hide your lost virginity?"

"You think I'm not a maid?" she murmured, her eyes filling with tears. She wished he had choked on his mead.

"Maids don't lie half-naked in meadows, covered with

flowers. But I don't care. You've cast a spell on me, and you're the one I must have."

Despite his cruel words, the smoldering need in his ice blue eyes made her heart race. She looked away, afraid her heart might break.

Wiping away a tear with his fingers, he admitted, "My male needs threatened to control me, and I'm not proud of it. That's what passion seems to do. I'm a Montbryce, an honorable Norman noble. I was tired after my journey. I thought you were a vision."

As he spoke, he gently eased open the bed robe and fixed his gaze on her breasts, which the diaphanous fabric of the nightgown did little to hide.

"Two perfect circles on two perfect globes," he murmured with a faint smile. He lowered his head and twirled his tongue lightly over each hard nipple, sending molten waves to the core of her being.

Her heart was pounding and she couldn't swallow. He kissed her softly, then, as the kiss lengthened and deepened in intensity, she parted her lips and welcomed his tantalizing tongue, warmed by the mead. His lips were sticky and he tasted of honey. With a groan, he wrapped his powerful arms around her, accepting the silent invitation, licking the corners of her mouth.

Sucking on her lower lip, he trailed one hand down her throat and cupped her breast. It filled his hand and he stroked slowly and rhythmically, his fingers straying closer and closer to the expectant nipple. His scorching touch through the silken fabric aroused feelings unknown to her before, and when he finally pinched the pert point between his thumb and forefinger, a spasm shook her. She arched up off the bed, wet heat flooding from a very private place.

What is happening to me?

With his other hand, he carefully peeled the nightgown from her trembling body. “I’ve longed to see you naked,” he whispered, “and to lose myself in you. You are as lovely as I imagined.”

She moaned softly as his big hands cupped both breasts. He lowered his warm lips to them, suckling and licking as he tenderly squeezed the other needy nipple. She arched her mons and felt his manhood heavy against her thigh.

His kiss then was slow and deep. She sucked his tongue into her mouth. Surrendering to an instinct that overcame the inner voice urging modesty, she opened her legs. With a deep grunt she felt in her toes, he used his hand on the top of her thigh to open her wider, pulling her leg over his. She felt the silken tickle of the hair on his legs, and the hardness of his manhood pressing against her. Still she was afraid to look at his nakedness.

His long fingers found her most intimate place. The sensations were overwhelming, but she didn’t want him to stop. She couldn’t breathe and had to break away from his kiss. She looked into his eyes, expecting to see censure at her wantonness, but instead saw deep need.

He smiled at her and whispered, “Don’t forget to breathe, Mabelle. Don’t be afraid.”

The sound of his seductive voice calmed her. He kissed her again, continuing to stroke harder and faster, the other hand squeezing a nipple. Intense heat coursed through her belly, shooting down her inner thighs. She dug her heels into the bed, wanting the sensations to go on—and on.

“Come for me, my lovely,” he whispered. “Come for me.”

She didn't understand his words, only half heard them, totally rapt in scaling a mountain of exquisite pleasure, and wanted to scream as her body cascaded from the peak and fell into bliss.

"Your screams excite me," he said huskily. "I want to see your face again when you reach ecstasy."

No man had ever spoken such words to her. She had entered a new world. She wanted to laugh and cry. She wanted all of him.

Where have these thoughts come from?

He bent his head to suckle, then ran his fingers lightly across her belly and slid one finger further inside, then another, curling them against the tender flesh, his palm pressed against her mons. She had never known such sensations and rapture came again quickly.

Ram held her tightly as her body convulsed.

Is that me screaming?

She opened her eyes and plumbed his blue depths again. He smiled and whispered, "It's time. You're ready now."

He came to his knees and spread her legs wider. She finally summoned the courage to look at his male part and gasped, "*Mon Dieu!*"

He chuckled and whispered, "I know. I'll go slowly—if I can."

His hand guided the tip of his manhood into her throbbing folds.

"I'm wet," she stammered, in whispered apology.

He groaned. "That's a good thing. Put your hand on me."

He took her hand and curled it around his long length.

"Silky," she murmured.

The memory flashed into her mind of how magnificent he had looked at the lake—a beautiful aroused male, his excitement barely concealed by his braies. Since that moment she had longed for him to join his body to hers. Surely he must see the lust on her face?

"You're beautiful, Mabelle," he groaned. "I've ached to make you mine."

"Please…Ram…please," she murmured, awash with desire, "possess me…take me."

He entwined his fingers with hers and pressed her hands to the bolster. Bracing himself, he held his breath as he pushed in.

She cried out, startled by the sharp twinge when he breached her maiden's gate.

He stopped and looked into her eyes.

"*Dieu!* I'm the *first*," he choked. "You're truly mine."

She should have been affronted at the tone of surprise in his voice but was too enthralled with the sensations building inside her. She tore her hands from his and grasped his hips, pulling him towards her, then reached up and brushed his nipples with her thumbs. His eyes glazed over as he gasped at her touch.

He withdrew almost completely and plunged in again, then thrust deeply, over and over, faster and faster. She had never experienced such a feeling of possession.

This man is mine.

Deep within, exquisite pleasure blossomed. She raised her arms above her head, and he entwined their fingers again. The overwhelming sensations Ram had brought to her body earlier were nothing to what surged through her now, an inexorably intoxicating bliss. Ram's skin sheened with perspiration. She wanted to tear her hands from his grasp and run them across his gleaming shoulders.

She felt his essence burst from his body and rush into hers. He reared his head back and a strangled gasp emerged from deep in his throat. Euphoria filled her. A shudder went through them both, and she screamed out her amazement with a sound she had never made before. He collapsed onto her, his breathing labored.

"Forgive me," he gasped after a minute or two. "Too heavy—can't move."

"You're not heavy," she whispered, her fingers lazily caressing his nape. His shoulders twitched. She loved the feel of his weight on her, his warm body covering hers completely, his heart beating in rhythm with her own.

Rolling away several minutes later, he saw the tracks of tears on her face. "I'm truly sorry. I thought you were not a maiden. You should have told me," he said softly. "Though you were a virgin, that was the most exhilarating…"

Mabelle blushed, elated she had pleased him, that he too seemed to have been moved by the experience.

"…you took all of me. You were tight, my lovely, but you were wet and welcoming. I could feel you throbbing around my shaft, and I wanted to stay inside you as long as I could."

How to respond? This man she barely knew, who had preoccupied her thoughts constantly, was saying intimate things that inflamed her. She wanted to arch her body to his, wrap her legs around him, rake her fingers through his hair—but then he would again judge her a wanton.

He has eyes that can make women do foolish things.

He went to the basin and poured water from the ewer

on to a cloth. "Would you like me to cleanse you, Mabelle?"

The deep tenderness in his voice brought tears to her eyes, and despite her discomfort at having a man, a warrior, wash her most intimate parts, she nodded. He smiled at her embarrassment over the bloodstained sheets.

"It wasn't a trick," she murmured, not knowing what else to say.

He kissed her nose. "I could tell."

She wanted to offer to cleanse him but was too shy to ask, and before she knew it, he had left the bed to take care of his own needs. She couldn't take her eyes off him as he walked around confidently and without embarrassment. He was so male, so muscled, so big, so dark, so naked, and so comfortable in this masculine room.

"Do you like what you see, *Comtesse*?"

A flush rushed to her face already heated by the stubble of his beard.

"*Oui, milord.* I confess to being the wanton you already know me to be. It's a weakness I didn't know I possessed. You've unleashed something I've never experienced before. Despite my mistrust of you, I can't say no to your passionate embraces."

He sat beside her on the bed and took hold of her hand. "First of all, never call me *milord.* I'm your husband and my name is Ram. Secondly, I'm conflicted. The irony of our predicament strikes me. You did indeed behave like a wanton, but that aroused me. Your actions were inappropriate, but I wasn't blameless. At least we have passion, if we don't have trust. I'm elated no other man has possessed you. I'm also overjoyed to have been the one to bring you to your first experience of ecstasy."

She was puzzled. "How did you know that?"

He traced a finger down her nose and laughed. "A man can sense these things. It was the look of utter surprise on your face. You're not a wanton, just a warm, passionate woman. We'll make beautiful children. I'm happy to have a wife who is passionate and lusty in bed. Passion is not a weakness."

"But I don't know how to be lusty."

"Don't worry, I'll teach you. *Je serai ton maître*."

His promise of mastery thrilled and dismayed her.

"Let's sleep now and perhaps in a while—"

He turned her, encircled her with his arms and cupped her breasts in his big hands, nuzzling the back of her neck. Sleep quickly claimed them.

~

Ram woke before dawn filled with an intense feeling of well-being, and slowly became aware of the naked woman sleeping beside him. His wife. Her back was to him, her breasts and belly pressed to the bed, one long leg straight beneath her, the other bent. One hand rested on the pillow next to her face. Her tangled hair lay like a coverlet over her back and shoulders. He had an urge to put his hands on her lovely round *derrière* but resisted. He wanted to watch her breathe for a few more minutes. They would have to rise soon to prepare for their journey, and he had already hardened at the sight of her.

His first glimpse of Mabelle had ignited a fire within him, and yet the intensity of their passionate joining was overwhelming. He was usually a man of few words when he bedded a woman but recalled sharing intimacies with

Mabelle he had never uttered before. What he had experienced with her was more than a bedding. She had claimed him, possessed him, just as much as he had possessed her. It elated him he was the first man to penetrate her. He had never made love to a virgin. Why had he been sure she was not a maid? Would she ever forgive his cruel words?

It had seemed natural to cleanse her, something he had never been motivated to do for a woman before. As he looked at her now in the early light of dawn, sleeping peacefully, he tried to imagine what life must have been like for her before they met. It felt good to have her here, beside him, in the chamber he loved but had never shared with anyone. "I swear to you, Mabelle," he whispered, "you'll never want for a safe place to sleep ever again."

He reached to fondle her hair when she stirred. She turned lazily and stretched. His need intensified and he gathered her into his arms, feathering kisses along her neck.

She blinked, seemingly disoriented for a few moments. Then she smiled. "Do we have time to do it again?" she asked.

His manhood reacted predictably to her sultry innocence. "We have time."

A NEW DYNASTY

"The Saxons are to endure the humiliation of seeing the Conqueror crowned on the anniversary of Christ's birth," Ram remarked as he and his wife and brothers were breaking their fast before the departure for the coast. "William has a strong feeling for form and law and he's resolved to let no ceremony pass that might strengthen his claim to be regarded as King of the English."

He turned to his brothers. "So we're agreed? You'll take care of things here and at Belisle and Domfort. I imagine you've had enough of England after Hastings."

Both men agreed readily.

Mabelle smiled timidly at Ram. "I can tell you're honored by the invitation from William, and nothing will keep you away. From the little you've told me, you played a large part in ensuring the victory."

He had shared something of the details of the battle, though he had decided not to tell her about his near decapitation. "Are you sure you want to accompany me?" he ventured, not knowing what he would do if she said she would prefer not to. She had never travelled by ship before.

"Will it be safe?"

"It's a short voyage, and, if we're careful to pick the right tides, you'll be safe with me. But the castle at Ellesmere isn't like Montbryce; we can't live in it yet."

Why did he feel a compulsion to take her with him? It would be a difficult and dangerous life, perhaps for years, and there would be a lot of traveling back and forth to Normandie.

"I don't want to be left behind, Ram."

Encouraged by her loyalty, he admired the way she sat a horse as they journeyed to the coast with a contingent of his knights. Decorum dictated she ride her mare side saddle, but she eventually confided, "My back is broken. It would be more comfortable riding behind you on Fortis. Then at least I could feel your warmth. I'm frozen to the bone."

He looked at her with a teasing smile and reined in his horse. Perhaps having a wife who had spirit wasn't such a bad thing. "I would enjoy feeling your beautiful breasts pressed against my back."

She flared her nostrils, causing him to chuckle, and soon she was mounted behind him. He patted her thigh. "I now see the advantage for me of your riding astride."

The winds were with them and they took ship for the English coast. She weathered the crossing well, but Ram was seasick from the moment they cast off. He had reluctantly advised her of his ailment. "I'm sorry. I did warn you. When I think of the last time I sailed to England, with

William, it seems a lifetime ago. I didn't know if I would ever see you again."

Mabelle huddled closer to him. "You thought of me?"

Another bout of retching prevented his response.

She wiped his brow. "I'm not a good wife. I have no idea how to help your malady."

Her genuine concern touched his heart. "Nothing can be done about it. Believe me. I have to stay outside, but if you're cold, you should seek shelter under the canvas they rigged for you."

"*Non*, I love the tang of the salty breeze on my face, and I would rather be with you."

Even in his misery, he believed she meant what she said. "This wind is filling the sail and should carry us quickly across the Narrow Sea. We're fortunate." He didn't want to mention this stretch of water could be deadly if weather and tides turned against them.

They came ashore safely. "Welcome to England, Mabelle. I'm glad you're here with me. This is our new country, the land of opportunity for us and our children."

William had arranged for an escort to accompany them into London. When the long and tiring journey was finally at an end, they fell asleep in each other's arms in the opulent accommodation at the royal residence next to the Abbey.

The next day, they woke early. "I have no yuletide gift to give you," he whispered.

To his delight, she shyly curled her hand around his morning erection. "I can think of a gift."

It was an exhilarating coupling, their first in England, but they couldn't risk being abed when servants came to prepare them for the momentous event.

Later, as they made their way to the coronation in the church of Saint Peter, called Westminster, Ram thought he would pass on to her something of the Abbey, so she would know the history of the magnificent building. "Edward the Confessor chose Westminster as the site for his palace and church because it lay close to the famous and rich town of London. It was surrounded with fertile lands and green fields near the main channel of the river Thames, an important trade route. Of course, London isn't the seat of government. That's in Winchester."

Mabelle gazed at the architecture. "I know the Confessor grew up in Normandie."

"*Oui*, and he looked to Norman architects to build his abbey, because they were more advanced in their craft than the English. He was aware of the great abbey churches built at Caen, and of the development of our architecture. The Abbey was Edward's great gift to the people of England, magnificent and innovative even by our standards. It was consecrated on Holy Innocents Day, in the year of our Lord One Thousand and Sixty-Five."

Once again, his wife surprised him. "But Edward was too ill to attend. My father and I were in Arques, and the castle was full of rumors of his imminent death. Like Moses and the Promised Land."

He squeezed her hand. "*Oui*, but, on this day, in the Abbey, William, *Duc de Normandie*, is to become the third man in this eventful year to wear the English crown. He will be king of his Promised Land."

Ram's chest swelled with pride as he escorted Mabelle into the Abbey. Her velvet surcoat dress was emerald green, trimmed with ermine, made for her by Bette, at Montbryce, before the terrible day of their intended wedding. Her girdle was of spun gold. The ruffled pleats of the sleeves of her satin chemise reflected the light of the thousands of candles. Over her dress she wore a voluminous semi-circular matching cloak, pinned in the center with a brooch bearing the Montbryce crest. The cloak too was trimmed with ermine. Her hair was closely coiled with a few curls at the forehead, and she wore a wimple wound about her golden hair and thrown over her shoulder. A snood of embroidered green silk held the wimple in place.

As they proceeded to their places, he whispered, "You look stunning. Even in this illustrious gathering you turn heads."

There was a substantial guard of Norman men-at-arms and knights posted round the church to prevent any treachery on the part of resentful townsfolk.

In the presence of the bishops, abbots, and nobles of the whole realm, Archbishop Ealdred of York consecrated William as King of the English and placed the royal crown on his head. The Archbishop of Canterbury had refused to officiate. The coronation robe was ornamented with gold and costly gems. Hundreds of amulets of gold and silver hung from it.

"Each amulet contains a saint's relic," Ram whispered to Mabelle.

When Archbishop Ealdred asked the English, and Geoffrey, Bishop of Coutances, asked the Normans if they would accept William as their king, all proclaimed their agreement with one voice, but not in one language. Ram shouted proudly with a resounding *Oui*, thrusting his fist into the air in salute to William, filled with conflicting emotions at the memories of the horrific battles, and what the victory had cost him. His other hand held Mabelle's tightly.

The Archbishop led William to the royal throne in the presence and with the assent of the bishops and abbots gathered there.

Suddenly, Ram smelled smoke.

Several voices shouted *Fire!*

Many in the crowd took fright, rushing out of the church.

"Ram?" Mabelle cried, clutching his arm as smoke billowed.

Her obvious terror tore at his heart. "I won't let any harm come to you. Hold on to me. We must stay together."

He led his trembling wife to safety, his arm firmly around her, sword drawn. He delivered her to his men-at-arms with instructions to take her back to the palace.

To their credit, the bishops and a few clergy remained in the sanctuary to complete the consecration. Ram decided his duty was to remain close by William in case the fire was a diversionary tactic.

After a quarter hour of anxious confusion, a Norman captain appeared from the rear of the church to inform William the fire had been extinguished. The new king reassured and thanked those who had stayed.

Ram elbowed his way through the phalanx of nervous clerics. William looked pale and seemed shaken by the course of events. "You will scarcely believe, my friend, that my own cavalry caused the commotion," he explained hoarsely. "When they heard the harsh English accents, they believed treachery was afoot. They set fire to some of the buildings surrounding the Abbey, putting people to the sword."

Ram shook his head in disbelief. "*Majesté*, you must make an appearance to the people, to reassure our fellow Normans you've been crowned."

The new king regained his composure, nodded and walked regally to the door of the Abbey. The sight of him in his coronation robes calmed the largely Norman crowd.

He squared his broad shoulders and proclaimed, "I've sworn to maintain the Church, and all Christian people in true peace, to prohibit injustice and oppression, to observe equity and mercy in judgments, and to rule my people better than the best of kings before me, if they are loyal to me. I am determined in my heart to make England a country where something other than anarchy can reign. I will pursue the King's Peace with warlike fervor."

As cheers resounded, he turned to Ram. "With the help of the Confessor's Norman advisors and allies like you, *Comte Rambaud le Noir*, I will be invincible."

~

Having shed the cloak and wimple, Mabelle paced back and forth, biting her nails, frantic for Ram's safety. She rushed to embrace him when he arrived back at the Palace.

"Everything is peaceful now. Our Duke is King William the First of the English, despite the best efforts of our own Norman soldiers to ruin the day for him."

"I heard the tale," she replied. "It's the talk of the Palace."

They looked at each other and laughed with relief.

"We shouldn't let your beautiful *ensemble* go to waste, *Comtesse de Montbryce*," he purred, undoing the girdle of spun gold, as he pressed her to his body. "This is a day for celebration."

As soon as he touched her, she felt the clenching low in her belly. They disrobed quickly, his need to join their bodies apparently as urgent as hers. She called his name over and over as he knelt between her legs, draped them over his shoulders, lifted her hips, bent his head and kissed her place of pleasure. He held her firmly as he made love to her with his warm mouth, his tongue as deft as his fingers had been. It seemed natural. She trusted him with her body. Why could she not trust her heart to him?

"I savor every tremor of pleasure vibrating through you, Mabelle."

He smiled the smile that made her quiver. Keeping her legs draped over his shoulders, he put a bolster under her hips and slid his manhood inside. She smiled back as their rhythmic dance inflamed her. Throbbing with release, her sheath welcomed his surging seed.

"Your hair's getting longer," she whispered later, as she twirled her fingers through it. "It smells of wood smoke."

~

Long days and nights of celebration followed the coronation.

"The king wishes to formally name me Earl of Ellesmere at tonight's banquet," Ram told his wife on the third day. "Beforehand, he wants to meet to discuss the problems in the Welsh Marches, and how he perceives my role in dealing with them. There's no definitive border between England and Wales, so we must establish our authority in the region."

When they were ushered into the king's antechamber, William strode to Ram and embraced him warmly. "*Non, mon ami*, you will not kneel. I wouldn't be wearing this crown today without your help. I am desolate about your father."

Turning to Mabelle, still in a deep curtsey, he took her hand and kissed it, pulling her to her feet. "My dear *Comtesse* de Montbryce. At last this fool friend of mine has had the good sense to marry you."

"Merci, Majesté."

"My dear friend," the king turned to Ram, wasting no time. "I want to talk about these irritating Welsh rebels."

"Sire?"

"You have time and again proven your worth, both militarily and in governance. The situation in the Marches requires such skills. You've been there and seen for yourself. I also need someone I can trust implicitly. I envision my Marcher Lords having more power than an ordinary earl. Rebellion is ever in the air. We need to consolidate our victory."

Ram gritted his teeth. He itched to tell William what he thought of the *castle* at Ellesmere that he had indeed seen for himself, and fervently hoped rumor of the fiasco with Rhodri had not reached the king's ear.

The monarch's next words broke into his thoughts. "Ah, here come d'Avranches, Montgomerie and Fitz-Osbern, the others chosen for the job."

I am indeed in illustrious company.

He wondered if the other men's castles were as dilapidated as his. After the appropriate introductions of the lords and their ladies had been completed, and the social niceties observed, the women withdrew to a nearby alcove.

The discussion continued for several hours, with William outlining the powers he planned to give to his four Marcher Lords. Ram's earldom of Ellesmere occupied an area close to Wales, between Chester and Shrewsbury, sites of two of the proposed earldoms. Hereford in the south was the other.

When time came for the feasting, Ram went in search of Mabelle. The ladies had long since left to prepare for the banquet.

"This is one of the proudest moments of my life," he whispered to her as they were announced, and he entered the massive hall, his beautiful wife on his arm.

"I'm happy to be here to see you honored."

"It's your presence here that makes me proud."

Why did I think she wouldn't make a good comtesse?

"I have mixed feelings," he admitted. "The king has indeed honored me beyond measure, but it's an honor that's not without its dangers. The Marches are not a safe place to bring my wife and start our family. It certainly won't be the comfortable life we enjoyed at our castle in Normandie, at least not for a while."

She leaned into him. "I don't care, Ram. I would rather be with you."

He touched his hand to her cheek. "I can't envision leaving you alone in Normandie, Mabelle, I need you by my side."

Before the food was served, King William called his four appointees to the dais and commanded them to bend the knee. "*Mes seigneurs, Comtes* d'Avranches, de Montgomerie, de Montbryce and Fitz-Osbern, I confer upon you the titles of Earl of Chester, Shrewsbury, Ellesmere and Hereford. You are hereby invested with greater powers than any noble has ever enjoyed before."

During the feast that followed the long ceremony, Ram and William Fitz-Osbern began discussing the castles they had been granted. He was aware his fellow earl was an accomplished castle builder.

"Hereford is in reasonably good shape," Fitz crowed. "If Ellesmere is in need of renovation, I would willingly give you aid with the task. We must work together to strengthen our position throughout the border regions."

"I accept your offer and I thank you," Ram replied, his heart lifting a little.

FLIGHT

While the Conqueror and his Marcher Lords were celebrating, Lady Ascha Woolgar spent a lonely Yuletide in the manor house at Ruyton, and by January suspected she had conceived. The possibility became a reality a few sennights later, and she was filled with elation one moment and dread the next. Morning sickness and worry wore her out. She was afraid the steward appointed by the earl would notice something was amiss.

She recognized her good fortune with Montbryce's generous arrangements. Many Saxons had been thrown out of their estates by the Norman invaders. Her stubborn Saxon pride would not let her grovel to the earl now she carried his seed. He would probably reject her and the child. Even if he acknowledged the babe, it would grow up with the stigma of bastardy. She determined to survive the ordeal alone. At least a son or daughter would be a cherished remembrance of her brief liaison with Ram. It was ironic that in all the times her brutish husband had used her, she had never conceived. Indeed, she'd assumed she was barren.

Her faithful maid was the only person in whom she confided. "No one can ever find out, Enid. We must tell people my child is the issue of my late husband, Sir Caedmon."

Enid shook her head vehemently. "That would be easier to accomplish if your tenants and servants didn't know Sir Caedmon left here well before the Battle of Stamford Bridge, my lady. If he was the father of your child, the babe would be born by May, but you'll not give birth until much later."

Enid was right, but Ascha could see no way out of her dilemma. She fretted to such a degree about her pregnancy becoming evident, she worried she might fall ill. "Steward Roussel will soon start putting things together and spread word of my condition at Ellesmere. He may tell Lord Rambaud. I'm sure he already wonders why the earl is generous towards me. Perhaps I'll just have to stay hidden in the manor house."

How impractical that would be. She couldn't hide a babe away after his birth.

"My lady, we should perhaps try to procure an abortifacient for you. I could—"

"Never, Enid," Ascha cried. "I want this child desperately. But Lord Rambaud must never know. We need a miracle."

~

Roussel was perplexed. The lady of Shelfhoc Hall looked worse every day. Should he mention this to Lord

Rambaud? He decided against it. His explicit instructions had been to take care of the house and estate. Nothing had been said about the welfare of the Saxon woman who lived there. The whole arrangement was strange as far as he was concerned. He couldn't understand why the Norman earl had taken on responsibility for this remote manor, far from his own lands.

"You're to administer the rents and the estate, and take care of the house," Gervais had told him. "And you're to provision the men-at-arms left there to safeguard the manor. All accounting and revenues are to be given to the lady of the house. The earl doesn't want to be bothered with it."

"Am I to take a commission on behalf of *milord*?"

"*Non*. You'll be recompensed directly by me, and then by the Ellesmere steward, Bonhomme, when he arrives."

Oui, the whole arrangement is very strange.

~

In the early spring, three riders were challenged by the Earl of Ellesmere's men as they approached the rampart protecting Shelfhoc. "State your business, Saxons," the captain sneered.

"Who are you to demand I tell you my business?" a burly nobleman replied angrily.

"I am captain of the guard assigned to protect this manor, and you will not pass until you tell me who you are, and what your business is with Lady Ascha Woolgar."

The visitor urged his mount forward. "I am Sir Gareth Bronson and she is my sister. I am accompanied by my son and my squire."

Seemingly satisfied, the soldiers gave way.

The three rode into the courtyard. Sir Gareth dismounted and rapped with his fist on the door of the manor. “Ascha! It’s your brother. Open the door.”

Gawain and Edward dismounted; Edward took the reins of the three horses then handed them over to a man who had emerged hurriedly from the stables.

“Gareth,” Ascha exclaimed as she flung open the door, throwing herself into her brother’s arms. She had not seen him in the two years since her marriage to Caedmon Woolgar.

“How do you fare, Ascha?” he asked as he strode into the manor, his arm around his sister, Gawain close behind. “I’m sorry I couldn’t come sooner. It’s impossible for Saxons to travel now with these cursed Normans everywhere. The Conqueror boasts about the *Peace of God* and safety for all, but—”

“Never mind, Gareth, you’re here now.”

“I should have come before, my dear, as soon as I received your message about Caedmon’s death at Hastings. I suspected he may have fallen there. You look pale. Are you well?” He embraced her. “How are you coping with his death?”

“As well as can be expected. I was never happy with him. He wasn’t an easy man to live with.”

Gareth took a good look at his sister. “No. But a woman can’t survive alone these days here in England, especially a Saxon woman. Who is the Norman who took our horses? And you have Norman soldiers guarding Shelfhoc?”

Has he guessed?

“He’s a steward assigned here by the Earl of Ellesmere

who has generously provided me with protection, and a steward to help me manage the estate. He furnishes an accounting of the revenues."

"Why would a Norman earl do that?" young Gawain asked, his voice laced with suspicion.

Ascha fidgeted nervously with her hair. "There's the ever present danger of attack from the Welsh here in the Marches. This is a valuable but vulnerable estate. He's protecting his own interests.

"Gawain, why don't you go to the kitchen and see what Cook can find for you? You must be hungry after your journey."

She was relieved when he smiled and left.

Her brother waited until Gawain was out of earshot, then continued, "Nevertheless, Ascha, you can't stay here alone. I'm getting the feeling you've already suffered at the hands of these Norman invaders."

Ascha's betraying hands went immediately to her rounding belly.

"As I thought."

She clenched her fists. "But where would I go, Gareth?"

He didn't hesitate. "You'll come with us to Scotland."

Her hands flew to her face. "Scotland?"

"King Malcolm Canmore hates the Normans as much as we do. He has made it clear he welcomes to his court in Edwinesburh any Saxons who don't wish to remain as subjects to the Normans. We'll make a new life there, free of Norman tyranny. Many of us have made the decision to follow the hundreds who've already fled."

Ascha pressed her fingertips to her temples. "But what about Shelfhoc Hall?"

Gareth considered, steepling his hands. "I'll speak to this steward and inform him you'll be traveling to my home for a while. He needn't know you're never coming back."

It's the answer to my prayers—but Scotland?

"As you have rightly guessed, Gareth, I'm with child but without a husband. Will such a woman be welcomed in the court of King Malcolm?"

Gareth put a reassuring arm around her shoulders. "You're my sister, Ascha. Many Saxon women have fallen victim to the rapacious appetites of these murderous Normans. You'll be under my protection. Gawain's mother died years ago. You and I will be good companions for each other. I'll safeguard your secret."

Ascha chewed her lip. "And you'll speak with Steward Roussel?"

Gareth thought for a while. "I'll instruct him to continue taking care of things as usual. I see no reason why he can't send you a yearly accounting, if we send back word of where we are once we arrive. Normans are obsessed with form and order. He'll probably be happier to be in charge of a manor where there's no-one to constantly look over what he's doing."

Ascha shivered. "True, perhaps, though he'll still be ultimately responsible to the earl, a powerful man I prefer not to cross."

Her heart was heavy as she remembered her brief but fulfilling liaison with Rambaud, a man she could never have. Would he be angry if he ever found out she had borne his child and not told him?

~

Three sennights later, Lady Ascha Woolgar left the land of her birth, fearful of what the future had in store for her and her unborn child. Gareth had taken care of the arrangements as promised.

A score of souls made the harrowing journey in ten grueling days. Upon their arrival, they were greeted warmly by the Scottish king and his queen Ingibjorg, and provided with help and support by other Saxons who had fled before them to make a new life.

By the time her son was born a short time later, Gareth had procured a house for himself, his son and his sister, along with their squire Edward, and her maid Enid. She named her son Caedmon. The name of her dead warrior husband would be perpetuated, if not his bloodline, and would make it easier to conceal the babe's parentage.

She could not choose a Norman name for him but gave him the second name Brice, which in her language meant *son of a nobleman*. She took satisfaction in knowing she would be the only one who knew the true significance of the name. But she vowed never to tell her son of his true father. It was a noble thing to be the son of a martyr of Hastings, whereas the bastard of a Norman—

In thanksgiving for her miracle, she swore an oath to devote her life to this precious child.

ELLESMERE TAKES SHAPE

The castle at Ellesmere gradually took shape. Ram decided it was at least habitable and Mabelle could move there after spending six months at the Palace. He missed her unbearably and suspected she missed him, but then Westminster was a lonely place for a Norman woman alone with only a loyal maidservant. Each time he came to visit she rushed into his embrace.

"How long are you staying this time?" she asked shyly on his third visit.

She's ached for me as I've ached for her.

"As long as it takes to pack."

"I'm returning with you?" she asked happily. His nod was the assurance she needed. She rushed off to get Giselle started on readying the baggage.

Ram had seen little of William during his previous visits to the Palace. Once, however, when he did manage a brief audience, he was amazed to hear the king remark on how useful he'd found some of Mabelle's intimate knowledge of Normandie. "It's astonishing, Ram, what people will say when they think they're speaking to someone unimportant."

The king was away often, riding extensively throughout his new kingdom, confiscating lands and building fortified wooden castles. Then he'd appointed his half-brother Eude and William Fitz-Osbern as co-regents, and gone back to Normandie.

Catching up with his wife, Ram told her, "We've been delayed by the rebellion that broke out in Fitz-Osbern's earldom shortly after he was named Regent. It took him away from work on our castle. However, he has suppressed it—with great brutality, I might add."

Looking around furtively he whispered, "I'm getting increasingly worried about the capacity for cruelty of some Norman lords."

~

Mabelle coped well with the long journey north, assuring Ram that she was used to traveling. He didn't want to dampen her enthusiasm, but feared her reaction when she set eyes on the unfinished castle.

It touched his heart to see her struggle to conceal her dismay.

However, little by little, she added her personal touches to the castle. *La Cuisinière* sent a young Norman woman from Saint Germain, whom she had trained in the finer arts of cuisine.

"Trésor is proving to be the treasure her name implies," Mabelle remarked to Ram one evening after they had supped in the half-finished hall. "She brooks no nonsense from the Saxon and Welsh servers and scullery maids, and her rule in the kitchens is supreme."

Ram patted his full belly. "I agree, and visitors speak highly of the fine food we serve here."

Mabelle dabbed at her mouth with a napkin. "Giselle is relishing her role as head of the household, selecting and training the maids and houseboys to meet her rigorous Norman standards."

Ram felt well-pleased. "*Oui*, now we have Fernand's son, Mathieu, here as our steward, it seems like home."

Haunted by the memories of the pestilence that had swept through the Calvados, Mabelle suggested to Ram they should have a healer on hand in their home, and he agreed.

They augmented their household staff by inviting to the castle a local Welsh healer recommended by the village midwife.

"Myfanwy has a special healing touch, your ladyship," said the stout, red-faced Saxon midwife.

Mabelle was reassured that, when she did conceive, she would be in good hands.

The Welsh woman was amenable, and Mathieu Bonhomme allocated her a small chamber within the castle.

Mabelle spent much of her time supervising the menus, preparing herbal remedies and salves under Myfanwy's supervision, and doing embroidery and weaving. She made wimples, chemises, shifts and dresses, and shirts for Ram, though most of her husband's clothes and the fancier items were made by local tailors.

Myfanwy debated long and hard when she was offered the place at Ellesmere. A position at the castle would ensure not only her future, but more importantly that of her daughter. However, she feared the earl might not approve of a woman with a bastard child. She decided to say nothing of Rhonwen.

"I am amenable," she finally told the countess. "It will be my honor to serve you and *Arglwydd* Montbryce."

The small chamber she was given was in a remote part of the castle. If they were careful, Rhonwen could come with her, and be hidden away. But what would the girl do? She was already becoming known in her own right for her healing skills.

It was safer for her to stay in the village.

The Montbryces enjoyed their first Yuletide in Ellesmere, and celebrated in the chapel with the usual religious observances, but also enjoyed the Festival of Fools. A jester was elected to be a mock bishop. He dressed in fake vestments and led people to church, where he delivered a service in gibberish nonsense and sang rude songs. It gave them a sense of being back at home in their beloved Normandie, and relieved some of their homesickness.

"I miss our beautiful Calvados," Mabelle confided later when they were in bed. They had laughed heartily at the festival and it had relaxed them.

"As do I, but as long as you're here, I can bear the

homesickness. When the weather improves, we'll return home for a visit."

He turned her so her warm back was tucked into his body, and enfolded her in his arms, cupping her breasts.

"When I hold your breasts, I'm in Normandie. I hold my homeland in my hands."

She felt his erection against her back.

"What is this spell you weave around me?" he whispered, nuzzling her ear. "I've only to touch you and I become insatiable."

They made love, pleasuring each other, until they tumbled together into mindless oblivion, calling each other's name, drugged by the overwhelming feelings of sensual rapture.

"You're my lifeline in this sea of foreign hostility," he murmured sleepily.

REBELLION

Ascha Woolgar wondered what the commotion was about when her nephew Gawain burst into the room where she was playing with her son.

"Have you seen father?" he panted.

She frowned. "I believe he's in his chamber."

"I must find him and tell him the news. Edgar the Aetheling's ship has foundered in a gale off the coast of Fife. He and his sisters have been rescued and brought to King Malcolm's court."

Ascha's mouth fell open. "The Aetheling? Our rightful king? Sailing off the coast of Scotland?"

Gawain nodded his head so vigorously, Ascha worried it might fall off. "He was part of Earl Morcar's rebellion in Northumbria against the Normans but was defeated. His plan was to flee to Hungary, the land of his birth, when the ship went down."

"The hope for ridding England of the Normans is still alive?" Ascha asked excitedly, stooping to pick up Caedmon, who had struggled to his feet, clinging to the folds of his mother's skirts.

Gawain swallowed and took a deep breath. "The other astounding news is the newly widowed King Malcolm is smitten with young Margaret, Edgar's sister. Apparently he rode from his residence in Dunfermline to welcome the royal refugees.

"Imagine if he marries her. What a political coup. It would bring Malcolm an alliance with the old royal house of England, and a large dowry from the King of Hungary. Edgar would benefit enormously from having a brother-by-marriage who is already a formidable opponent of the Norman usurpers. I'm confident Malcolm would support Edgar if he attempted to claim the throne again."

He stared wide-eyed as if he couldn't quite believe the words he'd uttered.

Ascha planted a kiss on Caedmon's nose, then put her hand on Gawain's quivering shoulder. "Your father will be delighted with this news. I'll help you find him."

As Gawain and the whole Saxon community in Scotland hoped, King Malcolm Canmore, the Great Chieftain, became besotted and soon married Princess Margaret. He agreed to support her brother Edgar in his campaign to claim the English throne. When a serious rebellion broke out in Northumbria early the following year, Edgar returned to England with other rebels who had fled to Scotland, to lead the revolt. Gawain and Gareth Bronson were among those who went with him.

After early successes the rebels were defeated by King

William at York, and Edgar again sought refuge with Malcolm. Gareth was wounded, bowshot in the arm, but Gawain managed to get him back to Scotland safely. Ascha took care of him and he recovered.

In late summer that year, the arrival of a fleet sent by King Sweyn of Denmark spawned a fresh wave of English uprisings in various parts of the country. Edgar and the other exiles sailed to the Humber, where they joined with Northumbrian rebels and the Danes. Their combined forces overwhelmed the Normans at York and took control of Northumbria.

Edgar then led a seaborne raid into Lindsey which ended in disaster, and he escaped with only a handful of followers to rejoin the main army. Gawain was among them, Gareth was not. He died instantly, felled by an arrow through the heart.

Ascha grieved for her dear brother, her protector and champion. Gawain, his heir, assured his aunt she and little Caedmon could remain in the house.

Late in the year, King William fought his way into Northumbria and regained York, buying off the Danes and devastating the surrounding country. After Yuletide he moved against Edgar and other English leaders, who had taken refuge with their remaining followers in a marshy region, and put them to flight. Edgar returned once more to Scotland. Gawain drowned in the marshes. Since he had no heirs his property devolved to Ascha.

~

Ram seethed with anger as he strode out of the recently furbished Map Room at Ellesmere into the corridor, where he bumped into Mabelle who was accompanied by a servant.

“What is it, Ram?” she asked.

“The news from Northumbria and York is dire. I hope we can resolve the Welsh problem without having to resort to the tactics William is using in the north,” Ram replied, running a hand agitatedly through his hair. He glanced at the servant, whom Mabelle promptly sent away.

“What’s he doing? Hasn’t the rebellion been quashed?”

“It has, but he’s bought off the Danes and is harrying the whole region. The devastation includes setting fire to the vegetation, houses and tools to work the fields. It’s inevitable anyone who escapes slaughter will starve. Walk with me to our chamber. I feel safer talking there.”

Once they reached their sanctuary, he continued, “After such cruel treatment, neither the people nor the land will recover for many years. You know I want the firm establishment of Norman rule, but William has let his anger get the better of him. It sickens me. He wants to terrify the English into obedience. These actions won’t benefit us in the long run.”

He could voice these treacherous notions to his wife. She would never betray him. “What worries me in particular is that in this region some of the other Marcher Lords are capable of similar atrocities.”

MORWENNA

LLYS POWWYDD, WALES

When Rhodri thought back to the year the Normans had come, he sometimes regretted he had not killed Rambaud de Montbryce when he had him at his mercy. However, he had to grudgingly admit the Earl of Ellesmere, for such he had become, was an able administrator who had brought growth and prosperity to Ellesmere in the six years since the invasion.

No one would now recognise the crude earthwork that had been Ellesmere Castle. It had become a well appointed Norman fortification, and the earl was constantly adding on to and improving it. He had even commissioned the building of a church. Rhodri's own *castle* was comfortable, but his *llys* would never match the opulence of Ellesmere, not that he wanted it to.

It galled him that the population of Ellesmere prospered and grew, whereas his own people eked out a life of poverty and deprivation. The Normans had encroached further into his country than the English Saxons and

William the Conqueror seemed determined to crush rebellion with an iron fist. It had been six years of grinding oppression and persecution and Rhodri felt the weight of his role even more than he had when he had first assumed his father's mantle. Life for him and his followers was perilous. If they were taken they would be tortured and executed.

Yet, the harassing raids had to go on, fueled by a need for food and a burning desire to regain what was rightfully theirs. The Welsh wanted the Normans out of their lands. Rhodri would not succumb to the widely held belief they could not beat the invaders. He would fight them to his last breath. It was his destiny.

He did succumb, however, to the insistent suggestions from Morgan ap Talfryn that he become betrothed to Morwenna. He wasn't sure why he agreed. He needed a wife, and he needed heirs. But his memories of the girl were tinged with apprehension. He invited her and her father to his *llys* at Powwydd to sign the documents.

Her entry into the *neuadd* stunned every male in the *hall*. All eyes turned to watch the flirty girl who had grown into a voluptuous woman. She was fair of hair and face with breasts and hips that promised fertility and pleasure. Her thick blond braid was coiled around one side of her neck and perched jauntily atop her breasts, rising and falling as she breathed. Her ever-present smile was bewitching, but her blue eyes assessed a man through long blond lashes in a way that belied her supposed innocence. Rhodri felt he was being stripped bare. Despite himself, he was aroused.

After the formalities were completed, Morgan suddenly announced his intention to leave Llys Powwydd.

Rhodri was taken aback. "I'd hoped to have a chance to get to know Morwenna. Will you not stay longer?"

Morgan slapped him on the back and laughed nervously. "I'm leaving her here with you, Rhodri. She doesn't want to return with me."

Rhodri considered the implications for her reputation. "She shouldn't stay here with me."

"Nonsense," Morgan replied. "In a *llys* this size you can provide her with a chaperone. It is your royal residence after all."

He had the uneasy feeling the man was relieved to be rid of his daughter.

After only a few days, he understood her father's wish to be gone. Morwenna's refusal to behave like a noblewoman had the chaperone up in arms. She often sought Rhodri out, sitting in his lap by the open hearth, grinding against him. He was torn between arousal and disgust. Festivities and dancing carried on around them in the *neuadd* and large numbers ate their meals in the timbered hall. She seemed oblivious to his embarrassment at the disapproving looks from his people. She flirted with other men, who shied away, no doubt wondering why Rhodri did nothing to restrain her. He was at a loss—a feeling foreign to him.

Before long, she chafed at the limitations of the *llys*. When he told her he and his men would soon be traveling to Cadair Berwyn, she flew into a rage until he gave permission for her to accompany them.

"I can be of use to you, Rhodri," she crooned, batting her eyelashes. "I could go to the earl's castle and spy for you. I've been there many times. No one notices me."

Rhodri doubted that was true, but considered her offer.

It might be useful to have a spy within Ellesmere.

SONS

Despite the ongoing problems with Welsh discontent, Ellesmere prospered. The spacious Great Hall was completed, and Ram proudly showed off the intricately carved tables and large tapestries—all brought from Normandie.

Mabelle grew to love the region around the town. She befriended some of the Normans who had settled in the area prior to the conquest. There were mountains, moorlands, farms, wooded river valleys, and quaint villages. Ram explained to her it had come to be known as the Marches, because the Anglo-Saxon word for boundary was *mearc*.

True to his promise, William granted Ram virtual independence and what amounted to kingship over his lands. Marcher lords ruled their territory as they saw fit, unlike other English lords who were directly accountable to the king. Ram could build castles, administer laws, wage wars, establish towns, salvage, claim treasure-trove, plunder and was allowed to fish for royal fish. The king's plan was to subdue the Welsh without having to do it himself.

Ram was often away dealing with Welsh incursions, holding courts which could try all cases except high treason, and administering his territory. He encouraged immigration from Normandie, established markets and expanded trade, especially in fine cloth and wine. Sheriffs received their appointments from him.

Occasionally, he had to confiscate the estates of felons, and redistribute them to more trustworthy folk. His experience administering the Montbryce family estate was of great benefit to him, and he became known in the Marches as a firm but fair ruler, and a soldier to be reckoned with. He believed if people had enough food and the basic necessities of life, and were treated fairly, they would not want to rebel.

He often told Mabelle, "I could do none of this without your presence here at Ellesmere. You've proven to be a formidable countess. I never worry about the castle when I'm away."

In recognition of Ram's contributions, King William granted him another vast tract of land in Sussex in southern England, which brought four score and three manor houses under his control. It was also an area vital for the defense of England. He decided to deed ten of the estates to Hugh and ten to Antoine.

Ram's power and wealth were growing, as he had hoped. He had succeeded more than he ever thought possible in bringing honor, wealth and prestige to the Montbryce name. There was only one fly in the ointment.

"The years are going by, Mabelle, with no sign of your getting with child. Why don't you ask Myfanwy's advice?

You're still relatively young at five and twenty, but I'm approaching a score and ten, and the lack of an heir is beginning to worry me."

"Me too," she admitted.

If I'm barren, he'll have to put me aside. I'll die of grief.

~

Myfanwy loved life at the castle. She passed on to the countess her recipes for herbal remedies and salves, and the two women got to know each other. They developed a fondness, and Myfanwy was happy Mabelle de Montbryce trusted her. Her healing powers, which some whispered were magical, depended a great deal on the trust of the person being treated.

She went often to the village to take coin and food to Rhonwen. She confided how worried she was the countess seemed to be having difficulty conceiving. "She and the earl have been married for years, without issue. Should I broach the subject? I have many herbal concoctions to offer."

Rhonwen shrugged. "Perhaps it's the husband who is the problem?"

Myfanwy laughed. "Pshaw, child. Where do you get these notions? He's a virile man if ever I saw one. Can't keep his hands off his wife."

~

Joy surged through Mabelle when, after only one month of Myfanwy's herbal ministrations, she missed her flux.

Ram often chafed Ellesmere was not as fine as the castle at Montbryce. He worked tirelessly to make improvements to the buildings and grounds, determined to make their home in this foreign land as grand as the ancestral one in Normandie.

Knowing she was pregnant, she waited until he once more began his complaints about Ellesmere. They were alone in their chamber when Ram finished his usual lament with, "I only want a castle suitable for my beautiful wife."

"—and child," she added.

It took him a few moments to understand her meaning, and then he leapt from his chair and embraced her. He picked her up and twirled her around until they were both dizzy, then set her back on her feet and kissed her deeply.

"Are you sure?" he rasped. "It's been so long."

"I've only missed one month but I'm sure."

"You're the perfect wife," he crowed.

Mabelle laughed. "Yes, I am, but I couldn't have done it without the perfect husband. Apart from you and me, only Giselle and Myfanwy are aware of it. Can we keep it that way for a while?"

He kissed her forehead. "Of course, my beloved. But it will be hard for me not to climb up to the battlements and shout it from the rooftops."

For as long as she lived she would remember the first time he'd ever called her his *beloved.*

The happiness and relief that swept over him confirmed Ram's suspicions.

I'm in love with her.

But he was first and foremost a soldier, the king's man. His steadfast commitment to William would bring more handsome rewards.

What is this alchemy we have between us?

He had only to touch her for his manhood to harden. Not even touch—the mere sight of her was enough. And now she would bear him a child. He was a happy man. He couldn't imagine life without Mabelle. If he had been forced to acknowledge his wife was barren and seek another—it was something he didn't want to contemplate.

~

As her confinement drew closer, Mabelle grew more nervous. She hoped Ram would return home from the sortie against the Welsh before the event occurred, though she was confident all would go well.

Her every need had been taken care of for several sennights, and she had grown bored. She felt fat, bloated and unattractive, despite the fact her husband told her repeatedly she looked lovely and lush. She lay in bed, longing for his attentions, unable to get comfortable, and resigned to being awake as the dawn broke. Gradually, she became aware of a dull ache permeating her belly.

She lay perfectly still. The ache passed. Perhaps she should call Giselle to prepare a bath for her, to soothe her troubled spirit.

As sleep claimed her, the ache came again, this time more forcefully and for a longer period. She had never borne a child before, and had assumed the pains of labor would be sharp, intense stabs. Now she wondered if perhaps these aches were signals her child wanted to be born. She rolled out of bed slowly, pausing as the pain caught her again.

Oui, something is happening.

"Giselle, Giselle, *viens vite*, come quickly."

The maidservant bustled in from the connecting chamber, her red hair uncharacteristically awry, her face flushed with excitement. "*Milady*, is it the *bébé*?"

Mabelle nodded so hard it made her dizzy. "Fetch the midwife, and Myfanwy."

Fifteen hours later, clinging to the birthing stool brought days before in readiness, bathed in sweat and screaming loudly, Mabelle feared the hour of her death was at hand. But the experienced midwife told her calmly everything was normal, and she saw no reason to be anxious. "It's a good idea to scream. It will make you feel better."

Bertha used simple and natural procedures, relying on pepper to provoke sneezing. "I'm confident you'll not need the shroud you had made at the behest of the bishop," she reassured Mabelle. "But it's as well you obeyed his insistence on confessing your sins."

Myfanwy comforted her with various soothing herbal remedies and oils.

Mabelle sought solace during her labors in praying to Sainte Margaret, the patron saint of pregnant women. As her child came into the world and her last cry of relief rent the air, a maidservant brought word that Ram had ridden into the bailey and been informed of events. She closed her eyes and thanked God he'd come home safely.

A few minutes later, he gasped her name as he threw open the door of their chamber. His wild eyes fell upon her as she lay back, feeling spent and disheveled. And then their child made his presence known with a lusty wail.

"You're beautiful," he called to her as she smiled at him weakly.

"My lord," Bertha cried, ushering him out, "you shouldn't be here. Don't worry. You have a fine healthy son, but your wife needs to rest now. I'll bring the child to you when we've cleansed him. He too has had a long journey."

As Ram was shooed out, the midwife said to Giselle, "Trust the father to turn up as soon as it's over."

The four women laughed, though Mabelle barely had enough strength left to do so as Myfanwy handed her a steaming bowl of chamomile tea.

~

Ram had ridden hard to get home, soon working up a sweat in the warm August weather, driven by a premonition his child would be born that day. Though exhausted, joy overwhelmed him that he had been at home when his son was born.

When Bertha appeared with his babe swaddled in warm wrappings to keep out the unavoidable draughts of the castle, he took his heir into his arms and gazed upon him. He could scarcely believe he and Mabelle had created this wondrous being he held. What a wife she had turned out to be. They would name the boy Robert, after the king's father.

"Robert de Montbryce," he murmured, cradling the

child, "I'm your father, Rambaud de Montbryce, son of Bernard de Montbryce. It's to my everlasting sorrow my father didn't get a chance to see you. What does life hold in store for you? You're the long-awaited heir to a rich Norman heritage. Wherever your travels take you, I hope you'll always remember that."

Ignoring the strident admonitions of the midwife, he strode off with the babe still in his arms, to the chamber where his wife lay. The women had cleansed Mabelle, combed her hair and assisted her back to bed. She was exhausted, but he saw only her radiance. Smiling, she reached out her arms for her child, and he carefully handed Robert to her. She coaxed the child to her breast and he tried to latch on.

Ram's shaft hardened. "I was nervous about holding a baby," he confided with a grin, "but I'm good at it."

Mabelle had noticed it too. "You are, Ram." She smiled at his obvious physical discomfort. "In many noble families the father never touches the babes. I know only too well how a child needs a father's love."

~

By February, Mabelle had conceived again over the previous Yuletide. As the time for the birth approached, she enjoyed sitting by the window with her ladies, sewing busily, looking up from her work to see the fields in lambing-time. She watched shepherds clad in warm sheepskins drive the sheep into enclosures.

Soon I'll have another little lamb of my own.

She liked being a mother. Robert was a strong, healthy lad. Everyone who saw him admired his dark hair and blue eyes, and commented on his resemblance to his father. She wondered what her next child would be like. She spent a lot of her time in the nursery with her son, and preferred to nurse him, instead of using a wet nurse. She told him often how much she loved him, words she had never heard from her own father.

How is it I find it easy to tell my child I love him but I can't tell Ram?

When Ram pined for Normandie, Mabelle chided him. "Remember, Ram, our son was born in this foreign land. It's his land."

Ram always objected. "Robert is a Norman first and foremost. When I'm gone, it's the Norman lands that will pass to him. They're the important holdings and titles, the ones passed down in our family before. The Montbryce legacy."

Idly patting her belly, he smiled. "Our second son will inherit our English lands and titles. Those lands I've won for myself. They are Ellesmere lands."

In September of the year of our Lord One Thousand and Seventy-Three, Ram and Mabelle welcomed their second son, Baudoin, another almost identical copy of his father. Again, everything went normally, and the midwife and Myfanwy saw her through it.

As time progressed, and the boys grew, Ram didn't get to spend a great deal of time with his young sons, but when he did, he treated them much as his own father had treated him—with a firm hand but with love. He often remonstrated with Mabelle that she doted on them too much. Robert and Baudoin were excited to see him return from his travels. Whenever he was away fighting the barbaric Welsh, Mabelle was consumed with worry for him.

The following year, Edgar the Aetheling returned to Scotland. Disillusioned by further disastrous attempts to regain the throne, he succumbed to Malcolm's urging that he abandon his claims and make peace with the Conqueror.

The despondency among the Saxon refugees in Scotland was palpable. They congregated more and more at Court, drawn by their patroness, Margaret, Queen of Scotland.

Many among the Scottish nobility resented what they considered to be the anglicization of their Celtic court, but they were afraid to voice their criticisms, given Margaret's well known piety, and her husband's besottedness.

Ascha felt isolated after the deaths of her kinsmen. Caedmon was her only solace. She instilled in her son, and encouraged among the Saxons at court, a sense of great pride that he was the son of Sir Caedmon Woolgar, a *housecarl* who had fallen with his king at Hastings. It was the stuff of legend that the royal bodyguards had fought to the death rather than surrender.

At seven years of age, Caedmon Brice Woolgar was a strong, affectionate boy, a mirror image of his real father. Ascha was unconcerned about the resemblance, finding comfort in it. She was confident the two would never meet.

ACCIDENT

One of the powers granted to the Marcher Lords was the right to raise militias. Ram often recruited and trained new soldiers. While the ranks might consist of local people, the commanders of these men were always Normans. Giselle frequently dropped hints to the earl that her sons would make fine officers if they were only given a chance to come from Normandie.

Mabelle didn't pay attention to any of the details regarding such matters, busy as she was with her home and children. One winter's day, she was in the hall, sewing with ladies of the household, chatting about the impressive tapestry they had heard Bishop Eude had commissioned to commemorate the conquest of England. It was being made by the Anglo-Saxon seamsters at Eude's *demesne* at Canterbury in Kent but would later be sent to Bayeux in Normandie.

Robert and Baudoin were playing with their nursemaids near Mabelle's feet.

"I hear rumors it will be over two hundred feet in

length," Giselle commented. "The Anglo-Saxons are famous for their needlework."

"Apparently, it will show the historic events of the battle, as well as those leading up to the invasion," added Mabelle. "If it's being embroidered, then it's not a tapestry is it? That would mean it would have to be woven."

One of the nursemaids asked, "My lady, why is it being sent to Bayeux?"

"Bishop Eude is building a cathedral there."

While they were talking, her husband entered with some of his commanders. She glanced over to watch him. Even among this group of physically fit, elite fighting men he stood out. She fought the urge to rush over and press her fingers into his powerful thighs. The soft black hair hidden beneath the fine linen of his shirt called to her, and she smiled, thinking how shocked the onlookers would be if she tore the shirt off his muscled body.

Heat prickled her skin as he shifted his stance, and her eyes went unbidden to his sex, just there, hidden under the long doublet, nestled, ready to spring to life if he looked up and saw her hungry gaze. She averted her eyes, aware her face had flushed, that she had almost drooled.

Pray no one noticed.

The men's voices drifted into her returning awareness. They were discussing a new Norman knight who was due to arrive soon to take over command of one of the divisions.

"Seems he asked to be assigned to Ellesmere, *milord*," Gervais remarked.

Ram arched his brows. "Interesting. I wonder why?"

He glanced over to see if Giselle was within hearing, clearly wishing to avoid that hornet's nest.

"I expect he knows where the power is, *milord*."

The other men chuckled their agreement with this assessment.

"He's probably aware you have sons. Your heirs will inherit your lands, and they won't revert to the king. That kind of stability leads to opportunity."

Ram smiled. "And the name of this wise nobleman?"

"Giroux. I've good reports on him. He arrived recently from Normandie. Good family. Capable soldier."

Ram picked up a chart and studied it. "Sounds familiar—but I can't place it."

Mabelle's heart thudded and she suddenly felt cold. Ram didn't seem to be listening. Had she heard correctly? Could this be the son of the man her father had blinded and mutilated years ago? It was not a common name, and why had he asked specifically to come to Ellesmere? She had heard nothing of the Giroux family since coming to England but they were partly responsible for the years of wandering exile she had endured. She resolved to speak to Ram about it.

Later that night he reassured her. "I'm sure there's nothing to worry about."

He had remembered where he'd heard the name before but was in the process of seductively undressing his wife. "After Arnulf's death, there was no rumor of any ongoing threat from that family."

She persisted. "But why would he ask to come here?"

"News of our power and reputation has spread throughout Normandie. He's probably an ambitious young man seeking opportunity for advancement with a powerful Marcher Lord. Don't worry," he cajoled, playfully rolling her hardening nipple between his finger and thumb, grinning at her, "I can assign him where you'll never have to meet him."

She lost coherent thought as the passion that always took hold of her the moment Ram touched her did just that.

~

Not long after his discussion with Mabelle, Ram mounted Fortis, intending to ride out to inspect the Saturday market. He had always been an accomplished horseman, and was puzzled as to why his favorite mount seemed frenzied. It was a spirited horse, but that was the sort of steed he liked to ride. He had been relieved the stallion had adapted well to his new life in England after the rigors of Hastings.

Try as he might, he couldn't seem to calm the snorting animal, which reared so suddenly Ram was thrown heavily to the hard ground. Giroux rushed from nearby to calm the distraught horse. Gervais ran to his earl's side, pulling him away from the flailing hooves. Ram was having difficulty rising, only managing it with the help of his lieutenant. He knew immediately he had cracked a rib or two.

"What the devil is wrong with that horse?" he shouted, as pain snaked through his chest, bending him double.

"I'll look him over, *milord*," Giroux answered. "He seems calmer now. I'll see to him."

"Gervais, help me to my chamber. I fear my wife will need to assist me. I believe I've broken something."

Mabelle had apparently heard the commotion and hurried into the bailey. Gervais, almost carrying his earl, told her what had happened. She issued commands to servants as she helped her husband climb the steps. They assisted Ram to their chamber, where he sat on the edge of the bed, shaking.

Giselle and Myfanwy arrived with armfuls of linen cloths. The Welsh woman prepared a potion for pain, and Ram downed it in one, knowing firsthand how effective her potions were. The women tore the cloth into strips and bound him after Myfanwy's gentle examination confirmed the likelihood of broken ribs.

"*Yr Arglwydd* Montbryce," the healer said with authority, "you must rest for at least a fortnight. The only time you may get out of bed is when I come to bathe you in knitbone. Only thus will the bones start to heal."

His protests became less forceful when the draught she had given him took effect.

"Thank goodness you've at least stopped shaking," Mabelle murmured with relief, helping tuck warm linens around him.

~

Rhonwen loved to listen to her mother's accounts of happenings at the castle and longed to assist with the healing there. Though she lived with the family of the village smith, and enjoyed his protection, they were not her kin. However, she was never bored, being called upon often to use her skills as her own reputation grew. Folk said she had inherited not only her mother's skill but also her mystical aura.

One evening, Myfanwy's exhaustion was evident as she staggered into the village. Rhonwen bade her sit and handed her a bowl of herbal tisane. Her mother took a long draught of the liquid and her spirits revived. "Thank you, daughter. I feel better now. What a day we've had at the castle. *Arglwydd* Montbryce was thrown from his horse."

Rhonwen sat down facing her mother, her eyes wide. "Was he hurt?"

Myfanwy nodded, inhaling the aroma of the tisane. "Yes. Badly. Broken ribs. I've bound them, and ordered him to soak in knitbone every second day for a fortnight."

Rhonwen made a face. "That will not be pleasant."

Myfanwy chuckled. "No, and he's a proud man. He won't like it. At the moment he's compliant because I gave him a potion, but once he's alert—"

"How did it happen?"

Her mother did not answer right away. She seemed uneasy. "It was strange. The earl has ridden that horse for years. It's his favorite mount. Yet the beast was apparently frenzied. The earl's lieutenant had to pull his lordship out from under the flailing hooves, and a new soldier, Phillippe Giroux, managed to grab the reins and calm the animal."

Rhonwen shivered. "Giroux loiters around the village. I don't like him. He ogles women."

Myfanwy put down her bowl and took hold of Rhonwen's hands. "My countess doesn't trust him. I don't know why, but she doesn't. Stay away from him."

~

Morwenna verch Morgan sat alone in the cottage her father owned near the village of Ellesmere. Her sire had given in to her insistent demands she be rescued from the boredom of Rhodri's fortress. He had delivered her safely and then left her to her own devices, as usual. She smirked. He was afraid of her, believing she had inherited what he called "the dark arts" from her long dead mother.

Villagers who had faith in hexes and spells sought her out and paid her well. The location provided her with a place from which she could spy on the nearby castle. No-one paid attention to a plainly clad maiden wandering around with a basket. Some acknowledged her with a wave and a smile if they had seen her before. The stables were a particularly useful place to overhear gossip.

And it was in the stables of Ellesmere Castle where she stumbled upon what she had been seeking—a Norman accomplice.

The soldier did not know it yet, but she had seen him tamper with the saddle of the horse that had become frenzied and thrown the earl. He had rushed forward in a show of calming the horse after the incident, unaware she still watched from her hiding place.

She would find out why one of the earl's own men wanted to harm him, and use the knowledge to her advantage. The man was handsome—tall and well-muscled. Perhaps there would be other benefits to an alliance with him.

She waited until he had carefully lifted the saddle from the still nervous black stallion before she crept from her hiding place and came up behind him. "He's calmer now."

The Norman whirled around, his arms full of the saddle, his jaw clenched. His eyes darted to the horse, then back to her. She took a step toward him, unafraid.

"Get out of here, wench," he said angrily, heaving the saddle onto the half-wall of the stall.

She held her ground, head cocked to one side, a finger

pressed to her chin. "What do you suppose would make a horse so frenzied one minute, then calm the next?"

The Norman eyed her suspiciously, his hand on the hilt of his dagger. He gripped her elbow. "It's no concern of yours. Be gone."

She batted her eyelashes at him. "Are you sure you want to shoo me away, Norman? Your interests may be the same as mine."

He grabbed her roughly by the waist with one hand and pulled her to his body. "Is this what you're after?" he asked sarcastically, pressing his hard male length against her.

She ground her hips into him and looked into his eyes. "Oh, that and much more. Find me in the village. Ask for the cottage where you've heard you can buy a hex."

He sneered, but held her more tightly. "You don't look like a witch."

She put her hands on his chest and pushed him away. "You might say I am someone as interested as you in seeing the earl fall."

He tensed and watched her leave, his face red with anger.

She smiled as she made her way home. When she next saw Rhodri, she would hopefully have a plan to offer for ridding the Marches of the earl and his spawn.

RECOVERY

Ram realized he wasn't an easy patient, protesting loudly at the indignity of being forced, every second day, to soak in a tub of hot water darkened by the green of the knitbone. It necessitated the removal of his bindings, and their reapplication afterwards. He was too big for the women to wrestle into the tub, and Vaillon had to enlist the aid of another male servant.

"That cursed Welsh woman will kill me."

Mabelle stood with hands on hips. "Ram, much as I adore your magnificent body, it's not a pleasant task for me to dry you after you've been soaking in the wretched comfrey. But it will ease the swelling."

Ram squirmed, aware he had imposed the duty on her. "I'm sorry. I don't want any of the servants doing it. It's humiliating."

Mabelle's eyes sparkled as she baited him. "You're ruining every pair of braies you have, with your insistence on keeping them on in the tub. The laundress is less than pleased."

"I don't feel very magnificent," he whined, secretly wishing he had the energy to display his magnificence for her. "And I'll not expose myself to all and sundry."

An active, virile man, he chafed at spending time in bed, particularly since he was unable to make love to his wife. It was torture. Her nearness in the bed at night, or when she came to sit with him during the day, never failed to arouse him.

"It's difficult for you too. We've never been able to temper our passion for one another."

After close to a fortnight in bed, he was stroking her breasts and bemoaning his plight yet again when she rose and knelt between his legs. "Lay still, Earl of Ellesmere."

She feathered light kisses up the inside of one thigh, and down the other. Bending his legs slightly, she tenderly stroked the backs of his knees. His erection had sprung to life before she had started the kisses, and now she grasped the base of his manhood. She leaned forward and ran her tongue up the length of him.

"Mabelle," he gasped, keeping as still as he could, flattening his palms against the bed.

She moved her mouth rhythmically on his rigid manhood, cupping his sac with one hand and echoing the movement of her mouth with the other on his shaft. He groaned with every tug. Reaching for her breasts, he rasped, "I can't wait. Straddle me."

She lowered her slick womanhood onto his throbbing phallus, the sensation of deep penetration sending a wave of well-being coursing from his toes to the top of his head.

"You're already wet, my lovely. I can't thrust. You'll have to do the work." He grasped her hips. "*Oui,* that's it. I can feel you gripping me. Ride me hard, *ma belle*."

Her nostrils flared, her strong thighs braced tightly against his hips as she rode, back arched, hands threaded into her golden hair, breasts thrust forward proudly. She looked like a wild woman. Glancing to where their bodies were joined seemed to inflame her more—the golden and black curls intertwined. She stared into his eyes and he stared back. She smiled at him, and he returned the smile. They crested and peaked together, never turning their gaze as fulfillment clouded their vision.

Mabelle was careful not to collapse on top of him. Rising from the bed, she went to the ewer and poured water on a linen cloth. "Now I'll cleanse you in the loving way you've always cleansed me."

Loving? Of course I love her but could I bear it if she doesn't love me in return?

She dried him with her hair, and kissed his sated manhood.

"Cursed horse," he moaned, touching his bound ribs gingerly.

"Didn't you enjoy that?" she teased.

"*Oui*, of course, but these ribs are not healing fast enough. I can't wait to be riding again."

Yawning, she curled into him as sleep claimed them.

~

Ram was a healthy, robust and active man, and it didn't take him long to heal. He was happy to play with his sons when they were brought from the nursery.

"I want to get back on a horse, but if Fortis is still acting wildly, I'll have to find another mount," he told Mabelle sadly. "Much as I appreciate a steed with spirit, I also need a horse I can rely on when I ride against the Welsh. It will be hard to replace Fortis."

He was pleasantly surprised, however, when the horse was demonstrably glad to see him, and he mounted easily, only a twinge pricking his abdomen. He rode out to the town market with his men-at-arms.

"So, you've recovered from whatever upset you that day, *mon vieux*?" he said lovingly, patting the horse's neck, still puzzled by the uncharacteristic behavior.

On his return, he mentioned it to Gervais, who showed Ram the small scar of a deep wound on the horse's flank that he had discovered, under the saddle, as if something sharp had been pressed into its flesh. "See. There. I didn't notice it at the time."

Ram examined the mark closely. "Perhaps there was something stuck to the underside of the saddle?"

Gervais shrugged. "Not that I could see, but I wasn't the first to handle Fortis after the accident."

CONSPIRATORS

Ellesmere Castle and its environs grew as buildings and defenses were completed. With prosperity and expansion came more people, and a need for more skilled healers. Myfanwy saw an opportunity to at once acquire more assistance and provide a means for Rhonwen to come to the castle. Her daughter was growing into womanhood. Myfanwy wanted her near, under her protection.

She judged it wiser to suggest two girls as apprentices. She had heard Morwenna verch Morgan dabbled in healing and asked Rhonwen about the girl.

Her daughter shrugged. "I don't know her. She lives on the other side of the village. People claim to have been healed by her potions."

Myfanwy visited the girl in her cottage and was impressed with her beauty and her friendly smile. Morwenna told her she would be interested in living in the castle as an apprentice healer, but would have to ask permission of her father.

Myfanwy went to the earl. “I need more help, *Arglwydd* Montbryce. Your wife and her maidservant do what they can to help me. I want to bring two girls under my wing, apprentices from nearby villages. I’m not getting any younger. If something happens to me, you’ll need others to tend the wounds of your men, and nurse the illnesses of your people.”

She hoped her wrinkled skin would convince him.

The earl looked at her with narrowed eyes. “Who are these young women?”

“Rhonwen from Ellesmere and Morwenna, a girl from a noble family, known for her healing skills.”

He nodded. “Very well.”

~

As Phillippe de Giroux suckled hard on her nipples, grazing them with his teeth, Morwenna gloated. “It’s falling into place, my Norman stallion. That foolish old woman was so impressed with my *skills*, she couldn’t wait to rush off to recommend me to the earl.”

She ran her hands over his close cropped hair. “I love to feel the prickly stubble. Why do you Normans shave your heads?”

Phillippe took a breath and leered up at her. “It’s cooler under a helmet. But I have another head you should be more interested in.”

She looked down at his swollen manhood and smiled slyly. “Mmmm. I see what you mean.”

She put her hands on his shoulders and pushed him down on the bed. “Tell me again of your castle in Normandie while I pleasure you.”

She gripped his shaft and took him into her mouth, moving up and down on him roughly, sucking hard. He groaned and put his hands on her head, twisting his fingers in her hair.

Remembering his homeland brought back the horrendous memories of his childhood at the mercy of his father whose madness had turned him into a sadistic monster. Phillippe prayed for the day when his father would die and he would become the *Comte* de Giroux. He wept inwardly for his brothers. François and Georges were still subject to the depravities of their sire.

But if convincing this Welsh bitch to help him destroy the Montbryces in revenge meant recalling his home in Normandie, he would do it. She had told him she had ties to the Welsh rebels. His liaison with her would not be without its compensations. She had a talented mouth. The pressure in his groin was unbearable now. He clawed the bed linens.

"Giroux Castle is—*Dieu!*"

She twirled her tongue over the end of his phallus. "Tell me," she commanded. "If I'm to be your countess, I want to know about my castle."

He rose up quickly and shoved her back, pushing her legs wide open. He gripped his shaft and positioned it at her entry. "If you're to be my *comtesse*, Morwenna, you'll need to provide me with Montbryce's head, and a hot, welcoming place for me to impale my lance."

She smiled up at him and licked her lips. "You can count on me for both."

~

Rhonwen was content with her chamber in the castle, though she would have preferred to share with her mother, rather than the other apprentice.

She did not know what opinion to form of Morwenna. The girl was certainly beautiful, but there was something dark about her. She treated Rhonwen with disdain and they never sat together for communal meals. Morwenna spent most of her time when not required in the castle off on what she called '*adventures*'. Judging by the company she kept in the hall, Rhonwen had the feeling these adventures involved persons of the male sort. She doubted if Morwenna was a maid.

She was torn as to whether she should mention her suspicions to her mother, but didn't want to worry her. Perhaps it was jealousy making her feel the way she did? She feared the Montbryces liked Morwenna better than they liked her. Her high cheekbones and big eyes suggested a state of constant surprise, whereas Morwenna had a look of openness and honesty. Rhonwen was suspicious of what lay behind that beaming smile.

Morwenna's blonde hair was always tightly braided, whereas Rhonwen preferred to let her black locks hang loose. Morwenna was more attractive to men. Was that why the earl seemed to favor her? Rhonwen cursed her own shyness. Whenever the countess spoke to her, she seemed incapable of replying without stammering. Morwenna was full of confidence. Rhonwen resolved to prove to the Montbryces she was a more than capable healer, for her mother's sake.

POISON

The new healers had been at Ellesmere a fortnight when Ram looked across the hall one evening to the two girls who sat at separate benches. "The apprentices are complete opposites. Where Morwenna is fair of hair and face, Rhonwen is dark, moody, and, I must confess, hard to read."

"*Oui*, Morwenna braids her long hair," Mabelle replied, "whereas Rhonwen's hangs around her shoulders like a black cape. Morwenna smiles a lot, and Rhonwen doesn't."

Ram took hold of his wife's hand. "Don't be angry, but I've noticed Morwenna has beautiful blue eyes with long blonde lashes, whereas Rhonwen's are round grey pools."

Mabelle feigned annoyance, wagging her finger and shaking her head, but then she smiled. "Have you noticed how Rhonwen's high cheek bones accentuate her look of constant surprise?"

Ram chuckled. "*Oui*, and Rhonwen is small and delicate, whereas Morwenna—well, a man notices these things. You know, breasts, and hips that bespeak fertility."

Now I might be in trouble.

He supposed Mabelle had decided not to rise to the bait when the smile returned to her face. "Both girls are quick studies, and Myfanwy is delighted with her pupils. I confess I like Morwenna, but I find Rhonwen uncommunicative and shy. However, I can't fault the way the girl works when faced with a wound to cleanse, or a fever to tend. It sometimes seems people heal faster when Rhonwen takes care of them. She has a special touch. I can tell Myfanwy likes Rhonwen the best. She treats her like a daughter."

Ram replied, "I'm pleased the castle now has three expert healers."

Mabelle blushed. "*Oui* and the four of us are spending many hours replenishing the stock of herbs, and mixing fresh potions and salves."

"Speaking of salves, I'm leaving for the border region on the morrow. Would you like to join me in our chamber and soothe my ache?"

~

One warm spring day, Mabelle and Myfanwy were gathering herbs together in the garden. The Welshwoman made an observation that they must be sure to replenish certain ones. Mabelle recognised them as herbs used in child birthing. She blushed, wondering if Myfanwy had guessed what she suspected. It would be useless to deny it to this perceptive Welshwoman, whom she had grown to love and trust.

"I believe you may be right, Myfanwy. I'm with child again, I think. I've missed my courses, and I'm nauseous every morning."

Myfanwy cackled with glee. "Does *Arglwydd* Montbryce know?"

"Not yet, but I know he'll be pleased. I plan to tell him on the morrow, when he returns from Wales."

The healer put her wrinkled hand on Mabelle's arm. "I can prepare something for the nausea, my lady, if you wish."

"*Merci*, Myfanwy."

Morwenna stole into the Still Room.

Myfanwy looked up from her work and smiled. "You're here late, Morwenna."

"Yes," she replied. "I saw the light. I wondered who was working at this hour."

Myfanwy was preparing a potion. "It's a draught for the countess."

There was a sparkle in the old woman's eyes. What did it mean? Why would the countess need a draught at night? She was not known as a woman who needed help sleeping. The draught was for something else.

She is with child.

She moved closer to the old woman. "I can take it to her."

Myfanwy shook her head. "No, I promised I would bring it."

Morwenna took another step. "But it's late, and the master's chamber is on the other side of the castle."

The healer clutched the goblet to her breast, shaking her head more vigorously as Morwenna held out her hand for it.

"Give it to me, old woman," she spat.

Myfanwy's eyes filled with alarm, but she held on to the goblet. Morwenna took out her blade. Myfanwy's mouth fell open and she backed away, edging towards the door. She hadn't seen Phillippe de Giroux lurking there, dagger drawn. Without a sound, he stole up behind the healer, grabbed her by the hair, jerked her head back and stroked his weapon across her throat. The scream died on her lips as blood gushed everywhere. Morwenna rescued the goblet before it slipped from the dying woman's grasp. Phillippe shoved the body to the floor, inspecting his tunic for blood.

Morwenna hastened to the bench and infused the potion with myrrh and coriander. "The countess is pregnant," she explained breathlessly to Phillippe, who was wiping his dagger on Myfanwy's tabard.

He snickered. "I suspected. Another Montbryce whelp."

She walked over to him with the lethal cup. "Not if I'm successful. I'll take this potion to her. If she drinks it, we'll have one less Montbryce to worry about. You'll have to devise a means to get rid of the body and this pool of blood. Couldn't you have simply strangled her? We don't want Rhonwen raising the alarm."

Phillippe was already dragging his victim to the door. He scowled at her. "It won't be a problem."

Morwenna retrieved a wooden tray, placed the goblet on it and went off to the countess's chamber. The earl was away, so it was likely only the maidservant would be with her mistress.

She tapped on the door and entered, smiling broadly.

~

That evening, as she sat in her lonely chamber, looking forward to Ram's return the next day, Mabelle heard a soft tap at the door. Morwenna entered carrying a wooden tray with a goblet, the usual bright smile upon her face. "My lady, Myfanwy has sent this special draught for nausea but says it must be taken before bed to be truly effective."

Mabelle was surprised the Welsh healer had evidently shared news of her condition with the apprentice but decided not to make an issue of it. She thanked the girl, dismissed her and took a sip of the potion. It had a bitter taste, and she could only drink a little at a time. She might prefer the nausea to this gall. She called Giselle from the next chamber to assist her to undress.

"You're no doubt looking forward to *milord's* return on the morrow," enthused the little Norman woman whom Mabelle now considered more a friend than a servant.

"*Oui*, I am. I love him dearly, and I miss him when he's away."

Giselle helped her lady lift the dress over her head. "So, you've come to see that what you feel for him is love?"

"*Oui*, for many years I didn't think I could experience love. As you know, I spent my childhood growing up with a father who didn't know the meaning of the word. And Ram and I—well—you're aware of the difficulties we had at first. I thought I would never forgive him, but he's the person I was meant to marry. He's the other half of me."

Giselle knelt to remove Mabelle's shoes. "Have you told him you love him?"

"*Non*, I'll probably never tell him. You know Ram. He's a man of action, a soldier. Such men don't allow themselves to fall in love. He's a good husband and father, and he cares for me, and our passion is sometimes…overwhelming, but for a man that's natural lust, and I wouldn't want to tell him I love him and receive no words of love in return."

Giselle smiled and patted Mabelle's belly. "*Milady*, you're mistaken. When he looks at you I see love in his eyes. When you tell him about the *bébé* on the morrow, why not tell him you love him?"

Now Mabelle smiled—even Giselle had guessed she was with child.

Suddenly the room tilted. Intense pain sliced through her abdomen, bending her double in agony—no time to reach the chamber pot before vomiting. She hugged herself, sweating, trying to still the shaking.

"*Aide-moi*. Something is wrong. Help me."

Giselle ran to the door of the chamber, calling loudly for help. "*Au secours! Au secours!*"

~

Morwenna and Rhonwen were roused by a loud banging at their door, and summoned to the countess's chamber.

The wide-eyed guard was breathless. "Where is Myfanwy Dda?" he demanded. "She's not in her chamber."

Rhonwen frowned, barely awake. Where else would her mother be at this time of night?

Morwenna shrugged.

Rhonwen averted her eyes and whispered, "I know not."

"Go then, quickly," he commanded. "I'll continue to search."

Rhonwen ran along the corridor, trying to keep up with Morwenna. "Mammie, mammie," she chanted over and over, hoping the litany would calm her beating heart. They burst into the chamber and rushed to help Giselle get the countess off the floor, where she writhed in agony. She doubled over in the bed, held in pain's thrall.

Giselle noticed the empty goblet on the tray. She seized it and inhaled. "Myrrh," she whispered breathlessly.

She put her nose closer. "And coriander."

"It's a potion. Myfanwy made it," Morwenna explained calmly.

Rhonwen's heart raced, but she said nothing as she bathed her lady's forehead with cold cloths.

"The Welsh witch has poisoned my lady," Giselle cried.

"No, it can't be true," Rhonwen exclaimed, shaking her head.

By dawn, it was heartbreakingly apparent the countess had lost a child despite Rhonwen's desperate efforts to save it, but she was hopeful she had staunched the bleeding and Mabelle de Montbryce would survive. For some unfathomable reason the Normans seemed to think her gentle mother had poisoned the countess. Giselle had sent Gervais off to arrest her.

Rhonwen withdrew into a corner of the chamber and

crouched down, sobbing quietly, confused and fearful for her countess and her mother. She called on the powerful forces of good to come to their aid. Morwenna had curled up nearby and fallen asleep. Rhonwen pondered why the girl had felt it necessary to throw suspicion on Myfanwy.

~

When Ram arrived home several hours later, Bonhomme awaited him, and he could tell by the expression on the man's face something was wrong. "My children?" he asked, as fear gripped him.

"Non, monseigneur. Ta femme, la comtesse—"

Ram's knees turned to water and his heart raced. How could he face life without Mabelle? "Where is she?"

"She's in your chamber, and the healers are with her. We're seeking Myfanwy. The witch poisoned your wife."

He didn't later recall how he got to the chamber but was gasping for breath when he arrived. What he saw made his heart clench with anger. He would kill whoever had done this. The bile rose in his throat as he looked at the ravages the poison had wrought on the fair face of his beautiful wife. She looked like she had been dragged to hell.

He didn't think he had uttered that thought aloud, and yet, as if sensing his presence in the room, Mabelle half-opened her eyes and murmured in a barely audible voice, "Ram, I was at the gates of hell. I wanted to spit in the Devil's face, but my throat was too dry."

He poured water from the ewer, then helped her sip the life sustaining liquid. She tried to speak. "Ram. Our baby. I've lost our baby."

"Baby?" he murmured, his fury intensifying. He clutched his wife's cold hands and brought them to his lips. The only sounds were Mabelle's sobs and his own heavy breathing as he struggled to control his emotions. He became dimly aware the two Welsh girls, looking exhausted, were standing in the far corner of the room. What struck him as odd, in that fleeting moment, was that tears streamed down Rhonwen's face, but Morwenna stood stonily expressionless.

Giselle entered and Ram ushered the women out into the hallway. "I thank you for taking care of her, for saving her life. What happened here? Where is Myfanwy, and why are my men hunting her?"

Giselle recounted the story, and Morwenna confirmed it was Myfanwy who had given her the draught and instructed her to take it to Mabelle. Wiping away tears with her sleeve, Rhonwen told Ram that his wife had miscarried a child and was still very ill.

Despair pressed at his temples. "She might yet die?"

Rhonwen averted her eyes. "The abortifacient she ingested was powerful, and it will take a long time for the poison to leave her body. We'll need to watch her carefully. Also, *Arglwydd* Montbryce, I hope you'll forgive me if I speak of these things, but sometimes when a woman loses a child, she loses the will to live, and my lady is already very weak."

An icy chill raced across Ram's nape.

This could kill her.

"Get some sleep now. I'll watch her."

He returned to his sleeping wife's bedside, dropped to his knees, rested his elbows on the bed and prayed, weeping for her terrible pain and his own.

IN NEED OF PROTECTION

The bloated body of Myfanwy Dda floated to the surface of a nearby lake two days later, her throat cut. Ram had left his wife's side only to visit with their children in the nursery, and to bring them to see their mother as she slowly grew stronger. When Gervais whispered news of the discovery in his ear, he left Mabelle with the two healers and went to discuss this latest development.

"Her confederate evidently didn't trust her to keep quiet," Gervais suggested.

Ram shook his head. "But why would she try to poison my wife, and kill our child? Though she was Welsh, she's lived in England peaceably for years. She had a position of honor and respect here as our healer. She's saved the lives of hundreds of our people. I had complete trust in her."

He returned to his wife's bedside and told her the sad news. She shook her head. "I can't believe Myfanwy would do this. What would she gain? Who would she conspire with, and why would they kill her?"

"Did she know you were with child?"

"*Oui,* she'd guessed as much and we talked of it in the herb garden. She told me she would prepare something for me to take, so I didn't question when Morwenna brought me the potion."

Ram rubbed his chin. "I do recall now that Morwenna brought it to you."

He turned to ask Morwenna where Myfanwy had given her the potion, but the girl had slipped out of the room.

Strange.

It was stranger still that Morwenna's hair was unbraided. Perhaps after a long and difficult two days, she had not had time to braid it this morning. With his Norman sense of order, he had a vague feeling something was not right, and it didn't sit well with him.

"Morwenna doesn't seem herself," he remarked.

"You're right. I hardly recognised her with her hair down. And the poor child has not smiled much today. I'm getting the feeling that of the two of them, it's Rhonwen who'll prove in time to be the better healer, and I wouldn't have thought that before. While I lay in pain, I could feel Rhonwen's compassion as she tended to my needs. It was mystical. I didn't feel that from Morwenna. In fact, I felt malevolence emanating from her."

"I'll tell Gervais to have someone keep an eye on her."

Two hours later his lieutenant reported Morwenna had fled the castle. The alarm was raised and the town thoroughly searched, but she couldn't be found.

"Perhaps she was murdered too, for her part in the plot," Ram suggested.

"*Non*, my husband. I think Myfanwy was a victim of this crime. I sense it was Morwenna who poisoned me.

What do we know of her? Until recently she still lived in Wales. Myfanwy knew only of her family. Perhaps we were blinded by the beautiful smile and braided golden hair."

"Ah," her husband replied with a wink, squeezing her leg. "It wouldn't be the first time that has happened to me."

As a familiar ache assailed her loins, Mabelle silently thanked God the poison had not destroyed her ability to feel passion for this handsome man she loved so dearly.

~

Rhonwen searched high and low for her mother, filled with dreadful certainty that something terrible had happened. When Myfanwy's body floated to the surface of a nearby lake two days later, her throat cut, Rhonwen was devastated, but not surprised. She and Morwenna were tending the countess and overheard Gervais when he brought the news to his earl. Rhonwen clenched her fists and shook her head, praying the tears wouldn't flow. Trembling from head to toe, she couldn't look at Morwenna, a terrible foreboding rising in her throat.

As the conversation continued, the other girl slipped out of the chamber. Dread constricted Rhonwen's throat. She sensed the earl's unease. Something did not sit well with him. Normans were known for their ingrained sense of form and order. Was he of the same mind she was?

The countess held out her hand. "I have a feeling it's you, Rhonwen, who'll prove in time to be the better healer."

Rhonwen wanted to weep in her lady's arms. Her value

had been recognised, but she had never felt so alone. She hoped her lady couldn't feel her trembling.

Face on fire, she bowed her way out of the room, emotion warring within her. The Montbryces recognized Myfanwy was innocent, but now Rhonwen was alone. Her mother was dead, and the killer gone, for she had no doubt Morwenna had played a role in her mother's murder.

~

Myfanwy's death was declared to be murder by persons unknown, and she was buried with dignity and solemnity in hallowed ground. Mabelle grieved for the Welsh healer, and knew in her heart the woman had not been involved in the plot to kill her. Whoever was responsible remained at large, probably with Morwenna. Rhonwen seemed inconsolable over the death of the crotchety old woman. She was probably the closest thing to a mother the girl had ever had.

Attending the funeral exhausted Mabelle, and Rhonwen helped her back to bed. "I learned much from her, my lady," she said haltingly. "Who'll teach me now? Who'll protect me?"

It was an odd choice of words, but Mabelle replied, "You have great inner abilities to heal people, a natural touch which will stand you in good stead, and never fear, we'll seek others to help us learn more. I'll protect you."

~

Ram suspected Rhodri was involved in the plots against

his family. He and his well-trained trackers tried many times to follow his trail into the mountains but always returned empty-handed. He couldn't understand these stubborn Welsh folk, with their strange Celtic beliefs, and their incomprehensible language. He grudgingly admitted they had difficult geography to deal with and admired the way they used the impossible terrain to their advantage.

However, he had a personal desire to see Rhodri captured after the humiliating incident at Ruyton, and was determined to put a stop to his interference in the future prosperity of England, and William's plans to expand his control into Wales.

He assumed Rhodri had spies in his own castle. Morwenna had been one. He didn't like to consider that any of the educated Normans under his command would ally themselves with a barbaric Welshman.

~

From time to time, Morwenna came to Cadair Berwyn when the weather permitted, or to *Llys* Powwydd. She was flirtatious, but Rhodri insisted they wait until their marriage before they lay together. He sometimes wondered what ailed him. Here was a gift being offered freely, yet he could not take it. Something held him back.

What was she doing when she was not with him? She had told him of an accomplice she had stumbled upon—a Norman soldier who seemed eager to do away with the Montbryces. It should have been good news, yet he was uneasy. Why would a Norman betray a fellow Norman to a Welshwoman and her rebel cohorts?

The two had already plotted and failed in their attempts to kill Montbryce. His gut tightened when Morwenna casually told him of the slain Welsh healer. She was on his lap in the chair by the hearth, fingering the fine amber beads he always wore. He wished she wouldn't touch them. His long dead mother would not have approved of Morwenna.

She twisted the tight braid at the side of his face. "I want to do my hair this way," she murmured. "I'm tired of one big braid." As she spoke she flicked the end of her plait provocatively in his face.

Despite his best efforts, interest stirred in his groin and her smile told him she was aware of it. She squirmed in his lap, licking her lips. "I wish I had an amber necklace," she pouted.

His manhood lost interest, and he stood abruptly, his hand under her elbow. She was angry as she struggled to keep her balance. "What's wrong with you, Rhodri ap Owain? I'm spying for you, taking the risks, but you won't even give me a necklace."

Watching her storm out, Rhodri exhaled and put his hands on his hips, leaning forward to ease the cramping in his gut. Murdering women and unborn children. That was not the way he fought.

NORMANDIE

In the late spring, Ram and Mabelle visited Normandie. He had made the journey many times in the nine years since the invasion. The defense of the castle merited constant attention given the volatile political climate in Normandie. His brothers were not far away in their own castles, but Ram had trained an elite garrison under the command of *Capitaine* Laurent Deschamps, a trusted comrade with whom he had fought. He was never disappointed in Laurent's preparations and felt Montbryce was secure. It would be years before Robert was old enough to take up his birthright.

On this visit, Ram and Mabelle took their sons with them. He had long felt it was important they visit the castle at Saint Germain. They were the sons of a Norman *comte,* and it was imperative they be familiar with their ancestral home. Despite the unseasonably fine weather, it took them a sennight to reach the coast. The crossing was calm and even Ram managed not to become seasick. Robert and

Baudoin enjoyed the voyage, excited to be going to Normandie.

As their cavalcade rode into the bailey of the home where he had been born, Ram was hard pressed to hold back his emotion. This edifice held many memories and so much history.

"How can I impart that to our children?" he asked Mabelle. "I hope this will be the first of many visits for them. One day Robert will be the *comte* here. Perhaps in time the Welsh problem will be solved, our king will no longer need my services in England, and we'll return to Normandie for good."

Mabelle sighed. "*Oui*, Ram, I would like that too. You have wealth and power, but it has been gained at a price."

Ram looked at her wistfully. "The way we Normans constantly insist on alienating people with our brutality, the less likely it seems there will ever be peace."

He took his children to show them the fields and orchards around the castle. Fernand Bonhomme, looking old and stooped, found a malleable horse so he could ride with Baudoin on his lap, Robert behind him, holding on to his papa, squealing with delight. Everyone was happy to see their liege lord returned, and commented on the handsomeness of his children. It was the first time they had ever spent time as a family with no external pressures.

"This is a place of intense memories for me," Mabelle confided to her husband. "I recall the dark handsome knight, conjured from the lake, who became my husband, a man who has brought me the most exquisite pleasures." The smile left her face. "But there are more difficult memories of my father and yours."

He noticed she made no mention of the wedding day incident, so he decided not to either.

They took the boys to the crypt, but it was evident the shivering lads were uncomfortable as they stared up at the long shadows cast by the flickering candles on the vaulted ceiling.

Mabelle picked bluebells with the children while Ram watched, and they exchanged smiles at the memory. The blue flowers held no interest for the boys, who preferred to chase each other through the fields, laughing and shouting. They took them swimming in their special lake, and Ram knew his eyes betrayed his need as they looked at each other close by the place he had first found her. The bitter-sweet memory washed over him like a rushing river. Trying to break the tension, he remarked casually to his sons, "*Maman* once threw papa's sword into this lake."

"Why, *Maman*?" Robert asked curiously. "You must have been very angry with him."

"Oh, *oui*, *mon fils*, I was angry," she replied, grinning at her smiling husband.

"It's a good thing you didn't stay angry at him, *Maman*," Robert said innocently.

Their contentment at being back in the land of their birth carried over into their bed chamber, and they made sweet love every night as their bodies joined with flow and grace. Ram loved fondling and caressing Mabelle's breasts. After the birth of two children, they were fuller and more sensitive and suckling them always enthralled her. The swell of her responsive bud at the slightest tender touch of his fingers exhilarated him and he never tired of feeling her inner textures. He loved to hear her call out his name in the throes of passion and wondered if she did indeed love him. She had never told him she did.

"Would you like to go for a picnic in the meadow?" he asked innocently one day. "You could pick bluebells. Fernand can look to the children for a while."

Mabelle eyed him curiously, and he struggled to keep his feigned composure.

"It *is* a beautiful day," she agreed. "And I do love bluebells. I'll get *La Cuisinière* to prepare a hamper."

She scurried off to the kitchens, leaving him to wonder if she had guessed his plan to get her to the enchanted pool. He wanted to erase any bitter memories they both may be harboring. Why did he care? Did he need her to love him? Were the physical pleasures not enough?

She came barefoot into the Great Hall, carrying the picnic basket and a blanket, and he was pleased she had changed into a simple chemise and belted sage green overdress.

"Will you be taking your sword to the meadow, *milord comte*?"

He laughed, taking the hamper and blanket. "I think not, saucy wench."

They strolled out of the castle, their bodyguards following at a discreet distance. He ordered the men-at-arms to halt outside the walls. They would keep watch from where he stationed them, and he deemed it safe enough.

When they reached the meadow, he spread the blanket, and lay on his side, his head resting on one hand. He felt comfortable in his linen shirt and loose fitting knee breeches, especially once he took off his boots.

His gaze followed Mabelle. She hummed, gathering the blue flowers to her breast.

She was doing this the morning I found her.

He cared too much for this woman. He suspected Mabelle would never forgive him completely for his accusations and suspicions, though he intended to try to erase that memory today. But could he let go of his pride, his fear of rejection? He came lazily to his feet, wandered over and took hold of her hand as she bent to pick another flower. The grass felt good beneath his bare feet.

"Would you like to take a swim, *milady*?" he drawled seductively.

Her grasp on the bluebells tightened, but when he kissed her, the flowers fell to the ground. "Gather them up and bring them to the lake."

He led her to the water's edge, out of sight of their bodyguards, took the flowers, then undressed her, brushing his hands against her breasts as he lifted the clothing from her body. He disrobed quickly, smiling at her naked beauty. As he led her into the shallow water, she reached out tentatively and grasped his erection in her long fingers. Even the cold water couldn't dampen his arousal as she slowly moved her hand on his phallus.

"I'm not a good swimmer, Ram," she teased. "I need to hold on to something."

He took her hand from his swollen manhood and lifted her. "You have other talents and skills which are far more important. I fear I may release too soon if you continue that," he teased.

She entwined her legs around his hips, locking her ankles behind him. He walked over to the shallows, where a smooth moss-covered rock met the water's edge. The friction of her wet female cleft against his shaft sent ripples of sensation up his spine. Leaning her back against the rock, he feathered kisses on her throat, neck and nipples.

She groaned with pleasure and swirled her tongue around the rim of his ear. "The moss feels like velvet against my back," she crooned.

His need had become intense. "Mabelle, I have to come now."

He thrust inside and her sheath clenched him tightly in response. Her legs gripped his torso, trying to draw him deeper as he pressed her body against the rock. She clung to him, keening her pleasure, her breasts rubbing against his chest.

In his passionate haze, he caught a glimpse of speckled trout flashing by in the knee-deep water. He curled his toes into the mud. She raked his scalp with her long fingers, and cried out his name as his seed erupted into her and a powerful spasm tore through her body.

She lowered her head to his shoulder and her hair enfolded them like a golden cloak. Staying inside her as long as he could, he carefully made his way to the deeper water, eased on to his back and floated for a while, with her on top of him, moving them effortlessly through the water with one arm, both of them completely relaxed.

"You're as light as a feather," he murmured into her ear.

She's purring.

He guided them back to the shallows and carried her to the grass, where he knelt to lay her down and spread out her hair. With great care, he took the bluebells and placed them reverently on her body. He posed her legs as he remembered them from that bittersweet day, as awestruck by the sight as he had been then.

"On the day of our intended wedding," he managed to say hoarsely, "I thought you were a vision. Your beauty struck me senseless, and you're more breathtaking today. What happened that day embittered us both, but if you'll allow me to continue to pleasure you today, *milady*, we can perhaps atone for our mistakes? I hope whatever you were dreaming of that day will come true for you."

A tear trickled down her cheek. "It has already come true, Ram. I was dreaming of being kissed by you, my husband."

Antoine was right. I'm an idiot.

~

The day of their departure, Mabelle awoke shortly after dawn, dressed and went to break her fast. Ram had risen before her, and she couldn't find him anywhere. She decided to make a last private visit to the crypt. A strangled cry escaped her as she entered the shadowy chamber. Ram knelt before the tombs of his parents. A tiny posy of bluebells lay atop each. She sank to her knees beside him and took his hand. They clung to each other.

"Swear to me, Mabelle, that if I die in England, you'll return here with my body, so that I may be laid to rest with my parents. I belong in Normandie."

"I so swear," she whispered, stricken by the notion of life without him.

PLANS LAID

Thanks to Ram's well tried and proven methods of governance, the towns and villages around Ellesmere grew and prospered. September brought with it the affirmation of another child firmly planted in Mabelle's belly. She and Ram were thankful the abortifacient seemed to have done no permanent damage. It had been a year since she had been poisoned. The resilience of her body surprised her, considering the difficult life she had led before she met Ram.

The long summer had been particularly hot, relieved only by gentle rainfall in the early evenings. She often felt uncomfortable and was nauseous every morning. But the weather produced a bumper harvest and there was much celebrating at the autumn fayres held in the towns and villages. No one would starve this winter.

Rhonwen continued to show great promise, but they heard tell of another renowned healer in the village of Whittington, which had not yet held its fayre. Mabelle received Ram's permission to take Rhonwen with her to the Whittington Fayre so they could seek out the healer. The young woman was gleeful at the prospect.

"Perhaps we'll convince her to return with us to Ellesmere, my lady?" she enthused.

Mabelle rubbed her hands together. "Perhaps we will. But if not, we'll try to learn as much from her as we can about the things we don't yet understand."

As planning for the excursion progressed, it occurred to Mabelle how wonderful it would be for her sons to accompany them to Whittington.

"They enjoyed the fayre at Ellesmere," she argued, when Ram was less than enthusiastic. "They have few chances to be little boys. Please let me take them. Giselle can accompany us and keep them busy while we're with the healer."

Ram relented, insisting they be protected by a company of ten men-at-arms as their escort, but he was uneasy that he couldn't go with his family. He wasn't interested in what they would be discussing with the healer but might enjoy the fayre with his wife and children. "We have too few opportunities to be together and enjoy life, as we did during our visit to Normandie."

"Don't be concerned," Mabelle laughed. "Your men will take good care of us. We'll be surrounded by people at the fayre and it will be perfectly safe. The Welsh won't encroach as close as Whittington. In any case, the beginning of October is too late in the season for them to leave their mountains."

Ram put his hands on her waist and leaned his forehead against hers. "You're right, but I still don't like the idea of my pregnant wife and my children leaving without me."

Since her flight from Ellesmere, Morwenna had not been able to return. Phillippe was relieved. He did not want to be seen with her anywhere near the castle. They held their trysts in an abandoned hunting lodge on her father's lands, not far from Oswestry.

Their joining was rough and both liked it that way, tearing off their clothes as soon as they arrived. The plotting began the moment the coupling was over.

Phillippe had thought long and hard on how to take revenge on the Montbryces. It had been a year since the failed poisoning. But now Fortune had smiled on him. He had learned the countess and her children would be going to the autumn fayre in Whittington. What better opportunity for a kidnapping?

"Kidnapping?" Morwenna exclaimed. "We would need Rhodri's help with such a plot."

Phillippe smiled inwardly, confident she would talk herself into the scheme. "Would it not benefit his cause to obtain a large amount of money?"

She snorted. "He doesn't care for money. He's a patriot."

Is she truly so dim?

"But he recognizes the importance of money to buy food and arms."

Understanding dawned on her face. "But would the earl pay a ransom?"

Now for the *coup de grâce*.

"That's the beauty of the plan. If he doesn't, we'll kill his family. If he does, he will fall out of favor with his beloved king for giving money to rebels. And he won't know we plan to kill them anyway."

His shaft surged with renewed interest. She grasped him, putting her mouth on his arousal. "I like the way you think, Phillippe. I'll convince Rhodri. When is the fayre?"

~

Rhodri was distracted while Morwenna explained the plan to kidnap the earl's family. She had not made any attempt to touch him though they were alone in his solar. What was her relationship with the Norman accomplice? She was a woman who craved men.

He forced his thoughts back to the plot she had suggested. It had merit. His people definitely needed coin. Food was in short supply, despite record harvests on the English side of the Marches after a glorious summer. The utter injustice of it rankled. Why not extort the money from a Norman?

He had the manpower. It could be done, and quickly. Time would be of the essence if they were to take the Montbryce family in October and have them ransomed before winter set in. They could sequester the hostages at Cadair Berwyn. The earl would never venture so far into Wales in search of his family.

He summoned his most trusted advisors. His father had relied on the good counsel of Aneurin ap Norweg and Andras ap Rhys. He would too. They listened intently.

"They'll have servants with them," Aneurin advised.

"We'll kill them," Morwenna replied.

Rhodri held up his hand. "There will be no unnecessary killing. If the earl believes we intend to murder his family anyway, he won't pay."

Morwenna was indignant. "What of the men-at-arms who will escort them? Shall we spare them too?" she asked sarcastically.

Rhodri nodded. "We will accomplish this with cunning, not brutality."

Aneurin and Andras nodded, both voicing their agreement. The decision was made. They would kidnap Mabelle de Montbryce and her two children from the Whittington Fayre.

"What ransom should we demand?" Rhodri asked.

Morwenna did not hesitate. "Two thousand pounds, preferably in Fleury pennies."

The men looked at her in shock. "Where would he put his hand on that kind of coin?" Aneurin asked, more than a hint of ridicule in his voice.

Morwenna smirked. "It's only one year's income from all his properties."

Silence reigned in the room. Rhodri tried and failed to comprehend how so much wealth could exist. "How do you know this?"

"The Norman told me."

She flounced out abruptly with a gleam in her eye.

Rhodri and his men set about making the final plans.

ABDUCTION

As soon as Mabelle met Caryl Penarth she thought the woman embodied the meaning of her name, which Rhonwen explained was the Welsh for *love*. Caryl willingly shared her knowledge of the healing arts with the two women and agreed to consider coming to Ellesmere, at least for a few months, to instruct the local women, as well as Rhonwen.

When they were not with Caryl they enjoyed the minstrels, theatre, jugglers, magicians, and human chess games. They laughed at the bright costumes of folk dressed as King Arthur, mermaids, and the fayre's king and queen. Mabelle had not seen her sons laugh as much since the journey to Normandie. They tended to be serious little boys.

Everyone enjoyed the fruits of the bountiful harvest, and the ale and wine flowed freely. The women and children were never without their armed escort, and Mabelle enjoyed herself immensely. After three days they mounted their horses a little after midday for the slow ride back to

Ellesmere. Caryl promised to come to the castle in a sennight.

They had traveled only a short distance when they entered a copse. Rhonwen commented on the beauty of the autumn leaves. Without warning, masked men clad in sheepskins and leather breeches dropped like stones from the trees. The Norman soldiers were quickly disarmed and dragged from their mounts. Mabelle could do nothing. The furtive attackers seized the reins of their horses and led them deeper into the wood.

Mabelle lost sight of Robert.

"*Maman, Maman,*" her son shouted.

"I'm safe, *mon fils*, don't worry. I'm here. Look to your brother," she called in reply, trying to sound braver than she felt.

None of the men made any move to harm them, and she considered that a good sign. It didn't seem they would be murdered at least.

Other brigands were concealed deep in the forest, with horses at the ready. The attackers mounted. One took Robert on his lap and another took Baudoin. Stealthily, the caravan made its way deeper into the woods. The men spoke to each other in a language foreign to her, but the terrified Rhonwen seemed to understand and Mabelle surmised it was Welsh.

Neither of her sons had cried since they were taken, but she constantly called words of reassurance to them, hoping her voice didn't betray her fear. "Don't be afraid, *mes enfants*, I'm here, as are Giselle and Rhonwen. We'll be safe. Don't worry."

It broke her heart to remember her children's joy at riding on their father's lap.

They rode at a steady pace for about an hour. Mabelle was relieved they had not travelled at a gallop. Perhaps the child she carried might survive this ordeal—if she did. She had a sense they were traveling west, probably into Wales. When she saw the village of Oswestry in the distance to her left, her suspicions were confirmed. Trying to occupy her mind and divert it from the sheer terror threatening to engulf her, she wondered how the bandits had known the Montbryce family would be at Whittington. This had not been a random act. She and her family had been targeted. The traitor within was still at work.

Other than comforting words spoken to the children, the three women said nothing, exchanging only glances whenever the track caused their horses to be close to each other. A bandit held the reins and they had no chance to control their own mounts. Escape was impossible.

Though there was no marker, Mabelle could tell an hour later that they had crossed into Wales when they reached the village of Rhydycroesau. Their captors became more relaxed. The scowling faces of the villagers told Mabelle all hope was lost. There would be no rescue. Ram would never see his family again. She prayed her husband would discover the identity of the traitor and cut out his heart.

After another hour in the saddle, Mabelle's body ached. She asked their captors several times if they might be allowed to dismount for a few moments for the sake of the children, but was ignored. Did the men speak her language? They reined in the horses at a cottage on the western edge of a tiny village.

"You'll sleep here tonight," one of the bearded men

said gruffly in Norman French, holding out his burly arms to help her dismount.

She didn't want to accept his aid, but would otherwise have fallen flat on her face. When her numbed feet hit the ground her legs gave way, and she had to lean on the horse. The man didn't take his hand from her elbow as she waited for the feeling to return to her limbs.

When he grew impatient, Rhonwen spoke to him in Welsh. She assumed the girl had told him her mistress was pregnant. He seemed surprised and allowed her more time to regain her equilibrium.

Once they were inside, the man bolted the door of the cottage, imprisoning his captives, and her sons ran quickly to their mother. Neither boy had cried throughout the ordeal and she told them how proud she was of their courage.

Baudoin struggled to control his fear. "Will Papa come to rescue us, *Maman*?"

"I'm sure he is already in pursuit, *mon petit*."

Judging by the worried frowns of Giselle and Rhonwen, they didn't share her optimism.

Bread and cheese and ale had been provided for them. The cottage was cramped but clean. It afforded a chance to sleep indoors and take care of their personal needs. With the limited means at her disposal Giselle did her best to tend her lady. Rhonwen massaged Mabelle's back and applied to her feet a salve Caryl had given her. Mabelle prayed the child within her still lived.

She slept fitfully on a pallet, which was furnished with surprisingly clean linens; her sons cuddled into her. Giselle and Rhonwen clung to each other on the second pallet.

At dawn the following day, a loud banging on the door

signaled departure. The leader entered with bread and honey. Fear made her choke on the food, but she was determined to eat, to keep up her strength. She encouraged the children to eat.

She leaned over to Rhonwen. "Do you know where we are?"

Rhonwen glanced around furtively, then whispered. "My lady, I think this village is Llansilin. I believe they're taking us to the mountains."

Fear crept up Mabelle's spine. Their suspicions were confirmed when they left the cottage. Their horses had been replaced by sure-footed Welsh mountain ponies. She smiled when Robert seemed to forget the terrible trouble they were in and exclaimed with excitement, "Look, *Maman*. Ponies."

~

"Trussed up?" Ram shouted. "Ten of my finest men-at-arms? Knocked out and trussed up like piglets for the spit? How can this be?"

He raked his fingers through his hair, scratching his head, completely distraught over the desperate news from Whittington.

"*Milord* Earl, it appears they were ambushed," Gervais replied.

Ram snorted. "Of course they were ambushed. They're Norman soldiers, supposedly prepared for ambush."

Gervais hesitated. "Perhaps they had enjoyed the delights of the fayre a little too much, *milord* —the ale—"

Ram stared coldly at his lieutenant. His voice dripped

ice as he replied, "Then I'll execute them myself. I entrusted my family to them and they failed me."

Gervais remained silent.

Ram could stand the silence no longer. "You believe they're already dead, don't you?"

Again Gervais kept silent. The minutes dragged as Ram paced.

"Summon my commanders to the Map Room. We'll pursue them."

Gervais threw up his hands. "But, *milord*, we don't know where they've gone."

"They've gone into Wales," Ram shouted, knowing only too well who had taken his family.

"But, *milord*, winter comes early to the mountains of Wales. We could easily lose our way and become trapped. The local people won't help us."

Ram pounded his fist into his palm. "I told you to summon my commanders. We'll follow them into Wales."

Gervais' shoulders sagged. "*Oui*, milord."

~

At least with the ponies the women were able to ride astride and hold the reins themselves. However, the track had become a narrow, twisting path. They rode single file, with some of the men in the lead and the others behind them. Flight was impossible.

Robert and Baudoin were now on a first name basis with the ponies they shared with their captors, and Mabelle was grateful they were distracted from their fear.

The path rose steadily for the next three hours. The scenery became wilder, the terrain more rugged. They entered a remote village. The men called out to each other, confirming the direction to take. Mabelle looked to Rhonwen who told her they were in Llanrhaeadr-ym-Mochnant.

She didn't know why she asked. She would never remember these tortuous names, and what did it matter anyway? Who could she tell?

"In your best estimate, Gervais, where do you think they've been taken?" Ram asked impatiently as he and his commanders pored over the latest charts they had of the area, not knowing if they were accurate or not.

Gervais traced his finger along the chart. "They may have taken the route through Oswestry, and crossed into Wales at Rhydycroesau. After that, it's more difficult to say. If Rhodri is behind this, we don't know where his camp is. They may have gone north west to Llanarmon, or south west to Llansilin. Or he may have taken them to Powwydd Castle."

Ram followed his lieutenant's finger. "Rhodri is behind this. Of that I have no doubt. But what does he plan next?"

Phillippe de Giroux stepped forward. "*Milord*, if he planned to murder them, why have we found no bodies? Why take them into Wales? Perhaps he has ransom in mind."

Gervais spoke again, looking directly at Ram. "*Milord*, I'm as anxious as you are to rescue my countess and your family, but you must see it's futile to ride into Wales. We could search for sennights and not find them. You know yourself how difficult the terrain is, not to mention the weather that will soon turn against us, if it hasn't already."

Gervais was right, but his heart was broken. He dismissed the other men with a curt, "Leave us."

He slumped into a chair. "You're correct, Gervais, but I can't sit and do nothing."

"You have no choice, *milord.* But it may not be long before they send a message. I think Giroux is right and they'll demand ransom. However, they too know winter is setting in and won't want to wait until spring."

~

It was getting colder. They had left Llanrhaeadr far behind at least an hour before, and were still climbing. The Normans had dressed for the warm autumn weather in Whittington and the children were shivering. The brigands had provided blankets at the cottage, but Mabelle's fingers and toes were freezing. Giselle and Rhonwen rubbed their hands together frequently, trying all the while to keep the ponies on the narrow track.

She became aware of the sound of rushing water. Judging by the roar, it must be a high waterfall. Suddenly they came upon a cascade which fell about two hundred and fifty feet through a stunning arched rock formation. The raging torrent was thunderous. Some of the water had formed ice crystals at the edges. The men called a halt as everyone gazed at this natural wonder. One of them took the opportunity to give each captive another hand woven *brychan.*

"Pistyll-Rhaeadr," Rhonwen yelled to her fellow

captives. “Myfanwy told me of this. It’s the most beautiful waterfall in all Wales.”

They headed into the woods. This path led into a wide valley. After a few hundred feet they were down in the valley floor, and then they turned onto a track going in the opposite direction up the hill on the other side.

They made their way on a trail that wound up from the valley floor. Once the tortuous path reached the head of the valley, the men turned in their saddles. Mabelle followed their gaze and the incredible vista took her breath away.

Even barbarians appreciate a beautiful view. I’m beginning to understand why the Welsh are passionate for their wild land.

The path forded then followed a stream, and soon they came across a sight which made the first stunning vista pale in comparison. There was a lake far below them in a deep crater, backed by craggy mountains and ridges. Mabelle hoped the faraway vista was not where they were going. She had never seen a lake of the same color as the one below them, as blue as the *bleu de France* favored by the heralds of the French king.

The leader signaled another halt, and the captives were allowed to dismount. They sat together on rocks in a clearing. One of the men gave them bread and cheese to eat and ale to drink.

“Ask them where they’re taking us, Rhonwen,” Mabelle urged, though she was hesitant to put the girl in danger.

Rhonwen received only a grunt and a disdainful look in reply.

The climb for the next two hours was strenuous. They came to the top of a crag and had to hug the side of the mountain. It was the strong hind legs of the ponies that saw them through. The path was wet and slippery. If they fell, they would fall to their deaths.

Once they had crested the crag, they headed along a wide ridge path. They reached a rocky knoll and Mabelle was astounded to see a wooden fortress loom out of the mist, built into the side of the mountain. Some of the roofs of the buildings seemed to be covered with turf, others with what looked like slate. Though she couldn't see the rear of the fortification, she was sure it was perched on the edge of a deep ravine. Any army wanting to attack would have to send its soldiers in one at a time. It was impregnable. This was probably the reason for the evident lack of armed men on the high balustrades. They had reached their destination and her heart plummeted. She surveyed the magnificent scenery of high mountains on every side.

It's a beautiful place to die.

CADAIR BERWYN

Darkness fell as the captives were led through the gates of the forbidding fortress. The towering palisades, made of stout trees lashed together, were as tall as two men. Once inside, they were led to a chamber. Mabelle had learned the leader's name was Andras. He lit several candles with speedy efficiency, and she gradually discerned that the room was clean, if spartan.

"We're expected," she whispered sarcastically to Giselle.

Five palettes piled high with sheepskins and furs had been installed at one side of the room, and a chamber pot placed discreetly behind a screen, along with drying cloths, a basin and ewer full of water. An empty wooden bathtub stood propped against the wall. A roughly hewn table and six stools completed the furnishings. The comparative warmth of the room led her to believe none of the walls was an outer one. They were completely within the fortress.

"My children are hungry, Andras," she began, but he

didn't reply. He bolted the heavy door after leaving. She glanced at her children and then at Giselle and Rhonwen. The women understood the necessity to be careful what they said in front of the boys. It was a relief none of them had been violated. With the natural curiosity of children, her sons began exploring their new surroundings, and the women sat down to wait.

They didn't have to wait long. Andras reappeared and ushered them to follow. He led them along a dimly lit corridor, outside across a rocky pathway, then into a great hall full of light from scores of torches. Mabelle blinked rapidly. It was difficult to believe such a place could exist so high in these bleak mountains. It must have taken considerable skill and perseverance to build.

The high, vaulted ceiling was supported by huge wooden crossbeams from which hung foreign-looking banners, wafting gently on the currents of air. The walls were covered with an haphazard collection of shields, weapons, furs and antlers. The air was hazy with smoke and heavy with the aroma of roasted game. At least a hundred dark-haired, swarthy men, bristling with daggers, lined the walls, standing erect. All were clad in sheepskin jerkins, leather breeches and boots. It was the devil's army.

At the front, on a dais, sat two massive wooden chairs, one slightly smaller than the other. Andras urged the Normans forward, until they were standing directly in front of the chairs.

A large, muscular man lounged in the bigger chair, his long fingers caressing the dragons intricately carved into the arms. He wore breeches and boots but no shirt, and a sleeveless sheepskin jerkin open in the front. His face bore the trace of a smile. A blonde woman sat on the edge of the other chair, looking malevolently pleased.

Giselle gasped. "Morwenna," she whispered to her mistress.

Mabelle couldn't at first recognize the girl. Her once tightly-braided hair now flowed in a wild tangle down to her waist, softened only by two braids on either side of her face. The end of each braid was adorned with brightly colored beads, and she wore a narrow leather thong around her forehead. She too was clad in leather breeches and boots, and a sheepskin jerkin. The smile Mabelle had been used to seeing was now replaced by a look of malice and triumph. She made a move to rise and speak, but the big man stopped her with a barely perceptible movement of his hand.

Mabelle knew without being told this man was Rhodri ap Owain. He had been a constant thorn in the side of the Marcher lords for a long time. Even before the invasion, his frequent sorties into the border counties of England from his stronghold in the Welsh mountains left a trail of fear and destruction in their wake. It was said he hated Saxon and Norman equally and burned with Celtic fervor for a Wales free of their domination.

She contemplated him, the cold sweat of fear trickling down her spine. He embodied primitive masculinity and vitality, with eyes like green jade and the tanned, weathered skin of a man who lived his life in the open air. Around each of his muscular biceps, a narrow band of Celtic knots had been etched into his skin.

He was intimidating to behold, and Ram had told her the mere mention of his name struck fear into the hearts of those living on the English side of the Welsh border. To them he was a feral force. To his own people he was a folk hero of mythical proportions. Though few had ever met him, all knew of his deeds, and the Marcher lords could get no information from the Welsh villagers to help them find him.

Mabelle swallowed her fear and exhaustion as Rhodri stood. At more than six feet he was a towering figure, with curly black hair which hung down his back, flowing freely, except for two tight war braids at either side of his face, each bound with amber beads. He was in need of a shave, but she suspected that was always the case.

"Lady Countess of Ellesmere, I bid you welcome, and I apologise for your difficult journey. I wasn't aware you're with child. Permit me to introduce myself. I am Rhodri ap Owain ap Dafydd ap Gwilym, Prince of Powwydd."

He bowed slightly.

Whatever Mabelle had expected from a Welsh rebel chieftain, this was not it. He spoke courteously, in her language, despite his primitive garb. A memory of her father rattling off his long list of lands and properties flitted into her head. However, she had learned enough about Welsh naming traditions to recognize this man's pride was in his ancestry, not his lands. She was also well aware this was the man her husband thirsted to kill after their encounter at Ruyton, though Ram had always seemed reluctant to tell her the full details of the rebel's escape. She supposed no Norman warrior wanted to be reminded that his wounds had been tended by a Saxon woman.

"Lord Rhodri," she stammered, trying to gather her scattered thoughts and appear in control of her fear. She returned the bow, but not too deeply. Courtliness aside, this man held their lives in his hands.

"My lord, my children and my serving women are in need of food and clean clothing." She took a deep breath. "And I am in need of an explanation as to why we have been—?"

He silenced her with the same slight movement he had used with Morwenna. "Forgive me, Countess, I haven't yet finished my introductions. I believe you're acquainted with my betrothed, Morwenna verch Morgan ap Talfryn?"

Mabelle looked straight at the girl and felt Rhonwen tense beside her. "*Oui*. Morwenna, murderess of my unborn child and of Myfanwy Dda."

Morwenna protested. "It wasn't I who murdered that foolish old woman—"

Again Rhodri silenced her with a look, and she sank back into her chair, scowling.

Mabelle now knew for certain there was a traitor in Ellesmere Castle.

Rhodri continued. "As to why you're here, Countess, it must be obvious by now we intend to ransom you to your husband. He and I have met before, you know."

Mabelle's knees went weak with relief. But was he referring only to her when he spoke of ransom? Seeking protection for her children and her companions she asked, "Do I have your assurances then, Lord Rhodri, that my children and my serving women won't be harmed while we're here? Your men have already killed my escort at Whittington."

Rhodri strode quickly from the dais and reached the captives in a trice, his hand on the hilt of the large dagger tucked in his belt. Before the exhausted Mabelle could react, Rhonwen moved to protect the boys, and stood defiantly between them and the aggressor.

Rhodri seemed to be taken aback for a moment as he glared at the healer, apparently noticing her for the first time. It was a few moments before he turned to Mabelle. "Not a single one of the soldiers in your escort was killed when you were taken. I give you my word, as Commander of Cadair Berwyn and Prince of Powwydd, that no harm shall come to any of you as long as you're in my care." He winked. "Unless, of course, you try to escape."

Suddenly he turned back to Rhonwen, and asked her name in Welsh. That much Mabelle understood, but she became confused when she thought Rhonwen replied in the same language that she was the daughter of Myfanwy Dda. She must actually have said she was a protégé of Myfanwy's. Rhodri looked at Rhonwen with surprise for a few seconds, and the usually timid healer met his insistent gaze.

~

Two things surprised Rhodri when his eyes fell on the healer. One was the strength of his unexpected arousal. The other was the feeling of calm that swept over him when he heard the lilting way in which she spoke his language. It was the Welsh of the Marches. The interview with the captives was something he had prepared for, though anticipation had filled him with nervous tension. Yet now, the intrigue, the plot, the ransom, all seemed somehow insignificant. Something in nature had shifted and he knew with certainty the change would affect his life dramatically. Who was this young woman he had barely noticed when the hostages were first led in? When she told him she was the daughter of the murdered healer, he wanted to reach out to console her, to explain it was none of his doing. He was drawn to this diminutive woman much more than to his glowering betrothed. But the healer was his captive and probably terrified of him. He turned away sadly and walked back to the dais, glad he was wearing his long jerkin.

Fear chilled Rhonwen but, strangely, it wasn't Rhodri she feared. His aura of primitive power drew her and brought on conflicting emotions. As a healer, she recognised and admired a strong, healthy body when she saw one. She was indeed the daughter of Myfanwy Dda, a truth hidden because of her illegitimate birth. The mystical side of her heritage, passed down through generations of Dda's, drew her to this warrior. She sensed an affinity that transcended the physical and it alarmed her.

She wanted to reach up and touch his dark face, fondle his braids, run her hands over his tattooed biceps, feel the controlled strength that radiated from him. His deep, sonorous voice evoked the memory of the rich, melodious Welsh folksongs they had enjoyed at the fayre in Whittington.

Her thoughts made her blush. How childish to expect a Celtic prince to welcome the attentions of a lowly woman such as her. She determined to quell her feelings, knowing with dire certainty she would avenge her mother's death by killing Morwenna, his betrothed. It was a harsh knowledge for a woman who had dedicated her life to saving others.

As Rhodri returned to his chair, Morwenna glared at Rhonwen. She had not failed to notice the brief exchange that had taken place between the chieftain and the healer. She smiled at him, but her thoughts were black.

You look at her while you're betrothed to me. A curse on you. I have another who'll give me much more than this windblown fortress.

"I want to kill the healer," she told Rhodri after the captives had been escorted back to their chamber, and food ordered for them.

He looked directly into her eyes, his voice cold. "You'll not kill any of them. I've sworn an oath they'll be protected here. They're worth nothing to us dead. We need the coin they will bring. It will allow us to buy the things we desperately need to continue our struggle. Our people have to be fed, clothed and armed. Many in the villages will starve without this ransom money."

He turned to Andras. "We don't have much time. I'll write the missive. Prepare four men to ride to Ellesmere. We must act before the weather turns against us. The countess is expecting a child, which I wasn't aware of. We don't want the babe born here, then he'd be a Welshman. When is our *loyal* friend from Ellesmere expected to arrive?" he asked with a hint of sarcasm.

Andras sneered. "On the morrow, Lord Rhodri."

Morwenna could scarcely wait.

RANSOM

Phillippe de Giroux arrived at the isolated fortress of Cadair Berwyn exhausted and frustrated. He had lost his way twice. Despite his peasant garb, he'd been unable to ask for help because he didn't speak Welsh and was afraid his manner of speech would jeopardise him. Once he found the right trail, his pony almost lost its footing on the high path.

The guards who challenged him didn't seem to know who he was, which added to his irritation until he finally made himself understood.

"Curse this wild country, and curse these ignorant Welshmen with their fanatical obsession of defeating the Normans," he muttered as he stabled the pony. "They'll find out to their sorrow we can't be defeated."

He followed the guards, hoping they were indeed taking him to Rhodri and not some dank cell. He soon found himself in an enormous hall where people were seated at tables and benches, enjoying a meal. The air was redolent with the aroma of venison.

A giant of a man presided over the gathering, Morwenna seated at his side. He had no doubt this was the rebel chieftain, the so-called patriot prince.

The chatter ceased when the crowd caught sight of him.

Affronted by the notion these Welshmen might think to treat him as anything less than a superior Norman nobleman, Philippe paused to help himself to a chunk of meat from the large trestle table at the side of the room, hacked off a piece of coarse black bread and poured a goblet of ale.

He turned and waited, confident the barbarian would come to him.

~

More amused than irritated by the Norman's typical arrogance and sensing Morwenna's obvious agitation, Rhodri came down from the dais and joined the traitor who had helped him secure the prize. Rhodri detested spies who betrayed their own countrymen but tried not to show his contempt.

Giroux glanced in Morwenna's direction and asked, "All went well?"

The man didn't even have the courtesy to introduce himself. "*Ydi*, yes. Very well. I thank you for your help."

"Has the ransom been sent?"

"*Ddoe*," Rhodri automatically replied in Welsh.

He saw how irritated Giroux was he had spoken to him in Welsh. "Yesterday, *hier*," he added.

Giroux had betrayed Montbryce for his own reasons,

not for the freedom of Wales, and he wondered what had caused the anger that drove a man to seek revenge at such a high risk.

"I didn't see your men on the trail," Giroux began, and then quickly changed the subject.

Rhodri knew then he had lost his way.

Giroux rushed on. "The weather is already bad in the passes. I hope they get through."

"They're Welsh, they'll get through."

~

Rhodri was mistaken. A blinding snowstorm howled out of the frigid peaks and caught the messengers unawares. Though autumn blizzards were not unheard of in these mountains, the sudden ferocity of this one forced them to seek shelter in a shepherd's hut.

The snow stopped after two days, but they had to wait another sennight before the weak autumn sun melted it sufficiently to make the track safe enough for travel. They had used up their supplies. If they got to Ellesmere, it was unlikely there would be time to return to Cadair Berwyn with the reply to the ransom demand they carried. If they were able to leave Ellesmere alive, they would have to winter in the foothills, and return to the mountains in the spring.

~

"*Mon Capitaine*?"

Gervais looked up from his task in the Map Room to

see one of Ellesmere's most trusted commanders. The man was clearly exhausted, and Gervais knew why. He braced himself. "What is it, Brémonde?"

The commander shifted his weight, evidently unsure how to begin. "*Mon Capitaine*, I'm a loyal servant of the earl. I came with him from Normandie. I grew up at Montbryce. I would never question anything he does."

Gervais waited.

Brémonde cleared his throat. "But, the men, well, we're exhausted. We're warriors, used to working hard, to rigorous training. But *milord* earl is pushing us beyond our limits."

Gervais had expected this conversation. "But he pushes himself just as hard."

Brémonde nodded vigorously. "It's true. He does, and we know he's grieving. We all want the safe return of our beloved *comtesse*."

Gervais chose his words carefully. "It's difficult for him. He blames himself. He cannot seem to break free of a deeper and deeper melancholia. He's lost interest in the affairs of the manors in Sussex. I have to admit, I'm at a loss."

They stood in uncomfortable silence. Gervais was on the point of dismissing the man when they were disturbed by another soldier, who knocked on the open door and entered.

"Forgive the interruption, *mon capitaine*, but there are four Welshman at the gates. They say they have a message concerning our *comtesse*."

Gervais ordered the messengers be taken to the cells, then ran to the hall, where his earl sat slouched in a chair by the hearth, gazing into the charcoal embers.

"*Milord,* messengers from the barbarian Rhodri are in the cells. Preparations are being made for their torture."

The promise Ram had made to his wife the morning after their marriage haunted him. "You'll never want for a safe place to sleep ever again," he'd vowed.

Roused from his constant berating of himself for not adequately protecting his family and household, he leapt to his feet when told of the messengers' arrival. "Take me to them."

It was evident the four prisoners had undergone a difficult journey. They were dirty, and battered, their beards unkempt. Yet there was dignity in their bearing. He could sense when a man was afraid, and these men showed no sign of fear as he strode into their dank cell. He wondered how long they had been on the road to his castle with the message.

Their leader didn't wait to be spoken to. "Earl of Ellesmere, *Comte* de Montbryce?"

His enemy was an educated man, a warrior. "I am he. Who are you and what is your message?"

"I'm Aneurin ap Norweg," he replied, withdrawing a small metal tube from inside his sheepskin jerkin which he handed to Ram. "I have a message for you from Lord Rhodri ap Owain, Prince of Powwydd."

Ram snatched the tube, willing his hands not to shake. He unrolled the damp parchment coiled tightly inside, squinting to read the blurred message.

To Rambaud de Montbryce, Earl of Ellesmere

Herein my requirements for the release of your wife, children and household servants.

Two thousand pounds in Fleury pennies to be brought back to Wales by the messengers.

If they are killed, and no ransom paid, you will not see your family again. I guarantee the safe return of the captives upon payment.

Rhodri ap Owain, Prince of Powwydd.

Ram's gut tightened. It was impossible. He shook his head. "I can't comply with these demands. This sum is the equivalent of a year's income from all my properties. For all I know they're already dead."

He could barely speak the words, and yet, in the depths of his despair, he had never sensed his beloved wife and children were dead. He thrust the document back at the Welshman.

Aneurin refused to take it. "My Lord Rhodri is a man of honor. He has sworn an oath that none in your family or household will be harmed, if the ransom is paid."

Ram smirked. "Your leader must have a different code of honor from ours if he thinks kidnapping women and children is honorable."

He spat out the words, though he knew some Normans thought such misdeeds acceptable in time of war. Aneurin remained silent. This *was* war and they were both warriors.

Ram stared at the Welshmen for long minutes, trying to gather his thoughts. The cool control that had stood him in good stead in many a skirmish helped slow his racing heart. "We're both aware of the atrocities men are capable of. However, I will not send you off with a chest full of coin. You wouldn't make it back before winter. I assume you've taken them deep into the mountains. My family would not be able to travel out in the winter. Why have you come so late?"

Aneurin reluctantly agreed, explaining the delay of the blizzard. "We'll take whatever message you send back to the foothills, and wait until the spring to return to the mountains."

Ram wanted to shout that his cherished wife was pregnant, that he feared for her life if she gave birth in the wilds of the Welsh mountains, but his fear made him swallow the words.

"But Rhodri will believe you've been killed," Gervais interjected.

"He may think that, but won't act upon his suspicions until our deaths are confirmed."

These men obviously held their leader in high regard. "I could order you be tortured until you reveal where Rhodri is holding my family."

It was an empty threat. Such toughened men would not succumb to torture.

Aneurin's expression didn't change. "I'll save you the trouble and tell you they are in the fortress of Cadair Berwyn. If you could find it and arrive there alive, it would profit you nothing."

A spark of hope flickered in Ram's heart. Aneurin spoke as though he truly believed they were alive and safe in some fortress. He paced in the dark cell, trying to ignore the bile rising at the back of his throat, brought on by the stench in this squalid place and his own dread.

He gave a curt order. "Gervais, escort these men to a

chamber in the North Tower. Provide them with pallets and a bath, and food. Bolt the door."

He left the cells before Gervais could protest.

THE DREAM

Rhodri granted permission for the Montbryces and their servants to sup in the hall, for which the countess was grateful. "Thank you, Lord Rhodri. It has given the boys a chance to mix with the other children in the fortress, and ease their boredom. It's amazing that children can ignore the circumstances that have brought them together, and treat each other as friends."

She and the other two women ate at a separate table from the Welsh, and as her pregnancy became more evident, she seemed to appreciate this bit of decorum and privacy.

Morwenna had badgered Rhodri with her demand for their deaths every day for a sennight. "Aneurin has not returned. It's been a month since they left. The earl has murdered him and his men. We must kill the hostages."

He too worried about the messengers, but why did the woman have such a blood lust? He deeply regretted becoming involved with her. He supposed he had been smitten with her beauty, but now hatred distorted her lovely face. Even her ample breasts did nothing to rouse his lust. She sickened him. He also suspected, if they married, she would not come virgin to his bed.

And now I love another.

He understood passion. He was as passionate as anyone for his beloved country, but had no personal hatred for the earl, whom he recognized as an able administrator, a fair man who strove to better the lives of the people who lived in his lands. He could have killed the earl years ago, at Ruyton, if he had wished, if he was the sort of man who killed adversaries knocked into oblivion by a blow to the head. He wanted none of the Norman usurper's earls ruling his own country, and would fight to keep them out, but saw no reason to slaughter the earl's wife and children. He had given his oath they would remain safe, and he reminded Morwenna of that again.

She rose to her feet abruptly and angrily stormed out of the hall. Though the hostages were too far away from the dais to hear what had been said, he suspected they were aware the woman thirsted for their deaths.

My constant staring probably makes them nervous too. They likely think I'm musing on how best to kill them. They would be surprised to learn who it is that draws my gaze. They must know the messengers haven't returned. The countess will have to soon accept her child will be born in these mountains.

~

That same night, the Prince of Powwydd had a vivid dream. He sat amid his children. There were five of them, and two had flaming red hair. A hazy vision of his grandfather, Gwilym, drifted into view, his copper hair ablaze in the sun. It was a happy dream, different from the ones he usually had when he returned from raids. He derived no pleasure from taking lives, and death often stalked his nightmares.

Like his Celtic ancestors, his belief in the power of dreams ran deep in his blood. Now, Arianrhod was revealed to him. It was a dream of hope and promise for the future. The virgin white goddess of birth conjured an image of the mother of his children. She was a diminutive woman with long black hair, high cheekbones and eyes like grey pools, the woman he had been unable to stop thinking about since setting eyes on her.

When he woke, he spoke her name, "Rhonwen." He gave thanks for the honor the gods had bestowed on him. She was not high born. Her mother was Welsh, but her father? She had never lived in Wales, only in the Marches, and he sensed she burned with a desire to kill his betrothed, to avenge her mother's murder.

He had to prove himself worthy of her and win her heart. Then the dream would be fulfilled.

~

The Normans had been escorted back to their chamber after the meal, and Giselle soon had the yawning boys tucked up in their pallets. In consideration of her condition, Rhodri had provided a bed for Mabelle, but the lads liked their pallets.

"What brave little soldiers you are," Mabelle whispered, gazing at their tousled heads.

A tapping at the door made them all instantly wary.

They were usually left alone at night. Rhonwen opened the door a crack, and Mabelle heard a voice speaking Welsh.

Rhonwen's shoulders tensed and she turned to her mistress. "Rhodri has sent for me, my lady," she whispered, her big grey eyes wide with apprehension.

"For you?"

Before Mabelle could do anything to prevent it, the healer was gone and the door barred once more. She and her maid exchanged desperate glances. Being called to Rhodri at this time of night could mean only one thing for the girl. They wept for the loss of her innocence, and for the failure of the barbarian Rhodri to keep his word none of them would be harmed.

A PERFECT MATCH

Phillippe didn't knock, knowing Morwenna would be alone in her chamber, pacing impatiently. They exchanged no greeting. By the time he reached her, she had torn off her shift and was naked. He devoured the site of her thrusting breasts and the heated promise in her eyes. Their kisses became ravenous. Their mouths remained locked together as they both worked frenziedly to remove his clothing. She sucked his tongue into her mouth. He bit her lip, then her earlobe. His hands squeezed her breasts roughly and she arched her mons to meet his erection. His tongue darted in and out of her mouth and she groaned huskily. "Phillippe, Phillippe. Fill me now. I need my Norman stallion."

Throwing her onto the bed, Giroux leapt on top of her and rammed his phallus into her throbbing sheath, already weeping for him. She sank her teeth into his neck. She liked him to be rough and that suited him too.

"We're a perfect match," he rasped.

After their passion had taken them both over the edge, they lay physically spent but still full of anger and plotting.

Morwenna pouted. “The weak-willed Rhodri refuses to kill them.”

Phillippe yawned. “He’ll come to his senses. I’ll make sure of that. Mabelle de Valtesse will pay dearly for her father’s crimes against my family.”

Morwenna cuddled into him, curling her finger into the hair on his chest. “And, my lusty Norman knight, you’ll repay me for my help by taking me as your bride to Normandie, and I’ll be the *Comtesse* de Giroux.”

Gooseflesh marched across his nape, but he would have to be careful not to let his disdain show. He mustn’t give away that he had no intention of taking this barbaric woman as his wife.

To Normandie? His family and friends would think him as mad as his father. When she had served her purpose, he would be rid of her, or perhaps leave her to make Rhodri’s life wretched.

He reached for his clothing. “I must return to my own chamber. We don’t want anyone becoming suspicious.”

He kissed her carelessly, opened the door carefully to make sure no one was in the hallway, and stepped silently from the room.

AMBER

Rhonwen trembled as she stepped into Rhodri's chamber. The escort remained outside. She was afraid of this Welsh warrior's intentions but had been drawn by his magnetism each time she'd set eyes on his Celtic beauty. She was equally afraid he *would not* do the wild things she'd imagined him doing to her. She too had Celtic blood in her veins.

He sat in a massive wooden chair by the hearth in the center of the room. He wore a pale red linen shirt, the sleeves rolled up to his elbows. The firelight glowing in the depths of a string of amber beads drew her gaze to his neck. She licked her lips, suddenly aware she was perspiring. His long, curly hair was tied back at his nape with a brown leather thong. The war braids were gone, making him seem less intimidating. Leather breeches clung to his muscular thighs. His feet were bare, and she noticed fleetingly how long his toes were.

His usual weapons were nowhere in evidence. The only light in the room came from the flickering embers. A bluish pall of smoke, wending its way up to the smoke-hole canopy in the roof, hung around him. The chair beside him was empty.

"Don't be afraid, Rhonwen." His voice was soft and held no threat. "Come, sit by me," he said in Welsh, holding out his big hand. "Let the fire warm you."

She shivered and walked towards him slowly. Her breasts tingled and a strange ache throbbed in her nether regions. "I'm not afraid, my lord," she lied as she sat in the other chair, her hands holding on to the arms tightly, in case she might have to flee suddenly.

Slowly, he leaned forward to rest his bare forearms on his muscular thighs, and stared at her. She blushed as the fire of his gaze warmed her body. She tried not to look at him but was held by the green depths of his eyes.

"It's as I thought," he pronounced huskily after several minutes. "You're as drawn to me as I am to you."

Rhonwen stared at her knees. "You're betrothed to my enemy, my lord."

He sat back in the chair, his frustration evident. "Ah yes, the lovely Morwenna."

He remained silent for several minutes. She couldn't take her eyes off his face as he wrestled with his demons.

"I'll not marry her."

Icy chills raced up and down her spine. It was what she wanted to hear but made the situation more confused. "My lord?"

He stood and said softly, "Please, call me Rhodri."

She suspected this powerful man didn't use the word *please* often. She trembled as he moved behind her chair and placed his big hands on her shoulders. When he touched her, she stifled a groan of pleasure as the heat of his body flowed into hers.

"My lord—Rhodri," she stuttered, "I cannot, we cannot. I'm your captive. I'm a maid."

He bent to whisper in her ear, "My Rhonwen, it's you who have captured me. I can't stop wanting you. But I'll not force you against your will. I'll resolve the problem of Morwenna and send her back to her father. He won't be pleased I've broken the betrothal, but I have no wish to live my life with her blood lust. It's you I want."

Her mouth fell open. The room had tilted. "But you've known me only a short while."

Rhodri chuckled. "The same could be said of you, and yet you've no doubt in your mind about your feelings for me. Do you?"

She longed to tell him her feelings for him threatened to overwhelm her, but remained silent.

He took his hands from her shoulders and a moment later she shivered when he fastened something cold around her neck. Reaching up instinctively, she felt the smooth amber beads. She looked down and saw how beautifully formed they were—an object an artisan had worked on lovingly, an object of great worth. The heat of his body lingered in the cold beads. She wanted to turn, to look up into those piercing eyes, but was afraid of what she might see there.

"Return to your chamber, Rhonwen. The fates have destined we meet. I know in my heart our future paths lie together. Accept this as a token of my pledge to you. You'll come to my bed when it's the right time, and you will be my wife."

He took her by the arm and helped her rise from the

chair. She was so stunned by his words, and his gift, she could barely make her legs work as he walked her across the room to the door.

He gave a terse command to her escort. "Take the healer back to her chamber."

~

Rhodri sank back into his chair, breathing deeply to calm the arousal brought on by Rhonwen's presence. He had moved to stand behind her so she wouldn't see her effect on his body. His erection turned to granite when he touched her. It was as well she hadn't turned to look at him when he fastened the amber beads around her neck. His mother would have approved of his gift, but looking into those round grey pools would have undone his resolve.

He had been afraid to kiss her when she left, fearing the emotions such a kiss might unleash. It had taken a great deal of effort to keep his voice steady when he'd spoken to the guard.

~

Agitated and conflicted, Rhonwen stumbled along in an effort to keep up with the escort holding the torch lighting their way. Her mind was a jumble of emotions. A squeak escaped her dry throat when a furtive figure emerged unexpectedly from the dark shadows.

The man paused for a moment when he saw them, but then resumed his pace, and she gasped as they came face to face. She recognized him as a Norman by his shaved head and was sure she had seen him before, in Ellesmere. Who was he and what was he doing here? She averted her eyes from his malevolent stare.

When she stepped hastily into the chamber, the other women mistook the cause of her trembling.

"What has that brute done to you, Rhonwen?" Mabelle demanded.

"No, my lady. Rhodri did nothing to harm me. He was kind to me." She felt her face flush. "But I've just had an encounter in the hallway that has scared the wits out of me. There's a Norman soldier here, one of your husband's men."

"It's Giroux," Mabelle hissed, clenching her fists. "I now see clearly the malevolent hand behind the earl's riding accident, Myfanwy's murder, the loss of my child, and my own near death after the abortifacient, and this last betrayal, our kidnapping and probable death at the hands of a Welsh rebel."

"Who is he? Why has he betrayed you?" Rhonwen asked.

Giselle told Rhonwen the story of how Guillaume de Valtesse had blinded and mutilated Charles de Giroux and consequently endured years of wandering exile with his daughter.

Mabelle slumped onto the edge of her bed. "I didn't know you knew the whole story, Giselle, but I'm relieved I didn't have to tell it."

Rhonwen had listened open-mouthed. "But if you and your father were cast out of your home, was that not revenge enough for the Giroux family?"

Mabelle sighed. "Apparently not. My father died

several years ago, and I inherited Alensonne, Belisle and Domfort. I can't believe his reckless actions have resulted in this threat to my own life, and those of my children and servants. From the grave he reaches out to hurt me and mine."

Rhonwen grasped Mabelle's hand. "Forgive me, my lady," she wailed tearfully, "it's not just that I saw the soldier. He knows I saw him."

"We must think," Mabelle murmured.

The three women sat huddled together on Mabelle's bed, careful not to wake the sleeping children.

"What did Rhodri want of you anyway?" Mabelle whispered.

Heat rose in Rhonwen's face. "He's drawn to me."

Giselle sneered. "You mean he lusts after you."

"No. He was kind and gentle. He spoke of—love—of my becoming his wife." It sounded ludicrous. "He gave me this necklace of amber beads." It was incomprehensible.

Mabelle looked at Rhonwen and whispered, "And you feel the same for him, don't you?"

Fearing the censure of her lady for her foolish feelings, Rhonwen could barely murmur, "Yes."

The countess squeezed her hand. "A woman never knows when love might come along and knock her off her feet."

Rhonwen couldn't believe she'd heard these words from the Countess of Ellesmere. She looked wide-eyed at Giselle, who for some reason was silently nodding her agreement. "We must hope Rhodri's love for you will protect us from Giroux," the maidservant whispered.

Phillippe burst into Morwenna's chamber. "They know it was I who betrayed them."

She looked up at him with a bored expression. "It's not a good idea to come here during the day."

He strode towards her. "That's not important now. The healer saw me."

Morwenna rose immediately from her chair. "Does she know who you are?"

He ran his hand back and forth over his shaved head. "Perhaps not by name, but I'm sure she recognized me as a Norman. It's only a matter of time before she and her accursed mistress deduce who I am. The earl believes I'm in Normandie, and must never find out who betrayed him. My life would be worth nothing."

"We'll wait and watch for a good time to kill them, my lover," she purred as she pressed her body to his and kissed him. "I suddenly like the idea of bedding you in the afternoon."

Giroux unexpectedly began appearing for meals in the hall and scowled at the hostages, his hatred and lust for vengeance plain to see.

Rhodri thought it curious but didn't reprimand him. He did notice, however, the occasional exchange of heated glances between Giroux and Morwenna. They had conspired together in England to trap the countess, and he had serious questions about their relationship now.

NO FUTURE

Rhodri sent for Rhonwen every evening. At first they sat in the chairs talking as before. Sometimes he ran his fingers through her hair, inhaling its fragrance, feeling the texture of it, remarking on its beauty. He gazed at her for several minutes at a time. He sensed she had resolved to keep a tight rein on her emotions.

She's drawn to me but can see no future for us.

As she became more at ease with him, he encouraged her to sit on his lap. The soft pressure of her small body against him was pleasant torture. He loved the feel of her slender form in his arms, and as long as they stayed in the chair, he was confident he could control his male urges. His steadfast belief that this woman was his soul mate strengthened him, and he didn't want to hurt her or drive her away. They talked of many things. Rhonwen told him of her love for healing and the things her mother had taught her. Rhodri shared tales of growing up in the castle at Powwydd.

One night, after she had sat upon his lap every evening

for a sennight, they were laughing over a story he had told her of a prank he and his brothers had played. Her smile gladdened his heart. He put his fingers on her chin, drew her face to his and kissed her on the lips. The kiss deepened and she responded to him, parting her lips as he coaxed with his tongue. She slid her arms around his neck.

She's not afraid.

They kissed for long minutes, exploring each other's mouths, necks, throats and ears. Rhodri was intoxicated by the innocence of her responses and her eagerness to please and explore him. He loved the feel of her small hands on his face.

"Rhodri," she whispered as he nuzzled her ear and bent his head to kiss her again, "what of Morwenna? She's your betrothed. Surely what we're doing is wrong?"

He tensed. "I'll send her back to her father in the spring."

She sat up. "But she risked a great deal for you. She murdered my mother, and helped deliver my mistress to you."

Rhodri sifted his fingers through her hair. "Morwenna didn't do what she did for me, or for Wales. Murdering your mother was not part of my plans."

She relaxed back into his arms. After a few moments, she took a deep breath and asked, "Do you think she's still a maid? I didn't believe her to be one when we shared a chamber at Ellesmere, and I have stronger suspicions now."

He smirked. "The Norman, you mean?"

She sat bolt upright and he felt her fear. "I saw him coming from her chamber. He knows I saw him. He wishes me dead, and my mistress and her family."

He stroked her hair, hoping to soothe her. "Why would he want you dead? There's no gain for anyone in that."

Rhonwen shivered. "He doesn't care about gain. It's revenge he seeks."

"Revenge for what?"

Rhonwen told him who Mabelle suspected he was, and why he was driven with a thirst for her blood as the daughter of the man who had blinded and mutilated his father. Rhodri didn't confirm her suspicions about the man's name, but resolved to double the watch on the Norman and on his betrothed.

They sat in silence for several minutes, listening to the beating of each other's heart. He wanted to reassure her. He squeezed her knee and turned her face to his. "I've given my sworn oath nothing will happen to any of you. I'll defend you with my life if necessary."

Rhonwen ached with the pain of knowing there was no future for her with Rhodri. She still could scarcely believe his interest in her. But when he touched her hair, all she wanted to do was curl her body into his, rest her head on his chest and bask in the warmth and comfort she experienced in his arms. She loved the soft tickle of his silky black chest hair against her nose. He never wore his braids when they were together, and she longed for the courage to untie the leather thong that kept his hair bound at his nape.

His kiss had rocked her to the core. For the first time in her life, she felt like a desirable woman. There was desire in Rhodri's kisses, and in his eyes, and in the delicate touch of his big calloused hands.

Was it a mistake to trust him? He could have taken her against her will, but he had not. His patient wooing warmed her heart. The bond she had sensed through forces beyond her understanding was becoming stronger and stronger. She wished each day away, longing for the sun to go down, anticipating his summons.

The parting would be unbearable.

Rhodri stood unmoved as Morwenna's fists beat against his chest.

"I defy you to send me back to my father. I defy you to break our betrothal."

"I'll not marry you, Morwenna."

She sprang away from him and spat in his face. "My father will kill you. You have no right."

He wiped the spittle from his cheek. "I have every right. A bridegroom expects his bride to come to his bed chaste. What will your father have to say about your rutting with a Norman soldier, a spy at that?"

She seemed taken aback for a moment, and then sneered, "And what of your precious Rhonwen, will she come to your bed chaste? I think not."

Rhodri grasped her wrists. "Nothing about Rhonwen should concern you," he said softly. "She is light where you are darkness, joy where you are hatred, innocence where you are corruption. Beware what you say and do while you remain here."

He released her hands, hoping she understood the quiet menace in his voice. "Go to your chamber."

Morwenna went as she was ordered, but glared at him defiantly, intense hatred in her eyes.

She'll seek revenge for my turning to Rhonwen.

"She must be watched at all times," he told Andras. "And the Norman."

"It will be done, my lord."

That evening, Rhodri told Rhonwen, as she sat on his broad lap, that he had banished Morwenna from his life and that the evil woman would be leaving as soon as the weather broke.

"It's still many sennights away," she murmured, returning his gentle kisses.

"I'm having both her and the Norman watched."

Rhonwen imparted this news to the other hostages when she returned to their chamber but didn't tell them how Rhodri had lovingly caressed her breasts, or how he had made her nipples harden with the strokes of his calloused fingers. She mentioned nothing of the wanton feelings these actions had produced in her, but did admit that Rhodri had again proclaimed his love for her.

Mabelle sensed the healer was deeply in love with the rebel chieftain. She felt sorrow for the hopelessness of the situation, and thought longingly of her husband, whom she had not seen for months. She was consumed with mixed feelings about Rhodri's declaration of love for Rhonwen.

Her husband Ram had never told her he loved her, though she believed in her heart that he did. But she had been slow to recognize she loved him. Now was probably too late. If they ever saw each other again, he would never believe she had not been raped while a captive. He would no longer want her, even if she declared her love for him.

~

"The Norman sleeps in Morwenna's chamber every night," Andras reported.

Rhodri grimaced. "I don't care, my friend. So long as the two of them stay away from the hostages, they can rut to their hearts' content."

He wished he could go to Rhonwen's chamber, but the other hostages were there. She would never accept a chamber of her own when her noble mistress had to sleep with her maid.

"Bring the healer to my chamber."

Andras nodded and left.

Rhonwen entered a while later. Would his body always react as strongly to her presence? This time he didn't wait for her to come to him at the chair but strode to her side, lifted her into his arms and returned to the hearth. She smiled and put her arms around his neck.

His lovemaking began with gentle kisses and progressed slowly to stroking and then suckling her breasts. He knew she could feel his erection against her bottom, and that she wanted to touch him, but he held her firmly, and slowly caressed the inside of her thigh beneath the woolen tunic. He had never cared much in the past about a woman's pleasure, but now he derived great satisfaction out of Rhonwen's delight in the new found awareness of her body.

"I want to bring you pleasure, my love. Let me touch you."

"Your touch brings me more pleasure than I've ever known," she whispered, but he could tell she didn't know what he intended to do.

Throaty murmurs escaped her as he stroked further and further up her thighs, until his fingers found the tight black curls of her mons. Still suckling her breast, he opened her legs and grazed his thumb over the swelling bud. Her eyes flew open and she almost fell off his lap, but he held her firmly and continued to stroke.

"Hush, my sweet Rhonwen. I won't hurt you."

She soon gasped his name, lost in the ecstasy of her first release. For long moments he cradled her, rocking gently, his heart full.

She recovered from her euphoria and became embarrassed when she saw she was sprawled on his lap with her tunic up around her hips, her legs open.

"Nothing we do here is wrong my love. You're my woman, and I want only to give you pleasure. When you're mine completely, I'll show you ways to paradise that will make tonight pale in comparison."

He felt her body heat at his words. He brought her to release after release that night, slowly sliding his fingers inside her. She cried out with intoxication and surrendered completely to the passion he was patiently teaching her to enjoy.

YULETIDE

At the Winter Solstice, Rhodri's people held a ceremony. He explained to Robert and Baudoin this was to encourage the sun to come back someday. Considering the remoteness of the fortress, it was well supplied. It had its own large communal kitchens made of stone which were separate from the wooden structure. There were two huge fireplaces for cooking. Most of the meals were surprisingly good and food was never wasted, but at Yuletide they enjoyed a special banquet, which began with mulled cider, followed by venison and fenberry pie. When Giselle asked where they had found fenberries, she was told they grew readily in the bogs of Wales.

Both Mabelle and Giselle almost fell off their bench when a roasted boar's head was carried in. "At least this one isn't green and yellow," they exclaimed together.

Giselle reddened. "Everyone is looking at us strangely, wondering what we're laughing at. It reminds us of feasts at Montbryce…long ago," she said wistfully.

An oak log was burned for twelve hours using the

remnants of the previous year's log to light it. Rhonwen explained that, once it had been burned, the people would keep the remnants for next year, but the ashes would be spread on the fields in the valleys below at the time of planting. This would encourage a good harvest.

The doors were decorated with holly. The Welsh believed the evergreen with its blood red berries was a sign of fertility, and its spikes would capture evil spirits before they entered.

That night Rhonwen had a dream. She and Rhodri were making love. It was so vivid, she was afraid she had cried out her passion. She awoke to find her fingers in an intimate place. But she felt no shame. Rhodri had taught her things about her own body she had never known and unleashed passions she had been unaware of.

If only it could be.

Mabelle heard Rhonwen cry out and recognised the sounds of anguish and longing. She had lain awake many nights, aching with need for her husband, remembering the touch of his hands on her breasts and the fulfillment of his hard manhood deep within her. Had she cried out in her sleep, as Rhonwen did now?

BIRTH

Robert and Baudoin were growing boys who often became restless. With Mabelle's permission, Rhonwen was teaching them Welsh, and they were proving to be good at it. Mabelle and Giselle learned a few words as they listened to the lessons. They passed the time sewing and weaving with the Welsh women in the camp, or spinning wool with a drop spindle.

Increasingly, Mabelle blamed herself for the kidnapping. She had been the one to insist they go to Whittington despite Ram's misgivings. Her carelessness might yet cost them their lives. Her husband would likely never forgive her.

Another worry nagged. If Ram had pursued her captors and been killed or injured in Wales, perhaps his beautiful body lay at the bottom of some deep crevice.

The weather was mostly foul and they were unable to spend much time outdoors. Rhodri and his men seemed impervious to the bitter cold, and spent hours honing their fighting skills in the frigid mountain meadow, keeping in good physical condition. The Norman women were amazed by the cleanliness and grooming of the Welshmen when they came to the hall, despite the fact they spent many hours in physical activity. The hostages were provided with hot water whenever they asked for it.

The young Welsh boys were included in the training and were equipped with small wooden swords, daggers and shields with which to learn the rudiments of self-defense and attack. One day, Rhodri asked Mabelle's permission to include Robert and Baudoin in the boys' training sessions. He brought with him a sword, dagger and shield for each of them. She noted he had waited until the boys were with her. Their eyes lit up when they caught sight of the miniature wooden weapons.

"*Maman*," Robert pleaded, "please say we can go."

They would benefit from the outdoor exercise, not to mention the awesome skills they would learn, but Mabelle thought it incongruous Rhodri should want to train the sons of his enemy, and she told him as much.

He seemed surprised. "There's no glory and no honor in defeating an unworthy enemy. The earl is a worthy opponent, as his sons will be."

She consented, and her children became Rhodri's pupils in the arts of raiding warfare. They loved it and were full of tales of their prowess when they returned.

She worried about her unborn child. Giroux's presence in the fortress frayed her nerves, and yet the babe seemed to thrive and grow. Morwenna and the Norman were seen rarely.

Mabelle had entered her ninth month when she experienced sudden hard labor in the hall. She collapsed to the floor with a strident shriek as the pain hit. This hadn't happened with her other deliveries and she panicked. Giselle and Rhonwen rushed to help, but it was Rhodri who reached her first. He lifted her effortlessly despite her bulk and carried her to his own chamber.

"Fetch the midwife," he yelled to no one in particular.

"You'll have privacy here, Countess," he rasped, laying her on his own bed.

She croaked her thanks that her children would not have to witness her labors, then the pain hit again. It was so severe, she vomited.

"I'll send clean linens. Warrior I may be, but I've no intention of involving myself in this battle for life."

~

The hours crawled by as the countess's screams echoed around the fortress. She called her husband's name over and over, not in recrimination, as Rhodri had heard people say women did in the midst of childbirth, but with longing and regret. He shut out the image of his beloved Rhonwen undergoing the same agony for him, but knew in his heart she would call his name with love when the time came.

His heart plummeted when silence suddenly reigned. He would be truly sorry if the courageous Norman noblewoman had died in childbirth. The Earl of Ellesmere must care deeply for this remarkable woman and would seek revenge. Then a thin wail pierced the still night air, and Rhodri smiled at the immense relief he felt that at least the child lived.

An hour later, he was sipping a tankard of ale with Andras in the hall when Rhonwen appeared, carrying a bundle. She opened the coverings to reveal a tiny baby girl, wrapped in swaddling and a *brychan*. "She can only stay a few minutes. She's come into the world early, and needs to be with her mother, but I knew you'd want to see her."

He stood and took the bundle, awed at the love on Rhonwen's face for this child that wasn't hers. "The babe is fair, like her mother. The lady lives then? She has survived her ordeal?"

"Yes, she's strong. I'm confident she and the child will flourish."

"She had a good healer to assist her," he said lovingly.

"No, the skill of the midwife saved them both," Rhonwen replied modestly. "And her own stubborn determination."

DEATH

A sennight later, Mabelle had recovered sufficiently to join the others in the hall for a meal. She brought the newborn for everyone to see. Rhonwen was honored to carry the babe around as people commented on the fairness of the blonde child who was already thriving. Most were aware the monk had baptised the babe Hylda, after the countess's mother.

After a while, people drifted away, off to their beds. Only Rhodri and the captives remained.

When Morwenna suddenly burst into the hall, brandishing a dagger, Rhonwen clutched the babe to her breast, frantically seeking a means of escape.

"You're mad," Morwenna shrieked at Rhodri, her distorted face reddened with rage. "This is the spawn of a Norman invader, a man you hate."

Heart beating wildly, Rhonwen bolted out of her way when the madwoman lunged at her.

Rhodri jumped to his feet and ran to disarm Morwenna, twisting her wrist. The dagger clattered to the floor. She sprawled at his feet sobbing and screeching, pounding the planking with her fists.

In the noise and confusion, Rhonwen didn't immediately notice Phillippe de Giroux enter the hall. The countess screamed when she saw him creeping stealthily in the shadows, sword drawn. "*Mes fils!* Robert, Baudoin!"

Phillippe grabbed her by the hair and forced her to her knees. "*Tais-toi,* Valtesse bitch. You'll watch in silence while I despatch your wretched spawn to hell, and then I'll kill you. Your cursed father turned my father into a raving lunatic."

He raised his sword. Rhonwen gasped in horror when she saw the sharp blade poised to behead Robert. The boy stood rooted to the spot.

"*Non,*" Mabelle wailed.

Suddenly, Phillippe's rabid eyes lost their focus. His death grip on Mabelle's hair slackened. His disbelieving gaze fell to the dagger embedded deep in his chest. He dropped his sword and slumped lifeless to the floor, a spurt of blood from his gaping mouth spraying across the front of Mabelle's gown. She lunged for Robert, clutching her son tightly, sobbing.

"Phillippe," Morwenna yelled. She had seen Rhodri throw the dagger that had ended her lover's life. She sprang to her feet and picked up the weapon forced from her hand. She ran towards Rhodri, who had crouched to retrieve his dagger from Philippe's body. He cursed as she thrust the blade, deflecting the blow intend for his heart. The steel sliced into his bicep.

Giselle gathered up the wide-eyed Baudoin.

Rhonwen rushed to place the new born into the safety of her sobbing mother's arms. Then she ran to aid Rhodri who was struggling with the frenzied Morwenna. She grabbed the hair of the woman who had murdered her mother, determined not to let her slay Rhodri. That she'd managed to wound him was alarming enough.

When Morwenna turned her attention and her wrath onto Rhonwen, she bolted and ran out of the door, down the passageway and through the gate to the outside, where she found herself lost in a blanket of thick fog.

Morwenna was in pursuit. She had to keep going, though she had no notion where she was running, having been outside rarely during her captivity.

She felt her way along the wooden palisades, glad she could draw Morwenna away from the man she loved. She could hear the demonic woman screaming curses not far behind. The mist cleared for a moment. She was on a narrow precipice. Before her yawned the chasm of the ravine.

I'm standing on the edge of the world.

She spread-eagled her body against the palisades, clutching at the rough bark, and raised her face, trusting her fate to the spirits of the mountains as a feeling of power surged through her.

A manic Morwenna appeared out of the smothering fog and lunged. Rhonwen looked into her eyes and saw death. They struggled briefly, but she felt no fear. Suddenly, her mother's murderer slipped, fell and was gone, swallowed silently by the stoic mountains.

I didn't hear her scream. Surely, she must have screamed?

She braced her back against the palisades, digging her nails into the wood, panting hard and now afraid to move. Fearing she might freeze or faint if she didn't get inside, she wasn't sure which way to go when she heard Rhodri calling to her. Reciting incantations whose meaning she didn't understand, she edged her way along the precipice towards the sound of his voice until she stumbled into him. He grabbed her away from danger and held her to his body.

"You're safe now, my Rhonwen, you're safe. I have you."

"Morwenna is dead," she sobbed, reaching out her frozen hand to touch the blood oozing from his arm. "You're bleeding, Rhodri. She's cut you. I must see to your wound."

But dizziness overwhelmed her and she fainted.

Rhodri took her to his chamber, removed her clothes and massaged her body with rosemary oil to warm her. Gradually, her teeth stopped chattering and she regained her wits. He covered her with furs and blankets and sat by her bedside until she stopped shaking.

Later, she stitched his wound and applied a healing salve of lady's mantle.

"Your stitches are so delicate, I'll bear but the faintest scar."

The small gap it would cause in the Celtic knot designs etched into his biceps would be hardly visible and unnoticed by most. She couldn't believe he barely flinched as she plied the needle through his flesh.

NEGOTIATIONS

Three sennights later, a sudden thaw made it possible for Aneurin ap Norweg and his men to make their way to Cadair Berwyn. He delivered the reply from the Earl of Ellesmere to the ransom note sent by Rhodri.

To the Prince of Powwydd

Be informed the Earl of Ellesmere agrees to pay in full the ransom demanded for his family and servants but proposes an exchange at the border village of Rhydy-croesau.

Safe passage is to be guaranteed by both parties.

The chests of coins will be carried to the middle of the bridge and left there.

The hostages will walk to the chests with an escort who will verify the contents and carry the ransom into Wales.

The earl gives his word for his part of the bargain and trusts Rhodri ap Owain to do the same.

As he read again the ransom reply, signed by the earl and bearing his seal, Rhodri sent for Rhonwen. He had already dispatched a message back to Ellesmere, agreeing to the exchange and detailing the date and time.

He put his hands on Rhonwen's shoulders, trying to keep his voice steady. "I want you to stay in Wales, with me. I'll free the others on payment of the ransom, but you are mine."

"I've dreaded this moment," she whispered, avoiding his gaze. "I cannot stay. My duty is to my lady who has trusted me and given me a place of honor in her household. She's been like a mother to me, since my own mother was murdered."

He lifted her chin. "Look me in the eye and tell me you don't love me."

Rhonwen shook her head, her eyes brimming with tears. "You're a powerful warrior, a man who must fight for Wales, for what you believe is right. I'm a healer. I fight to heal men, not to wound them. Our lives and our priorities are different. I'll always love you, and treasure what we've shared, but I don't want to be involved in war and bloodshed. I want peace."

Rhodri let go of her shoulders, afraid he might be tempted to force her to stay. "I too want to live in peace. I seek only justice for my people. Sometimes it's necessary to fight to achieve it."

~

Ram had endured many agonized months of not knowing how his family fared, but had a deep inner sense they still lived. Mabelle had become an essential part of his life, part of him. His body would have felt the loss. There remained no doubt in his mind that, despite his refusal to admit it, he loved her deeply.

Why had he never been able to utter those simple words to her? Why had his stubborn pride and ambition deprived her of the assurance he truly loved her? He prayed fervently he would have the chance to admit his love. He sensed she loved him too, though she had never confessed that to him. But he didn't care. He resolved to tell her anyway.

And what of his children? He had been a loving father. Unlike his wife, he had never spoken the words to them either. Why was it so difficult? He swore an oath to tell his sons how much he loved them every day of their lives if they were returned to him safely. And the child his wife was carrying when she was abducted? Did the babe live? Did he have another son, or perhaps a daughter? Could Mabelle have survived bearing a child in the remote mountains of Wales?

He worried the Welsh rebels would not agree to his proposals for an exchange. "I hope my caution hasn't cost my family their lives," he confided to Gervais. "Can we trust Rhodri?"

Relief flooded him when a messenger arrived with word from Rhodri agreeing to the exchange, and outlining the day and time, only a sennight hence. "Send out scouting parties to reconnoitre the area around the border village where the exchange is to take place. We've agreed to the idea of safe passage, but we must position bowmen in strategic locations as I'm sure Rhodri will do the same. The Welsh archers are famous for their skill and deadly accuracy."

He had already gathered the sizable ransom from his estates in Sussex, and it lay in his chamber in two iron chests. "Post a two man guard outside my door, and double the guard on the walls and gates of the castle. We don't need a surprise attack on the castle to rob us of the ransom money."

Gervais smiled. "*Oui, milord.* It's good to be doing something productive."

Ram was aware some questioned paying the ransom. The other Marcher Lords had been vehemently against the idea, suggesting pursuit and revenge instead. One earl had intimated their king felt the same way. "His Majesty is not happy with the idea of financing rebels."

But Ram feared pursuit and vengeance would result in Mabelle's death. He knew with dread certainty that if his king commanded him directly not to ransom his family, he would defy the order.

He had also learned something from an unlikely source. True to her word, Caryl Penarth had come to Ellesmere a sennight after the fayre. She had agreed to stay when told of Rhonwen's disappearance with Mabelle. Ram had questioned her about her knowledge of rebels in the area of Whittington. He had sensed there was something she wanted to say, but didn't. After receiving the ransom demand, he had gone to her again.

"There are those who say I shouldn't pay the ransom," he told her.

Caryl hesitated a moment before she replied. "Then many will starve, my lord."

Ram arched his brows. "Starve? The harvests have been good."

"Not in Wales. It's a blighted land," she whispered sadly.

Ram knew much of the *blight* had been caused by Norman brutality.

"How do you know what Rhodri intends to do with the coin?" he asked.

"I've heard the whispers of hope on the lips of desperate villagers."

~

On the eve of departure from Cadair Berwyn, Rhodri summoned Mabelle and her family to the hall. He had developed a great admiration for this proud Norman woman, who seemed to have taken her ordeal in stride and maintained her bearing and fortitude throughout.

"My Countess," he began, bowing slightly. Had she noticed it was the first time he had used the word '*my*' in front of her title? "On the morrow we begin our journey back down the mountain to the border, where you'll be reunited with your husband. I trust you have all in readiness? My men and I will accompany you as your escort, and see you safely delivered."

Mabelle returned the bow with a curtsey. She looked surprised that he would accompany them, but said nothing. She was aware of his love for her healer, but did she know he had asked Rhonwen to stay?

Rhodri continued, trying to keep his eyes off the woman he loved, and his mind on the matter at hand. "It was never my intention to have you killed. I wasn't aware of the reasons for Giroux's involvement in our plans, and Morwenna has paid with her life for her treachery against you, and me. It has been my honor to have you and your sons and servants as guests in my fortress home. You'll never forget your daughter was born in Wales, and I hope one day she'll come to love the country of her birth."

Mabelle bowed slightly and smiled. "I too have come to have respect for you, and your people, Lord Rhodri ap Owain, ap Dafydd, ap Gwilym, Prince of Powwydd. I assure you my daughter will be told of the land of her birth, and I'm sure my sons will carry with them stories of how a Welsh chieftain slew the monster who wished them dead. I thank you for the respect with which you've treated us—all of us."

He knew she was referring in particular to Rhonwen. He nodded his understanding of her words and intent. Did she know how he burned for Rhonwen, how hard it had been to not claim her body and soul, to make her stay?

Mabelle cleared her throat. "I would like to return to our chambers now to make final preparations for the morrow. I'm worried about how the little one will cope with the journey."

Rhodri wanted to reassure her. "The weather is good, and we should have an easy journey. I myself will carry your infant daughter as we descend."

Mabelle seemed about to take her leave but turned back. "One last favor, Lord Rhodri, could I trouble you for writing materials? Parchment—ink. I wish to compose a letter."

Rhodri was curious but replied, "Of course. The monk can serve as scrivener."

"*Non, merci*. I can write it myself."

Now it was Rhodri who coughed nervously. “Perhaps you could spare Rhonwen for a few moments? I would like to speak with her alone.”

Mabelle turned to her healer. “Of course, if you’re in agreement. We’ll go finish our packing.”

Rhonwen blushed and nodded.

DON'T GO

"Come."

Rhodri led Rhonwen to his chamber and motioned for her to sit by the hearth in her chair. They faced each other as they had done at their first meeting alone. After long minutes of silence, her eyes filled with tears. He longed to hold her, to wipe away the tears, to tell her he was sorry for her pain, that he loved her, that she was his destiny. His thoughts were confused and she was conflicted too. He wanted to beg her to stay with him. His dream had convinced him they were meant to be together.

"Rhonwen, don't go."

"I must," she cried, putting her hands to her face to hide the tears. "I can't endure the thought of living with you as a warrior, spending my days amid blood and violence, worrying if you're coming back from the latest skirmish, tending ghastly wounds. But I want some memory to warm the cold, lonely nights without you. I don't know if I'm brave enough to ask, or if you'll consent —Rhodri, I—want to take part of you with me."

"You're taking my heart."

"I'm leaving my heart here with you, but I want—I need to give you something else. You've brought me love and pleasure, without concern for your own needs. I want to satisfy those needs for you tonight, my love, and I want to go from this place as a woman. I want you to be assured you're the only man who'll ever possess my body and my soul."

She was gifting him with her maidenhood. It was folly, but he picked her up in his arms and strode over to his bed.

At least I'll have this memory.

His physical need for her was so great he couldn't stop if he wanted to, but he vowed to make it a night they would both remember for the rest of their lives apart.

Perhaps if I make her mine, she'll stay.

Slowly, he peeled the garments from her body, kissing her face and neck, feeling her quiver as she stood by his bed. When she was naked, he gazed at her.

"You're lovely, so pure and innocent," he whispered. He quickly removed his own clothing and stood at her side.

Her eyes widened and she gasped when she saw his arousal for the first time. "I'm a healer, Rhodri, and I've seen naked men before. But I've never seen a man as big and as proudly erect. Looking at you heats my body."

She smiled at him and his heart raced. He had never felt as admired as a man. She was nervous but not afraid. He didn't want fear to dampen the great passion he sensed she was capable of. It had taken all his considerable control to not let her touch him when she had wanted to. He stroked her hair. "Rhonwen, you have the pure honest soul of an angel."

He picked her up and laid her down on the bed, then lay beside her and took her into his arms, kissing and licking her face, her throat, her shoulders. He kissed her lips, coaxing her with his tongue. She opened for him and he drew her tongue into his mouth, as her groan reverberated through his body. She pulled off the leather thong that bound his hair, then raked her fingers through it as it fell to his shoulders, sending ripples of pleasure from his scalp, down his spine to his toes.

He kissed her dark nipples, flicking his tongue over the already rigid peaks. She arched her body when he suckled. He knelt between her legs and trailed his fingers slowly between her maiden's breasts and down across her belly.

She opened her legs wider. "I ache for you, Rhodri," she whimpered shyly.

Where his hand had led, his lips now followed and he traced kisses down the length of her quivering body until he reached the black curls at the top of her thighs, curls as black as his own. Glimpsing the diamond of her desire, he edged his broad shoulders between her legs, grasped her hips, lifted her slightly and licked the jewel in that most private place.

She cried out and her eyes flew open as his tongue brought her pleasure, but also a blush of embarrassment. "Rhodri—"

"Nothing we do here is wrong or shameful. It's a precious gift you're giving me this night and I want to taste you," he rasped.

She closed her eyes and keened as he covered her with his mouth, the sweet taste sending new blood rushing to his groin. Wet heat eased the way for his fingers as he slowly inserted them. He could wait no longer. He guided the swollen tip of his manhood into her folds. She opened her eyes and placed her hands over his, urging him to enter.

"I'll try not to hurt you," he whispered. "I'm big, and you're—"

She smiled. "I'm not afraid."

Her truthfulness humbled him.

He entered slowly, felt the barrier, and pushed through. She sucked in a breath and cried out, clutching his shoulders. He clenched his jaw at the effort of holding still.

"Don't stop, Rhodri, please don't stop."

His Celtic blood took over on hearing her words. He groaned, withdrew almost completely, then plunged in again and again. She screamed his name with wild delight when his seed burst forth into her quivering body.

Still inside her, he lifted her with ease and rolled over so she was atop him. Black hair entwined where their bodies were joined, making them one body. He felt her sheathe pulse against him as he softened. It would not be long before he could bring her to ecstasy again.

He had never known such fulfillment. His soul had left his body and met hers in some ethereal place. He rose from the bed and went to fetch a cloth and water then cleansed the blood from her thighs.

"Don't be embarrassed, Rhonwen," he whispered with a smile.

"I'm not," she said truthfully. "I'm humbled my warrior is tending to my needs this way. You brought me to rapture with your tender lovemaking before, but this was different. This was fulfillment. The sensations coursing through me as we joined brought me to a mystical release. I've entered a wonderful new world."

She fell asleep hours later, after they made love again. He carried her carefully to the chamber where the other hostages slept, and laid her on her pallet. He spread her long hair on the pillow and covered her lovingly with the furs. He gazed down at her and whispered, "You're my destiny, Rhonwen."

She didn't wake, and he left silently.

The only person awake in the room was Mabelle, who watched him place Rhonwen on the pallet, and heard his words. She wept for their heartbreak, and for the unbearable longing for her own husband.

THE BRIDGE

Rhonwen awoke early, disoriented to find she was back on her own pallet. Glancing around, she saw Giselle and her mistress preparing for the journey. She rose and helped herself to bread and honey. The others greeted her normally and she sensed no embarrassment from them. Rhodri must have carried her into the chamber, but no one gave any indication they had seen or heard anything.

She almost wished they had, then she could pour out her feelings and weep.

Robert and Baudoin were excited to be going home and looking forward to riding the ponies down into the valley. Rhodri told Robert he could ride his own pony because he had learned quickly in the practice fields. The child was ecstatic.

"I wonder if Papa will come to meet us," Baudoin asked.

"Of course he will," Robert answered, "And he'll bring a huge army and slay the Welsh barbarians."

Mabelle groaned. "Old habits and beliefs die hard I suppose," she sighed to Giselle. "Let's pray there won't be violence at the border."

The previous night she had written a letter to Ram. Rhodri had carefully explained the details of the exchange. If anything went wrong, she wanted her husband to know she loved him. She tucked the missive into the folds between her dress and chemise.

Rhonwen wrapped the infant in as many swaddling cloths as she could find and suggested to her mistress that she carry the child in a sling she had fashioned from blankets. Mabelle agreed, confident the healer would be better able to manage the burden on the slippery trails and unsure if Rhodri would indeed accompany them.

However, when they made their way outside, Rhodri was already mounted on his pony. "Give the child to me, Rhonwen."

Blushing, she carefully lifted the sling. The Welshman leaned down as she placed the precious bundle around his neck. Mabelle saw their eyes lock for a fleeting moment, then Rhonwen looked away, sniffling back tears. Rhodri cradled the baby to his huge body. Mabelle was reassured his heat would keep her child warm.

When everyone had mounted, Rhodri shouted, *"I Lloegr!"*

The warriors and their hostages began their long journey down the mountain to England, as he had commanded.

Few words were spoken, despite the captivating beauty of the valleys and glades they traversed, painted gold by carpets of newly opened daffodils. Mabelle sensed Rhodri and Rhonwen were wrestling with their own emotions, and she was full of fear something might go wrong. Would Ram accept her in his bed when she returned? Would the children remember him? Would they make it safely down these treacherous mountain trails? Her hand went to the letter concealed at her breast.

They stayed overnight in the same cottage where they had found shelter on the outward journey and were surprised to see their own horses tethered to a post. Lying on the palette, Mabelle thought about the things that had changed in their lives since she was last in this isolated foreign place.

She was the mother of a daughter she had named Hylda, after her mother. The monk had baptised the child. However, Mabelle felt there was something lacking and had decided to wait for the reunion with Ram to decide what other names the child should bear.

Her sons had grown. They had demonstrated courage and forbearance during the long ordeal, and she hoped, as they grew to adulthood, they would remember some of the good things about the Welsh people they'd known. Giselle had changed too, and Mabelle sensed she had a different perspective about her captors. As for herself, she recognised she loved Ram unconditionally. She hoped desperately he would still want her once they returned.

Rhonwen had undergone the biggest change. Mabelle suspected the healer and the chieftain had been intimate on their last night, yet she seemed intent on returning with them to England. She knew the girl loved this wild Celt who now carried her own child down the mountain. He obviously cared for the babe he cuddled tightly to his broad chest. Was he thinking of his own children, of what he might have had with Rhonwen?

"I don't like this mist," Gervais muttered. "We can barely see the bridge itself, let alone the other side. The archers will be hard pressed to find their target, if we need them."

Ram shifted nervously in the saddle as he and his men waited. "We've already been here over an hour," he replied. "If the wait goes on, the mist may clear."

He struggled to stay positive. He had been in many tense situations in his life, but they paled in comparison to the stress he felt now with the lives of his wife and family in the balance. It was as though the mist had seeped into his head. He dismounted to walk around and stretch his legs, trying to overcome the fear and nervousness he felt. As he strolled into the trees near the glade where they waited, his heart raced when he saw a swath of bluebells.

He felt Mabelle's presence and his mind went back to the day they had met. What if he discovered she had been raped during her captivity? They'd often jested together about the *Fairies of the Blue Thimbles* and he prayed to them now that nothing would go wrong. The Welsh bowmen were legendary and it was said they could hit a target with their eyes closed. He suspected Rhodri had men hidden ready to strike if necessary, as he did.

"I wonder if there will ever be trust between our two peoples?" he mused aloud. "Peace can only come with trust."

He was weary of the constant conflict that plagued the Welsh Marches. A warrior first and foremost, he was also a diplomat, a good one, and he resolved to use those skills to a greater degree than he had before. He picked bluebells while lost in thought then carried them to his horse and fastened them to the pommel of his saddle.

A faint whinny off in the distance, beyond the narrow humpback bridge, brought him out of his reverie abruptly. His gut tightened.

They are here.

A loud assertive voice came from the mist. "Earl of Ellesmere, Rambaud, *Comte* de Montbryce."

"I am here," he shouted back, peering into the impenetrable mist, to see any sign of his family. "To whom am I speaking?"

"I am Rhodri ap Owain, Prince of Powwydd. We've met before, you and I. Did you bring the ransom we agreed upon?"

Straight down to business then.

"*Oui*. I've brought it. How do I know my family is safe?"

There was a pause, then he heard Mabelle's strong, calm voice. "Rambaud? Ram?"

The urge was to charge recklessly onto the bridge. Tears threatened as he tightened his hold on the reins, gritting his teeth and squaring his jaw.

"Ram?" she called again. "We're all safe. Robert and Baudoin are with me, as are Giselle and Rhonwen. And your daughter. Lord Rhodri has taken good care of us. We're looking forward to coming home."

A daughter. Ram's throat constricted. "Robert, Baudoin, you and your mother are well?"

"*Oui*, Papa," yelled Robert. "I've taken good care of Baudoin—and my baby sister."

Ram coughed in an effort to conceal his momentary inability to find words. The expectant eyes of his soldiers were on him. Much depended on what happened next.

"My men will place the chests in the middle of the bridge as agreed. They'll leave them open," he shouted to Rhodri. "If you have the hostages mounted, I want their horses sent across the bridge first."

He didn't want to run the risk the Welsh would turn and flee with the hostages once they had the ransom. It would make it more difficult if they were on foot.

"Agreed," came the gruff reply a few minutes later. "Then we'll send your family across on foot with four of my men, who will retrieve the chests."

Ram didn't like it, but could think of nothing else that would lessen the dangers. The Welshman held the upper hand and could disappear into Wales without honoring the bargain, if he wished. Ram had to trust him. Mabelle had confirmed they had been well treated, and Rhodri had left him alive at Ruyton, when he might easily have killed him.

Ruyton brought thoughts of Ascha Woolgar to his mind. He'd been too much of a coward to confess his dalliance. Had Mabelle ever suspected what had happened there? He sensed she knew, yet didn't judge him. Did it mean she didn't care, or did she love him enough to forgive him?

He heard the slow rhythm of hooves approaching. A Welshman appeared out of the mist, leading the horses Ram recognized as belonging to his family and servants. When the man reached the center of the bridge, he slapped them on the rump and they trotted over to the English side, where his soldiers retrieved them.

Ram took a deep breath. “Gervais, send the men with the chests.”

Four of his men-at-arms lifted the heavy iron chests and tramped to the center of the stone bridge, where they put them down heavily and lifted the lids. The metallic sounds echoed off the walls and rough cobblestones of the narrow bridge, amplified by the mist and the rushing water of the river below.

Since Ram could see the coins from where he stood, he assumed the Welsh could also see them. His men turned and strode back towards him. He felt a surge of pride in these Norman soldiers who must be aware of Welsh arrows aimed at their backs, and yet they walked slowly, never looking over their shoulders.

Out of the mist came Giselle, leading his sons by the hand. Both boys had some sort of wooden shield strapped to their backs. Baudoin looked over his shoulder and waved. The maidservant walked nervously but resolutely to the humpback center of the bridge, passed the chests, and continued on to the English side. Ram dismounted quickly and ran to take his sons up in his arms. Two Norman soldiers hurried to aid Giselle as her knees buckled and she swooned. She looked at them gratefully, then gasped when she realized these were the two warrior sons she had not seen for years. She wept as they embraced her. She smiled her tearful thanks to the earl.

“Papa, papa, did you miss us?” Robert asked.

Ram choked. He was amazed to see how much his sons had grown, but angry he had missed that. At least they hadn’t been starved. “Of course I missed you. I love you. I love you both.”

That wasn’t hard after all.

He hugged them, noticing each carried a wooden sword and dagger tucked into the belts of their sheepskin jerkins and leather breeches. They looked like miniature Welsh rebels. He found it amusing, but resolved in that moment never to follow the growing trend of fostering sons out to some other noble lord for their training.

"We rode ponies, Papa. Can we have ponies when we return home?" Robert asked.

Ram didn't want his children to feel he didn't care about the ponies, but was desperate now to see Mabelle. As calmly as possible, he replied, "I suppose we could see to that. Now, I want you to wait with Gervais here, while I greet your mother. She's coming next is she?"

"*Oui,* Papa, she and Rhonwen are saying goodbye to Rhodri, and then they'll bring *ma soeur*. Rhodri carried her down the mountain in a sling across his chest."

Ram felt a pang of jealousy at the familiar way his family spoke of this Welsh barbarian. "What's your sister's name?" He felt like he had something lodged in his throat.

"*Maman* named her for our *Grandmaman*," Baudoin answered.

~

After watching her sons walk across the bridge and disappear into the mist with Giselle, the countess turned to face Rhodri and thanked him as he carefully placed the sling around her neck. "It's unfortunate, Rhodri, Prince of Powwydd, that our people can't find some common ground, and instead seem to be constantly at each other's throats. I've learned a great deal about you and your country during our stay in your beautiful mountains, and

I'll share much of what I've learned with my husband. He's a lover of peace and prosperity, and would wish that for both our peoples."

Rhodri bowed, took her outstretched hand and kissed it lightly. "Peace can only come with trust and respect my lady. I pray one day we shall find that. *Siwrne dda*. Good journey."

She stepped away to look towards the bridge. Rhodri turned to Rhonwen and took her in his arms. He could smell the dampness in her hair, taste the salt of the tears on her face as he kissed her. He couldn't speak. If he did his voice would betray his anguish. The experience of their union had enthralled him, but she intended to leave. He understood why, but couldn't accept it. If she left, he would never again experience the mystical passion their joining had brought him.

"Rhonwen," he faltered. "I can't change what I am. I'll not beg you to stay. Only you know your heart. But you're my destiny, and I am yours."

His hopes plummeted when she blindly turned away from his embrace and began the walk towards the center of the bridge, clutching her lady's hand.

~

New footsteps on the old bridge caught Ram's attention. He peered into the mist, thicker now, and saw his wife emerge with Rhonwen who clutched Mabelle's hand tightly. They were accompanied by four Welshmen.

Mabelle walked slowly and proudly, head held high, and Ram had never loved her more. Her steadfast Norman courage had seen her through an ordeal that would have broken many women. She walked across the bridge as if she was out for a stroll, a sling across her body that he knew held his daughter. He had a momentary vision of her throwing his sword into the lake. He had fallen in love with her that day. Why had he never told her?

Rhonwen was having difficulty and he wondered what ailed the healer. She walked with her head bowed. Was she crying? Her shoulders shook. Perhaps she was ill? The two women paused in the center of the bridge. The men stooped to pick up the heavy chests and walked back into Wales in the same slow and dignified manner his own soldiers had walked.

But why were Mabelle and Rhonwen not continuing to walk towards him? Something had gone wrong. His gut tightened.

FOR WALES

Mabelle took hold of Rhonwen's shoulders. "You must return to him. He's right. You're his destiny and he's yours."

"But my lady—my duty to you. I'm a healer. How can I live with a warrior, a man of blood and war?"

Mabelle increased her grip and shook the girl. "Because you love him and he loves you. You can't turn your back on a great love. It will destroy you both. It won't be easy living with a Welsh rebel, but to live without love is unbearable and creates only bitterness. I've wasted too much of my life trying to deny the existence of love. You must embrace it. You and Rhodri will bear many fine children, and perhaps one day our sons and daughters will live together in peace in these mountains and valleys."

Rhonwen looked back to Wales. "I can't see him, but he's still there. May I embrace you, my lady? You've been like a mother to me since my own was murdered."

As they embraced, Mabelle asked, "Why did Myfanwy not tell me you were her daughter?"

Rhonwen sniffled. "She was afraid you'd think she had chosen me because I was her daughter and not because of my skills as a healer. She was ashamed I was a base born child, the daughter of a Saxon knight. I said nothing when it was believed my mother had poisoned you, because I was afraid you'd suspect I was involved."

They both looked down at the sleeping child tucked between them and Mabelle suddenly knew her daughter's second name. "My daughter will be named for you, Rhonwen, in honor of your love and courage and as a token of hope for the future."

She kissed the girl on each cheek, turned her, and gave a gentle push. "Now go. And don't look back."

Satisfied the young healer had made the right decision, she resumed her progress towards her husband. As she reached the end of the bridge Ram emerged from the mist and strode towards her. She noticed flecks of silver in his beautiful black hair. "Ram," she breathed, tears rolling down her cheeks.

She felt the warmth of his arms as he encircled her waist and his eyes fell to the babe, sleeping peacefully in her sling. "I want to hold you to myself tightly, but I'm afraid I'll crush the child," he rasped.

Mabelle lifted the babe from the sling and handed her to Ram. "My lord husband, I present your daughter, Hylda Rhonwen de Montbryce."

He looked at the infant who opened her eyes and smiled. "She has your golden hair," he murmured. Then his eyes widened. "Rhonwen? Why have you named her thus?"

"I'll explain," she rasped. "You'll understand. I cannot speak of it now."

Swallowing hard, he took his wife's hand and, holding the baby firmly in the other arm, walked to where Giselle stood, supported by her sons. She seemed to have recovered from her momentary dizziness of relief. He kissed the babe's forehead, handed the child to the maidservant, and turned to his wife.

The simple touch of his hand can reignite my passion so quickly.

He had brought her warmest cloak. He retrieved it and draped it lovingly around her, never taking his eyes from hers. She held her breath. He pressed her tightly to his body, enfolded her in his own cloak and whispered, "Mabelle, I'm consumed with love for you. Thank you for this beautiful gift. I'm whole again now you're back safe with me. My life has had no meaning with you gone. Can you forgive me and return my love?"

Her legs trembled as happiness and relief flooded her. He had not asked if she had been violated, had uttered no words of blame. He had declared his love for her without any conditions. She returned his embrace and felt the familiar longings she had striven to suppress during her captivity. Suddenly she caught sight over his shoulder of the posy of bluebells attached to the pommel of his saddle. The memories engulfed her. She could hardly wait to get her handsome husband into bed. She pressed against his arousal.

"Oh Ram, I've loved you from the first moment we met, but I was too full of fear and resentment about the past to admit it."

He grinned, then swept her up in his arms and mounted his horse with her in front of him. "Giselle, please bring my daughter to me."

He nestled the infant into the sling her mother still wore.

"It's good to hold another babe," he rasped.

Mabelle leaned back against her husband's chest and the warmth of his body banished the chill.

"What of Rhonwen?" he asked. "Are we to wait for her?"

"She's gone back to Rhodri. She loves him. They are destined to be together."

His body tensed. "Rhodri ap Owain and Rhonwen?"

"*Oui*. They too share a conquering passion."

Ram shook his head. "To Ellesmere then," he commanded.

~

Rhonwen heard the horses leaving on the English side of the bridge. With them went her family, her security. Though the Montbryces were not blood kin, they had come to mean much to her. Ahead of her waited the man she loved with a force that threatened to consume her. She stopped before the end of the bridge and took a deep breath to clear her head. Her hand went to the fine amber necklace Rhodri had given her on their first night together, a token of his love. Was she making the right decision? Would he care she was the bastard daughter of a Saxon lord? He was of proud noble descent.

Suddenly Rhodri emerged from the mist. He had heard the Normans leave. She stood alone in the swirling mist. "Rhonwen? Is it you or a trick of my eyes?"

She smiled nervously. "It's me."

Rhodri grinned and folded his arms across his chest. "I

knew you wouldn't leave me. I had to see for myself you were gone. I trust in the power of my dreams."

Rhonwen held out her hands, shivering with cold. He took off his sheepskin and wrapped it around her, enfolding her like a tiny doll in his arms.

"Rhodri," she began nervously, "I must tell you something. You need to know that my father—well—he was a Saxon. He wasn't married to my mother. You're a prince—"

He looked into her eyes. "The real reason for your reluctance to stay suddenly becomes clear to me. You thought I'd be ashamed of your origins, your bloodlines."

Rhonwen nodded, biting her lip.

He tilted her chin. "Look at me and hear me well. I'll never mention her name again, but Morwenna's parents were both Welsh, both of noble blood, and yet she was as corrupt and rotten as a worm-eaten apple. You are purity, gentleness and goodness, and I need you to bring light to the darkness of my life. Being a champion for my people is not an easy burden."

She saw the sincerity and need in his eyes and hers filled with tears.

"Hush, hush, Rhonwen, my Rhonwen," he whispered. "*Mi wnaf dy garu di am byth.*"

"As I will love you, forever, Rhodri," she replied, elated he loved her so much her parentage didn't matter.

He lifted her and carried her into the land of her ancestors.

~

As the Montbryce family rode back towards Ellesmere

with their escort, they suddenly heard an ominous ear-splitting battle cry.

"Dros Cymru!"

It was a deep, guttural yell that echoed to the bone, and they reined in their mounts, sensing danger. They looked behind them. The spring sunshine had burned off the mist. On the opposite side of the valley, a tall man, mounted on a stallion, held a black haired girl on his lap. He thrust his fist up in salute to the Normans as he yelled his war cry again. "For Wales!"

Rhonwen waved then too, and Mabelle, Giselle, Robert and Baudoin waved back. For some reason he couldn't fathom, Ram raised his fist in a return salute. Rhodri ap Owain turned his horse and rode away, his wild shouts of joy echoing across the valley.

A FORTUNATE FOOL

"We'll need to stop for the babe," Mabelle told Ram as Hylda Rhonwen screamed her hunger. "The boys would benefit from a chance to stretch their legs."

They were half way home. Ram reined in his horse and halted the men close by a stream. Robert and Baudoin darted off to play by the water. "Take care, my sons," their father shouted, nodding to Gervais to keep an eye on them.

He lifted Mabelle and her precious burden from the horse and helped settle her on a fallen tree trunk, so she could feed the child. As she lowered her dress and chemise to bare her breast, the letter she had written on her last night in Cadair Berwyn fell from the folds. She'd been unsure of his love then; in the excitement and relief of their rescue she had forgotten it. He had seen the parchment, intent as he was on watching her suckle their daughter.

"It's a letter," she murmured, aware she was blushing. "A letter to you."

"From whom?"

"From me."

He held out his hand. "I would read it."

She handed it to him. He unfolded it with trembling hands.

To my husband Ram,

Mindful of the dangers we face on the morrow, which may yet prevent us from ever seeing each other again, I wish to share with you the feelings of my heart. I've known for many years I'm deeply in love with you. I've always hesitated to tell you of my love. This cruel separation we've endured has made me see the sheer folly of that. What was my fear? That you wouldn't love me in return? If you have longed for me as I've longed for you over these many months—

Be assured the children and I have not been harmed during our captivity. You will have already deduced it was Giroux and Morwenna who plotted against us. Both are dead, Giroux at the hands of Rhodri himself. It was Rhonwen who avenged her mother Myfanwy's death.

If the Fates decide we not be reunited, I cannot go to my grave thinking you didn't know of my love. I thank you for the deep passion we've shared. You have made my life complete. You're the other half of me. I long to see you again.

Mabelle

Ram refolded the parchment and tucked it carefully into

his gambeson, next to his heart. He looked over to his sons, who were throwing rocks into the stream. "You'd think they were returning from a picnic," he remarked with a smile.

He gazed at his wife and daughter. After a few minutes, he walked over to his horse and took from his saddle bag a loaf of bread and a wineskin. Bending his long legs to crouch down beside Mabelle, he broke off a chunk of bread and held it to her lips. She bit into it. "Mmmm—the bread in Wales was good, but there's nothing like Trésor's."

His blue eyes darkened. "Open your mouth."

She tilted her head back. He held the wineskin and poured the red liquid. Some spilled down her chin and onto her breasts. She gulped, and laughed. "I'm out of practice."

He kissed the baby's head and then licked the trickle of wine from her breast to the corner of her mouth, his tongue barely touching her skin. His eyes were full of longing, his body tense with need.

He patted his chest. "I'll carry this letter with me till the day of my death. It will be a constant reminder to me of what a fortunate fool I am. Nothing matters to me as much as my beloved family. I'll spend the rest of my life erasing the memory of the fear you suffered during your captivity."

He tore off a piece of bread, helped himself to the wine, and they continued to share a silent communion until Hylda Rhonwen was satisfied and sleepy. He took the babe, cuddled her to his chest with her tiny head resting on his shoulder, and sauntered over to the edge of the stream, where Robert and Baudoin were practicing with their miniature wooden swords.

Ram chuckled. "They're good at it," he shouted back to Mabelle.

"They had a good teacher."

That night Rhodri and Ram made love to the passionate women they adored, Rhodri by the hearth in the cozy cottage in the Welsh hills, and Ram in the opulent bed at Ellesmere, the heavy draperies cocooning him and his cherished wife.

Both noble warriors slowly pleasured their women, kissing and arousing them in the sensitive female places where they knew they loved to be touched. They rejoiced in hearing their women moan and cry out in fulfillment.

For Rhodri and Rhonwen, it was the beginning of their journey to know one another intimately. For Ram and Mabelle, it was a passionate reunion—learning about each other's bodies all over again.

Both warriors called out huskily in ecstatic euphoria as their essence filled the women they loved.

Love is like salt. It gives a higher taste to pleasure, and then makes it last.

SEQUEL

LLYS POWWYDD, WALES, ONE MONTH LATER

Rhodri's heart was full as he fidgeted with the sleeves of the doublet he was not used to wearing. However, a prince could not marry in a sheepskin jerkin.

He conceded to Aneurin he had a problem. "How can I continue attacking the lands of the Earl of Ellesmere now? Rhonwen considers the countess a second mother. She has a difficult enough time with the fact I'm a warrior. If I raid there she'll be mortified. She wants to be allowed to visit Ellesmere from time to time. I am like a godfather to the Montbryces' daughter, born in my own fortress, named for my bride."

"Well, my friend, there are other Norman earls to raid and harass," his comrade replied with a smile.

"I suppose you are right. Rambaud de Montbryce is not such a bad earl. Compared to Montgomerie and the others, he's a saint."

"Enough of this, we need to get you to your bride. You

actually look like a prince today in your red woolen doublet."

Rhodri laughed, brushing off his shoulders. "It's my favorite color, you know."

Aneurin slapped him on the back and the two friends strode purposefully to the chapel.

Because Rhonwen had no family present, Andras escorted her to Rhodri's side. She smiled at her groom, and his skin heated. He was anxious to get started on creating the five beautiful children he had dreamt of.

Mayhap my seed has taken root already.

It seemed the whole *commote* of Powwydd had heard the story of how he had fallen in love with the Welsh healer he had kidnapped. The tale was repeated often and only added to his considerable stature in the eyes of his people. It was a Welsh tradition that the groom *'kidnap'* the bride before the wedding and they felt Rhodri had more than satisfied the requirement.

He regretted their relationship had begun with an abduction, but she had seen the gratitude on many a gaunt face as he distributed grain in the villages. She told him it had given her an understanding of what had driven him to commit the crime.

Morwenna's father was at first belligerent when told of his daughter's death, but withdrew sadly to his lands, admitting the truth. Rhodri felt immense sorrow for him. The man had rambled on about his daughter inheriting the black arts from her mother. He prayed fervently his own children would be offspring of whom he and Rhonwen would be proud.

True to her nature, Rhonwen wore a lavender dress, and its simplicity heightened her loveliness. She carried a spray of ivy, symbol of fidelity, with a sprig of heather for good luck. As Rhodri took her hand he was overwhelmed by how tiny it seemed compared to his, and he swore to spend his life protecting this fragile woman. Her hair was adorned with fresh flowers, picked that morning.

Her grey eyes danced as she repeated her promises. "I, Rhonwen Dda, in the name of the spirit of God, by the life that courses within my blood, and the love that resides within my heart, take you, Rhodri ap Owain, to my hand, my heart, and my spirit to be my chosen one. To desire and be desired by you, to possess you, and be possessed by you, without sin or shame. I promise to love you wholly and completely, without restraint, in sickness and in health, in plenty and in poverty, in life and beyond, where we shall meet, remember, and love again. I shall not seek to change you in any way. I shall respect you, your beliefs, your people, and your ways."

She had committed herself so completely to him, warrior Rhodri feared emotion might hinder his ability to speak his vows. After taking a deep breath, he promised, "I, Rhodri ap Owain, vow to you, Rhonwen Dda, the first cut of my meat, the first sip of my wine. From this day it shall be your name I cry out in the night and into your eyes that I smile each morning; I shall be a shield for you as you are for me. No grievous word shall be spoken about us, for our marriage is sacred between us and no stranger shall hear my grievance. Above and beyond this, I will cherish and honor you through this life and into the next."

Dancing and feasting followed the ceremony and then a group of women spirited Rhonwen away into hiding. Rhodri accepted this as part of the tradition, but hoped it would not take him long to find her.

She giggled when he discovered her hiding place and his shaft swelled. He too laughed and lifted her, intending to carry her to their chamber. A boisterous crowd of well-wishers followed. She was giddy with excitement and kissed him joyfully, fingering his braids in her small fingers. He thanked the gods for bringing this shining light into his otherwise dark life.

He gazed into her eyes. "You own my heart, my Rhonwen, my bride." In those grey depths resided the love and courage of a woman who would stand by him in his fight. As a healer she fought death every day of her life. She was brave. She had challenged him when she believed he was a threat to the Montbryce boys.

"I am filled with love for you, Rhodri. You sweep me off my feet. I still find it hard to believe such a magnificent man could have fallen in love with Rhonwen Dda."

He put her down on the big bed, turned to the expectant crowd, folded his arms across his chest, and glared at them. One by one they abandoned their loud insistence on seeing the newlyweds disrobe, and left the chamber. Rhonwen burst out laughing when they had gone. "You intimidate them so."

"I had no intention of letting them see you, or me, naked. A man has to have something for himself."

She twirled her fingers in his hair. "You have me to yourself now."

They had made love in the cottage in the hills after Rhonwen had decided to stay with him, but agreed to observe the proprieties of the *llys* once they arrived there, and it had been several sennights since they had lain together.

They craved each other now, not only for the physical

fulfillment their lovemaking would bring them. Each revered the other's body as a finely wrought creation and their union brought them a mystical, even spiritual, release.

Despite his urgency, they made love slowly and savored each other's intense pleasure as they touched, licked and kissed, sucked and played. Later, lying in a stupor of pleasurable languor, a sleeping Rhonwen cradled to his chest, Rhodri did not think he could aspire to greater happiness.

~

Ellesmere Castle, Ten months later

Ram had been away in Westminster, summoned there by William the Conqueror for discussions with the other Marcher Lords. His wife was anticipating his return and went to meet him as he and his entourage rode in. As was his custom, he enfolded her in his cloak and kissed her deeply.

"What of the talks with the Marcher Lords?"

He shrugged and shook his head. "Let's get inside while I tell you. As I expected, it was the usual sort of discussion, me defending the benefits of diplomacy and positive action, and the others recommending tactics such as harrying, murder and mayhem. They cannot grasp we are making progress here. I did not risk my life at Hastings to bring fear and butchery to a foreign people. We Normans have so much to offer the world—fine architecture, arts, trade, and so on. Civil disobedience has to be punished, but they thirst for blood."

Mabelle could tell her husband was getting more and

more disillusioned—had known it for years. "Well, at least here in Ellesmere we have been spared the raiding of Rhodri since he and Rhonwen married," she said with a smile. "Speaking of them, a messenger arrived a sennight ago with news."

He accepted the tankard of ale a serving woman offered once his squire had removed his chain mail, and took a long drink. "*Oui*, we are spared, but the other earls are complaining loudly of his harassment."

She became impatient. "But you are not listening—Rhonwen has given birth to a baby girl. I am delighted to tell you they have named the child Myfanwy Mabelle."

Ram arched his brows. "You must certainly have made an impression on the Welshman during your captivity for him to allow that honor."

She giggled. "I suppose I must have. Rhonwen mentions in her message she would like to bring the child to Ellesmere once she is old enough to travel."

He snorted and almost choked on his ale. "I can't see Rhodri agreeing to that, but if Rhonwen maintains her relationship with you it can only benefit Ellesmere. She's thought of you as her mother since Myfanwy was cruelly murdered.

"I hope for all our sakes Rhodri doesn't come near Ellesmere. If he's captured I will have no choice but to hang him."

POSTSCRIPTUM

Rhodri ap Owain was never captured. His legend grew as the years passed.

William the Conqueror ruled with an iron fist for another ten years, during which time Rhonwen bore Rhodri four more children. Arianrhod had spoken true.

But, would Mabelle de Montbryce's words come to fruition? Would the children of the House of Montbryce and the Sons of Rhodri one day live together in peace in the mountains and valleys of the Welsh Marches?

DEFIANCE ~ BOOK II

ENJOY THIS EXCERPT FROM HUGH AND ANTOINE'S STORY.

En route to Domfort, Normandie, January 1067

Hugh de Montbryce tightened his grip on Velox's reins, but it didn't stop the uncontrollable shaking. He hoped Antoine hadn't noticed but suspected his brother was aware the hand tremor had plagued him since the eve of the Battle of Hastings.

That fateful October night, their eldest brother had sensed his turmoil. "There's no shame in fear," Rambaud had stated flatly. "I'm afraid, as is Antoine. Any man who tells you he isn't terrified of the impending battle with the Saxons is a liar. The important thing is not to allow fear to control you. Bravery is born of fear."

His brother's words had both reassured and annoyed him. "I can't stop shaking, but I'm not a coward."

Now, three months later, riding the frost-rutted route to Domfort with Antoine, Hugh recalled his outburst the night after the horror of the battle. "Why is it the thing a man feels most compelled to do after courting death is lie with a woman? The survivors in my brigade are hobbling round with tree trunks at their groins."

His shaking hand had gone to his rigid manhood. "Look at me. I can't help myself."

His confession had caused his brothers to shift nervously on their camp stools. The three were gazing into the dying embers of a fire they had hoped would dispel the October chill and warm their hearts after the sickening slaughter. He knew their discomfort was not caused by embarrassment at the uncharacteristically shocking remark from their baby brother, but because they understood.

Into the dark memory of those terrible days when the future of England and Normandie hung in the balance, Antoine's voice penetrated. "Let's hope Ram and Mabelle reached Westminster in time for the coronation of our Duke William as King of the English on Christmas Day."

Hugh glanced at his brother. "They'll have made it, if the tides and winds were favorable. After the festivities, I suppose Ram will be obliged to leave Mabelle in Westminster. He can't take her to live in Ellesmere Castle, given its dilapidated state."

Antoine nodded his agreement. "*Oui*. I don't blame Ram for being disappointed with the condition of the castle Duke William granted him. Compared with Montbryce, it's a ruin."

"Nothing more than an earthwork," Hugh added.

Antoine chuckled, his thoughts evidently on the same events. "I'm sure no one has ever been wedded and bedded as speedily as Mabelle."

"If Ram failed to show up at Westminster, he would surely lose his promised earldom, but he was willing to risk it to bind Mabelle to him," Hugh replied. "While he may not yet realize it, she's his soul mate."

His own words chilled his heart. He had resolved never to look for a soul mate. Hastings had changed him forever. The happy-go-lucky Hugh was gone, ground into the blood, muck and gore.

Antoine nodded. "I hope Ram comes to appreciate Mabelle more. She's the woman he'll need as he tries to establish his earldom in England."

"*Oui*."

"Especially in the dangerous Welsh Marches."

"*Oui*."

Antoine chattered on, pulling his cloak more tightly around him in the chilly air. "The brutality of our army's victorious crossing of the Thames at Wallingford sickened me. I was glad of the chance to escape the never-ending bloodshed and accompany Ram on his journey to inspect Ellesmere Castle. He certainly deserves the earldom granted as a reward for the building of our fleet for the invasion, but he and Mabelle will have their work cut out for them in Ellesmere."

"*Oui*."

"But Mabelle is strong. She's survived on her wits for many years."

"*Oui*."

Antoine frowned. "Is that all you can say? *Oui*? What happened to the talkative baby brother I used to know?"

Hugh shrugged. "He's no more. I'm sorry, I don't feel like making conversation."

Antoine shook his head and sighed. "Look, *mon frère*, memories of Hastings are painful for us all. I'll never be the same. The horror will always be with me, but I will not allow it to ruin my life. We were lucky all three of us survived and we should celebrate that.

"You fought well at Hastings, distinguished yourself in fact, and we were fortunate to serve under Ram's command, helping the Conqueror take Dover and Canterbury."

His brother was right and yet Hugh's dark mood refused to leave him. "I suppose I should be thankful to have survived with only a gash on my arm from a Saxon sword. I'll try not to be so sombre."

He rubbed his bicep. The wound had healed well, but the muscle ached still.

"Good. I've no wish to be talking to myself all the way to Domfort. Ram was concerned about you after Hastings, and I'm beginning to see why. He's appointed us overseers of Mabelle's dowry holdings at Domfort and Belisle, so we must live up to his expectations."

Hugh's shoulders tensed. "Of course we'll live up to his expectations. We're Montbryces. I haven't forgotten that. I won't let either of them down. You'll help me get established at Domfort, then journey on to Belisle."

They rode in silence for a long while before Antoine spoke again. "Hasten the day when Mabelle's father no longer holds Alensonne in his manic grip, then we can turn our talents to sorting out that castle as well."

Hugh sensed his brother's discomfort with his silence. "Don't worry. I'll be fine. It will just take a while to get over Hastings."

How to confess the slaughter had aroused him?

Ram had kept a mistress before he met Mabelle,

though he had been discreet about Joleyne. Antoine's reputation with the ladies was legendary. But Hugh had never pursued women, never felt the same rush of need he often experienced now. It was dangerous. If violence aroused him, he might kill a woman in the throes of passion.

ANNA'S STORY

Thank you for reading ***CONQUEST***. If you'd like to leave a review where you purchased the book, and/or on Goodreads, I would appreciate it. Reviews contribute greatly to an author's success.

You can visit me at www.annamarkland.com, and at my Facebook page, Anna Markland Novels.

Tweet me @annamarkland, join me on Pinterest, or sign up for my newsletter on my website.

Follow me on BookBub and be the first to know when my next book is available.

I am a firm believer in love at first sight. My characters may initially deny the attraction between them, but eventually the alchemy wins out. I want readers to rejoice that my heroes and heroines have found their soul mates and that the power of love has overcome every obstacle. For me, novels are an experience of another world and time. I lose myself in the characters' lives, always knowing they will triumph in the end and find love. One of the things I enjoy most about writing historical romance is the in-depth research necessary to provide readers with an authentic medieval experience. I love ferreting out bits of historical trivia I never knew. I based the plot of this novel on the true story of a Norman noblewoman who spent her early years wandering in exile.

I hope you come to know and love my cast of characters as much as I do.

I'd like to acknowledge the assistance of my critique partners Jacquie Biggar, Sylvie Grayson, LizAnn Carson and Reggi Allder. And a big thank you to beta reader Maria McIntyre.

81296385R00259

Made in the USA
Lexington, KY
14 February 2018